SHE WAS READY
FOR A MAN'S LOVING

His gaze was fierce, his kiss explosive and demanding, lacking any of the prior tenderness, but just as fiery and just as long and just as affecting. Under it, she melted inside, as if she had no bones.

Then he abruptly thrust her away, held her at arm's length.

She came up for air, stunned into merely staring at him. He struggled for air too, but anger stroked every line of his expression, his blue eyes reflecting some of the fire they had shared.

"Now, Miss Jesse Mae Banning," he said, his voice hoarse. "You think about that. The passion between us. And remember my mouth on yours and how my hands will feel against your skin. Dream of it. And imagine what more I can give you, the long nights of a lifetime together, and then . . . then you can tell me you won't have me!"

Dear Reader:

Just a moment of your time could earn you $1,000! We're working hard to bring you the best books, and to continue to do that we need your help. Simply turn to the back of this book, and let us know what you think by answering seven important questions.

Return the completed survey with your name and address filled in, and you will automatically be entered in a drawing to win $1,000, subject to the official rules.

Good luck!

Geoff Hannell

Geoff Hannell
Publisher

Books by Lee Scofield

Young Man's Darling
A Slender Thread
Taming Mariah
Sweet Amity's Fire

Available from HarperPaperbacks

Young Man's Darling

LEE SCOFIELD

HarperPaperbacks
A Division of HarperCollinsPublishers

This is a work of fiction. The characters, incidents, and dialogues are products of the author's imagination and are not to be construed as real. Any resemblance to actual events or persons, living or dead, is entirely coincidental.

HarperPaperbacks   *A Division of* HarperCollins*Publishers*
10 East 53rd Street, New York, N.Y. 10022

Cover illustration by R. A. Maguire

First printing: September 1995

Printed in the United States of America

HarperPaperbacks, HarperMonogram, and colophon are trademarks of HarperCollins*Publishers*

❖ 10 9 8 7 6 5 4 3 2 1

To all those sugar-and-spice redheads and flirtatious blondes who dominate my family—with love

1

"*You got yourself a fine* set of prize Hereford bulls there, Mr. McCarthy, a fine set. They should do your cows up proud. My foreman here will see they're properly taken care of, you don't have to worry none. And we'll see there's plenty of feed. All you have to do is feed and water them every day till you get them to your dropping-off place."

"It's been a pleasure doing business with you, Mr. Laskin," Luke replied and shook hands with the middle-aged man. He thanked him again, then tipped his hat in good-bye and nodded to the young cowhand who would oversee the loading of the prized animals onto the train.

Luke strolled away from the loading pens along the rails toward the small station house. The balding ticket agent looked up and nodded.

"Going to be a hot one today, Mr. McCarthy, even for May."

"Yes sir, reckon so. Sure gets muggy in Missouri."

"You have drier air out your way, do you?"

"Yep. But I expect Wyoming's colder than Missouri in winter, too."

"'Spect so. Well, have a good trip, Mr. McCarthy."

"Thank you, sir."

Smothering a yawn, Luke leaned against the wall. He'd been up all night in a poker game; he was tired. He should've walked over to the saloon for a cup of coffee before settling himself to wait for the train. He dug into his pocket for his timepiece. The train wasn't due for another thirty minutes or so.

The stationmaster's helper swept dust out of the station door. The broom swooshed in rhythmic motion. Tiny birds flitted in and out of a gap in the station's roofline. Once more, Luke yawned deeply.

On the verge of sleep, he was startled by noise—a scuffing, thump, and shuffle. He turned his gaze to the steps he knew to be on the other side of the station house. Another shuffle and thump sounded before a big, flat, quilt-covered object came into view, gliding a few inches above the ground. It appeared to have feet. Two black, tiny high-heeled feet. They took four or five miniature steps before the thing came down on the wooden platform with a thump.

It teetered a moment, then steadied. One corner of the old quilt slipped and Luke got a glimpse of what lay beneath it. A gilt-edged base glinted in the morning sun, with taut strings rising from it to disappear under the covering. A musical instrument, Luke thought. He'd never seen a harp before, except for a picture in one of Ma's magazines, but from the size and shape of the thing, it must be one.

He watched in fascination as a delicately gloved hand reached from behind the object to pull an old, scarred black bag along until it was even with the quilt-covered instrument.

The large package rose the few inches from the ground, and the small feet beneath began their shuffle of four or five steps. The black bag scuffed along behind. The process repeated itself three times before he got a glimpse of the carrier.

She was small and would probably come no higher than his chin, he thought. Her profile showed him only a small, straight nose and gentle cheek beneath a flat-topped straw hat full of feathers and blue ribbons that matched the dark-blue suit she wore. One long black feather drooped and bobbed against her cheek, jabbing close to one eye with her every movement. He could hear her muttering something under her breath.

The girl rested her large package against the wall next to the ticket window. It twanged and pinged in answer.

She threw a quick look over her shoulder in the direction from which she'd come, then, tugging her bodice into place at her waist, she stepped up to the window and addressed the balding man in charge.

"I want to go to San Francisco, Mr. Earhart. How much would the ticket be?"

When the ticket agent answered, the girl momentarily lost her bright expression. Her eyes dropped to study her toes. After a minute, she raised her lashes again and determinedly asked, "All right, then, how far will fifty-three dollars and," she counted something in her purse, "forty-eight cents take me?"

"That'll buy ya a coach fare to Salt Lake City, missy, but ya won't have no money left for eats along the way. An' are ya plannin' on takin' that there thing?"

Luke watched the girl give an affirmative answer.

"Well, missy, that'll be freight charges to boot. That thing'll have to go in the baggage car."

"Oh. I hadn't thought of that. What will freight charges cost?"

Mr. Earhart quoted the prices that would cover the transportation of her large object. She wrinkled her brow in earnest thought for another moment, then she turned her head, and her eyes searched the far end of the platform.

Luke noticed one flame-red curl bob against her shoulder as she swiftly turned back to the ticket agent.

"All right, Mr. Earhart. I'll need a ticket to as far as fifty dollars will take me and my, uh, freight." Carefully, she counted out dimes, nickels, and pennies, placing them on the sill in little stacks. "But please hurry, Mr. Earhart."

"Hold yer horses, missy. I gotta get it all straight."

The girl tapped her foot and nervously glanced back once more at the way she had come.

A long whistle sounded, and Luke switched his attention to the rails that disappeared into the distance.

"Train's comin'," called the boy who'd been sweeping.

A family of five moved in closer to the boarding side of the platform as the locomotive approached. The rumbling noise was deafening to Luke, and he wondered if the townspeople ever got used to the din. Little could be heard over the second whistle. At last the train rolled to a chugging, clackety stop.

Luke ambled down to the farthest edge of the platform. There he observed the man loading his precious bulls and, satisfied that all was going well, turned back to board the passenger car.

Above the train's noise, a bellow that wasn't one of the bulls rent the air around him. A wagon screeched to a halt in front of the station house. Its horses had been cruelly worked into a lather, and their mouths appeared cut. Luke frowned; he hated seeing animals mistreated.

A burly, coarse-faced young man dressed in over-alls leaped out, his heavy boots clumping hard as he jumped to the wooden platform.

"Jesse Mae," he roared, an ugly scowl in place. "Damn you, girl, where you at?"

The mother of the young family hustled her brood up the train steps. Luke noticed the redhead, her neck twisted so she faced away from him, scurry from the freight car's open doors, where her quilt-wrapped bundle was disappearing from view, to the car in front.

"Jesse Mae!" The bellowed shout assaulted the air as the man loped toward the girl.

Luke, now only a stride behind her, climbed one step. Suddenly he was shoved aside and pinned to the wall of the train car as the man thrust a tree trunk of an arm past him to grab Jesse Mae's slender one in a ham-fisted clamp. It must have hurt terribly, Luke observed, but the girl didn't cry out.

Twisting from her waist, Jesse Mae grated out a command. "Let go of me, George."

"You ain't a-gittin' on this here train, Jesse Mae." He gave a yank on her arm, careening her into Luke. "Yer comin' on home now an' we're gittin' married like we planned."

The girl turned Luke's way and flashed an apologetic glance. For that instant, Luke stared at her face. Her even features held a light dusting of freckles, but underneath them her skin showed milky white. Feathery auburn brows arched over wide eyes the shade of spring. They were the loveliest eyes he'd ever seen, and they communicated a quickly shielded flicker of panic. In that fraction of a moment, something very basic touched him.

Her lashes fluttered, and the tiniest muscle at the corner of her mouth quivered. She quickly shifted her attention to the other man. "George, you know I'll not marry you. I never said I would. I'm leaving now."

"Ya said I hadta wait till you was eighteen. Well, I waited." His little mouth twisted. "An' now yer sneakin' out on me."

Jesse Mae clung to the step rail and attempted to twist her other arm free, seesawing across Luke. Her head bobbed near him and the black feather on her hat tickled his cheek. He caught a whiff of vanilla.

"All aboard," called the conductor.

"I never told you I'd marry you," she said through gritted teeth. "I said I couldn't marry *anyone* until I was eighteen."

George scowled harder and yanked her forward. "Yer my woman an' we're gittin' wed."

Her chest intimately brushed Luke's as she tried to hold her position. "*No, we are not!* Now let go of my arm, you sniveling, overgrown son of a . . . a. . ."

She suddenly seemed to realize her proximity to Luke. She blushed beet red, the color traveling all the way to the roots of her hair.

Luke decided it was time to intervene. "Mister, I think you should let the lady go. She does seem to have declined your suit."

George threw him a nasty look, his jug ears red to the tips with fury, then ignored him. "Yer mine, Jesse Mae. If'n I'd knowed ya was gonna run away, I'd 'a jest taken you years gone by like I wanted to. Only waited 'cause Ma made me. 'Sides, Ma said ya stole some money."

"I didn't steal a doggone cent, George Jeter, and you know it!"

"How else wouldya git so much money to doll yerself up like ya are an' pay fer a train ride?"

"I *worked* for it, you dumb ox. Something you know

little about! I worked for every penny I saved, you hear me?" she enunciated clearly. "This money came from the extra eggs and butter and such. You know it's mine!"

The whistle hooted in signal that the train was ready to pull out. Luke heard the conductor's last call, and suddenly he wanted to put an end to the bickering. Without warning, he pushed himself more firmly between Jesse Mae and George and placed the flat of his hand in the center of the man's chest. He gave an almighty shove. Taken by surprise, George fell backward and tumbled over his own feet to the platform.

"You son of—" mouthed George, his voice lost in the all-covering noise of the train.

The train chugged and shuddered. Luke grinned. The whistle tooted again, and Luke could see George's thin lips flapping in rage. George made a lunge at the train steps, but Luke calmly put up one booted foot and heaved the burly body backward again.

The train rolled.

"Yer still mine, Jesse Mae," George shouted louder. "I'm gonna have ya. Ya cain't git away with trickin' me. You just wait, ya little bitch, I'll ketch up with ya an' I'll beat ya good, do ya hear? Yer mine, Jesse Mae."

Jesse Mae watched George disappear from view with a shudder of fear, trepidation, and overwhelming relief. Then turning her head—she stood on the step just above the curly-headed cowboy, which caused their faces to be on the same level—she found herself looking into a pair of discerning sky-blue eyes. The stranger returned her stare for a long, sober moment. Still shaking from her encounter with George, she felt it too close for comfort. The man had seen too much, she thought. Turning, she took the last step to enter the train car.

The stranger took her elbow with a guiding hand as he opened the door and escorted her down the aisle of the passenger car. Jesse Mae was grateful for his solicitude, but she hoped he didn't notice the frightened trembles that ran through her. The whole scene had shaken her far more than she wanted anyone to know.

George's demands had been growing more insistent for months in spite of all her deliberate rudeness and obvious distaste for him. She'd increased her watchful care never to be alone with him. Or even alone by herself. On the farm with Cousin Bertha and the kids, that hadn't been too difficult, for she always kept one of them by her side. Nevertheless, she feared his trap. Everyone knew George bided his time.

And George could be very ugly. She'd once seen him take an old horse that could no longer pull a plow and beat and torture it before shooting it. His laughter that day had frightened her beyond the ordinary.

He was just like his pa, people said. Jesse Mae knew different. True, his pa slapped Bertha and the kids around some, and she herself had been on the receiving end of an occasional backhand, but it was in a careless, indifferent way. George's cruelty had nothing to do with indifference; he planned it, savored it, as though it were the elixir of life.

Once, soon after she'd been left with them at age eleven, George had pinched her hard, twisting the flesh at her neck and arms brutally while she stood at the stove, her back turned and unsuspecting. She'd reacted with lightning speed. Swirling from the stove with a skillet of hot, sizzling grease, she held it away from her body.

"See this?" she'd threatened, indicating the popping liquid. "If you ever touch me again, George, I'll throw hot grease all over your ugly face."

George had laughed uproariously. He hadn't hurt her ever again, but she knew he wanted to and would, one day. If he caught her off guard.

Sometimes he talked to her, showing up wherever she was working—at the stove or in the chicken coop or at the washtub. Anytime he could find her without his mother around, he'd whisper threats, telling her what he would like to do to her. Horrible things that made her stomach roil.

Only a week ago, as she approached her eighteenth birthday, he told her just how he planned to take her. To his delight, she hadn't been able to hide her repulsion and fright.

It was no use to appeal to Bertha or anyone else for help. Bertha wanted her to marry George, claiming "the boy was just joshin' her," for Jesse Mae was the only real help the woman had. No one else cared. George's pa and his brother Abel thought "Georgie's courtship" great sport.

That was why Jesse Mae had planned this escape for so long, scrimped and saved so secretively, taking any extra job she could to earn money. She had to leave Sedalia and get away as far as she could. Nothing less would discourage George.

Well, now she'd done it! She'd finally left it all behind her.

The stranger guided her into a seat and then slid in beside her. She glanced at him nervously as he removed his hat and placed it on his knee, running his other hand through gleaming blond curls. He was very good-looking, she thought, with that strong, outdoors look of deeply tanned skin and crinkles about the eyes. The way his mouth curved at the corners as though he were perpetually amused appealed to her. She suspected he was a westerner—besides his low-slung gun belt, he wore a

Stetson and fancily tooled, high-heeled riding boots. He probably never walked anywhere.

His mouth spread to a smile, showing even white teeth. It was a charming smile and tugged at her heart-strings just the tiniest bit. Flushing, she jerked her gaze around to look out of the window. She had rudely stared; he probably thought she intended to flirt.

Well, handsome or not, she had no intention of setting up an acquaintance with a mere cowboy.

Cowboys and farmhands—she mentally shook her head in disgust—they drifted from place to place, seldom settling down long enough to save or build anything. Charming drifters were something she knew quite enough about, thank you. They were around one day, making you like them easy as you please, then gone the next, without any more than a "so long, I'll see you by and by."

That kind of man wasn't for her, no sir, and there was no need wasting her time with one!

Jesse Mae's father had been such a man. She and her parents had drifted from place to place as he got work. After her mother died, he'd left her on his Cousin Bertha's doorstep, saying he'd send for her after he found gold in the western mountains. But he hadn't and, truth to tell, Jesse Mae hadn't really expected him to. She'd never heard from him again.

No, even at eleven, Jesse Mae had known her father well enough not to wait for him. And the worst had already happened to her as far as she was concerned, when he'd dumped her at Bertha's. She'd ended up as a poor relation in a family living on a flinty, poorly managed and poorly producing scratch farm as just another child among ten. Cousin Bertha hadn't been unkind, just weak and demanding. She thought Jesse Mae had been left for her own personal convenience and ought to be grateful to have a home at all. It was only right that Jesse Mae work for her keep.

Bertha's husband was no better. Neither one of them knew how to make their farm pay off, and the family limped along from year to year barely eking out a living.

In spite of all that, Jesse Mae had thrived and learned. When she'd arrived in Bertha's household she was the oldest girl; only George and Abel were older. With four smaller children, it only followed that she became Bertha's staunch helper as well as a substitute mother for each new baby that arrived every year or so after that. As time droned on, most of the household work fell to her shoulders.

She'd become a good manager. She'd learned to cajole Bertha much of the time, plan and guide the younger children's schoolwork and chores, and even reason with Abel. It was George she couldn't handle.

But now she planned a good life for herself. By herself.

Jesse Mae glanced at the cowboy again. Yes, he was a handsome charmer—most women probably fell all over themselves for a smile from him. And he'd helped her get rid of George, but she didn't plan on letting that fact influence her. She'd keep her distance and he would keep his, she'd see to that. Such a man wasn't for her.

Even so, she owed him a proper thank-you.

Jesse Mae addressed the cowboy. "I want to thank you, mister, for your help back there. It was kind of you to take a hand with . . . with my . . . ah, problem."

He looked at her, amusement sparkling from his light eyes. "You're more than welcome, Miss Jesse Mae. I reckon I enjoyed it a mite, myself. I always take satisfaction in giving a bully a boot."

"It's Miss Banning," she prompted.

He held out his hand. "Howdy, Miss Banning, pleased to make your acquaintance. I'm Luke McCarthy."

Jesse Mae glanced at his proffered palm. It was large and long-fingered. And clean.

She wasn't used to shaking a man's hand, but she had no choice but to accept a handshake if she didn't want to appear terribly rude. Tentatively, she placed her gloved hand in his. "Well, Mr. McCarthy, thanks again. You've been most kind."

He nodded. "How far are you traveling?"

"Oh, only to . . . to . . ." Where was it she was going? Flustered, she realized she didn't know. Flickering a glance his way, she tried to keep her uncertainty from showing and gave a casual shrug. "Only down the line a ways," she amended.

Pretending to look out the window, Jesse Mae fiddled with her purse strings. She wanted to pull out the ticket she'd so hastily shoved in when she'd hurried to board. But she didn't want this stranger to know how ignorant she was, so she resisted yanking open her purse to look at the destination written on the ticket. It would make her appear more foolish than she already felt.

Embarrassment was definitely setting in after that scene at the station.

"Mighty fine morning to take a train ride," Luke commented. "Are you going to visit family, Miss Banning?"

"Ah, no, Mr. McCarthy. Not this time," she prevaricated, then quickly turned the direction of the conversation with, "Here comes the conductor." Thank goodness!

A dark-headed, middle-aged man seated across the aisle turned and, spotting Luke, spoke. "Howdy there, McCarthy. Didn't know you was goin' to be on this here train."

"Morning, Chandler."

"That was some poker game last night, wasn't it? Heard you was a big winner."

"I got lucky."

"Ol' Dick Everet was shore steamin'. He ended up so drunk they put him to sleep it off under the bar."

"It doesn't pay to drink while you're playing poker."

"Naw, it don't, at that. You an' your missus . . ."

Chandler trailed away as he looked at her, and Jesse Mae quickly returned her gaze to the window.

"Tickets, please," requested the conductor.

Jesse Mae opened her purse and found hers. As she pulled it out and passed it over, she surreptitiously noted the name of the town written there. Hinley. Western Nebraska. It wasn't nearly as far as she'd hoped to go, but it would have to do. She didn't mind as long as she could find work there.

Luke handed his ticket to the conductor, waited while the man punched the two, then accepted both back as though he'd every right to hers as well as his own. Annoyed, Jesse Mae sat forward and held out her hand. Luke placed her ticket there, but not until he'd quickly glanced at it.

She threw him a frosty look.

Amused, he smiled sweetly.

"Visiting friends, then?" he asked as though there'd been no break in the conversation.

"Not exactly."

"Not exactly, hmmm. Then a sweetheart? Was that why ol' George had his nose all out of joint?"

"No, Mr. McCarthy." Her voice grew more militant as each word tripped from her tongue. "I have no family there, or friends, and I certainly do not have a sweetheart there, or anywhere. And I do not *plan* to have a sweetheart there." She gave him a haughty, meaningful stare. "Or anywhere."

"Ouch. My apologies, Miss Banning. Out west you'd have every right to call me out for being so nosy."

Somewhat mollified, Jesse Mae relaxed and regally inclined her head. "I accept your apology, Mr. McCarthy. It's merely that I don't plan to marry at all and I've become a bit weary, I suppose, of the subject. I'm going to find honest work and live on my own."

"You want to be a spinster?" His disbelieving surprise was palpable. And a bit insulting.

"It's preferable," she said in disdain. "If I'm to work all my life, then I want to earn and own my own wages."

"Hmmm. That's an unusual way of looking at things. Most women of my acquaintance want to hogtie any man they can get their ropes on."

Jesse Mae arched a brow. "Most men, in my opinion, aren't worth the trouble of throwing a loop, Mr. McCarthy. They want a wife to cook and clean, all right" —she marched through her litany— "a woman willing to make their clothes, care for the house and whatever animals are about, grow a garden, nurse them when they're sick, share their bed at the drop of a hat, and produce their children. All without a whimper and very little reward for the wife. No, thank you! That is not for me."

Luke pursed his lips in a low whistle. "Whoo! That's quite a hat full. What about love? Haven't you ever been tempted by a handsome young face?"

She gave a delicate sniff. "No, and I never will be. Love, in my opinion, is a passing notion. However, I might be tempted by an older man. A much older man, one who's settled and steady." Thinking a moment, she added, "My mother told me a long time ago that it's better to be an old man's darling than a young man's slave. If I have to marry, I prefer to be an old man's darling."

Young, handsome, curly-haired Luke had the audacity to chuckle. His light eyes, crinkling at the edges caused her all kinds of nerve-wracking irritation. The nerve of him! If Jesse Mae could have moved at that moment, she would have, but the seat was too narrow to allow her to get past him without major physical contact. She'd save her dignity, but at the first opportunity she thought she ought to find another seat.

Feeling more militant than ever, she regarded him with a contentious stare. "You may laugh if you please, Mr. McCarthy," she said and nodded, her feather nodding with her, "but I'll never be subjected to any man's whim again, if I can prevent it! I don't mind working hard, in fact I'm quite used to it, but I'll not have *my* work go for the pleasure of a lazy lout whose main ambition is to spend his time in saloons and play poker."

2

Barely able to hide his amusement, Luke picked up his casual conversation with Chandler.

Occasionally, he sneaked a glance Jesse Mae's way, gauging her slowly relaxing features. She'd been strung tighter than a barbed-wire fence—her back was as stiff as a pole, her fingers clenched and unclenched her purse, and the enticing mouth he'd had such a delightfully close view of as they'd struggled on the train steps had folded itself into a straight line. But her barbs weren't nearly as sharp as she wanted them to be, he suspected. His interest hadn't been put off; if anything, she'd piqued it.

There was something about her that reminded him of someone. . . .

Luke wondered just how long Miss Jesse Mae had been planning her getaway. By all appearances, a long while. A good thing, too, from what he'd seen of ol' George. Nasty piece of work, was George.

After about an hour, the conductor came through the train car calling the next stop, Kansas City. They'd have a layover here of about forty-five minutes. Passengers exited; some boarded. Beside him, Miss Jesse Mae Banning scanned them all and then craned her neck to view the area outside her window. He caught her deep sigh of relief as the train started up once more.

She couldn't still be afraid of ol' George, could she?

Chandler rose to leave the train at the following stop. He tipped his hat politely to Jesse Mae, remarking, "Hope you have a nice trip home, Mrs. McCarthy."

The girl's head swung toward Luke, her eyes wide with offended accusation, but she remained silent. Luke tried to keep from grinning, but not very hard.

He intended to put the man straight, he honestly did, but somehow when he opened his mouth he couldn't resist a tease. "Thank you, Chandler. Actually, Mrs. McCarthy is traveling to her new home. This is her first trip west."

"Ah, I see. Well, well. My hearty congratulations, McCarthy. And best wishes, ma'am."

Chandler was three strides away when the explosion came.

"You . . . you bounder!" she said low between her teeth. Her voice had an odd, husky little quality to it. He'd been intrigued with it all along. "How could you do that? Tell such a whopper?"

"Ah, shucks, ma'am . . . I was only funnin'. . . ."

His mock apology didn't go very far. "And how dare you let people think we're married?" she sputtered as she stood. The black feather set up an agitated bounce. "I think, sir, I shall find another seat."

"Ah, now, Miss Jesse Mae, I'm right sorry I offended you."

Her chin lifted, her little nose in the air. "I accept

your apology, Mr. McCarthy. Now will you kindly move so that I may get out, or will I have to call the conductor?"

Luke, still trying to hide his grin, pulled in his long legs and rose.

Jesse Mae squeezed past, the back of her shoulder brushing warmly against his arm. Without looking at him, she stood in the aisle tugging her bodice into place as she glanced about her, assessing the accommodations.

She'd been so caught up in her byplay with Mr. McCarthy she hadn't noticed how many people were getting on; there were only two seats left. One was beside a scruffy, bearded fellow chewing tobacco; facing him were two other men whose acquaintance she didn't care to make.

The second was beside a young mother, wrestling a bouncing toddler on her knees. She started down the aisle. Seconds before she could reach the empty seat, a little girl of about three slid into it.

Jesse Mae looked in the opposite direction. Was there anything there? In the last seat against the back of the car, a respectable-looking elderly woman had a vacancy beside her. Satisfied, Jesse Mae started toward it.

Again, someone was there before her.

The conductor called his last warning, and the train began its creaking roll.

Drats! There was nothing for it but to sit beside that McCarthy man. Tightening her mouth, Jesse Mae hesitated a moment more before resolutely marching back to her former seat.

Languishing, with his legs stretched out and his arm draped over her empty seat, Luke glanced up, a half grin flashing his fine white teeth. "Enjoy your stroll, Miss Jesse Mae?"

Her gratitude toward him was no less than before, yet she thought him all too full of himself. She gave him a challenging look. "It's Miss Banning, and would you mind?"

"Mind?"

"I would like to sit down."

"By me?"

She closed her eyes momentarily and silently prayed for patience. "Obviously, Mr. McCarthy."

Luke took his time unfolding himself, but finally stood. He hadn't given her as much room as he could have, she noticed. The space between him and the back of the seat in front seemed about ten inches. Shooting him a glittering, reproachful glance, she leaned forward to gain as much distance between them as she could, and stepped in front of him.

The train gave a sudden precipitous, powerful lurch. Thrown backward, Luke abruptly sat down. Jesse Mae, her knees giving way, landed on his lap.

Instinctively, Luke circled her waist from behind.

Jesse Mae felt the shockwaves of his temporary possession as her back made solid contact with Luke's chest and her bottom was firmly cradled in his lap. Awkwardly, her legs dangled and bounced against his.

"Oh . . . let me up!" She jerked forward and struggled to get off his lap. Only, once again, she lost her balance against his muscled thighs. The splay of his hand at her waist firmed, sending tingles to the backs of her knees.

Jesse Mae felt her face flame.

"Now, Miss Banning, don't get in a flap. I was only trying to steady you."

Jesse Mae felt Luke's breath against the right side of her neck as he spoke. It sent the additional message of how close his lips were to her skin.

She had to get off his lap! People were looking at them!

"Well. . . ," she wiggled forward to get a foot on the floor, "I'll take care. . . ," she put her weight on one foot, prepared to rise, ". . . of myself, thank you!"

Jesse Mae finally gained her feet, but she was now imprisoned between Luke's legs. One masculine hand still held her waist while his other hand cupped one elbow to give her stability. It didn't help her unstable tummy much, she thought wildly. Not much at all.

"Shameless hussy," murmured a woman from across the aisle.

"Dreadful," agreed her companion.

More embarrassed than she'd ever been in her life, Jesse Mae wanted to cry. Except that she was too mad.

Her lips barely moved as she hissed out, "Will you kindly move your . . . your *limb?*"

Luke stood and she pushed past him. Seating herself, she once more gave the window all her attention.

"So glad you could join me, Miss Banning," came the low, wry comment at her back.

Jesse Mae refused to answer.

The hills flattened out and slowly the terrain became treeless. The monotony almost lulled her into sleep, for she'd been tense for days and wakeful for the last few nights. Afraid of sleeping past her time to slip away from the farm, she'd kept herself entirely awake the night before.

However, Jesse Mae was afraid to let herself relax even yet. George's threats disturbed her deeply. If only she'd been able to disappear sight unseen, then he would've had great difficulty finding out where she'd gone. She would have had time to lose herself in some way. And she'd hoped that given time, George—being the lazy lout that he was—would give up.

Now George not only knew just where she was headed, but on which train. What if he tried to follow her?

If? That was the sobering anxiety.

Needing to ease her tense muscles, Jesse Mae finally turned from the window and fixed her back against the seat, her toes barely touching the floor. Beside her, Luke slid lower, a huge yawn catching him. He propped his head against a palm, his elbow braced along the back of the seat.

The swaying rhythm was too much. Maybe she'd let her eyes simply rest.

A long while later, Jesse Mae came awake. What had disturbed her? The slowing of the train, she realized; they must be approaching another town.

Then awareness took root. Beneath her cheek was a mass of silky softness while something heavy lay against her shoulder. A fragrance of soap and masculinity assailed her nostrils.

She slowly lifted her lashes. Then, in alarm, her head. She'd been lying against the top of Luke's curly head while his cheek was against her shoulder! Appalled at the intimacy of it, she jerked up.

"Wha. . .?"

"Get off me, you oaf!"

His eyes at half-mast, Luke moved. About three inches. "You make an all-fired sweet pillow, Miss Jesse Mae Banning," he said in a sleepy voice, all innocent. "Y' know that?"

Jesse Mae refused to answer, but let him know of his offense by a long, hard stare.

"Freemont," the conductor called out.

The train rested at Freemont for thirty minutes. After visiting the ladies' retiring room in the station, Jesse Mae returned to her seat. Luke was nowhere in sight.

Perhaps he'd departed here, she thought. After all, she'd no idea what his destination was. Unaccountably, disappointment washed over her.

"Coffee, Miss Jesse Mae?"

Turning to see him holding two steaming tin cups, she felt caught off guard. She'd always been the servant expected to fetch and carry, and no man had ever offered her a cup of coffee or anything else without expecting something in return. Throwing him a suspicious glance—she wasn't sure what his motive was, but his expression was bland—she accepted one with a stuttered thank-you.

The brew was black and strong. Usually, Jesse Mae drank hers heavily laced with cream and sugar, but she didn't complain. Instead, she idled in the aisle and made small talk with Luke and another passenger about the weather as she sipped appreciatively. A moment later, they gave their empty cups to a young boy who collected them only moments before the train was ready to roll. The train slowly chugged out of the station and she and Luke started toward their seats.

A sixth sense made her turn her head, a rush of warning she usually associated with George. Then he was there, looming large and menacing. Worse, two of his cronies stood behind him: Eli and Archie Thoms. George was bad enough, but these three, together, terrified her.

Archie was a slow, blundering man, even more crude than George. But Eli . . . He was just as mean as George, but more intelligent—a sly demon. Back home, the whole county had whispered about the Thomses' nasty feud with a local family. When old man Jones was found beaten to death on a lonely road, it was commonly accepted, although never proved, that black-haired Eli Thoms had murdered him.

There were other things, none of which the brothers

had gone to jail for: the beating of a local merchant, found late at night in his store barely clinging to life; spilling grain of a neighboring farmer; threats to a young teacher, causing him to pack up and leave. All of the victims had been left too frightened to say who had harmed them. Worse were the rumors the men had raped a young black woman in town.

Jesse tended to believe most of the rumors, especially the one concerning the woman.

"Okay, Jesse Mae, ya had yer fun," George said, his tone threatening. "Now we're gittin' off this here train."

"No. . ." Clutching the back of the seat, Jesse Mae edged backward into it. She didn't stand a chance against the three of them, unless . . .

Passengers were rapidly settling into their seats for a long ride. Some glanced curiously her way. It was a straw she grabbed at. Here was her hope—she had to remain in sight of as many people as possible. George was wily enough to keep his meanness hidden, usually. He wouldn't likely do her real harm where anyone could witness his abuse.

Jesse Mae swallowed hard, then stood tall, finding her balance against the train's sway. She didn't look at the Thoms brothers, keeping her eyes focused on George. "I'm not going anywhere with you, George, I told you that. I have plans of my own, and they don't include marrying you."

George's piggy eyes shifted to Luke. "You an' him?" He took a threatening step toward her. "By gawd, I won't stand fer it, ya little bitch."

The Thomses remained where they were, saying nothing, but their eyes smoldered with danger. Eli's hand rested on his low-slung gun, while Archie cradled a shotgun.

"That's about enough, George." Not a scrap of Luke's

formerly teasing tone was left. His voice was quiet and even. Somehow Jesse Mae knew he wasn't afraid of George or his henchmen. She drew strength from the knowledge.

"I'll git to you, cowboy," snarled George. "Meanwhile, you stay outa this. She's my woman."

"I'm my own woman!" Jesse Mae found the courage to declare. "I don't belong to any man."

George's face turned nastier. "Is that so?"

"The lady already gave you her answer, mister. Now back away!"

"You been askin' fer a fight all along, ain'tcha, cowboy?"

George lunged forward, throwing a fist. Luke feinted and the punch whizzed past his ear. George, overthrown by the force of his swing, fell forward to his knees.

Jesse Mae's breath caught in her throat as she heard a metallic click. Swiftly, she pivoted. Eli's gun was out, aimed at Luke. "Stop!" she yelled.

A woman screamed, a child began to cry, and several men shouted, sending protests into an uproar all around them. A sudden loud clang added to the din.

"Break it up, here," shouted a slim man dressed in the dark blue uniform of the train company. "Break it up, I say."

"This is private business, mister," Eli warned.

"It ain't private when you're on my train, and I don't allow no fightin'."

"Now see here . . . I come on to git my woman who's run away," blustered George. "I got a right—"

"I'm not his woman," Jesse Mae interrupted desperately. "I have a right to go where I choose."

"This young lady is with me," Luke told the conductor.

George's face turned almost purple with rage. "Knew it, you lyin' little—"

The conductor held up his hand. "I don't allow no cussing on my train." The trainman's mouth pinched up in rueful assessment, then addressed George. "I won't put up with feuding. You have a ticket?"

"Don't need one 'cause we're gittin' off."

"The lady and I both have tickets," Luke remarked.

"Then you and the lady may take your seats while I straighten this matter out," the conductor said and nodded.

"We'll settle this without yer help," growled George.

"Not on my train, you won't." The conductor glanced between George and his cronies and Jesse Mae and Luke. "Now, mister, if you don't plan to travel with us, you must leave the train. Now! Otherwise you have to pay for a ticket."

Accusation glared from George's eyes toward Jesse Mae as he said, "How much to the next stop?"

The conductor quoted a price and George pulled out money and handed it over. "Fer them, too." He pointed at his friends and started to push past the conductor toward Jesse Mae.

"Hold it right there, mister." The conductor held up his hand again. "I've a whole carload of soldiers"— he tipped his head in the direction of the rear of the car where three soldiers stood at the ready—"about three cars back. I reckon you fellas might just as well cool off some—back there."

"I ain't leavin' Jesse Mae with him!" George glowered, jerking his chin at Luke.

The conductor thought a minute. "Okay, you can sit in this car if there's room. But you make one move toward this little lady and I'll have the soldiers throw you off the train. Is that understood? And your friends, there, have to give me their guns and find room in the car in back of us."

"I ain't—" started Archie.

"You will if you want to stay on this train," said the conductor caustically. "Miss, take your seat. You won't be molested again while you're on my train. Now you two. . . ," he held out his hand and waited while the Thoms brothers grudgingly handed him their weapons. "You can pick these up in the baggage car when we reach your destination."

The conductor marched the Thomses down the aisle and exited through the back door. Thankfully, he left two soldiers at the exit.

Jesse Mae slid into her seat, Luke following suit. Tightly, she folded her hands around her purse, trying to calm herself. She trembled all over.

Luke laid a large, comforting hand over hers. "It's over for now, Miss Jesse Mae. You don't have to face George without help again."

Unable to speak, she merely nodded. After a moment, she whispered, "Thank you."

"My pleasure."

Safe for now, but for how long? It was all so much worse than she'd imagined. George wasn't going to let the matter drop. Or let her go.

But George didn't know where she intended to get off the train; could she sneak off without him catching her?

She looked over her shoulder. George was there, all right, two seats behind her. The conductor hadn't searched for hidden weapons, and George carried a knife, she knew. Although she was certain he wouldn't dare use it in front of all these people, she still shuddered at his glaring, silent promise of retribution.

Licking dry lips, Jesse Mae stared at her lap. How

much money did she have left? No longer caring what Luke thought, she opened her purse and counted. Three dollars and fifty-nine cents. How far would that take her?

"Don't worry so, Miss Jesse Mae. He won't hurt you, I promise." Luke's low voice whispered in her ear.

She flashed him a glance. "You don't know him."

"I've met his like," he told her, not hiding his disgust.

"Mr. McCarthy, I appreciate all you've done, but. . . ," She hesitated, biting at the corner of her lip. Luke was just an ordinary cowhand, pulled into something more than he'd bargained for. She couldn't let him continue to defend her when he didn't know how dangerous George and the Thomses were. "George's friends are vicious. They wouldn't hesitate to—"

She stopped a moment, remembering how awful the store clerk had looked—she'd seen him several days after the beating he'd taken from the Thomses—and couldn't bear the thought of the handsome features in front of her suffering such abuse.

Taking a deep breath, Jesse Mae said all in a rush, "I can't let you get mixed up in my problems again."

"Like you, Miss Jesse, I make my own choices."

"But the Thomses . . . those men George brought with him. . ."

"I've met their like, too," Luke told her. Then he grinned his cocky grin. "What's the matter, Miss Banning? Think I can't stand up for my bride?"

Jesse Mae tried to smile for his effort at cajoling her from her worries, but she was afraid. She thought it best not to encourage his championship of her, so she returned her gaze to the window.

The train grew hotter as, hours later, the afternoon sun beat down on its metal roof. Several people slept.

Luke had taken her to the dining car for a midday

dinner. Ordinarily she'd have been impressed with the dining car—the chandeliers, beautifully set tables with lovely food, and stark white linens. However, George had dogged them to and from, sitting opposite them and malevolently staring the whole time. Luke had laughed, then ignored him and heartily enjoyed his meal, but however much Jesse Mae tried to overcome it, George's presence made her too miserable to eat.

The smell of onions lingered, left over from someone's noon meal. Other food smells, mixed with tobacco smoke hovering in the air and the odor of human bodies, served to make the air stuffy.

Jesse Mae longed to get up and stroll to ease her stiff limbs, but didn't dare. The one time she'd tried, George had been right behind her, whispering all kinds of threats. Thankfully, Luke had appeared at her side to escort her back to her seat.

After that, when Luke needed to leave her for a few moments, he beckoned to one of the young soldiers to sit with her until his return. One sat with her now. Luke needed to check on the bulls he'd bought for the rancher who employed him.

Someone behind her gave a huge snoring snort. It sounded like George. Could it be?

Jesse Mae twisted in the seat to peek over the back. Sure enough, two seats away, George was indeed asleep, his head tipped back, his mouth gaping.

She plunked back down, her mind racing. This was her chance, if she dared.

"Um, Private," she addressed the young soldier in a whisper. "I need to be excused. Please say I'll be right back if anyone should ask."

"Very well, ma'am. I'll stay to keep an eye on him." The soldier pointed a thumb behind him.

Carefully, Jesse Mae stood. Glancing over her shoulder, she saw that George still snoozed. She inched past the private, then, trying not to run, she raised her skirt a couple of inches to free her feet from entanglement and hurried down the train car.

The soldier guarding the door looked at her in question. She gave him her most brilliant smile. He opened the door for her with a flourish.

Taking extreme precautions, she peeked into the next car before opening the door. Good! Not one familiar face in sight. She sauntered through to that car's end, passed through the dining car the same way, and found her way into the baggage car at last.

The soldiers must be even farther down the line, she mused. As were Luke's bulls that he had mentioned. A bit worried, Jesse Mae wondered how much time she had before Luke made his way back to the passenger car and discovered her missing. And how long before George woke to find the same?

And she hadn't seen the Thomses. Where were they?

Well, she couldn't stand here dithering, Jesse Mae told herself as her eyes adjusted to the windowless car. She looked about her in the dim light. Now where would her old black bag have been put? And her harp?

Along one wall of the car were shelves stacked with various bags, boxes, and bundles. It took only moments to find hers, placed high over her head in a tight space. She had to wrestle with it while on her toes. A small grunt of satisfaction escaped her as it finally pulled free, and she swung it down, placing it on the floor by the door.

Pushing her way through stacks of freight, mailbags, and crates, she discovered the musical instrument wedged between a coffin and a huge crate marked Furniture. She almost moaned aloud. How was she going to get her harp out of there?

Resolutely, she bent and tested her strength against the coffin. It wouldn't budge. She wondered if it contained a giant.

Straightening, she looked at the crate. That, without a doubt, was beyond her.

Still contemplating the problem, she heard a noise behind her. Swiftly, she sat on the coffin and scooted herself back against the wall. She tucked her feet up, her knees under her chin, and hoped she'd be well hidden behind the harp and crate.

Eyes squeezed shut, Jesse Mae's heart beat in quick tempo as she heard someone coming. A low masculine murmur spoke to an answering one, but she didn't recognize who it was.

Until she heard what they were talking about.

3

"... *little vixen, sure 'nuff.* Where ya reckon George got her?"

Though she'd heard him speak only once, Jesse Mae knew it was Archie Thoms. His high-pitched voiced gave him away.

"Some sort of kin to his ma who's been livin' at his pa's farm," said Eli's heavy voice. "He said his ma threatened him off the girl till her say-so."

"Cain't think of George waitin' fer somethin' he wants."

"Ain't much like him. Don't rightly understand it, but he's a mite cowed by his ma. Woulda took the girl long time ago, else. Already waited overlong, by his account, when the girl sneaked out on him."

"That'd put any man in a sweat. That purty little gal might be more'n George c'n handle."

"Naw . . . Not when he gets aholt of her proper.

He's got a shack down in the hills he's gonna take her to—where no one c'n hear her holler," Eli said with relish.

George had once described the ropes he'd bought, saying they were for his secret place where he'd take her one day. And the whip. He'd licked his lips when he'd told her of it.

"He never said nothin' about her bein' so pert," Archie complained. "I like all that red hair, yessirree Bob. Fire on top, fire below. S'pose he wants to keep 'er all to hisself?"

"Yeah," Eli said. "Think he aims to marry this'un. Knew she was special when George offered to pay us'ns ta help get 'er back. An' he ain't a-wantin' his ma ta know his business, either, I reckon."

"That's so, I reckon," Archie said.

Jesse Mae heard a scratching sound as though fingers brushed through a beard. Eli spoke. "I wouldn't mind a turn at this'un, myself, before he beats all the fight outa her. That little gal's gonna be some real fun."

Jesse Mae clamped a hand over her mouth to keep from gagging while her stomach lurched. Two looming figures came abreast of where she hid. She prayed her corner was dark enough.

"But I won't," Eli continued, "if George is really gonna marry her. Don't feel right. 'Sides, messin' with another man's wife c'n be trouble on its own."

Every muscle in Jesse Mae's body remained frozen while she watched Archie reach for the door and pull it wide. Without looking her way, the two men passed through.

The car returned to its former quiet. For a long moment, Jesse Mae rested her head on her knees, shaking all over. She didn't know what might have happened if these men had found her alone in the dark baggage car. But their intentions toward her were clear. As were George's.

Get ahold of yourself, she silently admonished. *Keep a cool head.*

Taking a deep breath to calm her nerves, Jesse Mae eased herself out of the corner and stood in the dim light, thinking. Not only did she have to get away from George, but she had to give his friends another direction to their thoughts. They wouldn't have come on this journey if it weren't for George's claim and his promise to pay for their time. There must be a way to confuse them and tip the odds back in her favor.

Eli's tone had been a bit cautious when talking of "messin' with another man's wife." She thought of the earlier misconception of her being Luke's bride by the man Luke had gambled with, and Luke's own teasing. Perhaps if the Thomses believed her to be promised to Luke, they'd feel a reluctance to continue with George. Maybe she could fan the idea—if she had the courage to face them head on.

She'd have to, Jesse Mae decided, although she needed to talk to them without George's interference. She wondered how safe she'd be. She couldn't take a chance on waiting, though. Despite her fear, the time was now.

Gathering her ragged courage together, Jesse Mae marched boldly through the door and opened the next one into another boxcar. This one, fortunately, was illuminated with a couple of lamps. Its stalls held horses.

The Thomses lounged against a wall with a third man, smoking. When they saw her they all stared. Archie's roving leer almost undid her, but she held fast to her resolution and courage.

"I . . . I'm sorry to intrude, gentlemen. I'm looking for my intended, Mr. McCarthy."

They made no response, so she tried again. "Have you seen him come through? He's in charge of the bulls, you see."

"Ain't seen him," the unknown man answered.

Jesse Mae cleared her throat. "Well, if you should see him, please tell him his fiancée is looking for him. Thank—"

"Yer intended?" Eli asked, his voice terse.

Jesse Mae leveled her gaze at him. He'd jumped at the bait, but she mustn't overplay her hand. "Yes. Mr. McCarthy and I plan to be married as soon as we reach . . ." Oh my stars, where did Luke say he was going? "Wyoming. He has, uh, many fine connections there. And my father has settled in the West, you know," she threw in for good measure.

Eli's heavy brows lowered over narrowed eyes. "So ya are a runnin' off from George with another man?"

"Running off? Certainly not! My *cousin,* Mrs. Jeter, knew of my plans." She plunged into the lie, hoping her telltale face wouldn't give her away. "And I'm honoring my father's wishes."

"Ya mean ya never promised George?" asked Archie in an accusatory way. He made it obvious he didn't believe her, but she thought there was a doubt in Eli's mind.

"Whatever George would have you believe, Mr. Thoms. . . ," Her heart beat so fast she had to concentrate on not putting her hand over it to keep it from jumping out of her chest, "I have never given George any reason to think I would marry him. As to my engagement to Mr. McCarthy, why"—she sighed at this point, and did place a palm over her heart—"he's a fine, handsome gentleman, don't you think?"

"Is that so?" said Eli, his suspicions still showing. "How long you knowed this here McCarthy?"

"Oh, our acquaintance is of long standing. My father, you know . . ."

Satisfied that his Hereford bulls were traveling well, Luke bid good-bye to the youth tending the animals. He'd stayed longer than he'd intended, but the boy had needed a spell of company to break his boredom.

Luke had his hand on the door of the next car when a muffled movement inside made him pause. Years of dealing with frequent danger dictated caution, so he eased the door open a few inches and listened.

Jesse Mae's voice cut the inner gloom of the car, sweet and conversational, while she imparted information as though she were at a society tea. Who was she talking to? And what was it she was saying? He heard his own name mentioned and tipped his ear closer to hear better.

Then he heard Eli's sharp questions. Jesse Mae answered in raptured tones, her words scarcely tripping over the fairy-tale fabrication she was dishing out with a big spoon. The scheming little rascal! Telling the Thomses she was engaged to marry him—using him to put a barrier between herself and George, probably. Now who was telling whoppers? After she'd furiously objected to his teasing in the same vein, too. However, it was a clever ploy and tickled his fanciful humor. Next, she'd have the whole trainload of people believing it, and where did that leave him?

Mostly, he didn't care a snap, but he'd seen a man from his hometown of Wayside Station in the second car, and he didn't want the tale to get back to his mother. As farfetched as that sounded, Luke knew rumors had the ability to fly on the breeze.

Ma knew he didn't plan on marrying for a while or

want any entanglements until he decided he was ready for them. Even so, Luke didn't want her to hear exaggerations before he had a chance to explain things.

And what could he explain? How he'd taken a shine to a freckle-faced little redhead with lots of grit? Who had a way of lifting her chin in challenge and how, when she did that, displayed a lovely milk-white throat that fairly demanded he kiss it? Whose eyes spat out sparks of green fire when she was angry and who had a voice that would make a kitten jealous? Furthermore, one who thought she disliked men and fancied herself a successful old maid.

An old maid! If Luke could believe her. The girl was spinning a tale as long as his arm right now.

Jesse Mae's voice went on in its husky purr, telling of how her father and he had been friends for a long time, even partners in a mining venture, and how it was her father's wish that she marry Luke. Underneath all her bright talk, Luke thought as he listened, he heard a degree of desperation in the girl's story, and he couldn't resist going to her aid.

He eased the door wider and stepped through, quiet as an Indian. No one noticed him in the shadows. Only one of the horses pricked up his ears.

"How come George never heard none o' this?" asked Archie, his stare suspiciously drilling Jesse Mae.

"Oh, you know how George is. He gets something in his head . . ." she said, waving a hand. "Well, you can see, gentlemen, you might as well give up this fruitless journey and go back home."

"George has diff'rent ideas," Eli insisted. "We'll jest foller on what he wants ta do."

Luke stepped forward. "You'll be wasting your time, Thoms. Miss Banning is promised to me."

Jesse Mae's eyes widened before she swiftly dropped her lashes. Lordy oh lordy, she was in a tangle now!

How much had he'd overheard?

Enough, Jesse Mae thought, as Luke strode past the three men to slide an arm around her, hugging her close to his side. Wanting to scold him for his audacity, she was struck dumb. She could hardly reprove him in front of these men just after she'd claimed to be his loving bride-to-be.

Besides, an odd sense of safety—strange, because she had seldom ever found safety in a man's protection—and relief for his presence caught up with her. She'd been shaking in her shoes.

But still, she couldn't allow his intimacy.

When she pressed her lips together to give him her disapproval, she was treated to an additional pressure of strong muscles and warm fingers nipping her waist. His nose nuzzled her hair, leaving his mouth to brush the top of her ear.

"Where've you been, darlin'?" he said low in his throat but loud enough so the other men could hear. He sounded like a lover for all the world to hear.

The three men observing Luke's display were all eyes. She had no choice but to answer in kind.

"I . . . I w-was looking for you," she returned, barely above a whisper while the whole of her right side reacted with nerves. "Darling . . ."

His gaze never strayed from hers, giving their audience further display of his ardor and hinting at the promise of more as he murmured, "Well, you found me."

Luke turned her to the door, opening it with a sweep. Almost as an afterthought, he said over his shoulder, "Good day, gentlemen."

The minute they were through the door, then into the baggage car, Jesse Mae jerked from his grasp.

"You are a bounder, Mr. McCarthy, to take advantage of me in such a fashion."

"But, sweetheart, folks about to get married are allowed a little billing and cooing," he returned, unable to resist the tease. "I only wanted those gentlemen to understand my intentions."

"They understood all right, and so do I. Ohhh, George will be madder than ever."

"Miss Banning, you were the one socializing with those polecats that ol' George calls friends back there. Telling them such whoppers," he accused her with amused gentleness. "If you didn't want to tweak George's tail, why did you engage in conversation with his buddies?"

"Yes, yes, you're quite right, I know, but . . ."

Jesse Mae felt horribly guilty. Regardless of her prior irritation at him, she recognized that Luke McCarthy was only a cowboy trying to do her a good turn. But now Luke had taken the bit between his teeth, and after hearing what the Thomses would report to him, her cousin George would really target Luke for something deadly.

Oh, why hadn't she thought! It had never been her purpose to put Luke in danger. She'd only wanted to place doubt and confusion in the Thomses' thinking, to sway them away from George's plans.

"Shh!" Luke hissed. "Someone's coming."

"Oh!" Unable to express her frustration at him, she spun on her heel and marched to the other end of the car. Before the door flew open, an outraged George bellowed, "Jesse Mae!"

Jesse Mae instinctively stepped sideways and backward, her heart slamming into her rib cage in fear. She hovered in the gloomy corner behind the door. Muttering threats, George stomped blindly through the car.

Tentatively, she peered around her. "Luke," she whispered.

"Here," he answered, stepping out from the opposite corner. Strong purpose laced his voice as he said, "Let me get you back to your seat before I tackle that bastard."

Jesse Mae allowed him to take her elbow. However vexed with Luke she'd been a moment before, she was now too grateful for his protection to offer another word.

But Luke felt far too responsible for her, and she didn't want that.

The whole situation had blown up into a mountain of complication and now involved innocent people. What little control George had over his temper in front of others was wearing thin; no telling who might be hurt if he was pushed into mindless violence.

Furthermore, George hated any kind of authority or restraint; he would blame her for the soldiers and now he'd blame Luke, too.

Whatever doubts Jesse Mae had about leaving the train early fled. It was the best solution because she had to get as far away from George as possible. And if she left the train alone, leaving not only George behind, but Luke, too, George would likely forget about punishing Luke; he'd be more interested in looking for her. Then if her luck was in, George might go so far down the track before missing her that he'd have to give up the chase.

How could she do it? She'd probably missed her best chance when George had fallen asleep. With Luke constantly at her side, George staring holes in her back, and the army on guard, what scheme would work now? She wondered at how many more towns the train would stop before reaching Hinley, where her ticket ran out, and if any of them were large enough for her to hide herself.

Luke stretched his arm across the back of the seat as he stole a glance at the girl's profile. Miss Jesse Mae Banning was cooking something up; he could tell by the set of her mouth. Those pink lips pressed together in determination, while every so often her red-brown lashes flickered in his direction.

Obviously he couldn't force her, but he wished she would further confide in him. The girl was badly frightened of George and those two fugitives from a deep pit. And she needed more help than a few lies would provide, however much fun they had afforded him. All his hackles rose at the thought of her facing the situation alone. She'd be in real danger.

But the girl had braved facing the Thomses down with nothing more than wit, charm, and guts. He admired her courage. With George, she used mostly straight talk, but Luke suspected that tactic was a new one. He wondered how often she'd told George straight out she'd never marry him? Maybe never before today.

Luke studied her small hands tightly clutched around her purse. Small . . . yep, Miss Jesse Mae Banning was a little thing, but her size didn't disguise her womanliness. Nor did she normally let it deflect her from her purpose, he'd bet, if not faced with impossible odds.

The girl was up against the wall, though, he had to admit. He wondered what Jesse Mae would do when she reached her station with no friends there and only a few dollars to her name. If she weren't so proud, he'd offer her some money.

The sun slanted its western rays into the train car, edging her face and hair in gold. Luke, watching the attractive picture, finally spoke. "Miss Jesse Mae, I have to relieve my handler soon for a short spell."

"I'll be all right, Mr. McCarthy," she assured Luke. Jesse Mae had been watching for George's return, dreading his continued, unwavering stare. Yet she worried over what he might be doing. "Please go when you must."

Yet he remained.

The train slowed to a crawl. Luke asked the cause from one of the soldiers, and was told they had a water stop ahead.

The conductor entered the car, and she wanted to ask how far Hinley was, and if there were any towns before then, but was afraid Luke would hear and question her. If she could only think of someplace to hide . . .

Jesse Mae studied the countryside as the train continued to slow. Even the occasional farmhouse had become scarce. Far ahead, a water tower loomed like a lonely mushroom sitting on a level of moss. Such places must be rather stark, she mused, stuck out in the middle of nowhere.

Then it hit her. No one would expect her to leave the train where there was no town.

Should she chance it? She didn't relish being alone in the open country, especially at night, but it might be the best way to get away from George. Walking didn't scare her. She couldn't get lost if she didn't stray too far from the rails. If she could find a town or even a farm, she could look for work.

"I'll go now, Miss Jesse Mae. But I'll be back pronto."

"All right, Mr. McCarthy."

A soldier slid into the seat beside her. As soon as Luke was out of sight, Jesse Mae murmured something about visiting the ladies' retirement room, and squeezed past the soldier into the aisle. She made her way through to the dining car; George was there, looking mulish. White-coated waiters scuttled about, getting ready for the second rush of the supper crowd. Jesse Mae kept her eyes straight ahead, knowing the room set aside for women was at the end.

As expected, when George spotted her, he stood to follow her. At the door marked Ladies she suddenly turned a fierce glare on him.

"*Please,* George! You don't want everyone to think you need to hang on my skirts, do you?"

Flushing, he fell back a step or two. Glancing to the right and left of him, he stared poisonously at the smirking waiter a few feet away. Jesse Mae slipped into the private room and locked the door.

She waited ten minutes, counting off the time in growing agitation. The train wouldn't stop forever. She counted on George's impatience to work in her favor.

And it did. Opening the door a crack, she peered into the corridor. A woman waited to enter, her face weary. But thankfully, George was gone.

Jesse Mae casually glanced around her. No one paid her the slightest bit of attention. She went through to the baggage car just as she heard someone yell.

It came from the cattle cars; it was George causing the commotion, she was sure, and hoped the soldiers were close at hand.

The train jerked, a signal of its readiness to leave. Hurriedly, she found her bag and gave her harp a last yearning glance before struggling to unlock the sliding car door.

The train began to roll. But the heavy door wouldn't budge. Frantically, she put all her might into pulling it to slide in its tracks. Still, it remained stubborn.

Nearly weeping, Jesse Mae gave it one last try; the huge door slid open a few inches. She inched a shoulder to its edge and pushed it wide enough for her to slip through.

Looking down, Jesse Mae almost gave up her plan when she realized just how much speed the train had picked up. But waiting would serve no purpose. No, even if she killed herself in the jump, she'd be no worse off than being caught by George and his minions.

Taking a gulp of air for courage, she leapt.

4

Jesse Mae curled herself into a ball just as she hit the rough ground and rolled amid the tall grass that lined the track. It jolted her side mightily and knocked the air from her lungs. She clamped her teeth together against the pain and lay until she could catch her breath, listening to the noisy train recede into the distance, aware of the fading light and growing quiet around her.

She was cautiously jubilant. She had left George behind.

But now she was alone in the middle of nowhere and had to find some sort of shelter for the night. Perhaps she'd better return to the water tower.

Nearby, an animal gave out a demanding bellow. Even nearer, an angry man's curse filled the evening air.

"Damn it to hell and gone!"

It sounded like . . . like Luke McCarthy! But it couldn't be. Could it?

Painfully, she pushed herself to sit up. In the twilight she saw a man's silhouette heading through the tall grass toward two huge bulls. Hatless, his gleaming hair shone pale in what light there was left. It was indeed Luke.

Jesse Mae stood. Her once brand-new stylish hat dangled down her cheek, crushed beyond repair. She pulled it off, giving it a sorrowful grimace. The graceful black feather was in two pieces.

Almost in midstride, Luke spun on his heel, then stared at her in disbelief. "What the blue blazes—! Jesse Mae? Where did you come from? Er, never mind. How did you get off the train?"

A bit disgusted by what she thought was quite obvious, she said, "I jumped, of course." Rubbing her painful shoulder, she challenged, "And how did you, Mr. McCarthy? And why?"

"I didn't have a choice in the matter," he said, spitting his words out as he strode toward her through the tall grass. "Your ol' buddy George pushed me out, right as I discovered someone had driven my cattle off." He glanced over his shoulder to where his two bulls agitatedly bellowed. "What's more, all my gear got left on the freight car."

"I see. Well, why didn't you get back on the train, Mr. McCarthy?"

"Don't talk loco, Jesse Mae." Luke jerked a hand through the air impatiently. "The train was already moving, and I couldn't have gotten the animals back on if I tried."

"Oh, I . . . I'm sorry you lost your gear because of me. You shouldn't have mixed with my troubles."

"If you think I'm in a quandary now, it doesn't hold a candle to the heap of trouble I'll be in if I don't get those bulls to the M double C safely. They cost a lot more than my gear."

"The M double C?"

"The ranch I'm headed for."

"Oh." Jesse Mae frowned, then observed, "Your boss must be a tough man to work for."

"Yep. That he is."

"Would he . . . will you get fired over this?"

"Mmm . . ." Luke made a plaintive, low-in-his-throat sound and slapped his hat against his thigh to remove any dust before jamming it back onto his head. "Maybe not."

She nodded toward the bulls. "George and the Thomses did it, I suppose."

"Yep, that's the way I'd call it," he continued, the edge still in his voice. "They wanted me off the train because I interfered between George and you. But why in thunder didn't you stay on? There were soldiers there to protect you."

Jesse Mae felt miserably guilty over the predicament Luke had been put in because of her. Really, he had every right to be angry over it. Yet she was defensive all the same.

"For just how long, Mr. McCarthy? A few hours, until they departed and I was left to George's whims once again? Then what?"

Luke ignored her logic. "Hell's bells, Miss Jesse Mae! You could have killed yourself by jumping from a moving train, you know that?"

"I had to get off for my own safety, Mr. McCarthy," she insisted. "And I did try to tell you—those men are a nasty trio who like trickery any day better than honest dealing."

"Well, I hope they have a damned good belly laugh over this one, because it's their last dirty trick on me!"

He started away, indignant ire in every stride.

"Mr. McCarthy . . ." She straightened, ignoring her painful shoulder. Taking a moment to find her carpet-bag, she chased after him, feeling it bang her leg with every step. "Mr. McCarthy, I'm very sorry your journey has been disrupted. Really. It's all my fault, I know. Please, I . . . Let me help you get your animals home."

"You don't know what you're offering, Miss Jesse Mae."

"It doesn't matter. I owe you that much. How far do you have to go?"

"A far piece," he said, his thoughts and eyes gazing into the darkened distance before returning to address the problems at hand.

"Perhaps you'd better wait until tomorrow's train comes through and get on that one," she offered. "I can find my way to the nearest town."

"Do you think the conductor is likely to let me on just on my say-so? Ain't got nothin' to prove my getting off wasn't my doing." His manner softened while he contemplated her. "Did you hurt yourself in the fall?"

Her bruised shoulder throbbed, but she couldn't give him any more worries. She already felt guilty enough for being the cause of his present difficulties. He had to deal with taking care of his cattle. "Only a little."

"Here, let me see."

Swiftly, she stepped away as he reached to touch her. "No. It'll be all right. Shouldn't we see to the cows?"

"Bulls," Luke corrected her. He dropped his hand, speculating that she probably hadn't broken anything in her fall or she couldn't hide the pain it would cause her. Nevertheless, he took her bag and shortened his step to accommodate hers as they headed toward the water tower and windmill. "Does George know you jumped?"

"I don't think so."

"Well, I reckon he'll come looking for you as soon as he finds out you're no longer on the train."

"Yes, I suppose he will. I'd hoped he'd give up if I simply disappeared, but now . . ."

Luke wasn't deaf to the dread in her voice. "Now?"

"Well, you'll be gone too, don't you see?"

"Uh-huh." He understood her point. "George will take it into his head that we're really together after all," he said, verbalizing her newest fear. A minute later, he dismissed it. "Reckon it won't matter. We'll be long gone by the time he figures it out and gets back here. Right now we have more urgent problems to work out."

"Like where to shelter for the night?"

"Yep. Reckon our best bet is to wait it out by that shed till morning, then head for the nearest town. I'll need your petticoat, though."

"I beg your pardon?" Jesse Mae stopped. They were mere yards from the tiny structure that stood next to the water tower.

"Your petticoat. It will be flimsy at best, but it's the only thing I can think of to make a halter with. I can't leave my bulls to wander off."

"Oh." Jesse Mae thought of her two brand-new petticoats, one with the pink ribbons along the ruffle's edge. They were the first she'd had in years and she'd cherished them in secret, along with her other new things, for months before putting them on for the first time only this morning.

"Well, in the circumstances, I guess . . ." She could afford to give him the plain one, she decided. She headed for the shadows. "Turn your back, please, Mr. McCarthy."

Luke strode to the other side of the shed, where Jesse Mae heard him break open the lock on the door and then rummage through the tiny structure. Quickly, she removed her undergarment and hurried around to see what he was doing. "What are you looking for?"

"This." He hunkered down as he struck a match to the lantern he'd found. Lifting it high, he peered into the dusty corners, finding only a pick and shovel, a small wooden keg holding a few spikes, and an old tin lunch pail with a rusty hole in its side.

"Not much," she said.

"Nope," Luke agreed in disgust as he stood once more.

He leaned back against the shed and reached for her undergarment. A faint whiff of vanilla wafted from it, reminding him that he'd caught the fragrance from Jesse Mae's tiny form before. The poor woman's perfume, his sister, Josie, called it. Women who couldn't afford real cologne frequently used vanilla in place of perfume.

A swift glance at the girl's flushed cheeks hurried him on to the task at hand. "Here, hold the lantern."

Jesse Mae watched as he tore her white petticoat into strips before knotting them into a rope of a sort.

"Follow me, but don't make any sudden moves. You'll spook the animals."

"I have handled cattle, Mr. McCarthy," she replied pertly. "There is no need to speak to me as if I'm a complete greenhorn."

"What, a tame milk cow or two? Bulls ain't hardly the same thing, Miss Jesse Mae. They can be mean and ornery when provoked, and a body don't always know what they'll do. Anyway, I don't aim to go chasing after or running from one of 'em in the dark if I don't have to."

"No, of course not. I only meant . . ."

'Uh-huh. Well, start singing."

"Singing?"

"Yep. Don't know much about these here Herefords yet, but longhorns like singing. Settles 'em down."

"Oh, I see. Well, what should I sing?"

"Anything, so long as it's steady an' sweet."

She took a deep breath. "A froggie did a-courtin' go, mm-hmm, mm-hmm. A froggie did a-courtin' go, mm-hmm, mm-hmm . . ."

Jesse Mae lifted her husky alto in a soft offering as Luke approached the first grazing bull with unhurried movements. The animal sidestepped and moved away.

"C'mon, you dad-blasted stubborn beast," he muttered in a singsong and followed.

". . . won't you marry me, mm-hmm, mm-hmm," Jessie sang as the bull raised its head to look at her curiously.

Cautiously, Luke placed a hand on the heavy neck. The animal lifted its jaw and let out a plaintive bellow as if to answer Jesse Mae's song, allowing Luke's hand to stay. In a flash, he threaded the petticoat rope through the nose ring. After a moment of lowing protest, the animal returned to grazing.

"Good. Keep singing."

She complied. They slowly repeated the process with the second bull.

As the two huge animals seemed in an amenable mood, Luke heaved a deep breath in relief. "That wasn't near as bad as it might've been."

Jesse Mae broke off her song. "Thank goodness. Now what?"

"Reckon they'll make out passable for tonight, then in the morning we'll water 'em before starting on our way. Let's head back to the shed. Tomorrow ain't gonna be no Sunday school meeting, so we'd better get some sleep."

"Ah . . . yes, of course." In truth, Jesse Mae wanted nothing more than sleep. She felt purely exhausted. But the prospect of being alone all night with the handsome cowboy suddenly caused her hesitation over the propriety of it. Would she be safe?

Did it matter? Nothing could be as dangerous as the predicament from which she'd recently fled, and who was around to see that she spent the night alone with a strange man she wasn't married to?

Besides, after all they'd been through together since early morning, Luke wasn't much of a stranger any longer. The silliness of her own thoughts and fears made her chuckle.

"What's so funny?"

"Oh, nothing." She felt a flush creep up her face as he grinned back at her. He had a smile that would coax a flea circus from off a dog, she mused. And she discovered that, oddly, she didn't feel a bit frightened of Luke, in spite of his flirtatious teasing. But he did give her heart a pause.

Which jerked her musings back to soberness. She refused to go sweet on all that young male charm.

"Well, you got anything in that satchel that will do for a pillow, Jesse Mae?"

"I have an old cloak."

"That'll do for a blanket. Gets cool at night out in the open." He began to pick up rocks and throw them over his shoulder, working in an increasingly large circle. "What else?"

"Only my hairbrush, a nightgown, a couple of

dresses." They were work clothes, worn threadbare and too short, but the only ones she had beside what she wore. "What are you doing?"

"Making us a comfortable bed space," he said as he used the shovel to smooth the ground he'd cleared. It looked to be about the size of a double bed.

Her heart began to race. Maybe she wasn't as safe from Luke's amorous feelings as she thought. Men were men, weren't they? Her mother had always said that, and so had Cousin Bertha. In fact, that's what Bertha always said when she heard tales of her son George's escapades, as though that were all the excuse that was needed. Certainly, George would take such an opportunity as this to pounce on her.

"What do you mean, us? You don't expect—?"

"I don't expect anything more than a night's sleep, Jesse Mae, so you can quit imagining the worst. But it'd be best if we slept close to keep warm."

"I won't sleep there." Her voice was prim. Just because she felt guilty that she'd caused his current problems, Luke McCarthy needn't think that that entitled him to anything more personal from her than help with his animals.

He shrugged, though his eyes glinted bluer in the lamplight as though he found her amusing. "Suit yourself. But there's not much oil left to see by. You want to make your own bed?" He held the shovel out to her.

"I certainly do." She raised her chin and gave him a look that clearly told him she'd put up with no more nonsense. She grabbed the shovel and turned away. "Anyway, we can build a fire."

"Yep. Plan to." He was lining stones into a circle, even then. "But there's no wood in sight, not much out here on the prairie, and it's too dark to look for buffalo chips. Don't think there's much to make an all-night fire with unless we use the shed. Though the railroad authorities might object to that and besides, I don't see the need to tell anybody else who might be out there where we are if we don't have to."

"Oh." She felt foolish. She hadn't given a thought to those problems. Wood was a plentiful commodity in Missouri. Other than George and his pals, she'd ignored the possibility of confronting danger.

Standing still, Jesse Mae listened to the night sounds. A cooling breeze lifted her hem and tousled her hair. Far off, she heard a coyote yelp.

Coyotes didn't scare her, or any other natural creatures, she said to herself as she scraped away the surface rocks and flattened the grass in the place she'd chosen to sleep. After all, she was a country girl.

But the lantern abruptly went out, and for a moment everything around her lost shape. Tentatively, she reached out to nothingness. Her stomach went funny. She was a country girl, to be sure, but she was used to small, cozy spaces at night—for the last ten years she'd worked and lived in a tiny, overcrowded house and shared bed space with three little girls whom she suddenly missed—and she'd never been out on the wide open prairie before. Its emptiness felt vast.

"I suppose we can get along without one for all night, " she said slowly. "Just . . . just a small one will do for now."

Luke struck a match and touched it to a twist of dry grass. Jesse Mae breathed deeply as the meager supply of grass and leftover wood chips that Luke had found beside the shed flamed.

She hurried to finish her bed preparations in the faint light, then sat down on her old gray cloak, removed her shoes and wiggled her toes before pulling out her hairbrush. Taking her pins out, she proceeded to brush her hair. Long, soothing strokes were what she needed to help her think calmly and rationally. She'd always made her plans for the next day over this bedtime ritual.

Luke lay on his folded arm and watched her from under lowered lashes. All her movements dainty, Jesse Mae imparted a sweet womanhood that stirred his blood. Her hair reflected the firelight, its various shades of gold, red, and russet resembling escaped flames. Already, he knew her moods could also take on those elements of fire. A high flare of rushing indignation or, he suspected, a quiet, burning heat.

He couldn't blame ol' George for his attraction. He was damned intrigued with her himself.

Setting his hat over his face, he pretended to sleep until she settled at last. Hearing her breathing deepen, he allowed himself to drift.

"I think we should follow the railroad tracks," Jesse protested Luke's leadership the next morning. "We'll come up on a town eventually." She was thinking about what kind of work she might find to make her living. Her few remaining pennies wouldn't take her far.

"Those tracks are fairly well used, Jesse Mae," Luke stubbornly insisted, pointing to a dirt road of sorts that led northwest. They'd missed it the night before. "That means there's either a farm, ranch, or a town at the end of 'em. My guess is we can buy horses and enough supplies to take us to the next real town, at least."

"But won't that only delay you more?"

"My time schedule has already been blown to smithereens," he reminded her. "I'll be danged if I'm gonna herd these animals on foot all the way to the M double C. 'Sides, won't ol' George look for you in the first town along the railroad route?"

"Um, yes, there is that. But I must tell you, Mr. McCarthy, that I have to find work as soon as possible."

"You have work. You promised to help me get these bulls home." He'd already led them a ways down the wagon track.

"And how far is that exactly, Mr. McCarthy?" she shouted after him. "You never answered that question, did you?"

"Wyoming's a ways west. Might take a few days." He studied the twisted petticoat rope he was looping over his arm. Making do was all well and good, but he needed real equipment. And, the tolerance between the two bulls wasn't likely to last for long, so he had to devise a way of herding them so they wouldn't have to walk side by side.

"As far as Wyoming?" She took a few steps after him. "Well, as long as it's only a few days, I suppose—"

"Good. Let's get going, then."

"Hold on." Jesse Mae sat down to take her shoes off.

He leaned his weight on one leg impatiently. "What are you doing now?"

"Going barefoot. I don't want to wear out my only shoes. They're new."

"Jesse Mae, the ground's rough," he said, staring at her tiny feet and slender ankles as she pulled off her white stockings. "It'll likely tear up your feet."

Even as he said it, he realized her feet were tanned and, while shapely, showed that she was used to being shoeless. There was little sign of tenderness as she firmly planted her feet on the road.

"Not if I walk in the wagon track." She'd gone barefoot around the farm most summers since she was knee-high. "What about you? Those high-heeled fancy boots you're wearing will give you grief enough to cry over if we have to go far."

He looked positively affronted at her suggestion.

"Are you suggesting I take them off?"

"Might save your feet." For the first time in their acquaintance, Jesse Mae found herself on the upper end of an argument with the cowboy. It edged her lips into a grin.

"Nope. Can't do that." He shifted the short rope to his shoulder and stepped down the road.

She ran after him. "Are you shy?"

"Jesse Mae—"

"You are, aren't you?"

"It ain't that."

"What, then?"

He stopped cold. She almost ran into him.

"A cowhand in good standing never parts with his boots, Jesse Mae. It's a matter of pride. And anyway, I might have to chase the bulls."

"You're scared of what someone might say if they saw you barefooted?" Her mouth dropped. She couldn't believe it. "That's a little silly, isn't it?"

He sighed heavily. "Woman, don't you know it ain't healthy to call a man a coward?"

"I didn't exactly call you a coward, Mr. McCarthy, but . . . if the boot fits . . ."

Luke glared through narrowed eyes. "You cheeky little dickens—"

Jesse Mae giggled. Swinging her bag to one shoulder and her shoes to the other, she started briskly up the tamped-down track. After carrying heavy laundry baskets and animal feed for years, her bag felt easy. "If you'd rather have pride than feet, Mr. McCarthy . . ."

Luke stared after her for only a moment before

ungraciously sitting down in the middle of the track. She tried to hold her features steady while he struggled out of his boots and socks, muttering curses all the while. But she didn't quite succeed.

Heaven help him if his brother Will ever heard of this, or any of the M double C cowhands, especially Sandy, Crow, or Simeon. They'd laugh themselves to a standstill and never let him live it down. But he couldn't let that little package of femininity get the better of him.

A heavy snort above his ear reminded him he had to keep moving. His bulls weren't likely to take kindly to one another if given enough time to size each other up properly, and even though the Herefords' horns had been sawed off short, he didn't relish being butted by one of them.

"All right, Miss Banning. But would you mind singing?"

5

After walking about six miles, they came across a small herd of cattle and finally reached a small sod house, barn, and spindly corral. Clothing flapped in the wind from a short clothesline attached to the house's corner: two shirts, a woman's dress, and several white squares. Someone pounded iron, its clanging noise reaching them long before they saw anyone.

"Thank goodness." Jesse Mae spotted a well to the side of the house. She was thirsty enough to drink from the rusty pail they'd brought with them, but now she hoped for something cleaner.

Luke leaned against a nearby post and hastily shoved his bare feet into his boots. They were sore and pink from the sun, but by heaven, he'd kept up with the little redhead. He never would've believed it, but she'd almost outpaced him. Anyway, she could never call him a coward again.

Jesse Mae strode forward, calling, "Hello? Anyone home?"

A brown-haired woman stepped from the doorway, a baby in her arms. "John?" she called loudly and with a little concern. "John, you come on round front. We got comp'ny."

"I'm sorry to call on strangers like this out of the blue, ma'am," Jesse Mae addressed the woman, remaining still so as not to cause more alarm. "But we—Mr. McCarthy, and I—need some help."

"Well, I'll sure oblige you, if I can," the woman said cautiously. "What is it you need?"

A bearded man of medium height stepped around the corner of the house, a rifle cradled in his arms. He looked the two of them over carefully before he said, "What can we do for you folks?"

"Right now I'd be very grateful for a cup of water," Jesse answered.

The woman waited for her husband to nod before letting her expression soften. She took a tin cup hanging from a nail in the doorpost and offered it. "Help yourself, Mrs. McCarthy."

Jesse Mae set her bag down, tumbled her shoes on top of it, and then hurried to the well without bothering to correct the woman's impression. Besides, she was getting used to it.

She drank thirstily, then dipped her cup again and took it to Luke. He drained it in three long gulps, and Jesse Mae refilled it immediately.

"You neighbors er what?" the bearded man finally queried.

"My name's McCarthy," Luke replied, lowering the cup for the second time. "We ain't neighbors, just passing through. We accidentally got left behind when the train stopped for the water back a ways. Followed your road."

"How do, Mr. McCarthy," the woman offered. "We're the Pearsons, John and Effie."

"What befell you?" John Pearson asked, his notice of their dusty appearance obvious.

"Pleased to meet you, ma'am," Luke responded with a tip of his hat to the woman. Then he turned toward the man. "It's this way, Mr. Pearson . . ."

Luke told their story briefly. "I was headed to Wyoming on the train with two Hereford bulls when I had a run-in with a trio of polecats. One, especially, frightened Jesse Mae and I wouldn't stand for that. When the train stopped for water, I discovered my bulls had been let off the train. I got off to see about them, and the next thing I knew, Jesse Mae and I both got left behind." He finished with, "Jesse Mae had her satchel with 'er, but all my gear got left on the train."

"Sounds like something funny—some dirty dealin' to me," John remarked.

"Yep, it was that." But he offered no further explanation and John nodded in understanding that that was as much as would be said.

"Well, my stars," Effie exclaimed. "I never heard of the like. Nobody ever got off the train down there before. We seen railroaders nosin' about sometimes, though." She switched subjects without a breath. "You folks must be nigh starvin' if you ain't had nothin' to eat since yesterday. I got rabbit stew close to ready an' reckon we can make it stretch."

Jesse Mae recognized the woman's generous offer and gave her thanks graciously.

"Where's them bulls now, Mr. McCarthy?" John asked.

"Reckon they're mixin' with your cattle about a mile back, Mr. Pearson. Hope you don't mind, but it seemed safe enough to leave them there for a spell. I'm hoping you can sell us supplies and horses."

"C'mon into the house, Mrs. McCarthy," Effie invited. "Little Abe, here, is fussin' to be put down fer his nap."

Jesse Mae threw Luke a helpless glance. "I'm not—"

"Jesse Mae and I'd be pleased to eat at your table, Mrs. Pearson," he intervened with a smile, all the while patting Jesse Mae's shoulder in a patronizing fashion. She heartily wanted to dig her elbow into his ribs, but Effie watched them too closely. "And I can pay for supplies."

"Well, now, I ain't got nothin' but mules just now Mr. McCarthy, an' I need 'em, myself. But I got somethin' you can mount, if need be. Glad to get rid of the dad-blasted thing, too, if you're a mind to have it."

"What've you got, Mr. Pearson?"

"A camel. A she-camel with an uncertain temper."

A camel? One of those foreign things with brown humps? Jesse Mae'd heard about such animals when she had still been in school. Before her mother died. She'd continued her education on her own by sneaking talks with the Sedalia teacher and overseeing the Jeter children's homework.

But a camel? She barely concealed an unladylike snort. The high and mighty cowboy, Luke McCarthy, with his fancy boots and spiffy hat, was reduced to riding a camel? Curiosity to see the animal made her pause. It was all she could do to hide her laughter.

Luke controlled his surprise and disappointment with a pleasant nod toward John, but as the men turned toward the back corral, he flashed Jesse Mae a quick you'd-better-not-say-a-word frown over his

shoulder. She, in turn, smiled at him sweetly before
following Effie into the house. If she didn't miss her
guess, they were going to ride a camel out of this
place. Luke would ride anything rather than be caught
walking.

The little dirt abode was just as Jesse Mae had once
heard a soddy described. The Pearson's bedroom sat
in the back corner behind a blanket-hung wall, and
the kitchen-parlor took up the front half of the house.

Jesse Mae fell naturally into the routine of helping
with the meal preparation as well as picking up little
Abe when he fussed, carrying him over her shoulder
to soothe him back to sleep. Effie maintained most of
the conversation, relating how she and John had built
the house and barn, just the two of them, and what
effort it took to plow the grain field for the first time.

Jesse Mae mentally shook her head in compassion.
No wonder the woman looked thin and tired.

In her busyness, she barely took notice when Luke
entered with John, scarcely appeared to listen to their
talk of cattle breeding, or showed awareness when
Luke's gaze frequently focused on her. The kitchen
tasks seemed all too familiar. Except no one squabbled
or fought for food as they did in Cousin Bertha's house.

The Pearsons ate their midday meal with relish, but
with little talk to interfere. Luke smiled at Jesse Mae
across the table and followed their example. Jesse
Mae, used to the chatter and whine of almost a dozen
children, found the near-quiet refreshing, yet strange.

When the meal was finished, Jesse Mae insisted that
Effie sit and rest while she cleaned up the kitchen.
After Effie's protest was put aside, Jessie Mae breezed
through the task with an economy of motion. She
found a cloth and dusted the few pieces of furniture,
taking careful pains with the big black Bible that took

pride of place on top of their one chest. As her final effort to repay her hostess, she went outside and gathered the clothes from the line.

Inside again, she set the clothes on the bed in the corner and folded the diapers carefully, ready for use.

John excused himself to return to his work. Effie watched Jesse Mae from her rocking chair, mending in her lap. "My, my, Mrs. McCarthy, you sure know how to take care of a family, I'm thinking. Do you and Mr. McCarthy want a large one?"

"Oh, no . . . I mean, well . . . um . . ." In spite of herself, Jesse Mae found herself blushing. Drat it all, why hadn't she set these people straight in the beginning? If she tried to do so now, she'd look a fool, beside causing unneeded suspicion.

"We ain't had much time to palaver over it, ma'am," Luke replied for her. "We just met a short time ago. Ain't had time to get much acquainted except for . . . uh, well, ma'am, you understand."

"I knew it! You two are newlyweds. Brand-new, ain't you?"

"Your guessing abilities are mighty sharp, Mrs. Pearson."

While Effie preened at Luke's compliment, Jesse Mae held her annoyance with him at bay, pointedly going to the door and looking out. "The sun's about halfway down the western sky," she remarked casually. "Shouldn't we be on our way?"

"Yep, the day's getting on, Jesse Mae. There's something of a town west of here where we can get horses, John thinks, but if we start out now, with the bulls an' all, we'd be caught short of daylight getting in. John proposed we spend the night and proceed in the morning."

"That's a dandy idea," Effie said. "I don't get much

female comp'ny an' I'd be pleased if you'd stay longer. Ain't got nothing but the barn to offer fer a bedroom, but there's fresh grass to sleep on, an' I got an extra blanket."

Before Jesse Mae could protest, Luke accepted. "That sure is a godsend, Mrs. Pearson. The barn will do us just fine, won't it, darlin'?" He raised a brow at Jesse Mae, daring her to say a word against it. "Now, John needs some help on that busted axle he's fixing, so please excuse me. No need in wasting daylight, to my way of thinking."

"You folks take after our own hearts, Mrs. McCarthy," Effie said as Luke strode out of the door. She rose from her chair. "You ain't the shiftless kind."

"Thank you. But please call me Jesse Mae."

"All right. Now, I know you must be plumb dyin' for a good wash, dearie. After yer troubles yesterday an' yer long walk an' all. Little Abe'll likely sleep fer another while yet, an' I got outside work to do. Why don't you take a quick sponge bath while you got the house to yerself?"

"Oh, Mrs. Pearson, you are the soul of kindness," Jesse Mae answered gladly. If only Effie knew how rare it was for Jesse Mae to bathe without the company of three little girls and a watch set out against the boys. "I'll do just that."

She wasted no time in drawing water from the well and laying out fresh clothing. Long practice at piece-meal bathing gave her the ability of baring and washing one limb and torso area at a time, working from top to bottom.

When she'd completed most of her bath, she donned the best of her two work dresses, a faded green print, and sighed with pleasure. She did love to be clean, something for which Cousin Bertha had often laughed at her. In spite of Bertha's slovenly ways, Jesse Mae drew great satisfaction in the thought she'd left behind good bathing habits in the girls.

Tying her hem up around her waist, she stepped into the wash pan, wiggling her toes in enjoyment before sitting on the edge of the kitchen bench and hiking her skirt all the way to the top of her thighs. With care, she lathered and rinsed first the right and then the left foot and leg. Placing her feet on the bench, she patted her skin dry, then leaned back on her arms and stretched, pointing her toes.

It wasn't that he made a sound—perhaps she was used to being on the alert for that sneaky, dirty-minded George—but she suddenly knew that Luke was watching her. Her head snapped toward the door.

He stood statue-still, his hands at his sides, his face almost blank.

"What are you doing there?" she sharply demanded, jerking her skirt and muslin petticoat down. Her heart pounded with fear and a feeling of betrayal.

"Watching you," Luke said honestly. He slowly raised his gaze to hers and forced himself to keep it there. "I'm real sorry, Jesse Mae, I didn't mean to be a Peeping Tom. I didn't know you were washing. I only wanted to . . ."

What had he wanted to tell her? The sight of her milky white legs, shapely and long for her tiny body, had thrown him off his stride. Seeing her bare flesh had caused him a queer turn that he didn't understand, a gush of hot desire that embarrassed him. Shamelessly, he wanted to see those legs again, to find out if they were as silky as they looked.

Luke swallowed hard and mentally hauled himself up. He'd seen women's legs before. Granted, they'd been at the whorehouse, but it wasn't as though he didn't know what a woman looked like. He was acting like a prime greenhorn kid. His embarrassment, he guessed, was because she wasn't a whore. But that wouldn't take away the image of what he had seen.

"I'm right sorry, honey," he said quietly, his voice husky. "Excuse me."

He left as suddenly as he had appeared. Jesse Mae pulled a long, shaky breath into her lungs. Luke had actually apologized for his intrusion, something she'd never experienced before. Her cousins, the Jeter boys, would never have thought it necessary to do so. George, especially, would've tried to take advantage of the situation. She'd have needed to threaten George with the kitchen knife to have him leave her alone, and he would never have apologized.

Luke was different. He was a gentleman. Something about him assured her of that, yet she'd been aware of that flash of unadulterated desire in his gaze. It had triggered a response in her, whether she wanted to admit it or not.

Slowly, her nerves let go of their tautness, and when Effie came in, she could pretend that she was totally relaxed. Only she wasn't, perfectly. Because she found herself newly aware of an attraction toward Luke that she hadn't counted on.

Stubbornly, she decided she'd just have to ignore it. Her plans didn't include letting her feelings get out of hand for a good-looking cowboy who might be here in her life today and gone tomorrow. No sir. If she got tangled up with any man, an old man's darling was what she planned to be, a man who had something besides a sod hut to give her. A man who treated her as his best treasure.

She dreamed of having a house of her own, a real nice house, not too big but just right, and good furniture that she could polish to a high shine, and a really fine bed.

She'd never be a young man's slave, like Effie, here, who would likely grow old before her time.

The baby woke and began to cry. After a while, Effie put the child to her breast to nurse. He rooted and suckled, yet seemed unsatisfied and whimpered angrily until he started an all-out wail.

"My milk seems to be drying up. I don't know what to do," Effie said plaintively. "The little tyke's likely to starve if I can't feed him."

"Won't he take cow's milk?" Jesse Mae asked.

"He don't cotton to the bottle, that's fer sure. But 'sides that, cow's milk don't seem to agree with 'im. Don't know what to try next."

"What about goat's milk?"

"Goat's milk? I never heard of nobody feedin' a baby goat's milk."

"Well, Bertha's third from the youngest—that's the people I worked for—had lots of problems before we tried goat's milk. That seemed to work."

"Well, I'll have John look around town and see if he can find a nanny. Meanwhile, I surely wish little Abe would outgrow this colic."

"Here, let me walk him awhile." Jesse Mae held the baby upright over her shoulder until he burped, then lowered his little body until his head lay directly on her shoulder. It wasn't long before he quieted while she hummed.

"You seem to know a lot about babies," Effie remarked as the men came in for the evening meal.

"I've had lots of practice," Jesse Mae answered automatically.

*   *   *

"Hope you 'n' Luke'll be comfy, dearie," Effie half whispered as she handed Jesse Mae an old quilt. Dusk lay quietly on the land, and they'd finished supper hours ago. "Go on, now. There ain't nothin' more you can do fer me, an' yer man's awaitin'."

Jesse Mae knew she'd stalled long enough about joining Luke in the barn. Nothing would be gained by making one more excuse to stay close to Effie. Beside, John had given her a funny look when he entered the house a short while before, as though he wondered why she showed so little eagerness to be with her husband.

"Thank you kindly, Effie. For everything. We'll be leaving before sunup, I expect, so I'll say good-bye now."

"Yer comp'ny has been my pleasure, Jesse Mae," Effie replied, hugging her. "Now git along."

Jesse Mae trudged her way down the barn path thinking how sincerely kind Effie had been. She hadn't been on the receiving end of a motherly hug since her own mother had died. She'd been ten, and when she was scarcely eleven, her pa had left her at Bertha's.

She'd known only servitude after that. And survival skills against George. But it had taught her well, she firmly reminded herself, and no mere cheeky rascal of a male who made her heart flutter would undo her intentions to lead her own life according to her own design.

She picked up her pace and marched into the barn. All afternoon and evening, she'd been playing Luke's wife because of his letting their hosts think they were married, and she was about to tell him a thing or two. Her glance darted to where Luke already lounged on a pile of sweet grass in the far corner, away from the milk cow and mules.

Stomping over to him, she patted her foot in irritation.

Luke stared at her slender, tiny foot, and raised his gaze a jot to where her ankles disappeared under the dark of her skirt. The foot patted expressively. He'd never thought a foot could talk before.

"Now, Jesse Mae," he bit down on his lip and speedily sat up, then put out his hands as though to ward her off. "Before you explode, let me explain."

She tossed the quilt down. "Yeess . . .?"

"The Pearsons wouldn't have understood us traveling together without being married. They might've sent us off without much more than a cup of water."

"You lied, and you made me lie. I *hate* that."

"I'm sorry, honey, but it wasn't a lie, exactly. I just didn't see any need to correct them. Besides, you did your share of that when you lied to the Thomses."

"You put me in a humiliating bind," she said, glaring at his pointed reminder. "And I don't count what I said to the Thomses as lying. They're pure poison, and anything I said to them was for self-protection. But these are honest folks. Effie kept asking how we'd met and such. I had to tell her a friend introduced us—"

"Well, now, that's true in a way." Luke leaned back on his elbows, his eyes snapping with humor. "Ol' George brought us together right nicely, don't you think?"

"And that we didn't have much time to get really acquainted—"

"Mmm, very true." His I've-got-the-world-by-its-tail grin infuriated her. "But I'm aimin' to fix that soon's I can."

"I had to say that my family didn't approve, so we had to sneak away from Missouri."

"Uh-huh, that ain't no lie, either, honey." He crossed his ankles. "What else?"

"Luke McCarthy," she said with disgust. "You're a

scalawag. You won't take any of this seriously. Doesn't it bother you that you're fooling honest people?"

"A mite, I reckon. But not enough to change anything. We have to get on tomorrow, and I see no need to make more commotion tonight."

"You were mad clear through last night. You didn't find any of this funny then."

"Yeah, but tonight we're a lot more comfortable and tomorrow looks promising. The town has a telegraph, John says, and I can let Will know I'll be late getting back with the Herefords."

"Thank heavens for that. Is Will your boss?"

"Yep. And it shouldn't take us more'n the day, once we get to town, to find some riding horses and the supplies we need to be on our way."

"Okay." She picked up a pile of the grass and moved it about five feet. It was too close to him, in her opinion, but it would give her as much distance between them as the space allowed. "Will this Will fellow be angry about all the additional money he is spending? You know, after all the expenditure already paid out, won't he be upset over the need to buy horses and supplies?"

"He can afford it."

She sat up from patting her grass bed into shape. "Really, Luke, you should be more concerned about your boss's needs. If you care little about spending his money so freely, he might fire you for sure."

"Hmm, you think so?" Luke made himself busy by spreading the quilt on his share of the grass.

Jesse Mae studied him for a moment. His golden curls fell appealingly across his forehead, and he'd removed his neckerchief, which left his shirt opened at the throat. The thick blond stubble on his squarish chin barely darkened his skin; she wondered briefly about whom he'd inherited his features from, and where his family was now. Was he, perhaps, married?

The sudden thought made her blink with shock. Why hadn't it occurred to her before that he might be?

"Um, well, I guess he trusts you a lot or he wouldn't have sent you on such an important mission. I mean, those bulls . . ."

"Yep. Reckon that's so." Luke lay back on the quilt and closed his eyes. "Let me know when I should put out the lamp."

Jesse Mae scurried to smooth out her gray cape. She took her brush from her bag. "And I suppose you must be a good worker."

"I earn my keep."

"How big is the ranch you work on?"

"Pretty big."

"Most of the men are single, I suppose?"

"Yep. Most are. One or two married, though. There's a couple of cottages for the married hands."

"Oh . . . Well, is your boss married?"

"Yep."

"And . . . and do you live in the bunkhouse?"

He didn't, but he could see where her questions were leading. He lived with his mother in the original ranch house. It was small compared to Will's big one across the stream, but he'd always liked it and felt cozy there. It would be his one day.

"All the single men do," he prevaricated.

Satisfied, she began to brush her hair. He listened to the rhythmic strokes and folded his hands across his chest. He didn't have to see it to imagine the fire her hair reflected in the lamplight. He could call up last night's memory.

But the picture he couldn't get out of his mind was one of bare legs and slender ankles.

Fire on top and milky white legs below. He sighed with the languid thoughts of what was covered up in between.

She hummed a lullaby, and he then couldn't repress the image of her cuddling little Abe. She knew a lot about raising children, she'd told Effie, and he'd seen her settle the child down as though she were his own mama. This scrap of a girl was quite a package of womanhood.

So she didn't want to get married, hmm? Or, if she did, to an old man so that she would be queen of his house. The idea was ludicrous. He'd be hanged if he'd let her waste herself like that.

He'd be hanged if he'd let another man have her—young, old, or in between. Luke didn't know how he was going to manage it, but he was going to take this girl all the way home with him and marry her himself if he had to dodge the truth the whole blasted time. Because he wanted Jesse Mae Banning to marry him without knowing he was co-owner of the M double C, one of Wyoming's biggest ranches. He wanted the girl to marry him for himself.

6

The blackish brown camel was the tallest, weirdest animal Jesse Mae had ever seen. It rose up in front of her like a huge fairy-tale kind of a creature, the one hump on its back adding to the fancy. She hated to appear the wide-eyed country bumpkin, but it purely did make her wonder if a person needed a ladder to climb on with.

"Um, Mr. Pearson, are you certain a body can ride this thing? Luke, are you sure you can?"

"Never saw a mount I couldn't handle," Luke insisted. He wasn't about to admit that he, also, felt a mite uncertain, even an inch. "Ain't gonna be thrown by this one."

Jesse Mae cautiously approached the animal, her hand out to pet it. The animal promptly blew slobber all over her arm. A second later, the camel batted what appeared to be three-inch-long eyelashes as Luke drew near, and stretched her neck as though preening.

"I guess she likes Luke well enough," Jesse Mae murmured wryly, wiping her hand against the clean diaper Effie handed her.

"Mehitabel is a mite tetchy with women at times, Jesse Mae, but she's a fine pack animal an' can git you where you want to go. An' camels has been ridden since Bible times an' before," Effie reassured her. "We rode her lots when we first got 'er, but we don't really have no use fer her now. We're obliged fer the trade."

"Well, I suppose . . . But how do you get on it?"

"Just watch, Mrs. McCarthy," John said. "Down, Mehitabel, down. C'mon, now. Show the lady you can be a lady too."

The camel folded down and Luke threw a leg over the odd saddle that John had sold him along with Mehitabel, before extending a hand toward Jesse Mae. She gave him a doubtful look, and Mehitabel an even more uncertain stare, and didn't move.

"Scared, Jesse Mae?" Luke asked, his eyes glinting.

"No, of course not."

"Even a little?" He pursed his lips at her.

"Never." Setting her chin at the challenge, she marched forward and mounted behind Luke. Luke commanded Mehitabel to rise, and the camel did so, hind legs first, in its awkward, methodical fashion.

Jesse Mae caught her breath at being so high off the ground, then called her good-byes to the Pearsons as the camel began to move. The two bulls trailed behind them from a lead rope, one on each side to keep them separated.

Riding double was nothing new to Jesse Mae; she'd ridden with the Jeter children for years—that is, when the Jeter men had given permission for the use of their mounts—but riding double with a full-grown man was a first. Her legs dangled awkwardly, pressing against the back of Luke's legs without her control. The camel's saddle didn't allow her much room. Each time she tried to scoot back an inch or two, it wasn't anytime at all before she was smack up against Luke's back again.

"Will you quit wiggling?"

"I haven't anywhere to hold onto," she said, hiking her bag up once more to rest on her thigh.

"I told you to tie that bag down. Put your arm around my waist; that'll hold you steady."

"Maybe I should just walk." She leaned further away from him. Yet she couldn't maintain that position for long, either; her back would break.

"Don't go fool-headed on me, Jesse Mae. You ain't got proper walking shoes any more than I do, and you won't go barefoot again, not on this prairie." Then he added under his breath, "Not if I can help it."

"Well, it wouldn't be any more uncomfortable than riding astraddle on this animal," she responded. "I'm about to slide right over the edge of her. Really, Luke, I think I should walk."

"Nope. That'd slow us down."

"But I don't mind walking."

But Luke did. He minded the idea of her walking quite as much as he hated walking himself. He pulled hard on the reins. "Whoa, whoa there, Mehitabel. All right," he said on a note of disgust when the camel came to a stop. "Hand me your bag."

Mehitabel turned her head and gave them a haughty stare.

"Where are you putting it?" Jesse Mae protested.

"I'll tie it to the front of the saddle. Shoulda done this in the first place," he grumbled.

Behind them, the lead rope slackened and the two bulls began to graze.

"Maybe I'll just—"

"Now hold on," he instructed, as he twisted around. Before she could guess at his intention, he circled her waist with his hands and lifted her, pulling her around to the front of the saddle. In the process, she bumped against his shoulder and rolled against him, chest against chest, her forehead brushing his chin.

The momentary contact disconcerted them both, and Luke held her that way while he examined her upturned face, wanting very badly to put his face against hers, to find out if her lips were as soft as they appeared.

He resisted the impulse, though, knowing he had to wait his time. He didn't plan on making George's mistakes. She might be scared off before he'd had a chance to woo her.

Instead, he settled her crossways in front of him. "Now hook your knee on the pommel as you would a sidesaddle and you can rest your leg on the bag. There, now lean back against me. That should give you an easier ride."

Jesse Mae wasn't sure it would. Not with Luke's arm now snuggling her close. She had even less control over where their bodies met than before. His hand splayed against her waist far too intimately, making her much too aware of every finger against her middle.

"I'm not sure this is a good idea either, Luke."

"Quit fidgeting and fussing, honey. We'll make better time if you just relax. I'd like to make town by noon. I promise I won't take advantage of you. I'll only hold you steady."

Jesse Mae bit at her lip and stilled, trying to hide her agitation. It wouldn't do to let Luke know that he stirred her even a little.

Luke gave the command to move, and Mehitabel

went forward. Behind them, the bulls protested, then began walking again.

"I wonder how big the town is, did Mr. Pearson say?"

"Big 'nuff to take care of our business."

"Does it have a doctor or a lawyer, d' you suppose?"

"Mmm, doctor, I think. Why?"

"Oh, just wondering. Is he young or old?"

"Don't know. Old, I guess. John mentioned the man didn't make rounds beyond five miles outside of town anymore."

"Oh. Is he married, did John say?"

"No, John didn't say," Luke replied, annoyed with all her questions with no apparent reason for asking. "Why all this going on about a doc in town, Jesse Mae? You ain't sick, are you? And what difference does it make if he's married or not?"

"Oh, I was only thinking about my plan. You know, to be beholden to nobody and own my own wages. Or, barring that, to marry an old man. I could work for a doctor or lawyer really easy, you see, and that way I could either save my wages to go on to San Francisco or maybe, someday, I'd marry him. After I'd saved enough money of my own. If he was old enough."

Luke's hand tightened against her waist. This business of "her plan" was just about more than any red-blooded, healthy cowpoke could take. Throwing herself away on either of those ideas was downright criminal, to his way of thinking.

"Jesse Mae . . ." He trailed off because they were entering town. But he had to do something to dissuade her from trying to get work right away. That didn't suit his purpose at all.

"Guess not, anyway," she remarked casually, looking around. "This town is too small to hide in and too close to the railroad. George could find me here."

People stared as they entered the one-street town, but no one spoke. "Reckon they've seen Mehitabel before," Luke commented.

They found the tiny telegraph office next to the town's hotel. Jesse Mae looked the larger structure over carefully, mentally counting rooms. Catching her speculative gaze on the sign that read *Beekers,* Luke hurried to dismount.

"It would take a lot of work to keep up a place like that, wouldn't it?" she asked. "I wonder what kind of wages—"

Jesse Mae." Luke helped her to dismount, then handed her a twenty-dollar gold piece. "Get yourself some proper riding clothes and boots, honey, while I take care of sending my message. And a hat."

She stared at the shiny coin in her palm, then back at him, her eyes wide.

"I can't take this."

"Don't worry about it, Jesse Mae. I won quite a jackpot at poker the night before we boarded the train."

"I can't take it."

"Don't be ridiculous. You need a pair of britches and—"

"You don't understand. Your buying me clothing would be like . . . like . . . my being a kept woman." Pink stained her cheeks, and Luke suddenly realized she felt a little hurt as well as embarrassed.

"Aw, hell, Jesse Mae. It ain't nothing of the sort."

"It is! My mama always said that a lady never accepted anything except flowers or candy from a gentleman not her husband. I can't pay for new clothes."

She tried to hand the coin back to him, but he clamped his hand over hers, forcing hers to close around the money.

"Jesse Mae, you promised to help me get these bulls home, didn't you?"

"I suppose I did, but—"

"No buts. I'm holding you to your word. Count this money as an advancement of what I'll owe you for trail riding with me if you want to, but you go find the mercantile store and buy whatever you need in the way of trail clothes."

"Twenty dollars is too much. I-I'm the one in your debt, Luke; you wouldn't be in this fix except for me. Besides, I could never earn it out."

"Oh, yes, you will. We'll hit some rough country in the next few days, and I'll need you. Anyway, this is a special circumstance, Jesse Mae, and you said you wanted work." He tied one of the bulls to a hitching post and led the other to the next one over. "Now you work for me."

She opened her mouth to add to her protest, but he quickly intervened. "I'll meet you back here in about an hour, and then we can have some dinner and make our plans. Meanwhile, I'll try to find horses. Agreed?"

"I—"

"An hour," he insisted. Resolutely, he turned and headed into the telegraph office.

Surreptitiously, Jesse Mae glanced up and down the street before breathing a sigh of relief. No one paid her any attention.

When they met an hour later, Luke told her that he'd engaged rooms for them at Beekers. "Can't get mounts till tomorrow," he explained. "The livery owner says he can find a couple of saddle horses for us by morning."

"What about Mehitabel, Meshach, and Shadrach?"

"Mehitabel and who?"

"Um, the bulls. It seemed, uh, funny not to call them something."

Luke chuckled. "Okay. But now I'll be looking for Abednego to make an appearance somewhere along the way," he responded, referring to the fact that the three Biblical names were usually linked together. "Well, Meshach and Shadrach are having a long drink of water down at the livery stable, and Mehitabel is enjoying the attention of the local kids. They'll be safe enough until we leave."

Luke took her elbow, guiding her into the hotel, past the lobby and down the hall. "Room seven is yours, honey. I'm right next door in five."

She glanced at him suspiciously as they stopped in front of her door. "You're next door?"

"Don't go lookin' at me that way," he said as he handed her a key. "They ain't connecting. Now hurry with your freshening up. I'm starved."

Ashamed at her thoughts when Luke had done nothing to deserve them, she gave him a repentant smile. "I'll be ready in a shake of a lamb's tail." Halfway through the door, she turned back. "Oh, I almost forgot. Here," she said, thrusting a package into his hands.

"What's this?"

"New socks and shirt. I hope you like blue." It would match his eyes, she'd thought when she bought it. She'd spent more time deliberating over which shirt to buy him than she had over her own new clothes. There was also a razor and bar of soap in the package, but he'd find those fast enough.

"Why, thanks, Jesse Mae. Thanks a heap. How'd you know what size to buy?"

She looked him over carefully, estimating the width of his shoulders and the fact that she barely reached his chin, before letting her gaze rest straight ahead on his chest. It hadn't been hard. Not a bit.

"Oh, I suppose it's one of those things a girl does.

I've had lots of training, living with a large family, on how to guess what might fit somebody. Sizes, spaces—I'm good at sizing up anything and I hope it can help me in my next job."

"Well, it just did, didn't it? Remember, I'm your boss now. You're riding for the M double C ranch. Thirty dollars a month, room an' board."

She tipped her head to stare at him squarely. She hadn't quite put the whole matter in that context before now.

"What'll your boss Will say? D'you have the authority to hire a new hand? And women don't usually hire on as cowboys, do they?"

"Will won't have a worry 'bout it. 'Sides, I got just the job in mind for you, after we get to the M double C. You'll like it. Now get along an' clean up for dinner."

They ate supper in the hotel's tiny dining room, then strolled the town before turning in. They paused at her door. After two nights of having her close enough to touch, he felt almost bereft to know she'd be on the other side of a wall.

"Well, good night, Jesse Mae. Hope you sleep well."

"I guess I will. But I haven't slept alone in years," she said, thinking of all the years of sharing with the Jeter girls.

"Um . . . um . . . that can . . . be remedied any time you say so, honey."

She glanced up at Luke's funny sound. He opened his mouth but said nothing more. He was choking on laughter.

"What?" Then suddenly realizing the way her words had come out, she blushed. She felt the heat run up her face and down her neck. "Oh . . . oh, you . . . you!"

Swiftly, she pushed into her room and slammed the door behind her.

*   *   *

"This's the best I c'd do on short notice, Mr. McCarthy," the squat livery owner declared the next morning, referring to the two sorry-looking horses he offered for purchase. One was a swaybacked bay and the other an ancient gelding that was blind in one eye. "But I'm low, right now, on good saddle mounts."

They stood at the edge of the corral behind the livery barn. The owner, Mr. Sizemore, seemed only mildly interested in selling his stock. A boy of ten or eleven sat on the rail.

"You ain't holding out on me, are you, Mr. Sizemore?" Luke questioned. The man's asking price was overly high, making him suspicious of the trade. "Those the best you got?"

"Only ones free at the moment. Been a heavy season fer travel," the man offered.

"Pa, what about them mules Lester has?" said a boy.

His pa ignored the sally. "If you c'd give me a couple more days, I might c'd send down to Reddings an' get you sompthin' better. But it'd be two days goin' and two days comin'."

And the cost would be over the mountain, Luke mused. The man was a shrewd trader.

Jesse Mae glanced up at Luke through her lashes. After thinking it over, she had no desire to linger around this little burg any longer than necessary. It wasn't a good idea. It gave George too much catch-up time. "Where are the mules?"

Luke was beginning to know when the thought of ol' George panic-flashed across her mind, and it gave him pause for thought, too, but that didn't mean he was ready to throw a saddle over a mule. "Reddings?"

"He's a horse breeder over the Colorado border. Comes this way every fall with his stock."

"I think we should look at the mules," Jesse Mae said.

Luke stalled. "Two days' ride, hmm?"

"Them mules're young an' well trained, missus," offered young Bobby, upon which his pa gave him a dirty look.

"Luke . . .?" Jesse Mae murmured plaintively.

Her wide green eyes implored him. "All right, all right," he said, heaving out a sigh. "Let's see 'em."

"They's up at Lester's, behind the barber shop," Bobby said. "I'll take ya."

"You be sure'n tell Lester I sent you folks," Mr. Sizemore insisted as they turned to leave.

To Luke's relief and Jesse Mae's pleasure, the mules were as prime as Bobby had promised. It took very little time to come to an agreement with Lester on the price.

Jesse Mae felt disappointed when the mules already had names. "Yeah, they's called Remus and Romulus," Bobby told her. "Lester calls 'em Rem an' Rom fer short. He says mules is smarter'n horses, mostly."

"Know of any saddles going cheap?" Luke questioned the boy after flipping him a coin for his help.

"Sure 'nuff, mister," Bobby replied on a broad grin. "They's old, but Pa's got two-three. Don't let 'im charge ya more'n thirty dollars, though."

"I won't, Bobby. You can bet on it," Luke responded.

By noon, they were on their way at last. Luke turned in his saddle and surveyed their little cavalcade. Jesse Mae, appearing even tinier clad in boys' jeans and tan shirt, seemed comfortable enough on Rom. Mehitabel hadn't even groaned at the heavy supply pack they'd loaded to her saddle, but had merely given Luke a lovelorn stare and batted her lashes, to which Jesse Mae had, in turn, given him her ladylike derisive snort. He'd turned his glare on her; she'd only half hidden her laughter.

Luke headed due west, traveling at the moderate pace that Meshach and Shadrach required.

They camped that night in a depression of ground near a stream, surrounded by brush. Luke had picked the spot in an attempt to cover their trail a little. If George did follow them, Luke would make it as hard as possible for him to find them.

After a supper of bacon and biscuits, Luke spent time cleaning his gun and going over their equipment. At last he sat Indian fashion on the end of his bedroll and fed the fire. Luke had spread their blankets side by side separated by a mere yard.

"How far away is the M double C, anyway?" Jesse Mae spoke sleepily, her head pillowed in her arms.

"About ten days to a couple of weeks, I reckon, with the slow pace the bulls will need," he answered. "I've been thinking, though. Maybe we'll just drop down to Hinley and pick up your harp before we start north."

Jesse Mae sat up suddenly. "Oh, Luke! Could we? D'you think it's there?" In her excitement, she scooted on her knees to the edge of her blanket to face him. "I know that's as far as my freight charge carried it, but what makes you think they'll keep it for me? How long will they hold it, d'you know?"

"Well, I sent word for 'em to hang on to it when I telegraphed my bro . . . my boss. They'll hold it as long as need be."

"Are you sure? Oh, Luke, I'd do anything to get my mother's harp back. It's the only thing I have to remember her by. She played it beautifully."

"Then we'll do it. Mehitabel can carry it if we shift a few of our things to the mules."

"Luke McCarthy, you are one sweet man." Impulsively, Jesse Mae threw her arms around his neck, intending to simply thank him with a peck on the cheek, but instead tumbling him backwards. In a trice, his arms circled her, taking her with him.

Surprised, she lay atop him while her heart fluttered. Swallowing hard, she cleared her throat. Still, her voice came out in a whisper. "Thank you, Luke. Thank you kindly."

"It ain't nothin', honey," he whispered back, his mouth inching closer to hers. "Nothin' . . ."

But they each knew that what he was offering was more than a mere token. Going after the harp would take them out of their way by days. What he offered was a gift of effort, time, and expenditure.

"Nothin' . . ." His mouth closed on hers lightly at first, then with more urgency.

His lips felt soft as a feather, yet they gave her shooting tingles all the way to her tummy and drew her like a magnet. She'd never imagined masculine lips could evoke so much inner hunger before, never thought she'd feel so overwhelmed that she could scarcely breathe. She didn't want it to end.

Jesse Mae had never been kissed before, not properly. The few times George had tried, she'd been heartily revolted and fought him with anything she'd had at hand—a rolling pin, the iron skillet (which she'd kept by the attic pallet that she shared with the younger Jeter girls), or even, once, the chicken she'd thrown at him out in the chicken yard.

Now Luke's gentleness caught her by surprise. She sighed against his mouth and finally pulled away. Gingerly, on shaky limbs, she scooted back to her own blanket. He didn't move, but watched her from lowered lids.

"I ain't sorry, honey. Been wantin' that since the first day." His voice was low, husky.

Unable to speak, she nodded in acknowledgment. Slowly, he folded his arms behind his head and looked at the sky before he spoke again.

"Won't happen again, though, till you want it to. But don't go throwing your arms around me like that unless you mean it, hear? I don't reckon I'll be able to stop at one little kiss if you do."

Curling on her side, Jesse Mae stared into the fire. Her emotions were in a turmoil, that was certain, and it wouldn't take much for her to lose her head—and more—with Luke. Now she knew how her mother had allowed herself to get mixed up with her pa, even knowing he was a man with itchy feet.

She closed her eyes, remembering her mother's voice. All those hard years of near-slavery working for Pa's cousins hadn't dimmed her mother's advice. "Don't let yourself listen to sugared words, Jesse Mae, they'll lead you down the primrose path. Watch yourself, value what you are and what you have to offer a man. Choose a man who will treat you like a princess. Remember, my darling child, that it's better to be an old man's darling than to be a young man's slave."

I'm not going to fall in love with this cowboy, mama. No sir, no matter what. That kiss won't change a thing!

Across the narrow space, Luke heartily wished he'd brought a pint of whisky with him. It would be a long time before he could sleep. But then, again, a drink wasn't going to change his want for Jesse Mae. Not a jot.

7

They reached the outskirts of Hinley the next day at dusk and camped in a grove of cottonwood trees on the north side of town. Luke prowled the area like a cat before pronouncing the place safe. "Mehitabel won't likely to be spotted as easily in these trees," he said.

They staked the bulls at the wood's edge away from town where they could graze, then brought the camel and mules into the thickest growth.

"How soon do you think we can pick up the harp?" Jesse Mae asked as she unsaddled her mule.

"Freight office'll likely be closed by now. Rustle up some supper, Jesse, while I water the animals. Then I'll run on into town, take a look around and get the layout."

Somewhere along the way Luke had simplified her name, reducing it to merely Jesse. She liked it and decided to adopt the shortened address, though it made her feel a little different, as though she'd become a more adult personification of herself. Yes, she mused, as though she counted.

"You?" Jesse challenged Luke's intentions to leave her behind. "Why not both of us?"

"Don't think that's a good idea."

"Why not?"

Luke hadn't wanted to say it, but he thought George might be hanging around Hinley. If the dunderhead had been half-smart enough to figure out to watch her harp, he, or one of the Thomses would be keeping an eye on the freight office.

He planned to scout the saloons, too, and he couldn't take her with him there. But all he said was, "From now on, I'd like to draw as little attention to us as possible, honey, and besides Mehitabel, your hair doesn't exactly hide who you are. If George is looking for us, he'll be looking for the obvious."

Automatically, Jesse fidgeted with the blue neckerchief she'd worn to tie her hair back. It was true. Her cursed hair shone like a beacon.

After supper, Luke walked the perimeters of the little wood once more before setting off. Jesse sat hugging her knees next to the small blaze of firelight, feeling unaccountably lonely even before he left. She hated being left behind.

"Um, how late will you be?" Her voice sounded uncertain.

"Not late. You'll be all right if you keep close by camp," he assured her. He didn't like the idea of leaving her alone any more than she did, and hesitated. "Just keep that shotgun handy."

"I will," she promised.

After Luke left, she wandered over to pat her mule. "Hello, Rom," she said, rubbing his ears, offering him a handful of grass. He gently pushed his head against her arm. "You like that, don't you, boy? Are you lonely·without Rem?"

She'd gathered a large stack of thick prairie grass for Mehitabel earlier. The animal had ignored her and seemed content to just chew.

"Mehitabel is altogether too full of herself to bother with loneliness, I guess." Rom's ears flicked forward. With one last pat she left him to check on Meshach and Shadrach.

After observing that they, too, were content, she strolled back to the fire. Finding her brush, she gave her hair a thorough brushing, then fixed it in two long braids. She banked the fire, making sure it would hold its coals, before rolling up in her blanket.

But she lay wide-eyed, counting stars, counting minutes, counting the breaths she took. Funny, she thought, how much she could worry about that too-smart-for-his-own-good cowboy when she'd known him less than a week.

Luke tied Rem to the hitching post of the first saloon he came to and strolled casually through the open door. It was a Thursday night, so the custom wasn't as heavy as if it were Saturday. It took him only a moment to see that no one looked familiar.

He made the rounds of the town's business district, checking the establishments. As expected, the railroad station house was locked up for the night. The sign on the front door said its hours were from seven to six.

Satisfied, he started up a side street that paralleled the railroad track where a few of the seedier establishments were located. He paused outside of the saloon on the corner. A loud, raucous voice spilled out from the opened front window, its high insistence answering a heavy one of easy identification. Archie Thoms and George. It was a sure bet Eli was there, too.

Well, now they were up against the second go-round. Luke's fighting instinct began to boil, and his fists clenched. Those three had played a mighty dirty trick on him, and he wanted revenge. Ordinarily, he'd walk right up to them and face the men down; he was pretty good in a fair fight, and he'd take his chances on holding his own. But the polecats had already proven that they didn't fight fair.

Besides that, he couldn't draw attention to Jesse. If he tried for a showdown, they'd surely find her.

Slowly, he forced himself to relax. He had to think of both Jesse and his bulls. Getting Jesse to safety was almighty important, and soon she'd be safe at home, at the M double C.

He'd have to decide if he could sneak past George and the Thomses in the morning or if he'd simply leave the harp behind again.

Jesse would be deeply disappointed.

His temper simmered. He didn't want to face her and tell her she had to leave the harp behind once more. He danged well didn't. Jesse put a lot of store by her ma's harp, and he didn't see why she had to do without it because of these three bullies.

Luke lit one of his rare cigarettes and leaned against the building's window to listen. To anyone who might be watching, he appeared to be merely a lounger.

The men inside were arguing over whether they'd stay in town for another few days or leave to look for Jesse.

"Just let 'er go, George," Eli said. "We might 's well go on home. No female is worth all this fuss."

"No! I told ya afore. She's mine an' I ain't givin' 'er

up to a no-account cowboy. An' when I ketch her I'm gonna teach 'er a lesson she'll never fergit. She'll never run off from me again."

"Well, we ain't findin' her 'round here," Eli pointed out sourly. "We oughter go back and find where she went when she got off the train."

"Don't make no sense watchin' a harp," Archie added, bored. "Ain't no fun."

"If you knowed how Jesse Mae felt about that harp ya wouldn't say that," George insisted.

"Still think we oughta go home. Wastin' time, here," Eli said, more irritated.

A moment passed. Luke heard only shuffled movement. Then George spoke again, at first reluctantly, but then with growing enthusiasm. "I reckon a bit of fun would help the night pass. Reckon we c'ud find us a woman."

"That's what I want," agreed Archie. "A real lively woman."

"That sets okay by me," Eli agreed. "Reckon we can hang around Hinley one more day. But when we find that little . . ."

"Yeah, when we find 'er . . ."

Luke moved quickly. He had to get Jesse out of reach. Hell, he knew they'd been having it too easy these last couple of days. Jesse's nerves had settled down nice as you please, and she'd grown freer with him each passing hour. He'd made real progress in getting her to trust him, and he planned on broaching the subject of taking her home to stay any day now.

The sound of scraping chairs sent him on. He cut through to the next street, and just to play it safe, ducked into the Three Aces. He ordered a beer, then settled at a table in a back corner so that he could watch the comings and goings while he thought about things.

"Luke McCarthy." Someone called his name from the bar, and after a moment, he spotted a man whom he remembered had once worked a season for the M double C as a bronco rider. Like many cowhands, he'd left to see other parts of the country. "Well, I see you done growed up since I last laid eyes on you," the man said.

"Boswell, ain't it?" Luke responded as the older man came forward.

"Yeah, that's me." He wore the remnants of a cavalry uniform, his big frame nearly popping his shirt buttons. "What're you doin' in this neck of the woods, Luke? Kinda far from home, ain'tcha?"

"Oh, just having a jaunt, so to speak," Luke answered. "Sit down and tell me what you've been up to lately."

"Workin' my way back north, I reckon. Tired of the desert ranges and hot Texas summers."

"See you did a spell for the government," Luke remarked, pointing to the man's army jacket.

"Yep, tried that, too."

"So you're looking for work, huh?"

"Reckon so. Is Will needin' any hands? I wouldn't mind workin' for you folks again. Gotta say, though, I'm past my bronco bustin' days."

"Don't reckon we need a horse specialist right now, anyway, but . . ." An idea was forming in Luke's head. "Uh, Boswell, you got any ties in this town?"

"Naw, just passin' through, like I said. What you askin' for?"

"Hmm . . . Have you got your own outfit?"

"You mean a horse? You tryin' to insult me, Luke? You know I'd never be without a decent mount."

"Glad to hear you say it, Boswell. How would you like to ride for me right now?"

"Now? You mean tonight?" The older man scanned Luke's face in surprise. "Doin' what?"

"Well, it's this way. . ." Pushing his hat back, Luke lowered his voice and leaned across the table. Boswell stretched to meet him.

Luke recounted the story of how he and a partner had been shoved off the train when they had a difference of opinion with three men of low character, and their need to get their bulls safely to the M double C as soon as possible. "The trouble is, Boswell, I need something out of the train's freight storeroom down there at the Hinley station, and that trio of sidewinders are watching it. I, um . . . aw, hell, Boswell. Right now ain't the right time to square off with 'em, and I need that package."

"Uh-huh." Boswell gave him a sideways look as he tapped tobacco into his pipe bowl. "Mighty curious. Never knowed neither of the McCarthy boys to back down from no one. What's in that there package, anyway?"

"Um, well, um . . ." Luke trailed off. If he told Boswell what it was, the old coyote might beg off. "I'll tell you later. Will you do it or not?"

"When you want it?"

"First thing in the morning, soon 's the office opens. There'll be less chance of those candidates for a neck-stretchin' party catching on to the freight being lifted."

"Bad'uns, eh?" Boswell said around his pipe stem.

"As I said, a nest of sidewinders. Well?"

"Sure, Luke. But I want to hear what you ain't tellin' me, okay?"

Luke stared at him, deciding he could trust him, then rose. "All right, but later. Right now I gotta be on my way." He jerked his chin to indicate he wanted Boswell to follow. When they'd reached the street, Luke asked, "Where're you staying?"

"Planned on sleeping in the livery loft where my outfit is stashed."

"Well, we—that is, my partner and I—are camped out in that cottonwood grove just north of town. Get your gear and meet me there."

"Must be somthin' mighty important goin' on," Boswell muttered, turning away.

"Boswell?"

"Yeah?"

"There's just one more thing you gotta promise me."

"What's that?"

"You keep your dad-blasted humor to yourself when you come into camp."

"What's that?"

"You can't laugh when you see the outfit I'm trailing."

Jesse reared to a sitting position, her heart beating hard, when she heard a twig snap.

"It's me, Jesse."

"Well, for heaven's sake, Luke, you could've made more noise than that." She scrambled out of her blanket and stood glaring at him over the campfire. He'd been much later than she'd expected and she'd begun to worry. "You just about scared me out of a month's growth."

"Now that would be a shame for sure, honey, losin' a whole month," he teased. He bent his tall frame, putting his hands on his knees to see into her eyes squarely in the dim firelight. Though she tried to hide it, her gaze told him that she'd been overanxious. Had she been very frightened while he was gone? "Is that how you lost out before, someone scared you outa your natural growth? Is that how you come to be no bigger'n a minute?"

"Luke McCarthy, you stop that insufferable grin," she scolded, although she was glad enough to see it to want to throw herself at him. Feeling safe, her heart found its normal rhythm again. "I'm big enough to hold my own, thank you, and don't you forget it."

"Hmm, no, I won't. Sure don't want you riled at me more'n I can help it."

She dropped to sit by the fire. "What took you so long? What did you find out?"

"The freight office opens at seven in the morning. We can get the harp first thing."

"Oh, Luke, that's wonderful. I'll—"

"Jesse, you'll have to stay in camp."

The cautious way he said it made her uneasy. "Why?"

"George and the Thomses are in town."

"Oh." Her heart sank at the news.

"But don't worry, Jesse, I have a plan," Luke spoke with confidence. "I met an old friend, a man by the name of Boswell. He used to work for the M double C. He'll be here any minute."

"Already here," Boswell called from the edge of the trees. "Can I come on in?"

Jesse rose again, her stance wary. Unconsciously, she moved closer to Luke.

Luke was aware of her by his side, and he noticed and delighted in the growing trust she felt in him. "Yeah, Boswell, come and meet my partner."

Boswell stared at her for a moment before turning his brown-eyed gaze toward Luke, the corners of his mouth twitching. "Mighta known you was totin' a woman with you from what you wouldn't tell."

"Uh, yeah, well, you ain't seen the half of it yet." Luke shoved his chin out in defense as he turned to Jesse. "Honey, this broken-down old galoot once rode for my . . . the same outfit as me. He don't look like much, I know, but he's a hard man to come up against in a fight and we can count him on our side."

Boswell shed his hat and nodded to her. "Them's

kind words, ma'am, for an' old coot like me. Glad to meet ya, ma'am."

"Same here, Mr. Boswell. I'm Jesse Mae B—"

Luke cut her off. "It's Jesse's package we're after, Boswell."

"Yes, it's my harp. I had to leave it behind when I left the train before my destination, you see."

Boswell's eyes twinkled. "Harp?"

"Yeah, a harp," Luke said with a hard edge. "It belonged to Jesse's ma."

"All this fuss is over a harp?"

"Not just the harp, Boswell," Luke pointed out. "Those three polecats are after Jesse."

Luke's edgy tone was not lost on the older man. Boswell's eyes lost some of their twinkle. "Did you go robbing another man's nest, Luke?"

"Naw, nothin' like that. But ol' George set up his mind to see it that way."

Jesse squared her shoulders. "This situation is all my fault, Mr. Boswell, and I have no right to expect your assistance. Even Luke, here—"

"Working against becoming a victim ain't no fault, Jesse," Luke cut in again, "it's just good sense."

"Still, we . . . you wouldn't be in this mess except for me," she added, flashing him a look of misery.

"Un-un, honey. None of that. The reason we're in this fix is George thinking he owns you." Luke turned to his friend. "Now, are you still game?"

"Sure 'nuff, count me in," Boswell declared.

Behind them, Mehitabel gave out an angry guttural call and one of the mules answered. An unearthly, ear-splitting screech rent the night air.

Boswell burst out with, "What in tarnation?"

"Rom." Jesse took off like a shot to see what was wrong with the animals.

"Get down, Jesse," Luke whispered urgently as he sprinted behind her. "Stay out of sight."

Jesse stopped abruptly, staring into the dark. Mehitabel was on her feet, her nose high, and the mules moved skittishly, but she saw nothing else, nothing that should have caused an uproar. Luke clamped a hand on her shoulder, ready to shove her behind him, his gun in his other hand. Boswell stepped to just beyond her, his sidearm drawn also.

Out of nowhere, a small furry body launched itself onto Boswell's shoulder with a loud thud and a screech. Jesse whirled, her heart in her throat.

"Damn it, cat," Boswell exploded, a note of familiar affection in his voice. "You near got yourself killed."

"A cat!" Luke said on a note of disbelief.

"A house cat?" To Jesse it had sounded like a full-grown bobcat.

Even so, it was no small animal. Boswell lifted the black cat carefully by the back of the neck, but its claws had dug into the cloth of his jacket. "Let go, Abednego! Ain't you done caused enough trouble?"

"Did you call it Abednego?" Jesse interjected.

"I must be hearing things," Luke said, shaking his head.

"Look what you done to them animals, why—!" Boswell stared, getting a good look at Mehitabel for the first time. He rubbed his eyes and looked again. Finally, he slid a glance toward Luke. "Uh, is that a camel?"

"Yep."

"Yours?"

"Yep. The mules, too."

Boswell glanced around the area where they'd picketed the animals. "Where's your ridin' animals?"

"You're lookin' at 'em."

Boswell paused. "You ain't joshin' me, are you?"

"Nope." Luke waited, his mouth pursed.

"Mules?"

"Yep."

The laughter started low. Then it began to roll. "Not you," his friend sputtered. "Not one of the fine McCarthy boys."

"Boswell," Luke warned.

"Mules." The man's glee soared. "I"—he haw-hawed some more—"never woulda believed it."

"That'll about do it, Boswell."

"Whatever do you find so funny, anyway?" Jesse asked innocently, a little put out. "These mules are fine animals. Besides, they're the best we could find on short notice."

"A camel and two mules?"

"Yes," she said defensively. "And Remus and Romulus are good, steady mounts. I don't see a thing wrong with riding mules." She tipped her head at Luke, looking for confirmation.

"Uh, not a'tall," Luke responded, nearly choking on his words. Boswell gave him a smirking grin, for which Luke returned a stare promising retribution to come.

"Besides," she said as she turned to stroll back to the fire. "They give Meshach and Shadrach security."

"Who?" asked Boswell.

"Luke's bulls. And Mehitabel likes them, too."

"Mehitabel is the camel, I take it?"

"Uh-huh." Jesse settled herself at the fire once more. "Though she can be a bit of trouble at times. She sure has taken a shine to Luke."

"Females usually do," Boswell said as he stroked his cat. And grinned like the proverbial Cheshire one.

"Never knew you to be a cat lover, Boswell," Luke said, trying to even things out.

"Never was, before I ran into this ugly alley feline.

But he's a good mouser and fights like he was spawned by a mountain lion. We get along just fine. He won't bother nobody now that he's gotten acquainted."

"How did you come to name him Abednego, Mr. Boswell?"

"Dunno. How come you named your animals such queer names?" Boswell let go of his cat and took out his pipe.

Jesse giggled. "Well, I don't know either, but with the bulls as strong and staunch as Daniel's friends in the Old Testament, it seemed right. Anyway, with all three names now accounted for, I suppose we're a set. Luke said he'd be on the lookout for it."

Luke noticed Boswell's awareness of the easy way Jesse coupled herself with him, and knew his own gaze toward her was filled with uncommon pride and affection. Luke began to squirm under his friend's knowing look. It was one thing to privately admit he wanted to keep Jesse Mae Banning for himself, but it was quite another to appear to all the world as a lovesick puppy. Even though he was beginning to admit to himself that he was.

He decided it was time to turn the subject. "You can picket your mount with the others, Boswell, then get yourself some coffee. We have some planning to do before morning."

8

The morning was overcast, promising rain. Luke frowned at the sky as he ambled into town on foot, sincerely hoping the rain would hold off until they could accomplish their mission and get out. He didn't relish the idea of fighting bad weather while trying to make a quick getaway. Or leaving easy tracks behind for anyone to follow.

On the other hand, a good rain would wash their tracks away if it came just after they'd left.

He positioned himself at the corner saloon, leaning in the same spot he had the night before to observe the activity around the train station, although his view was mostly of the rear and side. The freight office was a small wooden building attached to the tiny brick station. Activity around it was slow; the clerk was ten minutes late opening the door.

He saw no evidence of either George or his pals,

but Luke remained cautious. He'd underestimated their cunning once before and he had no intention of being caught unaware again.

Glancing down the opposite street, he saw Boswell enter town just as planned. His friend rode his big black gelding toward the station at a slow gait. Without appearing to do so, Boswell looked his way. Luke gave Boswell the "everything clear" nod, and hoped to heaven it was. He'd given the older man complete descriptions of George and the Thomses; if Boswell saw any of them inside the station house, he would merely ask the clerk a useless question and leave.

Boswell dismounted and threw his reins in a loose loop over the hitching rail, then disappeared behind the freight office door. Luke held his breath, giving his friend time to ascertain if the harp was there. Then he'd move up to help load the thing onto Boswell's mount.

Luke was about to leave his post when from the corner of his eye he saw a familiar lumbering figure exit the bawdy house across the road. It was George, all right, heading toward the station. Luke turned his back and sped around the edge of the saloon's building. From this vantage point, he could still see most of what might happen.

"Damn the luck," he muttered to himself. He waited until George had his back to him, then put his little fingers into his teeth and blew. The shrill sound rent the quiet with startling force. Luke ducked out of sight, hoping that George would be curious enough about the sound to delay entering the freight office, and counting on Boswell to hear the warning.

He counted to ten. He blew again, three sharp notes, then cut between the buildings to the next street over, tracing the path he'd taken last night.

He glanced up and down the street. A dog barked

and a window slammed shut. For a moment, he felt jubilant. By golly, he'd created the commotion that he'd hoped for.

In the near distance, he heard an answering shrill whistle. Startled, he thought only a second before he knew it was Jesse. The answering whistle repeated his notes exactly. His jubilant feeling vanished; he felt like shaking her. She was supposed to have stayed out of sight in camp.

Where was she now? Was she in trouble?

He didn't wait to think more about it. Making a huge circle, all the while on the alert for the Thomses, Luke came up on the station from the opposite side.

George had moved away from the station and stood staring at the point where Luke had been only moments before. A woman, out to do her early shopping, did the same. A couple of heads poked through windows, curiously surveying the area.

"Who's making that racket?" asked one.

"Somethin' on fire?" asked one of the men coming out of a closed saloon.

"Don't think so," the shopper answered.

George was out of sight from the front of the station, Luke observed, but if he turned and walked only a yard or two, he'd have a clear view of it.

"C'mon, c'mon," Luke muttered through his teeth, willing his urgency onto Boswell.

George started to turn, then was stopped by one of the passersby. Luke let his taut body relax an inch.

Okay, so he knew where George was, but where were those damned polecat brothers? And where was Jesse?

Boswell sidled through the freight office door, the large musical instrument in his arms. He glanced around quickly, then headed for his horse. Taking his chances, Luke darted up to Boswell, jerking his chin in George's direction.

Boswell nodded, and together, they strapped the harp to the gelding's back. Luke stayed on the horse's far side where he would be less noticeable.

Jesse edged around the corner and hugged the back of the hardware store two doors away, then ran down the alley toward the station. She daren't whistle again; she'd heard nothing more from Luke.

He was likely to be in a rage about now, she thought, at her ignoring his command to stay in camp. But it had been impossible. It was her harp and her problem. She'd stuffed all her hair inside her hat, pulling it low, and had even gone to the trouble of rubbing dirt on her face. She prayed it would be enough of a disguise.

Following Luke and Boswell at a distance, she'd positioned herself on the second-floor porch of the hardware store, where she could watch the freight office and street. Her enemy had been easy to spot. She'd been dodging George for years, and when she saw him leaving the brothel, she automatically hid behind a rain barrel and waited.

When Luke whistled, she'd answered, hoping for the confusing effect of the unexpected. Afterwards, she'd pounded down the wooden staircase and raced toward where Luke had disappeared. Now she skidded to a stop at the side of a mercantile store and peeked around it.

Finding nothing alarming, the townspeople started on about their business and the street became more crowded. George, his expression always suspicious and now more so, turned purposefully toward the station.

She swiftly glanced about her. Where had Luke gone? And was Boswell still in the freight building?

Desperately, she cast about for another distraction with which to delay George. She couldn't let him get to the front of the station yet.

Picking up a rough-edged stone, she fingered it longingly. Dare she? She could run back between the houses and be out of sight before he reached her.

Two boys hurried toward the scene. Looking for excitement, Jesse guessed, unaware that nothing more was happening. They crossed the street close to George. Thinking them a perfect cover, she took quick aim and hurled the rock at George. It hit him square on the back of the neck. He whirled, his glaring menace landing on the children.

Jesse held her breath.

The smaller boy shrunk back against the taller, and a sense of anguished guilt assailed her. She shouldn't have done that—involved those kids, even innocently.

"Which one o' you brats did that?"

"We didn't do nothin', mister," replied the younger boy.

"Oh yeah?" George started for them. "I'll teach ya."

Without hesitation Jesse picked up another stone, this time a bigger one. About to let it fly, she held up when one of the passing men stepped into George's path. "Leave it be, mister. Those kids ain't hurting you."

George snarled something back, whereupon an altercation broke out between them.

The boys darted away in different directions, and Jesse let her breath out. Confused about what to do next, she turned to run back the way she'd come. Barely missing the Thomses as she raced passed them, her reaction was instant. She kept her head turned and speedily directed her path to join the older of the dodging boys.

Jesse's heart beat like a hammer and the skin along

the back of her neck itched with the desire to look over her shoulder. But she thought the Thoms brothers hadn't recognized her at all and she couldn't take a chance on giving them a second look. She herself slowed down and fell into step with the youngster.

As soon as they turned the corner out of sight, the youth stopped and stared at her oddly. Jesse paused too, sparing the boy only a nod before cautiously assessing the street, behind them. The argument had broken up but the Thomses and George seemed to be rooted to the middle of the crossroad.

The younger boy caught up with them, looking at her curiously. "Was 'at you what did that?" he asked.

She couldn't bear to lie to them. She'd nearly caused them harm by making George think they had thrown the rock. However, they were safe now, and chances of their running into the overgrown bully again were slim.

"Yeah, it was." Jesse flashed an impish smile. Then she appealed to their sense of children's honor. "But you won't tell on me, will ya? He's a mean cuss an' I'm runnin' away from 'im."

The older boy scrutinized her face a moment, his dark eyes wise, then nodded his agreement. "We won't tell."

"Thanks. Um, would ya mind walkin' a ways with me?"

"Naw, we wouldn't mind," he pronounced. "M'name's Ralph. This'un here's Lennie."

They didn't ask for her name and didn't seem to expect her to give it. At the edge of town, Jesse turned. The woods were just ahead and she didn't want the children to see Mehitabel. What they didn't know, they couldn't tell.

From the corner of her eye, she spotted Boswell climbing the eastern slope, heading toward camp. An oddly shaped mound sat on his gelding's back. Her heart leapt with joy; they'd gotten her harp.

But where was Luke?

She dug in her jeans pocket hurriedly, pulling out a handful of pennies and nickels. "I'm most obliged for your company, but I must get on, now. I'd take it kindly if you'd each have a piece of candy for your trouble of, um, escorting me."

She placed a nickel in the older boy's palm and five pennies in Lennie's. "Thanks, Ralph. Thank you, Lennie."

"We's glad to help, ma'am," Ralph said. The children turned and raced down the slope.

Luke hissed at her from the trees. "Jesse Mae, you ornery little scoundrel, hurry. George almost saw you! And who were those kids?"

"Only some town youngsters, Luke. They won't tell anyone about me."

Luke grabbed her arm as soon as she was in reach, hurrying her toward their camp. "You foolish girl. They're not the only ones who saw you, you know. One of those, um, sportin' ladies hanging out of a window was watching the whole thing."

"I'm sorry, Luke, but I hid my hair, and dressed like this, I thought mostly everyone would take me for a boy."

"Honey, no one who looked at you close would ever mistake you for a boy," he said, giving a quick glance down her body. "Not even that kid back there. What made you come after us, anyway?"

"George is as sneaky as a weasel. I thought you needed another spy, and a good thing, too. George was about to check that freight office right when Boswell was in there. He would've seen Boswell take my harp. And by the time I got close to the station—"

She paused to take a breath, her voice a bit on the wobbly side. "I didn't know where you'd got to. I was afraid."

The rain finally began to fall, big fat drops at first, but swiftly turning to a hard pelt.

"I've told you before, Jesse, I can take care of myself. I've handled men like George before."

What he didn't tell her was that there would come a day when he'd take George on with willing righteousness on her behalf, but he wanted to pick the time and place. He didn't want to confront George until he had her somewhere safe where she didn't have to be afraid.

"Come on, let's go," he urged.

Under the trees, they were protected from the worst of the rain. They reached the camp, where Boswell already had the harp unloaded. He held Mehitabel's harness tightly in one hand, but the animal strained away, snorting and making the old bronco buster madder by the minute. "Here, Luke. This dad-blamed ill-tempered animal is your beast. You do the packing," he insisted, throwing up his hands.

Luke laughed, and calmed Mehitabel, then wasted no time in packing Jesse's harp and the remaining camp gear.

The whole kit and caboodle of them would be a lot slower than he'd like. Right now he'd give a whole lot to have a string of fast horses on which to flee rather than two mules, a camel, and two bulls who needed a lot of care.

They left as hurriedly as possible, driving the bulls in front of them for a change. At the creek, they stopped long enough to water the animals and make sure the pack was secure, then moved on.

The rain cleared; the land steamed. They rode until

almost full dark, making their camp with an eye toward self-defense if needed. They ate a cold supper of leftover beans and biscuits in near-silence.

Jesse limped to pull out her bedroll from the pile of supplies. Her entire backside was sore and she was so tired she thought she mightn't ever consent to ride again when this was all over. She longed for her hairbrush, but had no energy with which to look for it.

She laid her bedroll out a little closer to Luke's than she'd done before. She refused to admit that she needed the comfort it would afford, but she did think she'd feel a little safer that way. She lay for a long time, thinking and worrying about the morning past.

They had narrowly missed coming face to face with George and the Thomses; she shuddered at the thought of what they could've done to Luke. Would've done. The unreasoning outrage on George's face when she'd hit him with the rock made her break out in a sweat.

"How long do you think it will take George to come after us?" she asked quietly.

Hearing the anxiety in Jesse's voice, Luke rolled on his side to face her, resisting his desire to hold her until her fear subsided. Her mouth pressed together as she waited for his opinion.

He wouldn't insult her by being less than honest. His answer was straight. "Depends on how long he waits to actually check the freight office for your harp, but he's stupid enough for it to take some figurin' out. After all, he never saw either of us at all. And then, he might give it up and not come at all."

"That's what I'd hoped, that he'd give up chasing after me. I should've known better, though. I should never have agreed to go after the harp," she said regretfully. "We nearly got caught."

"It doesn't make any difference, Jesse." He reached

across the space between them and stroked a lock of her hair. It lay wild where one braid had come undone. Even tangled, it felt silky.

"Of course it would've made a difference. We could've avoided Hinley altogether."

"That's not what I mean." He inched his hand deeper into the mass of her hair, tempted to pull her face toward his. "I suspected George would be there, and I could've changed my mind after I knew he was."

"Why didn't you?"

"Go to sleep, Jesse," he said with a sigh, letting her go. "We'll talk about it another time."

Jesse felt the warmth of his palm against her scalp withdraw, brushing her cheekbone in the process. She fervently wished she had the courage to snuggle against his hand for comfort without adding more guilt to her already overladened conscience. It hadn't occurred to her that Luke might want her to have her most valued possession above any other consideration simply because it meant so much to her. It hadn't been her experience that anyone would do so much, go so far, to please her.

Her debt to the cowboy was piling up faster than she could count, and that fact concerned her not a little. It would surely take her months of hard work to repay him.

George's glare was ugly. His face appeared squashed and tight, his eyes slits. "Whataya mean that there harp was got yesterday?" he asked the station freight clerk. "I was hangin' 'round all day an' I din't see nobody pick it up."

"I assure you, someone came for it."

"A woman? Was it a little 'un?"

"I couldn't say. I wasn't the clerk on duty yesterday," said the little man with the big side whiskers.

"Who was? Where is he?"

"Really, sir. . ." The clerk didn't like the nasty way he was being addressed. He didn't like the looks of the riff raff trio standing in front of him, either.

George's hamlike fist grabbed a piece of the freight clerk's jacket. "Tell me."

The little man swallowed and called across the room nervously. "Er . . . M-Mr. Terry?" He swallowed again. "Perhaps you would come and speak with th-this, er, gentleman."

A taller, gray-haired man stared at them over his glasses and came to see what the commotion was about. "Yes?"

"I wanta know who got that harp that was left here," George insisted. "Was it a man 'er a woman?"

"I don't know. Do you have a claim on it?"

"Ya bet I do, an' the woman, too."

The man looked George over carefully, and let his gaze drift scathingly over the men at his back. "Be that as it may, I don't have the package now," he said coldly. "Could I see your claim stub, please? Or perhaps you wish to fill out a missing freight form?"

George pivoted and angrily clumped out of the office. "It's that McCarthy bastard, that's who. They'd 'a noticed iffen it was Jesse Mae. But she was here, I know it. It couldn't 'a been got without 'er."

"Whatcha want to do now, George?" Archie asked. "No need a-waitin' around here any longer."

George gave his companion a scorching stare at his obvious statement.

"Well, it ain't."

"Gonna find 'er. Gotta search out who mighta seen 'er," George snarled, ignoring Archie.

"Might look to that fracas from yest'day mawnin'," Eli suggested. "Seems to me it twern't nothin' but a storm in a teacup. Yit, her harp's gone missin' since then."

"That's right, Eli." George's eyes lit up. "Right good thinkin'. Let's see who might have been a-watchin'. An' after, I got a idea where we c'd get us some money."

"Where at?" Eli gave George his full attention.

"Notice that bank ever bein' guarded heavy?"

"Reckon I noticed it ain't. You ponderin' on takin' it?"

"It'd be easy, don'tcha think?"

Eli gave his version of a grin. At last George was makin' sense.

Two mornings later, Jesse woke to the low tones of a debate. Luke and Boswell huddled against the predawn skyline, looking at lines in the dirt between them.

"But the trail over the mountain will cut our time by at least a couple of days, Luke." Boswell emphasized his statement by jabbing a stick at the map he'd drawn on the ground. "I thought Will wanted you to get them bulls home plenty pronto? Why all of a sudden d'you wanta take the roundabout?"

"Boswell, the shorter trail's rougher, rockier. Didn't you notice Jesse limping last night? She ain't used to hard days on horseback, not to mention that she's taken it on herself to watch out for those damned bulls."

As much truth as there was in what he'd just said, Luke had to admit to himself that he also wanted more time with Jesse on the trail before he subjected her to Wayside Station. Or his nosy family. But he'd be danged if he'd tell Boswell that.

"Yeah, I noticed. She babies 'em like they're the jewels of England. Hell, she even feeds 'em by hand.

Never saw no two bulls behave as well as when she's around, specially one bull around another."

Luke chuckled. "Yeah, she seems to have a way with 'em, all right. And she's afraid Will would throttle me for sure if anything happens to 'em."

"Hell's bells, Luke, ain't likely nothin' will happen to them cattle now. They don't really look none the worse for wear, do they? We could take it easy an' still save time by going over."

Luke shook his head adamantly. "I ain't gonna push Jesse, I tell you. She's stretched as it is—"

"No, Luke," Jesse said, standing over them, letting her temper show. She flashed him a glare she hoped would singe his tail feathers. How dare he imply she wasn't up to the rigors of the trail? "I'm fine, do you hear me? Just fine."

Luke hid his mixed frustration. Jesse was more stubborn than the two mules put together.

She turned to Boswell. "Are Meshach and Shadrach really up to the mountain trail?"

"They're a little footsore, but I think so, if we're careful."

"We'll need to graze 'em longer before going over," Luke insisted, glancing at Jesse. "They need a couple of days' rest, too."

"So is the mountain trail really shorter, or is it about the same as going around?"

"Over the mountain is still the direct route," Boswell said as he stroked Abednego.

"And how long then till we get to this place Luke works for? The M double C?"

Boswell gave her a curious glance, then shifted his gaze to Luke. Luke's face became unreadable.

"'Bout three-four days over the mountain trail, I reckon, at the pace we're goin'," Boswell answered.

"But we'll havta go through Wayside Station first, anyway. Trail leads right through it."

"Luke?"

Luke answered her impatient stare with one of speculation. "I reckon that's about it."

"Then we'll take the mountain trail. I'll not have you getting fired because we took another week," she said, her mouth firm.

They took the turnoff about midmorning the next day. Luke watched the rise of land in the distance and thought it might take most of the day to reach the foot of it. The Herefords seemed to have slowed their pace, he noticed; Boswell had made mention of their condition, too. Luke knew the bulls hadn't been allowed enough time to rest and graze.

"We'll reach the river about when the afternoon sun hangs halfway," Luke told Jesse, nodding toward the vista in the distance. "We'll make camp early and let the animals rest before we start up the mountain tomorrow. They'll have several daylight hours to graze."

He wouldn't push the morning start, either. That would give Jesse time to rest, too, he thought, regardless of her protests. Lord knew, they all could use the rest.

Boswell spotted a rabbit and raced after it through the brush, disappearing over the crest of a hill. He was gone a while before Luke heard the echo of his rifle.

"Something beside bacon and beans for supper," Luke said in triumph.

Jesse smiled at him. In truth, their supplies were beginning to thin out some and they'd all welcome a change.

To camp, they picked an open spot close enough to

the river to hear its musical sound as it rushed over boulders and rocks. Plenty of grass lined its boundaries for the animals to graze.

Signs of old crossings scarred the ground; Jesse gazed at them for long moments, wondering about the wagons and people that had come this way before. She was sidetracked in the need to help unload the animals and make camp, but later she found a perfect place to draw water at the river's edge, and thought that other women must have found it, too. It gave her a sense of kinship. She carried a pot of water back to the camp, but decided she could bathe a few yards upstream later. The thought gave her spirits a lift.

Scattered stone lying on a blackened flat rock in the ground suggested there had been other campfires. She began to set them into a circle. Abednego began circling, meowing for something to eat.

"You're getting spoiled," she scolded him teasingly. "Why don't you go hunting on your own? There must be mice in all that brush over there. Go on."

Suddenly, one of the bulls let out a distressed bellow. Jesse rose swiftly to gaze down to the river's edge where she knew Luke and the beasts to be. She saw only their rumps between boulders. What was wrong?

But then she heard Luke's "Confound it to hell and gone."

9

Jesse stumbled over the rough ground leading toward the river. Luke stood knee-deep in the water alongside the two Herefords. He leaned on Meshach's heavy forequarters, shoving with all his strength. The bull kept bawling and refused to budge.

"Move, you dad-blasted troublesome beast." A thread of pain laced his speech.

"What's the matter, Luke?" she called worriedly.

He glanced over his shoulder. "This blighted animal is standing on my foot and won't move. Where's Boswell?"

"Still hunting." Jesse waded in, feeling the cold water reach her thighs. "Is your foot crushed?"

"Can't tell yet. Would be for sure if the river bottom wasn't so muddy. My foot keeps sinking."

Jesse put her shoulder next to Luke's. Together they shoved the bull with all their might. Meshach turned to stare at them, his eyes stressed, his bawl plaintive. But still he didn't move.

"Hold on, Luke. I'll be right back."

"Don't reckon I'm going anywhere at the moment, Jesse."

She waded out again, the breeze on her wet legs making her shiver, and picked up a halter before heading for the mules.

"C'mon, Rem." The mule moved away from her, eyeing her as he continued to graze. *Whoever thought mules were dumb?* she wondered idly. Rem knew he'd done enough work today.

"All right, then, Rom." She turned toward the other and coaxed, "I know you like this tall grass, but I need you."

Gently, she patted Rom's neck and rubbed his ear. "See? I'll give you another rub if you help me now."

Rom raised his head and chewed placidly. Finally, he allowed her to slip the halter in place and lead him down to the river. But at the water's edge, the mule balked. "Oh, Rom, not now," she wailed.

Luke watched as she manuevered the mule. Sweat poured down his face. He thought he might go to his knees at any moment. "What's the matter with Rom?"

"Don't know. Something spooked him, I guess." She moved into the water and tugged at Rom's halter. "C'mon, mule."

The bull let out another frightened bawl, which communicated itself to Rom. He began to back.

"Jesse, throw me the halter. Quick."

She tried, but the leather ends fell short. "Blast."

Wading out, she picked them up and pulled. Luke leaned forward as far as he could, grabbing the ends as she threw once more. "Okay, now. Sing, honey.

Don't know why, but those mules like your singing as much as the Herefords do."

"A froggie did a-courtin' go, mm-hmm, mm-hmm . . ."

Rom's ears flickered forward, and Luke began to sing along. "That's it . . . a froggie did a-courtin' go, mm-hmm, mm-hmm . . ." He threaded the reins through the nose ring.

"Back, Rom, back." At Jesse's guidance, the mule backed another step. The bull protested, but his head turned.

"Good boy, fine fellow," she praised as Rom continued to back, coaxing the bull to move. A moment later, Meshach pulled free of the mud, and Luke was released.

Jesse dropped the reins and splashed towards Luke, slipping her shoulder up under his armpit and circling his waist. "Lean on me, Luke. How is it? Can you walk?"

She was hardly big enough to give him a crutch, he thought, amused even in his discomfort. Yet she was game to try. He moved his weight onto the foot and winced. He waited for the wave of pain to pass.

"Not as bad as I thought," he answered. And it wasn't, but he was enjoying her attention a mighty bunch. "Reckon I can make it to the bank if you stay with me."

"Sure, Luke."

They limped up the bank and hopped toward the camp circle. Jesse eased him down on a nearby rock, then dragged a saddle in place for him to rest his foot on. "Sit still and I'll get your boot off in a trice," she instructed.

He obeyed and leaned back on his arms. Soaked, the boot created a stubborn resistance. Placing her hand on his heel, she tugged gently.

It made a sucking sound and he hissed in pain.

"Sorry," she murmured. "Can you bend it?"

He complied. "Think it'll just have to come off in

the usual way, honey. Turn around and grab it between your legs . . . er, limbs."

She bit her lip at the pain she heard in his voice. But turn she did, grasping the boot of his damaged foot while he placed his good one square on her fanny and pushed. He groaned as the boot came free and she stumbled forward to her knees.

She twisted to look at him, his boot in her hand, her breathing slightly heavy with exertion. His blue gaze held the edges of pain and relief, but his lids drooped and his eyes began to fill with open hunger the longer she stared. It was an odd sensation. The whole thing felt strangely intimate, as though they'd engaged in . . . in lovemaking instead of a mere incident of kindness.

The flush rushed up her body like a lightning bolt. What was worse, he was aware of her reaction. Instantly, she looked away. She remembered too clearly the touch of his lips on hers.

No . . . No, she wouldn't—couldn't—entertain such thoughts. Briskly, she set about to examine his injured foot. Going on her haunches, she peeled off his sock; the skin already looked black and blue, but there was only minor swelling. Lightly pressing, she ran her fingers up and down his arch and instep, and over his straight toes.

She heard his sharp intake of breath.

"Does it hurt particularly bad in any one place?"

"Mmm . . ."

"Where?"

"Um . . ."

"Here?" She made the mistake of glancing up at him then.

Luke shook his head, his sleepy contemplation telling her something quite different than what came from his lips. "No, just . . . all over."

She rose, letting his foot rest on the saddle. "Well, I don't think it's broken. Though it'll hurt like the dickens for a while."

"I'm sure it will."

"It might swell, even yet."

A heartbeat's pause. "I'll live through it."

"You might not be able to get your boot back on. It'll be tight."

"I'll make sure I can get it on by tomorrow," he murmured. "My ma always says things will look better by morning."

She backed up a step. Her mama had said that often, too, but there was something in the way Luke offered it that sounded different from the way it was usually said. "Well, I'd better go see if Meshach is all right and let Rom get back to his grazing.

"Sure, honey. Thanks."

As soon as she was out of sight, Luke waggled his foot. Yep, it was sorely bruised. But not as much as he'd let on. And it didn't ache as much as he did for her.

"You gone and done what?" Boswell exclaimed later when he'd returned with a couple of rabbits.

"Meshach stepped on it and then got stubborn. Wouldn't move. Coulda been worse, though. The soft river bottom protected me some."

"How'd you let a fool thing like that happen? Ain't like you to be so careless."

"Had other things on my mind, I reckon. . . ."

Boswell followed Luke's gaze toward the girl. He saw the damp denim tighten around her derriere and long thighs as her small, graceful form bent over the fire. "Um, yeah, guess you do, at that."

Boswell cleared his throat. "Miz Jesse, I reckon I'll just string up a line for them wet things to dry if you wanta change. Luke, too."

"Oh, yes, Boswell. That would be wonderful. I'll run along and take a quick bath in the river and be back pronto to help with supper. If . . . if you'll help Luke get into his dry things?"

"Sure 'nuff, Miz Jesse."

Luke slept fitfully. Every time he turned, his sore foot let him know he was alive. So did his thoughts of Jesse.

Finally, he lay still and stared into the coals. Beyond the faint light, Jesse barely made shadows against the night. This time she'd made her bed on the opposite side of the fire.

Not for the first time, he tried to understand why she might be so afraid of their growing feelings for each other. The attraction had been there from the beginning; the spark had been lit the instant she declared so forcefully that she planned to be an old maid.

It was impossible to imagine Jesse as an old maid. Or the wife of an old man. In spite of her tiny form, she was all woman, full of a woman's passion and life. And ready for a man's loving even if she wouldn't admit it.

What had she told him? That her ma'd died when she was ten and her pa'd left her with the Jeters. She hadn't heard from him since. That might explain her determination not to love anybody again, afraid they might not be around long enough to invest in love. And she'd hurt too bad if she got left behind once more.

She'd also made a reference or two to her pa's hopping from job to job, finally selling her ma's things— all but the harp—to pay his way west. Might that set in her mind poorly? She sure had an intolerance toward shiftlessness. She'd kind of tarred him with that brush when they'd first met.

He wasn't like that, not at all—he and his brother Will generally put in harder days on the ranch than their hands—but he suddenly realized he'd have to prove it to Jesse. She was kind of like those Missouri mules. They had to be sure of what they were doing before they'd move.

Well, he couldn't do anything until he got her home. He only hoped he could figure a way not to scare her off before he had a chance to show her that she'd be all right with him.

Jesse staked the bulls to graze in a new circle of grass, then led the mules down to water. Mehitabel had uttered her loud protest that it was Jesse instead of Luke who handled her this morning, so she simply let the animal be. But it wasn't long before the camel came of her own accord to drink at the water's edge beside Rom and Rem.

It was a pretty morning, with the sun slanting the landscape with soft colors, and she could see a long way east and south. The mountain lay to the west.

Breathing deeply, she pulled the fresh scents of morning into her lungs. It smelled so cleanly different than the farm had; the Jeter house and barn odors were stale and closed in, their very land having taken on the feel and smell of neglect and abuse. No matter how hard she'd worked—on the chicken coop, on the house—it all smelled the same.

She liked the way this country smelled.

They would climb the mountain trail tomorrow, she mused. Then only a few days later they'd come to their destination.

Luke declared he'd be fine in a day or so, even though his foot had darkened. But the swelling was minimal, and she doubted if they would linger here another day.

She tried not to worry about what was behind her. Maybe, as she'd hoped, George had quit looking for her.

"Don't know whut you thinkin' to find here," complained Archie as he, Eli, and George walked their horses into the town nearest to where they'd pushed Luke and his bulls from the train. George was convinced that Jesse was with the cowboy and he'd discover where they were sooner or later. "Too many days gone."

George didn't bother to answer. He was too busy trying to see all of the town at once. It sure wasn't much, he noted, only a few buildings and one main street. If Jesse Mae was here, it wouldn't take long to find her.

"Livery down yonder," Eli pointed out. "Iffen they were lookin' fer mounts, reckon he'd know what horseflesh he sold to a body."

They headed toward the livery.

"A man an' a little redheaded woman, you say?" Mr. Sizemore asked. He pursed his mouth and arched a shot of tobacco juice to the side, wondering if the three men were willing to pay for the information they wanted.

"Yep. Have ya seen 'em 'er not?" George fairly growled his demand.

"Maybe I have. Maybe I haven't."

"Whut kinda answer is that?" Archie asked.

"Means show me yer money an' I'll tell you what I know," Mr. Sizemore said. He suddenly wondered if he'd done the right thing when the heaviest of the trio gave him a hard look of pure malice. "Bobby," he instructed his young son. "Run up to Lester's and ask 'im to step down here a minute."

George let the boy go. Damn the bastard—he knew something for sure. He didn't even try to hide that sly expression on his face.

He considered beating the man standing in the livery barn door, beat him good—he wanted to, if for no other reason than that it would relieve some of the rage building inside his head. But it was still daylight. He didn't cotton to getting caught. Beside, it might be quicker to just pay the money, get the man to tell what he knew, and then take his money back.

"Ain't got much money, mister. How much you want?" While George negotiated, he watched Eli slowly, unobtrusively edge toward the rear of the barn.

"Ten dollars?"

"Five."

"All right. Five." Sizemore waited while George dug five coins from his pocket and flipped them at his feet. From the corner of his eye, Sizemore saw Eli dismount and poke about, as if his only purpose were idle curiosity. Sizemore didn't like it, not one bit. He had a queer feeling about this bunch.

"Hey, mister. I don't 'low nobody back there." He hollered, then watched until Eli came around where he could see him again before continuing. "Well, they was here, all right. Came into town on that camel of Pearson's."

"Camel?"

"Whut's a camel?" Archie whispered.

"Yeah," Sizemore responded, looking through Archie. "Only one around here, so I know it was Pearson's."

"When? How long ago?"

Sizemore scratched his head. "Last Sat'day, I guess."

"Where they headed?"

"Well, now, mister, they didn't rightly say."

George gave him a disbelieving, hateful stare. Sizemore began to wish he'd never had truck with the skunk.

"Where's this Pearson at?"

"He don't live in town."

"Didn't ask where he wasn't, mister. Asked where he was."

"Out east of town, 'bout five miles."

"That all you got to tell?"

"That's about all five dollars gets, I reckon."

"What would another five buy?" George's voice was suddenly cunning.

Sizemore decided he'd told all he was going to. "Nothin', mister. Don't know no more."

Three days later, they were on the far side of the mountain when the storm hit. The sky took on ominous shades of blackness and Jesse watched Shadrach and Meshach grow more nervous with each peal of rolling thunder. She stretched to stand in her stirrups to see ahead, looking for any sign of the men. The narrow trail was silent and empty.

Over the last hour, she'd let Luke and Boswell put too much distance between them. Boswell had taken the lead at scouting the trail and leading Shadrach, complaining that Mehitabel was as touchy as if she had boils and it was clear as daylight that Luke was the only handler that the ornery camel would tolerate. They'd also discovered the animal did better if she didn't follow the bulls. Consequently, Jesse brought up the rear with Meshach.

Another lightning streak and thunder roll had Meshach huddled against a juniper tree. The bull let out another low bawl and refused to go another step. Jesse didn't like the lightning either, and dismounted her mule. "All right, fella. We'll stay put awhile."

Jesse heartily wished she had her cloak. The temperature had dropped, and she shivered in the frigid air. Then suddenly the heavens opened and began to spit hailstones the size of marbles and fifty-cent pieces. The bull bellowed in protest and even Rom showed his distress by kicking out. She grasped his halter at the cross piece and held tight.

"A froggie did a-courtin' go, mm-hmm, mm-hmm . . ." Jesse sang nervously. Then she couldn't sing at all. Hail slapped her cheek and chin and she ducked her head against Rom's neck to avoid the worst of it, yet felt its force against her shoulders and hat. She barely heard Luke's call.

"Jesse Mae! Where are you?"

She stared into the gloom but couldn't see him. She answered with a shout, and it took only moments for him to reach her. She was never so glad to see anyone in her life.

"Jesse!" Luke shouted to be heard. He took her arm with a strong grip and urged her forward. "Come on, there's a cave up ahead."

"What about the bull and mule?"

"I'll come back for 'em."

Slipping and sliding, Luke led her to a dark slash in the mountainside. By the time they reached it, the hail had slackened into icy-cold rain.

The entrance was rather narrow, but it led to a roomy enough cavern. Luke had a tight hold of her shoulders and practically carried her inside.

When she could, Jesse looked around. Mehitabel

knelt contentedly against one wall, and the other animals crowded toward the back of the cave. The cavern smelled of and felt deeply cold, but at least they were out of the weather. Thankfully, Boswell already had a fire blazing.

"Move in here, missus, an' warm yourself. You're about froze."

Jesse thanked him through chattering teeth and sank to the floor, holding her hands close to the flame. Luke pawed through the packs until he found her cloak. He wrapped it around her shaking shoulders before turning back toward the cave opening.

"Hey, Luke, hang on there. Where you going?" asked Boswell.

"After the bull and mule."

"I'll go," Boswell insisted. "I got my heavy gear on. You stay with Miz Jesse."

Luke merely nodded and didn't argue. He felt nearly frozen himself. He found one of the bedroll blankets and hunkered down beside Jesse. Noticing that her fingers looked blue, he drew her between his legs and pulled her back against him, his blanket covering them both like a tent, yet opened to the warmth of the fire. He tucked her hands beneath her arms, wrapped his own around her tightly and remained still.

"N-never s-saw it h-hail in th-the s-summer before," she stuttered, pressing into him for body heat. "D-does it-t d-do t-this very often?"

"Pretty high up. Sometimes get surprised," he mumbled.

Warmth began to seep through to them finally, and Jesse slowly became aware of Luke's arms cradling her. His hands gently rubbed her arms, aiding her circulation. After a few moments, she started to feel more than just the cold. He lowered his head and nuz-

zled her hair. His lips were cold, and his nose felt
chilled next to her ear, but she didn't pull away.
Instead, she turned her head, ever so slightly.

Luke didn't wait for a second invitation. He turned
her until he could find her mouth.

His lips opened against hers in hungry need, and
when she opened her mouth slightly, he instantly,
hotly sought more. Jesse felt the tip of his tongue on
the inside, stroking her teeth, touching her tongue,
and shuddered in response. Even through all the layers of cloth, she knew he felt it, for he acknowledged
her response with more of his own, deepening the kiss
for long moments until he suddenly pulled away.

Luke leaned his head back, his eyes tightly shut.
When he could breathe again, he swallowed hard.
"Oh, Jesse, honey, you shouldn't ever kiss a cowboy
like that . . . if you don't plan to make an honest man
of him."

She lay against his chest weakly, wondering whatever had happened to her good common sense. Hadn't
her mama warned her against this very pitfall?

Embarrassed by her own actions, she didn't answer
him; she didn't know how. Sitting up, she separated
their heated bodies. The cold air outside their small
circle served as shock waves of sanity.

Without looking at him, she turned away. Luke
caught her wrist. "You're going to, aren't you? Marry
me?"

"Oh, Luke. You know I can't."

"Why not?"

"I don't plan to marry anyone, really. I . . . you . . .
Luke, I won't be like Effie, living in a sod house with a
dirt floor that you can't ever keep clean, or one of
those wives who has a baby every year, subsisting on
backbone and determination and little else. I . . . I

admire those women, but . . . they end up working like slaves and dying young."

"It ain't always like that," he protested. "And there ain't much work out there for a decent woman."

"No, not a lot. But I told you before. I don't mind the hard work, but I want something of my own to show for it, I want to own my own labor. If I do marry, I won't settle for a mere cowhand, I want—"

Luke pulled her into his arms again, this time laying her across his lap while his hand wrapped around her chin. His gaze was fierce, his kiss explosive and demanding, lacking any of the prior tenderness, but just as fiery and just as long and just as affecting.

Then he abruptly thrust her away, holding her at arm's length.

She came up gasping for air, stunned into merely staring at him. He struggled for air too, but anger stroked every line of his expression, his blue eyes reflecting some of the fire they'd shared.

"Now, Miss Jesse Mae Banning," he said, his voice hoarse. "You think about that! The passion between us! And remember my mouth on yours and how my hands will feel against your skin. Dream of it. And imagine what more I can give you, of the long nights of a lifetime together, and then . . . then you tell me you won't have me!"

He got up and stalked outside. In misery, Jesse stared after him, at the sheets of rain beyond the narrow cave opening. She'd hurt him. It was the last thing she'd intended to do when she owed him so much. Even her life.

She blinked back tears and drew her cloak closely around her shoulders. Her clothes were still damp, and outside the small circle of fire-heated air, it was almost arctic.

10

Only moments later, Boswell came in with Meshach and Jesse's mule. He said something to her, but she barely answered. After settling the bulls at the back of the cave, he began to make soup; she sat where she was. Abednego mewed and rubbed against her. Absentmindedly, she petted him, but let him go when he jumped from her lap.

It wasn't until Luke returned to the fire that she was able to move. He was soaked through and scarcely looked her way. Getting up, she took the blanket and placed it about his shoulders, trying to apologize with her action.

Boswell coughed, then glanced at each of them in turn. Keeping his gaze on the soup, he said, "Better shuck them clothes, Luke. You too, Miz Jesse. Don't wanta catch your death, ya know."

Jesse knew Boswell was right. It cost her some

pride, but she made a husky-voiced attempt at appearing normal. "Yes, Luke," she urged. "Please get out of those wet clothes."

Luke rose, gave her one glance that told her he was still angry, then said, "I'll change in the back corner where the light don't reach."

Jesse took her turn in the dark corner, and then Boswell. Luke wore his extra shirt and wrapped a blanket around his waist, thrusting his stockinged feet close to the fire. Jesse sat across from him in her yellow checked dress, tucking her bare legs beneath her skirt.

"Reckon I c'n rig up somethin' to help this stuff dry," Boswell said to no one in particular. "Yep, that's a good idea," he answered himself when nobody else did. "Right smart idea."

The cave grew less chilled after a while, but Jesse slept fitfully that night. Beneath her the ground was rough and uneven, and she kept waking with cold in spite of the fire. She was up before dawn, pulling on her good stockings and petticoat although she'd intended to save them for town wear.

Glancing out of the cave entrance, she felt the faintest lifting of night. A cold, damp gust of air blew her way. It would probably rain all day, she suspected.

She checked the drying clothes and turned them over so the damp parts faced the heat. She used the last of their drinking water for the morning coffee.

Boswell coughed harshly, the sound coming from deep inside his chest. He turned uneasily in his sleep, his face looking flushed.

Luke rose and hunkered down beside her at the fire. "Boswell doesn't sound good," he remarked as he poured himself a cup of coffee. "He's been hackin' all night."

She glanced at him. There seemed to be little left of Luke's ill humor toward her from before, which lightened her heart considerably. His present concern was for his old friend.

"Yes, it worries me a little," she admitted. "He's feverish. Is there anything in the packs that might help him?"

"Don't reckon I packed any medicinals. My ma usually has a store of medicines, though. Soon's we get off this mountain it'll take only a day to get home."

"You didn't tell me you had family," Jesse said with a mixture of emotion, not the least of which was a bit of dismay.

"Uh, yeah, sure 'nuff." Luke could've sworn at himself. He'd wanted to wait for a better time to introduce his ma into the conversation. "What'd you think, that I hatched from an egg?"

"No, of course not, only you didn't mention living kin. I thought you were, um, you know . . . just a cowboy."

"That's exactly what I am, Jesse Mae. Just a cowpoke. Only I have a mother, too. I told you once that I had a job for you. Ma's getting older an' she could use some help in the house."

Jesse stiffened. Be at the beck and call of another woman in a house not her own? With no time for herself at all? It didn't fit her picture of ideal employment; what she hoped to find was waitressing or clerking in a store, with set hours. If she did find she had to keep house for someone, she hoped it would be for an elderly bachelor.

So Luke lived with his mother, hmm? She wondered if perhaps that was why he had proposed to her. His mother needed someone to care for her, either a servant or a daughter-in-law.

A daughter-in-law wasn't usually paid to take care of family. Was that what he wanted her for?

The idea distinctly disquieted her. It even hurt a little.

Well, she wouldn't do it, she couldn't compromise

her goals. Not even Luke, with his kisses like heaven and fire all wrapped together. Even after learning about his devotion to his mother and realizing that that did say something good about his ability to stay in one place. She wasn't about to get tied down in another family situation not of her choosing, with no life other than running to and fro and unpaid work.

Yet she did owe Luke money. And time. And her life.

At her continued silence, Luke abruptly jerked his pants from one of the drying sticks and went to the back corner. Quick, scraping sounds told Jesse his actions held anger, his heavy stomping into his boots and resultant low groan of pain adding to her belief.

Now he was angry at her again, and she didn't know how to smooth things over. What bothered her was that she wanted to. Very much.

He stalked to the cave opening and leaned against his forearm as he contemplated the weather for long moments.

"Jesse, come here."

His request was quietly made, his anger gone. Jesse rose slowly, and joined him.

While the rain had let up, the world beyond was a mass of fog. Only the nearest trees and faint path were visible. The only sounds were from the soft movements of the menagerie inside the cave.

It made her feel oddly safe and peaceful. Because if they were closed in, then everyone else was shut out. At least for a time she didn't have to worry about where George might be or if Luke's mother worried about him or if his employer would fire him for getting his bulls home so long overdue. Or if she could overcome her growing feelings toward Luke.

She tried to imagine having this peace all the time.

It seemed more than she could hope for, something beyond dreams.

They didn't speak as they watched the swirling, dripping fog until the fire popped, its piny odor filling the space around them.

"We're low on wood," she murmured, remembering.

"Yeah, I know," he said on a sigh, as though sorry their moment of accord was over. "Sit tight for a bit, honey, and I'll look for some."

Jesse pushed away her own feeling of sadness. Reality always intruded at the worst of times if you didn't prepare for it, she thought.

While he was gone, she counted over what foodstuffs they had left. There wasn't much.

Luke came in and tumbled an armload of sticks and pinecones beside the fire. It was wet, but the only small stuff he could find.

Jesse glanced at Boswell's sleeping form, then whispered, "Luke . . . we used the last of the bacon yesterday. And we don't have much flour left."

He slowly nodded. "Yeah, I know."

He turned suddenly and wrapped his hands around her shoulders. "Jesse, I've been thinking. Will you be all right for the morning if I go hunting?"

"Yes, of course, Luke, but are you sure? If the trail's bad . . .?"

"I can manage if it's only me."

"All right. Yes. Go. We could use fresh meat."

"I'll be back by midday," he told her. He gathered his things, took Rem with him and left quickly.

Jesse busied herself by seeing to the animals as best she could. When she returned to the fire, Boswell sat up.

"Any of that soup left from last night?" he croaked. His eyes looked bleary and his breathing sounded strained.

"Sure, Boswell. Here, why don't you move closer to the fire and I'll dish it up for you."

Spreading her blanket, she helped him to resettle.

"Dad-blamed cold. Don't feel so good."

"Well, a little of this soup should help."

"Where's Luke got to?" he asked between sips.

"Hunting. No need to stir yourself."

Boswell handed her his cup before returning to sleep. She tucked her cloak around him, hoping its added warmth would give him some deeper rest.

Still feeling the cold herself, she put on every piece of dry clothing she could from her bag.

She had no way of judging time. What little light filtered into the cave told her nothing but that it was daytime. She propped up the sticks Luke had brought in so the moisture could evaporate, kept turning the heavy denim pants and other clothing until they thoroughly dried, and fed the last of the good wood to the already meager fire.

Though he'd slept throughout the morning, Boswell struggled to sit up as if he had to fight to stay awake. Jesse gave him the remainder of the soup, telling him she'd already eaten her own.

"Thank you, lassie, you're a good girl. Don't 'member the last time I felt so poorly. Must have the grippe." He leaned against the cave wall. "Wanta play some poker?"

"Poker? I don't know the game."

"Look in my pack over there, Miz Jesse, an' find my cards. I'll teach you."

Luke came in about an hour later, carrying a grouse already dressed and ready for the fire. He put the bird down, and set about making a spit. His boots and pants were muddy up to the knees, and Jesse noticed he had dried mud on his hands.

"So this is what you do the moment I turn my back,

you old reprobate." Luke joked over his shoulder, assessing the scene, giving close attention to Boswell's flushed face. "Teach Jesse all your bad habits?"

"Had to keep the girl entertained, didn't I?" But Boswell barely had the words out before he went into another spasm of coughing. "Well, how's the trail down the mountain, boy?" he asked when he could. "Is it passable?"

Luke shifted his glance toward Jesse. Behind her smile flashed uncertainty and worry, but what she said was, "I've won three hands, Luke. We're playing for stones, see?"

"Yep, the little lady is right lucky. If I was playin' for real," Boswell said on another cough, "I'd owe her a heap."

Luke placed the grouse over the coals and stood. "The trail's blocked some. Mud's heavy in a couple of spots. Reckon we'll let it dry out for a day or so before taking the bulls down."

"'Fraid of that," Boswell muttered. "Well, beggin' your pardon, Miz Jesse, but since we ain't movin' for a while I think I'll just go back to sleep till supper."

"You do that, Boswell. Sleep's the best thing for what ails you," she replied with the old axiom. But she wasn't too sure about it.

"Sure, Boswell. We'll wake you when the meat is tender," Luke added. The moment the older man rolled in his blanket, Luke motioned her to the entrance of the cave.

Jesse glanced out, breathing deeply of the fresh air. She hadn't realized the cave air had become stagnant.

"The fog is lifting," she noted. "Do you think it will clear by tomorrow?"

"Likely," he commented, then lowered his voice. "Jesse, I've got some firewood to haul inside. It's a big piece and I need your help . . ." He let his voice trail, then asked in puzzlement, "What in the world have you got on?"

"Oh, uh, well, it's my nightgown."

He pushed his hat to the back of his head. "Hmmm?"

She glanced down at herself then up at him. "My night—" She stopped when she noted the twinkle in his eyes.

"Do you usually wear all those things under your nightgown?"

"No, of course not. I was cold, so I put on more clothes," she said defensively.

"Reckon a husband would have to peel away layers half the night to find out if there was a woman under there, wouldn't he?"

"I guess so," she said primly. "But since I've renewed my vow not to take a husband, the matter will not be discussed. Now what was it you needed my help with?"

Jesse carefully watched how Luke took her declaration, but he didn't give her the satisfaction of a reaction, for he only shrugged. "I've got Rem hooked up to haul a big log up to the cave, but I need you to take his head."

"All right, just a minute." She hurried to the back corner and stripped down to her underthings and then donned her jeans and heavy shirt once more.

Stepping out of the cave made her feel as though she'd been isolated far too long. The fog had lifted enough for Jesse to see down the mountain side for quite a ways. She spotted Rem waiting patiently off to the side of the trail, his head down, cropping grass.

The ground was a soggy mess. Immediately, her boots were caked with mud. She and Luke half slid their way down to the mule, and it took her careful leading and Luke's urging from the rear to get Rem to move up the slippery path.

"Good boy, Rem," Jesse praised when they reached the cave entrance. At that moment, the sun broke through the clouds and she paused to catch her breath. Blue jays squawked nearby, then flew off. From a distance, she caught the faint sound of jingling.

Puzzled, she glanced at Luke's profile. He'd heard it, too.

"Get inside the cave," Luke commanded, low.

"What is it?"

"Get inside," he repeated. "Wake Boswell."

There hadn't been enough time. Not enough warning. No time to conceal their presence from an enemy. Luke cursed his luck, frantically searching his mind for a way to deflect the oncoming party, whoever they were. But there was no way. The best he could hope for was to conceal the entrance to the cave.

He backed Rem down the trail a few yards, then left him there in plain sight. Then racing and sliding in the mud, he descended the treed slope opposite the cave until he found what he sought. Brush in abundance. Grabbing hold at the roots, he pulled until he had a mass of it, then raced back up, avoiding the mud as he could, but dropping dirt and loose rock in his wake.

Luke climbed higher, reaching a point where he could look down on the trail. Yesterday's footprints had been erased in the storm, but those of today were clear-cut and telling. His large ones and Jesse's smaller ones, plus Rem's, all leading from the cave.

The oncoming visitors were closer, though he heard little sound.

He positioned himself then let the brush fall. It tumbled and scattered, yet landed where he wished it—right in front of the entrance, covering the most obvious signs. If they were lucky, the party would pass it by when they saw Rem, the log, and the greater mass of churned mud.

They would be looking for him and not Jesse.

At Luke's pressing command, Jesse dropped Rem's harness and ran inside the cave. "Boswell," she called, close to the sleeping man's ear. "Boswell, wake up. Luke needs you. Someone's coming."

Boswell shook his head and blinked, then staggered to his feet, his handgun drawn. The black cat, which had been curled alongside him, shot forward and out of the cave as though it had been kicked.

Boswell ran out into the open, looking this way and that.

"Ssst," Luke signaled.

Jesse ran to follow in Boswell's wake, but hovered at the cave opening. Luke had backed Rem a few yards and left him standing in the middle of the path. She saw Boswell's nod, and knew there had been a silent agreement between the two men. Boswell turned and lost himself in the trees. Suddenly, a mass of vines and bush landed at her feet, covering the muddy imprints that showed the cave's use. Looking up, she spotted Luke on the slope above.

"Luke?" she murmured.

"Stay out of sight, Jesse," Luke whispered.

A moment later, she realized she could see neither Luke nor Boswell. Where had they disappeared to? she wondered.

She waited, scarcely breathing. Then she heard a sound, or rather felt, movement, a sort of vibration. Long moments passed. Through the trees, a low male voice murmured, the speech unintelligible. She couldn't tell for sure, but it sounded like neither Boswell nor Luke.

A shaft of late afternoon sunlight filtering through the trees caught a flash of moving color. Horses and men. They came from the trail they'd come up yesterday. How many, she didn't know. Jesse shrank out of sight against the inner cave wall, her heart almost in her throat.

Had they been followed? Who was it? She was certain it couldn't be George and the Thomses; they wouldn't have the least notion where she and Luke had gone. Besides, Luke said the trail was washed out; wouldn't that mean their tracks had also been obliterated? But then, wouldn't the interlopers discover them the moment they spotted fresh tracks and Rem hitched to a log?

She listened for all she was worth, long seconds of silence punctuated occasionally with sounds of movement: a horse blowing heavily, a faint hoof on a stone, a low grunt.

Then a not-so-low exclamation, a guttural one. The very obvious muddy scars in the track had been seen. And Rem.

She counted shadows that flickered on the edge of the entrance stone as bodies passed. Three. Four. Five.

Five men who spoke in another language, excited over finding the mule. A bloodcurdling yell made her jump, and then she knew. Indians!

The quiet broke in a dozen ways. Hoofs thudding along the trail, shouting and yipping, and Rem's frightened bray. Brush crashing and rolling pebbles.

Rom took that moment to answer, trampling in an agitated circle as the stone cave echoed his harsh bray into rebounding waves. Alarmed, Mehitabel suddenly stood up, her eyes bugged, her nose high. The Herefords added their bellows.

"Shh, hush," Jesse hissed at them, swiping up a

long stick from the pile as she raced toward the dark shadows. But even her whisper echoed and she wondered why she hadn't noticed how loud it sounded before. Grabbing Rom's ear, she rubbed it as Meshach and Shadrach huddled against the wall, crowding each other. Afraid of making more noise, afraid that the bulls might choose that moment to start a fight with each other, she squeezed herself between them, nearly getting stepped on in the process. Recklessly, she grabbed a stubbed horn and pushed at their heads.

A nearby rattling of stone caused her to look up. A man stood at the cave entrance, muscular and tall, dressed in breechclout, knee-high moccasins, and a white man's shirt. His drawn knife gleamed in his hand. His black eyes darted everywhere, noting the fire and their scattered equipment. Jesse pressed her back into the stone wall.

Another Indian entered, his hair falling loose around his shoulders, holding a long rifle in his hand. Unconsciously, she gripped harder on Rom's ear. Her mule snorted a protest and the two pairs of eyes turned her way.

She held her breath. Outside, the noise of Rem, still braying, and the remaining Indians gave her no clue as to what was occurring with Luke and Boswell.

The taller Indian took a cautious step forward, turning his head in an effort to peer deeper into the shadows. Another step, more confident. His companion was right behind him.

Jesse felt buffeted between Meshach and Mehitabel. Wanting to reassure the animals that she was there, she placed a hand against the camel. The usually jealous female backed, turned her head, and nibbled at Jesse's shoulder. With abrupt reaction, Jesse swatted the camel hard on the behind with her stick.

Mehitabel gave out a great roar and plunged toward the two men, dancing into the firelight's edge. Rom twisted and kicked out, adding his bray as he went. Meshach and Shadrach dashed away from the wall and bucked in a circle, butting at anything in their path. Suddenly, fantastic shadows rose on the cave walls, all enlarged and blobbed together, heaving and twisting. It appeared to be one mammoth monster.

Jesse stood frozen against the back wall, her heavy stick clutched tightly in one hand.

But the Indians didn't even see her.

The two men's eyes went wide with sudden terror. They screamed, turned, and fell over themselves to get out. Mehitabel, seeing the entrance light, dashed after them.

Outside, the terror was contagious and pandemonium broke out. Jesse heard gunshots. She raced to see what was happening.

At the opening, Jesse pushed against Mehitabel, who had stopped in the middle of it, taking up most the entry. The camel's long neck stretched out; Mehitabel bared her teeth.

The two Indians from the cave babbled at the top of their lungs and waved their hands wildly as they leaped to their mounts. From above, stones and mud began to roll down, bouncing into the area like petrified hail. A turbulent keening yell followed it, as though a giant troll held claim to the mountain.

Without another hesitation, all five of the riders plunged down the trail.

Jesse waited until the sounds receded before stepping into full view. Luke came sliding down the mountainside, his backside mud-coated, and folded her in trembling arms. She buried her face against his shoulder.

"It's all right, honey. They're gone," Luke said, patting

her back awkwardly. He wasn't so sure he was all right, though. He'd come near losing this girl once again and he thought he might not live to tell about the next time.

Boswell ran from the trees, breathing harshly. "What the damn hell was all that?"

"Unplanned visitors," Luke answered.

"Yeah, Luke, I knowed that," he said disgustedly. "They was Arapaho, if I don't miss my guess. But them Injuns came skidding down that trail like all the demons of hell was after 'em."

Jesse couldn't hold it in any longer. All her bone-jarring fright had turned to uproarious laughter at the memory of the dancing, bucking shadows the cave wall had reflected, which had saved her from possible death. She erupted in side-splitting, rolling laughter.

"Jesse, honey, are you all right?" Luke asked as he worriedly searched her features.

Jesse raised her face, her merriment uncontrolled. She couldn't say a thing. She nodded instead.

"You ain't havin' the hysterics, are you?"

She shook her head no. Then changing her mind, nodded again. "Uh-huh . . . it was . . . it was s-something I'll n-never forget as long as I live," she said between giggles. "Mehitabel . . ." She pointed to the tall animal who had wandered completely out of the cave and stood sniffing the air with disdain. "And then Rem and the Herefords . . ."

At that point one of the bulls let out another bellow, the sound changing and magnifying in the cave. It sent Jesse off again.

Boswell looked at Luke over her head. "You been feedin' this girl loco weed while I been laid up?" he accused.

"'Course not, Boswell," Luke replied, his eyebrows raised in affront. He patted her back again. "She's only having herself a little case of the hysterics. Said so, just now."

"N-not the b-bad kind, Boswell," Jesse finally got out, getting some control at last. "It's only that . . . you'll never believe it."

She related the events as they'd happened. Luke punctuated her account with his comments.

"I fired from above," he said. "I was comin' down as fast as I could when those two came tearing out of the cave. Hadn't seen 'em go in, just surmised it after—but then the caterwauling sent 'em all churning. I couldn't tell what was going on."

He didn't mention how horror had nearly curdled his blood at the fear of finding her dead in the cave.

"D'you think they'll come back?" Jesse asked when she grew serious again.

"Naw," Boswell replied. "Fact is, this'll be a place them folks'll likely shy away from after this." Then, rubbing his chin, he said thoughtfully, "Y'know, I kinda think this here odd-lookin' animal has saved us both today. I was hid behind a boulder, tryin' to keep a bead on them Injuns, but truth is, I had another coughin' spell. They'd of heard me for sure if it hadn't been for all that noise."

"Well, reckon we'll set guard just the same," Luke remarked.

11

The next afternoon, they came to the bottom of the mountain. They didn't linger nor did they rush. They were all tired and hungry, but it was Boswell that Jesse worried about. His cough was worse and she wondered how he clung to his saddle.

"Almost there," Luke had said to her an hour ago. He'd glanced worriedly toward Boswell and tried to encourage the older man as well. The last hour, Luke rode side by side with him, frequently placing a hand against his shoulder to steady him. Jesse wasn't sure if Boswell knew nor even cared. His eyes looked glazed. The man needed a real bed and medicine.

When Jesse finally saw Wayside Station's first building from a distance she thought she never wanted to leave civilization again.

"I'm gonna set you down at Mrs. Fry's roomin' house," Luke said as he led the cavalcade up a side street. He guided them into an alley, then directed them to the back door of a large, many-windowed white house with black shutters.

"Get you a room an' Boswell a doctor," he told her as he swung her down from her mule. Together, they helped Boswell dismount.

"C'n walk," Boswell murmured. But Jesse knew he was on the verge of collapse. They practically carried him up the three painted steps.

Luke rapped on the back door, but didn't wait for it to be answered. He opened it and swung the three of them inside the kitchen, lowering Boswell to a chair immediately.

"Howdy, there, Miz Emma," he said to the startled cook. "Get Mrs. Fry back here, please. And send for Dr. Reed pronto. Boswell needs 'im."

The cook hurried off, and Mrs. Fry rushed in. Taking one glance at Boswell, whose head was on the table, and then a lightning gaze at Jesse, she exclaimed, fluttering a handkerchief, "Oh, my stars, Luke McCarthy, what have you gone and done now?"

Mrs. Fry's disapproving expression pegged Jesse as an undesirable element that she wouldn't touch with a long stick. Jesse felt as though she might as well be one of the rag-tag kids from the big city, Kansas City, or even Chicago, without a hope for a crumb of compassion, or deserving of one, either, as far as this woman was concerned.

"Ain't done nothin' to hang for, Mrs. Fry," he told the plump, middle-aged figure. "Just brought you a couple of payin' guests for a few days. Boswell, here, has a bad case of the grippe. Been coughing bad and can't breathe very well."

"Oh, the poor man," Mrs. Fry sympathized, her handkerchief over her heart.

Jesse wasn't too sure how deep the woman's sympathy lay. Their hostess's gaze seemed a bit calculating.

"Well, let's get him up the back stairs," Mrs. Fry continued. "He can have room ten. It's closest to the kitchen."

"Kin' o' you, ma'am," Boswell said with an effort to sit up. His face still flushed with fever, Boswell stared through bleary eyes. "Miz Jesse . . . Abednego . . ."

"Don't worry about him, Boswell," Jesse said. "I'll take care of him."

Luke and Mrs. Fry gathered up Boswell and headed up the back stairs. Jesse trailed after them, not knowing whether she should stay in the kitchen or go with them.

She stood shyly in the bedroom doorway and watched Mrs. Fry loosen Boswell's clothing as soon as Luke laid him down.

"What room do you want Jesse to take?" Luke asked.

Mrs. Fry gave her a flicker of a glance. The woman was very polite, Jesse gave her credit for that. But there was the slightest downturn to her lips. "Room fifteen."

"Okay. Put the bill for both rooms on the tab, Mrs. Fry. Uh, on *my* tab," he amended.

"Don't worry, Luke. I'll see to it."

"Did someone go for Doc Reed?"

"Donny went," Mrs. Fry answered, speaking of her son. "He'll be along any minute."

"Fine." Luke addressed Boswell. "I'll be back later. Doc Reed'll fix you up, okay?"

"Yeah, Luke," Boswell whispered. "Ya gotta take care o' your missus . . ."

Luke seemed not to notice the status Boswell gave her, but Jesse did. So did Mrs. Fry, she noted, for the woman's eyes widened slightly.

"Maybe room seven would be better for the girl,"

Mrs. Fry said. "It's in front and gets the morning light."

Jesse opened her mouth to correct the woman's misunderstanding and to say that room fifteen—which she strongly suspected was at the back where she wasn't as likely to be noticed—would be just fine, but at that moment Luke took her arm. "Walk back down with me, Jesse."

When they reached the kitchen, the cook, Emma, was there. Her black face fell into a hundred lines and Jesse couldn't even guess at her age. She looked up at them while buttering thick slices of bread.

"When's supper, Miz Emma?" Luke asked.

"You know very well, Mr. McCarthy, that we serve at six sharp. And Mrs. Fry won't stand for in-betweens," she said primly, giving Jesse a quick, knowing glance. "It ruins her meals, besides playing havoc with my work. I have enough to do besides catering to every tinker, drummer, or cowpoke coming through my kitchen."

"Sure, 'nuff, Miz Emma, but my girl Jesse, here, has had nothing but a flour 'n' water biscuit to eat since morning. Couldn't you find her a crust 'er something?"

Jesse blushed to the roots of her hair. In all the time she'd worked for Cousin Bertha, she'd never gone without food, even though she'd sometimes scraped the bottom of the pan. And she'd always worked for her keep, she thought with pride. She couldn't imagine Luke begging for her.

Her hand flew to her hot cheek. "Oh, don't, Luke. I can wait for supper at six. I—I'll just get the cat . . ."

The woman's eyes began to dance. "Miz Jesse, is it? Well, I do concede we might need to feed her up a bit." She slapped a thick slice of ham on one piece of bread and then another. "Have you been starving the girl?"

"No more'n myself, Miz Emma." Luke returned the

woman's smile. "Honest. Don't all this trail dust speak for itself? We've been traveling for days."

Jesse looked from one to the other. Why, they were joking!

"Yes, I do see," Miz Emma said, topping the ham with a slice of onion. "And I'd suggest you clean yourself up some before you present yourself to Miz Annabelle. You know she hates to see her boys in such a state."

"Miz Annabelle?" Jesse murmured.

"Luke's mother."

"Is she in town?" Luke asked.

Jesse saw a slight wince cross his face. Did he hope to avoid his family?

"Was this afternoon. Took luncheon with Miz Fry."

So, his mother and the starchy Mrs. Fry were friends. If Luke didn't want to see his mother right away, did that mean he was ashamed to introduce her to his ma? But no, that couldn't be the case, because he wanted her to work for his mother. Didn't he?

Or was he only being kind?

"But she's gone home now?" he asked.

Jesse held her breath. She wasn't ready to meet any of Luke's family.

"Yes, I think so," Miz Emma said, handing one of the thick sandwiches to her and one to Luke.

Thank you, Lord. Thank you. She didn't have to face Luke's mother tonight looking like a ragamuffin.

Jesse gazed at the bread and ham longingly, then added another thanks to her silent message.

"Unless she's still at Miz Josie's," Miz Emma added. She set two large mugs of milk on the table. "Now sit. Let this child eat."

Luke groaned. "Well, I don't haveta go through town. Gotta get my cattle home, anyway."

"I'll take some soup to Mr. Boswell now," Miz Emma said and left the room.

Who was Josie? Jesse wondered as she sat and bit into the sandwich.

Luke wolfed his sandwich in four huge bites and downed his milk in one gulp. He sprung from his chair and headed out of the door. "Jesse . . ."

He was departing. After so many days together, Jesse felt suddenly abandoned.

"Yes . . . I—I'll just get the cat." Leaving her food half eaten, she followed him outside, looking for Abednego in Boswell's open saddlebags. The cat came to her readily, but then jumped to the ground and raced under the house.

"Oh, drats! Now I'll have to go hunting for the rascal." At least she would have something to keep her occupied for what was left of the day.

"Forget the cat," Luke said, swinging her bag to the steps. "It'll show up."

She started to call. "Abednego . . . here, cat."

"Jesse," Luke said, irritated. He grabbed her shoulders in his big hands and turned her. "Look at me!"

Jesse raised her lashes slowly. She was caught up in his expression, his eyes seeming bluer than the sky, his face stubbled in a golden beard.

"Jesse," he said hesitantly. "I hate leaving you here, honey, but I can't have the, um, animals untended. Now I want you to rest up, Jesse Mae, while I settle my business. Have a nap. Don't go running around town till I get back, hear?"

"How long will you be, Luke?"

"A while, I'm 'fraid. Might even be morning. Have to settle up with my . . . with Will. He's waiting for Meshach and Shadrach, you know."

"All right," she agreed, however reluctantly. Jesse

thought of all Luke had done for her. He'd been her champion, her knight in shining armor. She owed him so much, and oh, my goodness . . . She owed him *money!*

She had to find work, and soon. Somewhere. "How . . . how big is this town, Luke? Wayside Station . . . How d'you suppose it got its name? Is there much call for clerking and such?"

Knowing where her questions were leading, Luke insisted, "Don't, Jesse. Don't worry so. Just sit tight, okay? Have a bath," he said and then grinned his impudent grin, the first she'd seen in days. "Put on those town-fine shoes."

Don't worry? He thought it was so easy.

Well, she wasn't his responsibility. She could take care of herself.

"Oh, I will, Mr. McCarthy." She straightened her back and raised her nose. "A woman must make the best of her opportunities, my mama always told me. I most certainly will dress in my good shoes and dress. One should look one's best for one's prospects, don't you think?"

Luke felt a hard wrench at leaving her. For the first time in his life, he couldn't stand the thought of turning his back and riding away from a woman. He'd done that very thing a few times. Simply flirted and danced with a girl, then walked away. Not one of them had held his interest for very long.

Not one of them held his heart.

Jesse looked tiny and vulnerable, standing on Mrs. Fry's back steps in her oversized boy's shirt and too-big hat. And adorable.

Lord A'mighty, was she ever.

Her green eyes had shone misty for a moment back there, and he knew she'd felt the wrenching, too. In spite of all her protests, she couldn't deny they'd been through enough together to tie some firm knots.

As it happened, she hadn't even noticed that he'd taken her harp with him along with all of the animals. Mehitabel still carried it. It was his insurance against her stealing out of town without him; he knew she wouldn't leave without her ma's harp.

Luke was beginning to feel more empathy with ol' George. Hell, he was even *sounding* like ol' George, and that was a downright disturbing thought. Miss Jesse Mae Banning was to be wooed, not coerced. He wanted her in his arms willingly.

He faced forward. Before he could begin a proper courtship, he had responsibilities at the M double C, and a lot to answer for as soon as he reached there. Between his big brother Will and his mother, he'd be riddled with questions. They'd want to know everything. So would his sister Josie.

Plus, Sandy and Crow and the other cowhands would be as curious as a passel of raccoons. He was in for the ribbing of his life when they saw his mount, for he'd always taken great pride in his own string of fine horses, among the best on the M double C. And Mehitabel. Yes, sir, he'd get an earful over the beast.

Well, he could ride it out. He'd given his share of joshing over the years; he reckoned he'd let the men have their fun. Anyway, when they saw the woman he'd finally bring home—when he was able to convince Jesse to marry him—they might be laughing out of the other sides of their mouths. Jesse wouldn't allow anyone to say a thing against those mules.

As soon as he turned off the road onto M double C land, it started. Crow, a young half-breed and one of their best riders, raced toward him on his Appaloosa mare. "Howdy, Luke. Glad to see you home. Will's been actin' like he done drunk soured milk 'cause you're so late getting here, and Miz Annabelle's been worried as a duck in the desert."

"Well, I'm home now, and I ain't been settin' on my south side all this time."

Crow rode a loop around Mehitabel. "What you got there, a overgrown new kinda moose? Nope. Ain't got no horns. Mebbe it's a funny-lookin' giant dog."

"Careful, Crow. That all-fired fine beast is a camel. Come from Africa, once upon a time. She's got personality, and she don't take to every two-bit, half-baked cowhand that don't know how to treat her like a lady. It makes her skittish. She bites."

"A lady camel, huh? Like some of that bunch that the army used a while back? What's that there you ridin'? You lose a bet or somethin'?"

"Now don't go insulting my mules. They've showed their good qualities."

Sandy came out of the huge barn, his hands on his hips, and stared. He shook his head in disbelief. "Naw, say it ain't so. Say I ain't seeing what my eyes say it is. Are you Luke McCarthy, that young spruced-up dude that left here more'n a month gone, or an impostor?"

"How do, Sandy," Luke replied, smiling good-naturedly. "Know where Will is?"

"Yeah, reckon he's over to his house." Sandy thumbed toward the huge stone and wood house in the distance. He opened the corral gate and Luke herded Meshach and Shadrach through. "Mattie's getting set to have that next young'un, an' you know Will. He don't like to be too far."

Luke was crazy about his sister-in-law, Mattie, and knew she'd had a rough time giving birth to her last boy. For the first time Luke thought he really did understand his more serious older brother. Will worried for his wife; he'd be wild if anything bad happened to her. More than that, Luke thought he might feel the very same way if Jesse were having his baby.

The idea of Jesse having his baby sent his thoughts shooting sky-high, but it wasn't the time for indulging his fantasies. Besides, Jesse had once mentioned she didn't plan on having young'uns, so he had a lot of tall talkin' to do both to persuade her to marry him and to convince her that having her own children would be desirable.

She must have had a hellish time at the hands of those damned cousins if she was the same woman he'd seen taking such loving care of Effie's babe. Jesse was too natural at it for him to truly believe she wouldn't want a couple of her own.

"I'll ride over an' let him know you're home, Luke," Crow offered.

"Do that," Luke agreed as he dismounted. He led Rem inside the barn while Sandy took Rom and Boswell's black gelding.

"You look like you're runnin' down faster'n a two-dollar watch," Sandy remarked, beginning to unsaddle the gelding.

"Yep, just about am," Luke replied. Truth to tell, he couldn't remember the last time he'd been so tired. He hoped Jesse and Boswell were getting some real rest.

"Trip that tough?"

"Some."

"That so, huh? Reckon you got a tale to tell around the campfire."

Sandy, so called for the color of his hair, had been with the M double C for a number of years. He was wiry and homely as a mud fence, but he'd been Will's best friend since the day he hired on as a youth. Luke had been only eight or nine at the time. Will had been boss at the family ranch from the time he was fourteen.

"I do, sure enough. Reckon I'll wait for Will and Ma to get here to tell it, though."

"Where'd you pick up the camel?"

"Back in Nebraska. And that ain't all I picked up. Did Will tell you how come I left the train?"

"Didn't know enough to tell, now did I?" Will said as he slid off the rump of Crow's mount. "Damn it, Luke! Where on earth have you been? And what was that telegram all about? Where are the Herefords?"

"Don't go gettin' up on your hind legs, Will. Meshach and Shadrach are safe and sound out in the—"

"Who?"

Luke grinned. Will would eventually appreciate the humorous names, but at the moment he wasn't in the mood. "The bulls. They're fine, Will. I might've pushed 'em a little hard, but they ain't hurt. They'll fatten up again in a week's time."

On the verge of turning on his heel to go see his prizes, Will spied the camel and stopped cold. He watched silently as Luke commanded the beast to fold down. Through narrowed blue eyes, he took in the two mules that Sandy was unsaddling and the big tarpaulin-wrapped package that Luke carefully set inside the tack room, out of harm's way. "All right, Luke," he finally said quietly, "What kind of a thorny patch did you hit?"

Annabelle McCarthy stepped into the barn. "My word, son, where in the world have you been all this time? I've been so worried, and Will has just about ridden a new rut in the road up yonder looking for you."

"Howdy, Ma." Luke greeted her with a grin. "Any chance of a bath before supper?"

"Yes, of course." She looked him over carefully. "You wouldn't be allowed at my table looking like that, you may be sure."

But the glad-to-see-him smile in his mother's eyes denied that she'd ever turn her son away.

At Will's command, Crow took the mules and Mehitabel out to pasture. "All right, Luke. We'll save the explanations until supper. But they better be good."

Jesse stood awkwardly in the kitchen watching Emma baste the roast she was preparing for the evening meal before she finally asked directions to her room. She hardly knew what to do next, she felt such a letdown at Luke's absence. Something she'd better get over, she reminded herself.

Emma responded kindly, then promised that bath-water would be sent up presently. "There's a hip bath-tub in the upstairs closet," she directed. "I'm sorry that I can't be of more help to you, child, but with you and Mr. Boswell in residence, we pretty nearly have a full house at the moment and I'm the only one to do much. Lost the maid last week. Up and quit without notice," Emma finished, then added under her breath, "just like the last one."

Jesse's attention immediately went on the alert. She stepped forward eagerly. "Is Mrs. Fry looking for help, then? What does the job require? I'm looking for work, you know, and I can do most anything a board-inghouse might need. Make beds, clean rooms. I can cook, too; I could help you."

"Whoa, there, Miz Jesse. What would Luke McCarthy have to say about your working here?"

"Why, nothing." She raised her chin. "Nothing at all. I don't look to Luke for approval of my actions."

"Oh, my, my, I can see trouble brewing."

Jesse laughed. If only the woman knew the trouble they'd already faced in recent weeks.

"Don't worry, Miz Emma, I can take care of myself where Luke is concerned. Now tell me, what tasks does Mrs. Fry take care of?"

"Just Emma will do, child. Well," Emma paused to think a moment. "Mrs. Fry sees to the business side of things, to be sure. She does the ordering and presides at table. Donny sometimes helps."

In other words, Mrs. Fry didn't handle much of the real work. That left only Emma, and she definitely needed an extra pair of hands. In a happier frame of mind, Jesse made the climb up the back stairs. Hopefully, she wouldn't have to go far to find a real honest-to-goodness wage-paying job.

She popped her head in to see how Boswell was, but found him asleep. Then, getting the bathtub, she went around a hall corner to find her room.

Yellow roses adorned the wallpaper in the front bedroom that was room seven, and a yellow bedspread with a ruffle made the room feminine. Jesse thought it the prettiest room she'd ever occupied. It overlooked the town's main street, with its shops and businesses.

Answering a knock on the door, she found a young man holding two buckets of steaming water. He was dark and slight of build, and it didn't take but a moment to discover he was rather simple-minded.

"My name's Donny," he said. "Are you Luke's missus?"

"Um, not really. Please set the buckets right there on the stand." Excited to have a real bath, she gazed happily at the hot water.

Donny remained in the doorway. "You must be Luke's missus," he insisted. "Ma said so."

"Well, you see, there was a mistake. I—"

"You don't look like a missus. You don't dress like a girl, even. Ma says you look like something the cat drug up."

Jesse swiftly turned to the small mirror over the dresser. Did she look that bedraggled? If Mrs. Fry was so critical of her, she'd certainly hesitate to give her a job, wouldn't she?

Oh, she did! No wonder the woman had looked at her askance. Her braids were unkempt, the skin across her nose sunburned, she was dirty, and she smelled like mule and trail dust.

"Here, Donny, let me help." Jesse took a bucket from him and poured it into the hip tub. The sooner she got cleaned up and presentable, the sooner she'd feel better. Perhaps Mrs. Fry would change her opinion of her.

The boy shifted from foot to foot and stared at her.

"Ma says Miss Rosellen won't like you," he told her, tipping his head. "Ma says she'll be in a snit. A right royal fret. And she says only *heaven knows* what Mrs. Annabelle is gonna think."

Jesse commandeered the second bucket. She planned to avoid meeting Mrs. Annabelle, at least for now. However, she couldn't resist asking, "Who is Rosellen?"

"That's doc's girl. She's awful pretty, too. She's sweet on Luke. She's been sweet on Luke for a hunnert years. She saves every dance for him at the Saturday dances. Everybody in town knows she's sweet on Luke."

12

An uncomfortable feeling grabbed hold of Jesse's chest. So Luke already had a sweetheart? Jesse wondered if he had ever given Rosellen any of his heart-stopping kisses or made any promises to her.

"Well, thank you for bringing the water, Donny."

"Yes, ma'am."

An hour later, Jesse felt enormously better. Her hair was still damp from a thorough washing, and she had it piled high on her head, letting only a curl hang down over one ear. She'd been able to clean the worst stains from her one good suit, the navy blue, and hoped to pass Mrs. Fry's inspection. While she couldn't say that she was a fine lady, as least she felt like a grown woman and capable of conducting herself as one.

Jesse wanted to see Boswell before she went down to supper, and so she headed toward his room. She heard him coughing as she reached for the doorknob. Swinging the door wide, she discovered a youngish man with salt-and-pepper hair leaning over him, using a stethoscope to listen to the sick man's chest. She stepped inside.

The doctor gave her a fleeting glance, but then addressed Boswell. "You have the grippe, all right, Mr. Boswell. Chest inflammation."

"Thought so, doc," Boswell replied hoarsely. "Had it before."

"I can leave you something for the cough and fever," the doctor said, "but the best thing for you is to stay in bed and let nature takes its course."

Mrs. Fry sailed into the room. She didn't see Jesse, half-hidden behind the door. "Oh, there you are, Dr. Reed. I feared you might not come until evening, after Donny said you were out at the Sanderson ranch. However, you're in time for supper. Can I count on you and Rosellen tonight?"

"Just got in, Mrs. Fry. Have another patient to see," the doctor said evenly. But Jesse got the idea that he held his impatience in check.

Boswell appeared to have dozed off again. The doctor took Mrs. Fry's elbow and guided the older woman out into the hall. "Rosellen will join you for supper as usual, Mrs. Fry. Now about Mr. Boswell, here. He'll need some care for a week or so. Feed him soups and soft foods."

"Oh, dear." Mrs. Fry sighed dramatically as she pressed her handkerchief against her heart. "Yes, I suppose we can manage, doctor, though it will stretch me to the limit. You must know we are short of servants. We lost Katie last week. The girl simply left without notice," she said irritably. "I suppose Donny will have to do it."

"Donny will be all right if you give him close supervision, Mrs. Fry," the doctor insisted. "But you must not leave it all to him, you understand?"

"Well, you needn't speak to me in that tone, Dr. Reed. As though I shirk my Christian duties."

"No, no, Mrs. Fry. I only mean . . ."

Jesse moved from around the door. "Um, excuse me, please, Dr. Reed. I can nurse Mr. Boswell."

"Can you, young lady?" Dr. Reed gazed at her in speculation, his brown eyes dull with fatigue. "And who are you?"

"I'm Jesse Mae Ban—"

"This is the young woman that Luke McCarthy brought in along with the sick man today," Mrs. Fry was quick to say. The older woman gave her a reassessing glance. Her expression told Jesse the woman still had doubts, but that she was definitely relieved at her appearance. She went on. "Mrs., um, Miss, that is, Miz Jesse has taken the yellow bedroom at the front."

It was the boardinghouse's best, and the significance wasn't lost on the doctor. His eyes took on new interest.

Jesse addressed the doctor. "I'm used to nursing, Dr. Reed. Children mostly, but I know what to do for common ailments, and I know Mr. Boswell."

"I trust you can, ma'am. All right," the doctor capitulated. "If he should get worse, let me know. I'll stop in tomorrow if I can."

Jesse watched the doctor stride away, then she turned to Mrs. Fry. "You needn't worry, Mrs. Fry, about the extra work Boswell and I create. I'll not only take care of him, but I can clean his room and my own for a few days."

If she could prove her worth before asking for a job,

maybe Mrs. Fry would be happy to hire her. Or Dr.
Reed. She wondered if he needed an assistant, or if he
already employed one, and where he conducted his
practice. Fleetingly, she wondered how his daughter
occupied her time, or if he had a wife. But it seemed
odd, if he was married, that his daughter would take
her evening meals at the boarding house.

"Why should you wish to do that, my dear?" Mrs.
Fry said, bringing Jesse back to the moment at hand.
"Luke McCarthy is paying for your keep."

Jesse felt the heat steal up her cheeks. Mrs. Fry,
though keeping her tone polite, meant something very
insulting. Between embarrassment and anger, Jesse
thought she might explode. "Mr. McCarthy isn't—"

"Hey, Ma!" Donny shouted from the bottom of the
stairs. "Ma? Miz Emma needs you, and there's a cus-
tomer in the parlor."

Mrs. Fry winced. "I've told that boy until I'm blue
in the face not to shout. I must go. Do as you like, my
dear. I'm sure Emma will welcome the help."

Jesse watched the landlady descend the wide front
staircase, her footfalls softened by the blue wool carpet. Then she headed toward Boswell's room. She had
yet to see the public rooms of the house and wondered
how much upkeep they required.

Well, she thought, perhaps she'd better turn her
mind toward making a good impression on the doctor,
for it was certain she wasn't likely to make one on
Mrs. Fry.

Determined not to let Mrs. Fry get under her skin,
she took the water pitcher from Boswell's room and
headed down the back stairs to fetch more water. No
one, she'd noticed, had offered to bathe the patient, and
she guessed Boswell felt just as grimy as she had earlier.

"There is a cat howling at the back door, Miz Jesse,

wanting to come in," Emma said as Jesse headed toward the kitchen pump. "A black cat. I don't know what it's doing there or where it came from."

"Oh, that's Abednego. He belongs to Boswell."

"I was afraid of something like that. Mrs. Fry discourages the presence of animals of any kind in the boardinghouse," Emma said, giving her a sympathetic glance as she stirred a pot on the stove.

"Oh, dear. Well, I promised Boswell I'd take care of him, Emma. Don't be concerned, I won't let him into the house. May I feed him some table scraps? He hasn't had much to eat lately."

"Reckon so. There's a broken dish there by the side of the cupboard you can use, and you can give him a little of that milk on the table," Emma said. "But don't let Mrs. Fry catch you. Or Donny. The poor boy doesn't know the meaning of the word secret."

"So I've concluded," Jesse answered wryly. She found the dish and poured a little milk into it. "He, um, he told me all about Rosellen, Dr. Reed's daughter, and how she's sweet on Luke."

"Well, that's true enough, but you needn't worry. Luke could've married her any time these last two years if he'd had a mind to."

Jesse stepped back into the kitchen from setting the milk in front of the cat. "Oh, I wasn't worried. I only remarked about what Donny told me."

"Mm-hmm. I see. Well, I have to get supper dished up and served. Better find a seat at the table, child."

"If you don't mind, Emma, I'll just take some soup upstairs along with Boswell's and eat in his room."

"I don't mind, Jesse, but Mrs. Fry does. She doesn't cotton to the idea of folks eating in the bedrooms. She makes exceptions for only those who are too sick to make it to table. And she likes her guests to be prompt."

Jesse thought she'd better not upset the applecart, so she hurriedly carried the fresh water upstairs to Boswell. Since he was awake, he thanked her and insisted he could take care of himself for the evening.

"Are you sure, Boswell?"

"Sure as shootin', Miz Jesse. Now you run along. Ain't seemly for a young woman to take care of an old coot like me, anyway. You tell Donny to come up after supper. He'll give me a hand."

Jesse laughed, knowing Boswell felt more comfortable with the idea of Donny helping him bathe rather than herself. His voice grew huskier with his effort to speak, so she turned to go, not wanting to tire him further. "All right, then, Boswell. But I'll check on you later to make sure you've taken your medicine."

"That'll be all right, I reckon." As she reached the door, he said, "And Miz Jesse . . . you sure do look mighty pretty in your female duds. I can see why Luke is so smitten."

Jesse felt a lively curiosity about her supper companions and a great appreciation of the lovely table Mrs. Fry presented when she entered the dining room. Her memories included a few nice table furnishings from her mother's things; much to her sadness, all of them had been sold after her mother died.

"Oh, there you are," Mrs. Fry remarked in mild vexation. "We do like to seat ourselves promptly at six, my dear. However, you are here now. You may be seated," she nodded regally, indicating a chair near the foot of the table.

"I'm sorry to have kept you all waiting," Jesse murmured, flushing. These last years her meals had been catch-as-catch-can, and she reminded herself that she had much to relearn of society manners, things her mother had taught her when she was little. She gave close attention as Mrs. Fry's picked up her fork.

The supper company were mostly men, and they held a variety of occupations, Jesse discovered as Mrs. Fry graciously said their names. Two drummers; a cattle buyer from a Kansas City meat packer; Jeffrey Banes, the town lawyer; Mr. Jackson, who owned a bootery in town; Mr. Wittle, a railroad surveyor; a rancher and his young son; and a couple of men who, though Mrs. Fry didn't say, Jesse thought by the mere look of them were desperadoes. And Donny, naturally.

Of the women, there was Mrs. Fry, of course, who held social court from the head of the table; a Miss Hallows, Wayside Station's thin, somberly clad schoolteacher, who continually cast longing glances at Mr. Banes; and lastly, Miss Rosellen Reed, a young dark-eyed, red-lipped beauty.

This was the girl who saved all her dances for Luke.

Rosellen glanced at her curiously. But Jesse was soon ignored. From her position near the top of the table, Miss Reed thoroughly enjoyed the attentions of the younger men and seemed to expect it as her due.

Jesse sat quietly between the rancher's son and one of the drummers. It felt strange to sit waiting to be served even when the food was passed around the table family-style. She was so used to being the one doing the serving. Her active life hadn't prepared her to simply watch and not do. It almost pained her to observe the hurried, overworked Emma make a dozen trips to and from the kitchen, carrying too many hot bowls and heavy trays without help.

Everyone of the company seemed at least casually acquainted, with the exception of herself and the two desperadoes. The drummers, Clyde Shonhorst, a salesman for a hardware company, and Davis Smith, a salesman for ladies' clothing, told her they passed through Wayside Station about four times a year. Mrs. Fry's boardinghouse was a favorite stop with many of the traveling men, Clyde said. Miz Emma's cooking drew them.

Jesse noticed Donny speaking into Rosellen's ear soon after the vegetables had gone around. The girl's mouth pinched tighter and her fork paused. She looked at Jesse with open hostility.

Jesse turned her attention to Clyde's description of his travel route. Had she offended the girl in some way? Was she upset because of Luke's involvement with Jesse?

After the meal, the company dispersed quickly except for the ladies. Mrs. Fry led the way into the parlor, never once looking back. "We shall have a little music," she pronounced. "Perhaps some of the gentlemen will join us later."

Rosellen sailed out of the dining room in Mrs. Fry's wake, her charming attention focused on Mr. Banes. Miss Hallows followed meekly, her thin mouth drooping with sadness.

Without fanfare, Jesse picked up a tray and loaded it, carrying it into the kitchen.

Emma, eating her supper at the kitchen table, turned in surprise. "What's got into you, Miz Jesse? What are you doing?"

"Helping you," Jesse said as she began pumping water into the heavy teakettle. She placed it on the back of the stove to heat.

"Oh, child! No need to, you know. Mrs. Fry wouldn't like it. You're a paying guest."

Jesse sighed. Yes, she was. Or rather, Luke expected to pay her bill. But it made her feel no less guilty for remaining idle while Emma was overworked. And it didn't make her feel any better to realize she couldn't afford to stay at Wayside Station's best boardinghouse without Luke's help. She seemed to be getting deeper into Luke's debt every day.

She missed the confounded cowboy. Why, she didn't know, because she wanted to get on with her own plans as soon as she could and they didn't include him. No, sir. They couldn't. But it did seemed like days instead of hours since they'd parted.

If Luke came to see her tonight, Rosellen would be there, too. So, she challenged herself, why should that upset her?

"You're worn out, Miz Jesse, you don't have to do those dishes. Why don't you go on to bed."

"Emma . . ." It was hard to keep despair out of her voice. "I can't do that just yet," she answered, keeping her back turned. Whether she earned a wage for it or not, she was going to help Emma with the cleanup, else the woman wouldn't leave the kitchen until ten. Besides, if she kept busy, she wouldn't have to think about how confused she felt.

Luke swallowed the last of his coffee and put his cup down. He leaned back in his chair wearily. Across from him, his mother, Will, Mattie, Josie, his sister, and her husband, Bart, all stared at him. He'd told them everything about his trip except those private moments between himself and Jesse.

"God A'mighty, Luke. What possessed you to get involved with a stranger's business like that?" Will asked.

"I didn't have much choice. I couldn't let a man like George Jeter and his pals take possession of a helpless girl. They meant her every kind of harm. You'd have done the same if you'd been there, Will. He's the worst kind of bastard—excuse me, Ma, but he is—and the very thought of being caught in his clutches sends Jesse Mae white to the hairline. If it had been Josie . . ."

Luke's hand quickly fisted as he flung an appeal for understanding toward both Will and Bart. They'd have acted no differently than he if caught in like circumstances, and they all knew it.

The room grew quiet for a moment. Finally, his mother remarked, "Well, of course you did the right thing, son. And from the sound of the rigorous trail, I guess we're lucky to have the bulls safely home at all. And this girl willingly helped you?"

"Uh-huh. Willingly and cheerfully. And Ma . . . I sorta, um, promised her a job."

"Oh?"

"Yes. She needs the work, you see."

"We can always use an extra clerk in the mercantile for a few hours each day," Josie said, referring to the store she and her husband owned. "But we don't need anyone for a whole day."

"Thanks, sis, but I'd hoped we could put her to work on the ranch. It would be better for Jesse to keep out of sight for awhile."

"Well, I daresay I can use someone around for a while," his mother conceded.

"That sounds like a grand idea, Luke," Will said, suddenly enthusiastically. "If you don't want her, Ma, we do. Mattie?"

"What are you talking about, Will?" Mattie protested. "Just because I'm not as light on my feet lately?"

"Mattie, darlin', you need a little help these days," Will coaxed. "Ma's been saying it and so has Josie. If you don't have to chase after those two wild'uns of ours, you can save up your strength for the new one coming. Ma can't be over to our house every day, you know."

Mattie flashed a guilty look to her mother-in-law. "I suppose you're right, Will. I have been taking up far too much of Mother's time."

"Nonsense, Mattie dear. I love watching after the boys. But Daniel and Christopher are a handful, and if the girl is as industrious as Luke says, I think hiring her would be the very thing. We could share her time."

"Please, Mattie," Luke begged. "You'll love Jesse, she's good with kids, I've seen her. And she's like you, some. Inside, I mean. She's sweet and funny and . . . different."

"Ah-huh," Will drawled, while Mattie and Josie chuckled. Ma merely raised a brow. "How different?"

Luke scowled at his brother. That was the trouble with families, he fumed. They wouldn't let a fellow forget anything he'd ever done, even his past peccadilloes. True, he'd flirted with lots of girls in the past; it had been easy, for they'd flocked around him like birds. But too many times he'd wondered if they really liked him or liked the idea of being the wife of a wealthy rancher.

Now Luke was in love with Jesse, but wanted her to return that love without strings. Luke wondered, not for the first time, how to explain Miss Jesse Mae Banning's thoughts for her future, how to explain what she believed of him, to his family. They would certainly understand her struggles to better her life. He did, himself, and he wanted deeply to provide that better existence, but . . .

Luke stared at the five people who had made up the years of his life. He'd known only love and kindness from them. What had Jesse known? She'd been so frightened of getting involved with him, of believing he loved her. Or that love could mean anything but slavery.

He wanted to ask his ma, he needed to know. After hearing about the Jeter family and how Jesse'd existed these last years, after knowing what she would've faced at George's hands . . . was it right for him to test Jesse so?

Probably not. But something stubborn inside him persisted.

"You'll find out about Jesse soon enough," he said, bringing his thoughts back.

"Reckon so. Reckon I'd better run into town to see Boswell, anyway," Will said, standing. He reached a hand to his wife. "Better get on home, darlin'. The boys might have Sandy hung up by his thumbs by now."

"There's still something I haven't told you," Luke said quietly. He rose, too. "Jesse thinks I'm only a cowhand here. She hasn't put it together yet that the M double C stands for McCarthy. She only knows of you as Will. She half thinks you're a tough old codger and I'm about to get fired for being so careless." He chuckled at the expression on Will's face, then grew serious again. "And she half suspects my motives toward her. To her"—Luke glanced between Will and Mattie—"love spells a trap. She's scared to death of it. I have to have time to prove her wrong."

"All right, Luke. We'll do everything we can," Will said, slapping his brother's shoulder gently. "But you know she'll find out pretty quick anyway. Can't keep a lid on the whole town."

"Don't expect to. I only need a few days, I think."

Will snorted. "Confidence or conceit," he teased.

"Gut-level determination," Luke returned, "that I learned from you."

*   *   *

At midnight, Sheriff Ned Carey, elected only the previous year to his office in the small town of Wayside Station, picked up the mail from his desk and shuffled through it. First time in two days he'd had time to pay it any mind.

The usual mixture, he noted. Stock lost, suspected rustling. Petty thievery, most likely. Mischief going on along the cattle trails. A gambler over in Kansas shot; another card player caught cheating. A bank robbery down in Hinley, Nebraska.

He rubbed his hand across his dark stubble and yawned, then settled back in his chair to read the notices more carefully.

The bank robbery interested him most. Too many gangs imitating the James boys these days. This wasn't any of the usual imitators, though, he decided as he read the communication. This gang had waited until the last teller was left in the bank. Covered their heads with pillowcases. Only three men, the bank teller reported. Two heavyset, one smallish. One had a high, distinctive voice. He'd called another of the three "George." Got nearly two thousand dollars.

Must be a new bunch. Ned didn't know of a gang that fit such descriptions.

They wouldn't likely head their way, though. Wayside Station was rather off the beaten path after the railroad had passed them by. Besides, after the town had cleaned up that big rustler gang a few years back, they hadn't had a lot of trouble with outlaws and the like.

He lay the communication aside and yawned.

13

Jesse woke the next morning with the sun. Dressing with haste in her cleanest work dress, she hurried down the back stairs, and greeted Emma cheerfully. She had so many plans for her day.

"My, my, child. You don't let any grass grow under your feet, do you?" Emma's black face reflected her approval.

"Morning's the best time, Emma, don't you think? Here, let me do that for you," she offered as the cook brought out a ham to be sliced.

"Mr. Boswell feeling any better this morning?" Emma asked, going back to cutting biscuit dough while Jesse attended to the ham.

"A little, I think," Jesse affirmed. She'd learned that Dr. Reed was expected right after the noon meal, and she planned to be ready for him. She'd sound him out about needing an assistant.

Also, she'd taken a peek at room fifteen last night. As suspected, it looked out over the alleyway and was tiny, but it would do very well for her, and she was sure it cost much less than the yellow front room. If she could work during the day, she reasoned, and perhaps exchange her room and board for helping Emma in the kitchen, then not only would she earn her keep but she could begin to repay Luke.

"What are you doing in the kitchen, may I ask?" Mrs. Fry inquired from the doorway. "I don't allow my guests to roam the service rooms."

"I'm making breakfast for Mr. Boswell, Mrs. Fry."

"Oh. Well, I suppose that's all right, then. Carry on."

"Wait." Jesse laid the knife down, and approached the landlady. "May I talk to you, please?"

"Why, certainly. What is it you need, my dear?"

"I'd like to change my room to room fifteen."

"Would you?" Mrs. Fry frowned. "Don't you like the yellow room?"

"Oh, yes, I do. Very much. But I . . . I really can't afford it, you see. I thought—"

"Oh, if that is all that is worrying you, you must forget it. If Luke McCarthy says he'll stand the expense, then he'll do so. The McCarthys take care of their own, you know, and you should count yourself a very lucky young woman to have caught Luke's eye. I won't hear of you changing rooms. Now if you'll excuse me, my dear."

Mrs. Fry left the room.

"But—"

Jesse stood still, wondering how she was ever going to straighten out the misunderstanding if she couldn't get Mrs. Fry to stay in one place long enough to listen.

Later that morning, Jesse hauled all her clothes

except what she wore to the shed out back where the laundry was done. Everything she owned was dirty and much of it mud-caked. First she brushed her clothes vigorously, then soaked them in cold water before scrubbing them in hot. Lastly she rinsed them twice.

The clothesline stretched high above her and she had to stand tippy-toed to reach it. Remarkable, she thought, how much less work one person's clothes were to wash compared to the dozen she was used to from the Jeter family. She smiled happily. That was behind her now.

A jingling spur caught her attention and she whirled, her hand clutching a clothespin, her fist in the air.

"Whoa, there, Jesse," Luke said. "It's only me."

"Luke. Oh, don't do that, please." She fell back a pace, her hand over her racing heart. "Don't creep up on me like that."

"Sorry, honey. Didn't mean to scare you." And he was, too. She looked a bit white over it. He wondered how long it would take her to get over her fear of finding George about to pounce.

"What were you planning to do with that thing in your hand, anyway?" he asked, trying to josh her out of her fright. "Stabbing a man with a clothespin might give you a fierce reputation."

"Oh, hush," she said, blushing.

"Might even incite other women to take up the practice. Reckon some might call you to a duel. Miss Jesse Mae Banning, the fastest clothespin draw of the west."

"Luke, you scalawag."

Luke laughed along with her, enjoying her sparkling green eyes and wide mouth, noting for the hundredth time how even her teeth were. She wore her hair in a tight knot today, and his fingers itched to take the pins out.

"What are you doing in town so early?" she asked, turning to pin her good navy suit to the line. She was hoping it would dry enough so she could iron it before Dr. Reed's visit. "Did Meshach and Shadrach settle into their new home all right? And how's Rem, Rom, and Mehitabel?"

Whirling again, she held her dripping unmentionables tightly clutched in one hand. "Oh, Luke, I forgot. What did *Will* have to say? Is he horribly upset with you? Oh . . . that's not why you're here, is it? To tell me you've been fired?"

He pulled the rope line lower for her to reach, growing pensive. "If I, um, told you I was let go, would you leave town with me? We could go farther west, like you've wanted. San Francisco, even. That's where you wanted to go, wasn't it?"

Jesse bit at her lip. Will had dismissed him after all. It upset her no end and now here Luke was, looking as handsome as you please with no regrets in plain sight over losing a good position and asking that she go jaunting with him. It didn't help matters that she wanted to, Lord help her.

"With what, Luke?" She pressed her lips together tightly in an effort to fight her sudden tears and fingered her underdrawers. "How much of your wages have you saved this last year? I'll bet you spent them all on . . . on poker, and those boots and the like . . . the boardinghouse . . ."

"Well, maybe I have spent a goodly amount."

"You see?" She didn't want to feel triumphant, but there was the proof. He didn't know how to plan for a rainy day.

"Yep. Mehitabel, the mules, and all the equipment took about six months of my pay."

"Oh." She was crestfallen. She should've guessed that he had paid for all of that from his own pocket. Now he was probably totally broke. "Well, I guess I thought . . ."

"That Will paid for them? Nope."

"But wouldn't he?"

"Don't think so. 'Fraid he don't care much for mules. He hasn't made up his mind yet about Mehitabel."

"Oh. That's a shame. Did you tell him about Mehitabel's good qualities? And Rom and Rem's?" She looked at him hopefully.

"Yep. Did that."

"He wasn't . . . wasn't . . ." Her thought faded as he shook his head sorrowfully. "Oh. I'm sorry, Luke. Well, what can you do besides cowboying?"

"Hmm, not much else, at that. But I'm good at it." His voice grew low and tender. "Don't reckon I'd ever let you go hungry, Jesse."

"Not if you could help it," she said sadly, nearly under her breath. Life didn't always play fair. Before she died, her mother had sometimes gone a day without eating one meal, even though she always found a way to feed Jesse. Her mother hadn't realized she'd known, but she had.

Perhaps her father had done the best he could, too, by leaving her with his cousins. But that hadn't made it the better choice.

Jesse changed the subject. "Have you brought my harp?"

Luke studied her face, but kept his thoughts to himself. "Not this time. Had too many other things to do. Gotta make up for lost time."

"Yes, I suppose you do at that." She laid a hand on

his arm. "I'm sorry for all the troubles I've brought on you, Luke."

"Troubles? Well, my ma always says that troubles have a way of finding you without any help, but it's up to us to make the good times roll in."

Her face lightened. "Oh, my mama used to say something like that, too." She started pegging the rest of her wash onto the line. Yes, she remembered her mama telling her that sometimes a body had to make things happen for the better. "Tell me, Luke. Where might this Will person be found?"

"Why d'you want to know?"

"Because I want to talk to him. If I explain everything just as it happened, surely he'll reconsider firing you. He must realize it wasn't your fault. Now, where is he?"

"Jesse, I didn't *exactly* say I was let go."

"You said—"

"I asked if you would stick by me, go with me if I was. You know what I asked before . . . back at the cave."

She ignored his reference to the marriage proposal. "You mean you *didn't* get fired?"

"Uh, not exactly. . ."

"Why, you—"

Her temper sometimes matched her hair color, and now she let it fly. She hit him with her wet muslin underdrawers, leaving damp marks on his shoulder. He'd deliberately mislead her, playing on her guilt.

"Jesse, honey." He held up his hand, trying to appear apologetic. But his lips curled suspiciously and his eyes danced into blue diamonds.

"—ornery, low-down—"

"C'mon, you little fire-eater." A wet stocking hit him over the nose, dripping water down his chin.

He'd tried to extract a promise from her. Under

false pretenses. Knowing, *knowing* that she didn't want to marry a man with no prospects, and a young man at that!

"—skunk!"

She hit him again for good measure.

Emma came into the yard from her morning shopping. "Morning, Mr. McCarthy," she said, picking the white stocking from his chin and handing it without comment to Jesse. "I see you made it back to town in sprightly time. No doubt to see how Mr. Boswell is faring. Well, Dr. Reed's on his way to see about Mr. Boswell right now."

"Now?" Jesse gasped. "I thought he wasn't due until afternoon?"

"I just saw him coming out of the livery. Said he'd come on by immediately because he had to make a call that might keep him out till late."

Oh, drats! Her good clothes wouldn't have time to dry. Jesse brushed a hand down the faded yellow checked dress she wore. It was too tight across her bosom and still smelled a little smoky from the cave, but it couldn't be helped.

Jesse swung on her heel and marched into the house in Emma's wake. Luke followed in his own good time.

"Is Boswell any better?" he asked.

Jesse grabbed a clean apron from the stack that Emma kept in the corner cupboard, putting the top loop over her head and tying it in the back. It would cover most of her front, she thought, and make her appear ready for work. She hoped Dr. Reed would notice.

"He must be," Emma replied. "Jesse has been bathing his head with cool cloths to keep his fever down. He ate a good breakfast, Jesse said."

"Jesse did . . ." Luke murmured, watching Jesse's actions.

"Yes, Jesse has been seeing to him mostly," Emma supplied.

"Where has Donny been?" Luke fumed. They had traveled hard and rough for days, he'd wanted Jesse to take it easy for a while, and that lazy no-account kid of Mrs. Fry's should've been the one to fetch and carry for Boswell.

"Oh, you know Donny," Emma replied.

Yes, he knew Donny. The boy was seldom around when you needed him for real work. However, he couldn't help his mental condition, and he was harmless enough. Everyone always excused him.

"Oh, Donny was very helpful to me last night," Jesse finally interjected into the conversation. "He brought my bathwater up to my room. And he's very entertaining. He told me all about Miss Rosellen who pines for some local cowboy and saves all her dances for him."

"Rosellen?" Luke almost cussed out loud. Had he just thought Donny harmless? Luke scowled at Jesse's mock-innocent expression. Oh, fine! Donny had given her an earful, he was sure. The boy didn't know when to keep his mouth shut. Now she probably believed that he flirted with every pretty girl he knew. "Jesse, I—"

"You owe me no explanations, Mr. McCarthy. It has nothing to do with me." Jesse raised her chin. Turning her back, she climbed the kitchen stairs, arriving at Boswell's room just as Dr. Reed came up the front staircase. Luke joined her there.

"Morning, Mr. McCarthy," the doctor said. "Haven't seen you around lately. Hear you went east for some errand of Will's."

"Yeah, Doc, I did."

"Well, I know one young lady who is glad you're home."

Luke ground his teeth together, but all he said was, "Thanks, Doc. Brought Boswell with me."

"Ah, yes. How is our patient this morning, Miz Jesse?" the doctor turned to her and asked.

"Oh, much better, I think. He coughed some through the night, but slept fairly well."

Luke glanced at Jesse. How did she know, unless she'd spent the night checking on Boswell? That explained why she still had dark circles under her eyes. She wouldn't look at him. Instead, she looked steadily at the doctor, as though she hung on his every movement and word.

Boswell opened his eyes as they entered the room. His breathing still sounded heavy, but Luke noticed he appeared in far better condition than yesterday. Relief flooded him; he'd been more worried than he'd let on.

"Morning, Luke. Did you get them bulls home?"

"Sure did, Boswell, sure did. Will said to tell you he's mighty grateful for your help. Said there's an empty bunk in the bunkhouse with your name on it."

"Sounds jim-dandy to me, boy. It'll be good to work steady again. How come you didn't take Miz Jesse with you?"

The doctor moved to the bedside and put his stethoscope to Boswell's chest. "Quiet, now," he ordered the sick man. After a minute, he looked at Boswell's eyes.

"Um, well, she, um . . ." Luke tried to form a plausible answer to Boswell's question. He wanted nothing more than to take Jesse home with him, but under the right circumstances. He'd been scheming about how to offer her a job she would accept.

"What, and leave you?" Jesse intervened teasingly.

"Dr. Reed has delegated me your nurse, and I couldn't miss the chance to prove my skills."

"Good thing she's on hand, too," Dr. Reed remarked casually, giving Jesse an appreciative smile.

Doc's smile made him appear younger, Luke suddenly realized. And he'd never thought about it before, but Doc Reed was a right handsome man. Those creases in his cheeks might appeal to women.

"Well, young woman," the doctor continued, "keep up the good work and I'll try to stop by tomorrow again."

Jesse beamed. Dr. Reed had noticed.

Luke frowned. He'd noticed, too, and he didn't like what Jesse Mae was thinking. Not one little bit.

The doctor turned to leave and Jesse, murmuring, "Be right back," followed him into the hall.

"Uh, Jesse . . ." Luke caught her arm. "Wait a minute."

"Oh, Luke, not now." She craned away from him only to see Dr. Reed disappear around the curve in the stairs. She sighed and turned back to Luke. She'd have to try again tomorrow. "What is it?"

"I have to leave now, but I'll be in town tomorrow. I'll take you to dinner."

"Oh, I don't know, Luke. I have my duties here, and I—"

"C'mon, Jesse. Dinner. There's someone I want you to meet."

"Who is it?"

"A friend. Someone who might have a job for you."

"Oh." Her face brightened. "What kind of job?"

"Not a hard one, honey. Just a little light housekeeping and . . . and a little, um, companionship."

"Companion? You mean like those ladies in the East and foreign countries hire to fetch their needlework and read books and things?"

"Well, um, sort of. Yeah, I reckon that's part of it."
Luke shifted his feet, hoping to heaven he wouldn't get
hung high by this whopper. His ma had never sat
around doing mere fancywork in her life. She was far
more likely to turn beds or beat rugs or make pickles in
her spare time. But she did read occasionally; besides
the Good Book, she actually sometimes read a novel.

But *he* definitely wanted Jesse's companionship.
And more. Lots, lots more. He wanted the right to
touch her, to sweet-talk her. He yearned to kiss her
again and let the loving take its natural course.

"And a few outings with a couple of lively boys," he
was quick to add in all honesty.

He observed her face carefully. With all her procla-
mations of never wanting children of her own, he
knew she responded well to them in spite of herself.
She couldn't keep her true nature down. But he didn't
want to scare her off. His job offer couldn't come
close to sounding anything like she'd experienced
before. "Only two," he said.

"Only two?" Her green eyes blinked.

"Well, sometimes three," he answered thinking of
himself. "But never more than that," he insisted.

"How much does the position pay?"

He named a generous figure. With that kind of a
wage, Jesse could begin to repay him in no time. Her
hopes lifted.

"That's a lot."

"Housekeepers are hard to come by out here," he
said.

"Well, it can't hurt to meet this person, I suppose,"
she agreed. "I'll go if Boswell is feeling better. I don't
want to be too far away if he needs something."

Luke wanted to shout with joy, but all he said was,
"All right. We can set Donny to be with Boswell."

"I guess that would do. I can't promise to take the job, though, Luke. I have to keep all my options open. You know as soon as I can save enough money—after paying what I owe you, you understand—I'm off to California. I hear there are some real opportunities there."

"Sure, honey," he said quickly, not wanting to give her a chance to change her mind. "Noon, tomorrow."

"I ain't given up, an' that's all there is to it!" George snarled at Eli. "'Sides, we've had some fun along with the chasin', ain't we?"

The three of them sat around a campfire well west of where they'd burned a barn and robbed that sod-buster and his wife. Hadn't found no money to speak of, though, George thought disgustedly. But they still had some money left from the bank they'd robbed in Hinley.

"Yeah, that's so," Archie replied gleefully. "'Specially them saloon women. When're we gonna find us another 'un?"

Eli whittled a long stick, carving the end with care. It began to take on the image of a snake. He licked his lip and recalled the things they'd done in the last three weeks. Yeah, he'd concede they were having themselves a time. Beat stayin' in Missouri.

He didn't like chasing that particular woman, though; McCarthy was real trouble, and George was a fool to think the little redhead'd be better than any other woman. But he did like the money they'd gotten, and he liked the way it made him feel. People respected a man with money. They yes-sirred and no-sirred real good to a man who could pay for whatever they were selling. Reckon he'd go along with George a while longer.

"Okay, I'll stick by you, George. But I reckon we're gonna have to get more money soon. Got me a notion to likin' it. Let's see if that town up north has a bank."

"A right good notion, Eli," George said. "Let's leave here at sunup an' do some scoutin'. An' reckon we c'n find us a woman somewheres, Archie. Now that we know where my Jesse Mae has got to, we c'n take our time a-gettin' there."

Jesse dressed in her carefully pressed suit and spent a long time on her hair. Too bad she'd lost her hat, she lamented; a lady never went to town without one. It had been so smart, too, with its feather and crisp straw. And she'd spent a whole two dollars on the thing!

The only one she had now was the old felt man's hat Luke had bought her on the trail, but it couldn't be worn with a dress.

She gave her hair a final pat and turned this way and that in front of the mirror. Satisfied that her hair lay smoothly against her temples and the knot against the back appeared sufficiently neat, she picked up her gloves and left her room.

Luke waited for her in the front parlor, dressed up in a gray town suit, his boots cleaned and polished to a high shine. She thought he could've stepped from the pages of a men's picture magazine.

"You look very fetching, Jesse, honey. Shall we go?"

Jesse couldn't help herself; she gave him her best smile.

Between her nursing duties and helping Emma in the boardinghouse kitchen, she had yet to see much of the town. Now, excitement filled her.

Placing her hand on Luke's arm, they strolled down the street. Several people spoke to Luke, and glanced at her curiously. He returned the greetings politely, but didn't linger to talk.

They passed Mr. Jackson's Bootery and a surveyor's office. She spotted Mr. Banes's name on the window glass above the feed store. Several saloons, a vegetable store, a hardware store, and a dress shop lined the opposite side of the street.

Up ahead, a tall brown animal with spindly legs came into view, hitched to a railing outside of a large mercantile store. "Mehitabel," she exclaimed. She hadn't expected to feel any sentimentality for the animal, but then, there it was. She smiled like a child in sweet clover.

"Oh, Luke, you brought her to town."

"Yep. Kind of grown fond of the silly-lookin' thing."

"Hello, girl," Jesse said, stopping to pet the camel's neck. Mehitabel actually allowed it. Maybe the animal had grown fond of her, too, she thought. "Why have you left her here?"

"Oh, I had some business close by and it was as good a place as any." Luke glanced swiftly at the store windows—his sister often worked in the mercantile along with her husband—spied Josie's face there, then looked away again. He'd cautioned Josie that he wasn't ready to throw the whole family at Jesse yet. The good-natured teasing he'd endured had been endless.

They moved on, and at last came to Brown's Saloon and Restaurant. Inside the front door were two more doors. Above the left one, a sign read, *No ladies allowed.* Subdued male voices came from behind it. Jesse was curious, but Luke guided her through the right door, above which was a sign that said, *Ladies welcome.*

Luke led her to a table that already had a woman seated there. With brown hair mixed with gray and a plump figure, the smartly dressed woman smiled at her while her eyes searched Jesse's face.

Jesse returned the smile tentatively.

"Hello, my dear," the woman said.

"Jesse Mae, I'd like to introduce you—"

From the doorway, a man poked his head in and shouted, "Luke McCarthy?"

"Yeah?" Luke answered and turned.

"That yer animal out yonder a-makin' all that commotion?"

"Mehitabel? What's the matter?"

"It's Sat'day," the man answered as though Luke had asked a very stupid question. "A buncha them cowhands are already drunk. They're a pesterin' the poor beast."

Luke swung on his heel, muttering, "Sorry, ladies. I'll be right back."

"Oh, poor Mehitabel," Jesse murmured, glancing apologetically at the older woman. "If you'll excuse me, ma'am, I'll just run along and see what I can do to help."

14

Jesse lifted her skirt and ran down the street toward the noise that came from half a block away. Mehitabel, bellowing loudly, ran loose through the road's center, scattering people in her way, while two men hooted from the sidelines. One pulled his gun and shot into the air. Luke dived toward the frightened animal and caught a hand in the camel's harness. Mehitabel lifted him from the ground.

"Sing, Jesse," Luke shouted.

Jesse jumped high as another gun went off, and wrapped her arms around Luke's muscular one. Her feet left the ground as Mehitabel swung them around.

"Sing," he ordered.

"Um . . . a froggie did a-courtin' go . . . mm-hmm, mm-hmm . . ." Mehitabel slowed. "A froggie did a-courtin' go, mm-hmm, mm-hmm . . ." Together they brought Mehitabel's head down and then concentrated on calming her.

"Harry Long, you stop that this minute." A female voice scolded the man whose gun was out. Jesse glanced over her shoulder to see the woman Luke wanted her to meet. She'd walked right up to the man and shook her finger at him. "And you, too, Fred Myers. Shame on you two, torturing a helpless beast that way. Now get along and sober up or I'll call the sheriff to lock you in jail."

"Aw, hell, Mrs. McCarthy," Fred protested. "Just havin' a little fun."

"I mean it," said the woman. "And you watch your language."

"Sorry, ma'am," said the other cowboy, ducking his head. He holstered his gun with a little difficulty. "Won't happen again, Mrs. McCarthy," he said as he stumbled away.

Jesse let go of Mehitabel's bridle and stood perfectly still under a load of awe. This formidable woman was Luke's mother.

A lump of confused emotion swelled her chest. Luke's mother. He was about to introduce them; it was she who would employ her. But did the woman really want to? or need her? Or was Luke playing her hero once again?

A man with a star pinned to his vest arrived on the scene then, and Mrs. McCarthy began talking with him. Jesse glanced at the store window, noticing the quick withdrawal of a feminine face full of amusement.

Mehitabel had calmed down, so Luke hitched the animal to a rail, talking to her in a low tone. Jesse headed back toward the boardinghouse.

"Jesse!" Behind her, she heard Luke's call, but she marched on. "Jesse, wait."

He caught her, irritably turning her to face him. "You're going the wrong way."

"Am I?" She raised her chin, her manner accusing. "You didn't tell me, Luke. You never warned me that I would be meeting your mother."

Luke had the grace to look embarrassed. "You're right, honey. I didn't because I was afraid you might not come."

At least he hadn't tried to beg out of it, Jesse thought. Owning up to his fault counted for a lot with her. "You guessed right, then," she admitted, mollified. "I might not have."

"Well, my ma really wants to meet you, Jesse," he said gently. "Won't you come now?"

"I—"

"Please?" His eyes pleaded for her yes.

Mrs. McCarthy walked up to them. "Oh, my . . . I hate to remind you, Luke, but I did tell you not to hitch that camel in the middle of Main Street. Well. All the excitement is over now. Let's have our dinner."

Luke took his mother's elbow. "Ma, I'd like you to meet Miss Jesse Mae Banning."

"I'm Annabelle McCarthy, Miss Banning," the older woman said, holding out her hand. "I'm very pleased to meet you. My son has told me much about you."

Jesse rolled her eyes at Luke. What had he said? "I, um, wish I could say I knew more about you, Mrs. McCarthy. But the truth is, I never expected to meet you. At least, not today."

Annabelle laughed, and Jesse watched her mouth spread in a warm familiar pattern. Luke's.

"Well, come along. I'm plumb starving after all that excitement. You have such lovely hair, my dear. The colors of pure fire. Reminds me of a girlhood friend."

"Thank you." Jesse flushed at the compliment. The three returned to the restaurant.

"Now, Jesse. I understand you are looking for work?" Mrs. McCarthy asked as soon as they were seated.

"Yes, ma'am."

"What kind of work have you done in the past?"

The waiter paused beside their table, and Luke urged the women to give their orders before he gave his own. Jesse shyly ordered what Annabelle did.

"All kinds of housekeeping, ma'am," Jesse answered as soon as the waiter left. "Washing, ironing, sewing, cooking, cleaning, gardening, canning, milking, raising poultry, raising children. And helping them come into the world."

"Oh, my!" Annabelle McCarthy responded, her eyes widening. "All that at such a young age? You have actually helped with birthing?"

Jesse was suddenly embarrassed. It sounded as though she were bragging. And she'd never discussed the subject in front of a man before. "Yes, ma'am."

"Well, we could certainly use those skills out on the M double C. My dau—" Annabelle glanced at Luke and decided to rephrase her statement. "We expect a birth in about two or three weeks or so. Now, my dear, I understand Luke has offered you a wage."

"Yes, ma'am."

"And is it agreeable?"

"Oh, yes, ma'am, it—it's very generous." Suddenly concerned, she looked at Luke from the corner of her eye. Where was he going to get the money to pay her? His income couldn't be that much. However, the house he and his mother lived in was on the ranch, he'd once said, so they didn't have to pay rent. Still, it would be very convenient for him to simply subtract what she owed from her pay. Maybe that was what he planned, making it easy for her to work off her debt.

Still, she hesitated. "I wouldn't want to leave Boswell before he's well," she said.

"Very commendable, my dear."

"I'll talk to Doc Reed," Luke said. "As long as Boswell's fever is down, he won't object to us taking him out to the ranch."

"Give me a couple of days." Jesse had to think this thing through. She wasn't sure if working for Luke and his mother would carry her plan forward or not. But then, it would pay her debt.

It would mean seeing Luke every day, and that was becoming dangerous to her heart.

"Done," Luke agreed. He could hardly keep his satisfaction hidden. After that, they concentrated on their meal.

Mrs. McCarthy took her leave at the restaurant door. Laying a light hand on Jesse's arm, she said, "I'll be pleased to have you come, my dear."

"Why, thank you, ma'am." Jesse felt a bit startled by Annabelle's obvious sincerity. She didn't want to admit it, but she rather liked Luke's mother.

Luke escorted Jesse down the street. "Jesse."

"Yes?"

"There's a dance at the town hall tonight. I'd like to take you." He was crazily taking a chance on asking her, a chance that she'd find out during the evening that he and Will were brothers. But most times people merely called him Luke. There wasn't likely to be a reference made to his co-ownership of the M double C.

Eventually, he'd have to tell her. And he would, if that was what it took to reassure her feelings.

"Won't Miss Rosellen be claiming all your dances?"

"Ah . . ." Of all the answers he expected, that wasn't one of them. Dad-blame it! He knew he would have to answer for more of Donny's mischief. He thought fast. "Miss Rosellen has many beaus to choose from, and she seldom sits on the sidelines. She won't be pining for me."

"That isn't the way Donny tells it."

"But that's the way I call it, Jesse." He was quickly losing his temper over the way everyone around him wanted to horn in on his courtship of Jesse. Ma had insisted on meeting her, Josie had watched from behind the sign in the window of her store, and Rosellen was letting everyone think he was her beau. "Donny isn't the keeper of my love life."

"Well, I don't know. I can hardly take more time off from my nursing duties. What would Dr. Reed think?"

"What has Doc got to do with it?"

"I'm trying to be a good nurse." Jesse knew she was being overly cautious after accepting Luke's job offer, but old habits of self-protection haunted her. "Maybe then I can apply to work as Dr. Reed's assistant."

"That's loco. If you're thinkin' to hook up with him, your luck is out. Dr. Reed never works with one. 'Sides, he only has a couple of rooms, him and Rosellen, over the hardware store. Why d'you think Rosellen eats at the boardinghouse?"

She refused to feel daunted. "Perhaps Dr. Reed just hasn't had the right candidate before now. I heard today that he's been a widower for quite some time and that's why he didn't care to find himself a house. However, Donny said that his mother remarked that Dr. Reed has lately been giving thought to searching for larger quarters. It sounds to me as if he might need an assistant."

"Jesse Mae Banning," he said, losing patience, "you just agreed to work at the M double C. I'm holding you to your word. Now, how about the dance?"

Working with Luke would only foster his hope of marrying her, Jesse thought. And it would weaken her position, too. She might not be able to hold out if she continued to be beholden to him. If she continued to feel as though her day was incomplete until she saw him again.

His eyes were so blue she felt lost in them, and his mouth curved in equally pleasing lines whether he was irritated or happy. It startled her how much she remembered how his lips felt, and how much she wanted to experience them again.

"All right, Luke. I give you my word to work for your mother. But perhaps you should take Rosellen to the dance."

Those blue eyes slowly grew hot. "Well, maybe I just will," he said, and stomped off.

Luke called the next evening just before the supper hour, entering the boardinghouse through the kitchen as he had before. He caught Jesse by surprise; she had just taken freshly baked bread from the oven and had flour on her cheek. "Please set another chair for supper, Miz Emma," he announced lightly.

"That's fine with me, Mr. McCarthy," Emma responded with twinkling eyes, "if it's fine with Mrs. Fry."

"Mrs. Fry knows I'm here, Miz Emma. I'll be here every night until I can collect Jesse." He gave Jesse a meaningful glance.

"Oh, I can't go tonight, Luke," Jesse was quick to tell him. "Dr. Reed wasn't able to get by today."

"Is Boswell worse?" He raised a brow.

"No . . . no, I couldn't say he is worse." Jesse bit at her lip. She couldn't tell him a fib and get away with it. "He is just not better."

"Well, I'll run up to see for myself after supper."

"I'm sure he'll welcome your visit, Luke. Now, I must see to his tray."

"Not this time, Jesse." Luke took her elbows and spun her around, untying her apron. He allowed himself one long second to gaze at the back of her lovely neck where tiny curls danced. "Donny will take care of Boswell's supper tray."

Luke had thought long and deep last night about his pursuit of Jesse. He'd even talked to Ma about it. It had helped him realize that he was trying to rush Jesse too fast, pushing his suit too hard. He had to take up new tactics if she was worth winning. He had to allow *her* to choose *him*.

He turned Jesse to face him again and lifted the apron from around her neck. Gently, he used a corner of it to brush the flour from her cheek. She needed tender courting, he'd decided. And slow. She was like a delicate flower, willing to open, but needing the sunlight to do so. He planned to shine all over her.

She wore the green print dress today, he noticed, and she smelled clean and scenty, like soap. Only he thought it was laundry soap. Which reminded him she liked to smell nice; he remembered she'd smelled of vanilla the first time he met her.

Why had he been such a dunderhead? he suddenly thought. He should've brought her a courting gift. He'd get Josie to help him pick a perfume from her store for Jesse tomorrow.

Jesse gazed at him with wide eyes, trying to figure out what Luke was up to; there was no sign of his anger from the night before, but there was too much speculation, soft though it was, in his eyes to make her feel completely comfortable.

Even though he had threatened to, she knew he hadn't taken Rosellen to the dance. Donny had told her so this morning.

The hall grandfather clock chimed six times. Murmuring voices drifted in from the dining room.

"C'mon, honey. Let's go." He took her elbow to escort her into the dining room.

Supper was a far less formal meal in the boarding-house on Sunday than at any other time in the week. Cold meats, salads, fruit, fresh bread, and two cobblers sat on the buffet for people to help themselves. Frequently, guests who did not stay as boarders came to partake of Mrs. Fry's Sunday suppers. Emma had told her they never knew the final head count until everyone was seated.

At Mrs. Fry's direction, Jesse had helped set the plain white dishes on the dark mahogany sideboard in an attractive pattern with the two dozen newly laundered rolled napkins standing tall in the glasses. She had enjoyed doing it, finding the task had little relationship to preparing meals for the Jeter family.

"White or dark meat, Jesse?" Luke asked. He served her plate, choosing the best piece of chicken from the platter, then his own. He placed a generous portion of bean salad there as well, and a slice of ham.

The company constantly changed in a boarding-house, Jesse had discovered, aside from the longtime residents. The two salesmen had left on the early stage that morning, but three others had arrived. They would be in Wayside Station two days, they told Mrs. Fry. The desperadoes had disappeared after the first evening; Jesse, never having learned their names, wondered where they'd gone. But Mr. Banes, Miss Hallows, and the others helped themselves from the buffet and sat down as usual.

Tonight Sheriff Carey joined them.

Jesse allowed Luke to seat her, pleased that he took the chair next to hers. Rosellen breezed in, murmuring apologies for her lateness. Luke gallantly rose and seated Rosellen on his other side. It wasn't Rosellen's usual chair, Jesse noticed, although the dark-eyed girl didn't seem to mind. Not a bit. She gazed at Luke with delight and fluttered her lashes as though she'd captured butterflies there. She forgot all about flirting with Mr. Banes.

Throughout the meal, Luke was pleasant and sweet-tempered, and showed equal attention to Jesse and Rosellen. When Luke got up to refill Jesse's glass with water, he refilled Rosellen's glass as well. He brought them desserts at the same time. When Rosellen suggested a round of music in the parlor afterwards, she received not only a nod of approval from Mrs. Fry but an encouraging grin from Luke.

"That's a fine idea, Miss Rosellen," Luke pronounced. "Love the way you play the piano."

Jesse's nose felt a little out of joint. She hadn't expected him to take her at her word so quickly. In spite of her many pronouncements that she wished to marry an older, established man, or that she might choose not to marry at all, she liked Luke's very personal attention. Now he seemed to be spreading it around.

As the company rose, she looked at Rosellen. She was very pretty. And she could play the piano. Jesse admitted she was a little envious of her talent. Well, a lot, if she was truthful.

A sadness for the fact that she'd never learned to

play her mother's harp came over her. She'd planned to, one day, and she did remember a few chords. But her one day had slipped into years of survival at the Jeter household. Learning the harp was an accomplishment yet to be realized.

Rising quietly, Jesse began to clear the dishes. From behind her, Luke's strong, masculine hand wrapped around her upper arm, the bowl she held was taken from her.

"Not tonight, Jesse." Luke led her through the foyer and into the parlor. "C'mon and sing your froggie song."

"Don't be silly, Luke." Jesse blushed as Mr. Banes and Miss Hallows looked at her. "I—I can't s-sing in public."

"Sure you can, honey. You have a fine alto. Why, Jesse, here"—he turned to the few folks who had followed them into the parlor—"can outsing the birds. The Herefords love her serenades. The mules do, too. They responded all the way across the territory with her singing to them. Even Mehitabel likes it."

Mr. Banes smiled at Luke's boast. Miss Hallows said, "How sweet to see a man so proud of his little wife."

Mr. Banes appeared slightly surprised at Miss Hallows's statement, and Mrs. Fry wore an "I told you so" smugness.

Rosellen gave Luke a misty-eyed gaze of hurt, and then shot Jesse a look that could cut granite.

"Luke," Jesse whispered in mortified protest.

Luke either didn't hear or pretended not to. "Miss Rosellen, play that song you were keen on early in the summer," he directed. "I bet my Jesse here knows it."

"Luke," Jesse protested louder. She began to pull away, but he held her arm tighter.

"Just listen to it, honey. Rosellen wouldn't mind playing it through once. Would you, Rosellen?"

"No, of course not, Luke," Rosellen responded. Jesse wondered if anyone else heard the edge in the girl's tone.

Rosellen swivelled on the piano stool, her mouth tight. Her fingers struck the keys in a run, giving the notes vigorous, pounding life. After a moment, she softened the sound and settled into a lilting, poignant melody.

"Yep, that's the one," Luke said. "Rosellen does a right nice rendition of it, too. Heard it in a . . . ah, in—" He'd heard it in the saloon the night he'd played poker in Sedalia, but he didn't want to embarrass Rosellen by mentioning it. "Um, while I was away. Wasn't half so pretty as Rosellen does it," he finished.

Preening at his compliment, Rosellen began to sing in a soft soprano, and the others soon joined her. Jesse didn't know the song; there had been no time at all for the pleasures of parlor music in the Jeter household, but she could hardly explain that to Luke in front of all these people. However, the tune was easy to learn and after the first round, she was able to join in.

Music did lift her spirits, Jesse admitted an hour later when the company dissolved and went their separate ways. She couldn't remember the last time she'd enjoyed an hour so much.

Rosellen made a halfhearted bid for Luke to walk her home, but the sheriff stepped in and said he'd see to it.

Jesse drifted into the kitchen while Luke looked in on Boswell. Emma was putting away the last of the dishes. Automatically, Jesse began preparations for the next morning by filling the kettle, checking the sugar bowl and eggs.

"Walk me out, Jesse," Luke said as he prepared to leave.

Jesse followed Luke through the back door. His horse was tied to the back post. A big, dark bay, with black mane and tail, the stallion lifted his head and softly blew. A fine animal, she thought. Luke's saddle was one more evidence of Luke's taste—excellent leather, well fitted and tooled.

She paused on the last step while he pulled his reins loose. He came back to her and stood, their eyes on an equal level, to bid good night.

"Wish you were coming back to the ranch with me tonight, Jesse," he murmured, taking her hand.

"I really can't yet—there's still Boswell."

"Yeah, I know." It bothered him that Jesse was becoming all too settled in the boardinghouse routine. If it was routine she responded to, then, by gum, he wanted it to be the M double C's. And his and hers. "Well, my ma wouldn't say so, but she can really use your help, too. She, uh, has the lumbago, you see. Can hardly get around some days."

Another whopper he'd have to answer for eventually.

"Oh, I'm so sorry to hear it. I didn't notice anything amiss yesterday."

"No . . . no . . . Ma was all right yesterday."

"Maybe she'll continue in her good spell for a while."

"Mmm . . . maybe . . ."

"Well, good night, Luke."

Dusk fell softly around them. He wanted very badly to kiss her, yearned to travel her face with his lips. Saying good-bye was becoming harder each time he had to do it. "Good night, Jesse."

Jesse thought her heart had turned all the way inside out at the look Luke gave her. She backed up a step.

"Good night," she said again. She turned and hurried inside. She had to do something about the way her emotions ran riot in the cowboy's presence, she really did. It would do her no good to allow herself to fall all the way, no holds barred in love with him.

Taking the position on the M double C would throw them together again. How was she to resist him then?

She wondered when she could get away to visit Dr. Reed's office rooms. She'd have a better understanding of his practice if she could see them, and know whether she had a real hope of gaining employment with him or not. Mrs. Fry had made little mention of her voluntary help; Jesse doubted that she could look there for a wage. And, except for yesterday's excursion into town, she hadn't had a chance to see what other opportunities Wayside Station offered.

Sighing, she went to bed. She could do nothing at the moment. Still, she tossed and turned until late. She wanted to repay Luke, she *needed* to repay him for her own pride.

But to be once more in his company every day? Or to say good-bye and mean it?

Either way, she was asking for heartbreak.

15

The next evening Jesse swung through the kitchen door and almost smack into Luke.

"Whoa there, Jesse," he said, laughing. He took the huge platter of meat loaf from her hands and set it on the sideboard. "You aimin' to run me down?"

"No, of course not. What are you doing here, anyway? I thought you had lots of work to catch up on at the ranch?"

"To have supper with you, and uh-huh, I do."

"Oh?" In spite of herself, she couldn't prevent a smile from forming. She was so very happy to see him when she hadn't expected to.

"Came in to do an errand and to talk to Doc about Boswell."

"Oh."

"Yep. Doc said he'd be here for supper this evening."

"Oh?"

Luke didn't like the way Jesse brightened. She rushed back through the kitchen door, pulling at her apron strings.

"I brought you something—" he said, following. He extended the brown-wrapped package. He'd remembered to bring a courting gift this time. Josie had helped him choose the finest cologne she had in the store.

"Emma, I think we're short a place setting," Jesse said, ignoring Luke and reaching for another plate. "Dr. Reed is joining us tonight."

"My, my, so we are," Emma remarked. "All right, Jesse, we can make do if we set the end of the table double."

"Luke," Jesse said, "grab that dish of mashed potatoes, please. And have you seen Donny? He hasn't been around all afternoon."

Luke set his package on the table. "No, haven't seen the boy. Jesse, I—"

"Here, carry the cabbage, too," she ordered, shoving a second bowl into his hand. "I do hope he's on time."

"Jesse, why are you worrying about the boy? Let his ma do that."

"Well, I hoped he'd sit with Boswell again through supper," Jesse said, blushing. Then quickly, "It doesn't matter. I'll get Boswell's tray together in a moment. Come on, Luke. Emma is busy stirring gravy. Let's get these vegetables on the table."

Luke plunked the bowls down. "Jesse—"

But she was gone through the door. Disgustedly, he picked up the bowls again and followed her into the dining room. With lightning moves, she shuffled the table places to ease one more setting at the bottom end.

At five minutes until six, the dining room doors slid open from the front hall. Escorting Mrs. Fry was the handsome doctor.

"Good evening, my dear," Mrs. Fry acknowledged Jesse graciously. "Evening, Luke."

"Good evening, Miz Jesse. How's our patient getting along?" asked the doctor.

"Much improved, doctor." Jesse gave the report.

"Good. Good. Seeing a lot of the McCarthy brand these days," Dr. Reed remarked to Luke. "What's the word from the M double C?"

"Um, everything's just fine, Doc," Luke answered, swiftly glancing at Jesse to see if she'd caught Dr. Reed's reference. "So far."

Jesse's attention had turned to the new boarders. The company included a couple of circus people tonight; they'd engaged rooms for three days, according to Mrs. Fry. Jesse's eyes had widened like a child's at the acts the man described coming through town in about ten days.

A circus . . . He'd take her to the performance, Luke decided. Jesse'd like that, and most of the town would go.

"Yes sir, our trapeze act is the finest now touring the western states," bragged the tall, thin man. "And our trick riders are humdingers! We even have a real live tiger and a couple of bear cubs."

The clock began to chime. Luke waited behind a chair to seat Jesse.

"A tiger?" Miss Hallows murmured. She smiled shyly as Dr. Reed seated her. "Oh, I would like to see a real tiger."

"How big is the show?" Mrs. Fry asked as Dr. Reed seated her as well.

Luke waited impatiently for Jesse to come around the table. Her expression became rapt at the circus man's description. He began to plan the outing in his mind. It would be fun.

"Big enough to hire some local men to help it set up," replied the circus man. "We have almost a dozen wagons now between performers and equipment."

Luke saw the dreamy gleam grow in Jesse's eyes and nearly groaned out loud. He recognized that expression. It nearly shouted that she was cooking something up in that fertile mind of hers.

Luke thought he had enough tenderness for Jesse to last three lifetimes. But how was he going to pin her down long enough for her to believe him? or trust him?

How in heaven was he to keep her out of the circus?

Rosellen came in on Mr. Banes's arm, and the rest followed singly. Sheriff Carey brought up the rear.

The echo of the last chime faded and the chair he held remained empty.

Jesse disappeared through the kitchen door again just as Donny raced in, much to his mother's displeasure. He kept trying to tell a tale about one of the ladies at the bawdy house up the road chasing a gentleman out of a window in only his drawers. No matter how often Mrs. Fry tried to shush him, he kept bringing it up.

Luke waited in vain to seat Jesse. She came and went once more with pitchers of water.

This was no way to conduct a courtship, Luke stormed in frustration. Every time he tried to talk to Jesse there was an interruption. And hordes of people about.

It wasn't only frustration, he suddenly realized. A feeling more like anger started to build. Luke hadn't paid attention to how much work Jesse had actually taken on at the boardinghouse. That lazy Donny hadn't even offered to help, and Mrs. Fry seemed totally uninterested as long as the work was done and didn't interfere with her hostessing duties.

What did Jesse think she was doing?

"Excuse me, folks," he said suddenly. Marching out to the kitchen, he paused. Jesse had set a tray with enough food for two. "Make it for three, honey. I'll go up with you."

"It's all right, Luke. You go along and have your supper in the dining room. I usually take my meals with Boswell anyway."

"You're not a servant here, Jesse Mae," he insisted hotly.

"But I am Boswell's nurse."

"Not for long," he muttered under his breath. He hadn't realized the issue had become mountainous for him, but it doggone well had. "Not if I have my way about it."

He picked up the heavy tray and led the way upstairs.

"How're you doing, there, Boswell?" he asked his friend as he entered the room. He set the tray on the small bedside table.

"Tolerable, I reckon. Right tolerable." Boswell pushed himself to a sitting position. "You been taking good care of my gelding?"

Jesse spread a napkin over Boswell's knees, then handed him a filled plate.

"Yep, he's been chomping out our best pastureland alongside of Mehitabel. Rom and Rem, too." He handed Boswell a cup of coffee, then took his own plate from Jesse. "Damndest thing the way those four think they're a set. If one of 'em is in sight, then they're all there."

Boswell chuckled. "Well, thank you kindly, Luke. Been too sick to care much before now. It's good knowin' a man's friends are takin' care of 'im. Miz Jesse here's been an angel. Taken sprightly care of Abednego. Seen him this morning."

"Reckon you're up to makin' it to the ranch tomorrow?"

"Sure, sure. Anytime, now. Doc says my chest is sounding lots better. Got up today. Walked 'round downstairs for a bit. Talked to Miz Emma."

"You did, huh?" The patient was in better shape than Luke'd thought. Had Jesse been exaggerating how much nursing Boswell still needed? "Well, that is good news, yes sirree. I tell you what. I'll come in first thing in the morning with Ma's carriage. It'll give you and Jesse a nice easy ride out."

So it was settled, Jesse thought. She had no more excuses for staying longer in the boardinghouse.

About to take his leave, Sheriff Carey approached Luke. "Luke, did you hear from Henry down at the telegraph?"

"No. Was he looking for me?"

"Yeah. Said he had a message for you that came in a couple of days ago from a fella over in Nebraska. Said it got lost in the shuffle and now he wanted you to have it right away. Said to come knock on his door if it weren't too late."

Nebraska. The only people he knew in Nebraska were John and Effie. An uneasy feeling ran up his spine. Luke glanced at the clock. Eight-twenty.

"Reckon I will," he said. If John Pearson had sent him a telegram, the matter must be pressing.

And there was only one connection that he could think of that would precipitate an urgent message; they were close to the railroad water tower where he and Jesse left the train.

Had George tracked them that far?

Luke bid a quick good-night to Jesse, telling her

briefly to be packed and ready to go in the morning, then made his way into town. He sought out Henry's room above one of the saloons and rapped at his door.

"Evening, Henry," Luke said as soon as the man opened the door. "Hear you got an important message for me."

"Yeah, Luke. Just found it. Came in about noon two days ago when I was away from the telegraph office. Thought you should see it right away. Sounds to me like you could be in for a bit of trouble."

"Let me see it," Luke said.

He stood for a long moment, reading the three sentences.

ATTACKED A WEEK AGO BY THREE MEN
LOOKING FOR YOU. LETTER FOLLOWS.
BE WARNED.
  JOHN PEARSON.

George and his henchmen? It had to be; there was no one else he could count as that much of an enemy. Luke briefly wondered why John had sent a telegram and a letter—except that he must've felt the matter pressing. Had the attack been that bad? And had the letter arrived?

A sudden need to get Jesse to safety overwhelmed him.

Luke mounted his bay and heeled him into a spanking pace back to Mrs. Fry's boardinghouse. Calling himself all sorts of a fool, he wished he hadn't left his guns at home. He'd thought of himself as a courting man, and a man bent on winning his woman didn't have need of them, did he? Not blasted usually. But he wouldn't be caught without his again. From now on he'd double-pack his weapons and be on the alert for Jeter and the Thomses.

By heaven, he wasn't going to leave Jesse in town another night. He'd take her to the M double C immediately.

He dismounted at the back steps and tossed his reins loosely around the post. He pushed through the rear door, taking in the empty kitchen at a glance. Where had Jesse gone? And Emma? The kitchen had been alive only thirty minutes before.

He took the back stairs two at a time. He rapped twice on Boswell's door before swinging it wide. "Jesse in here?" he asked. But even before the words were out, he saw that she wasn't.

"Naw, Luke. Ain't seen her since you two left."

He strode down the hall, turning the corner to room seven. He knocked sharply.

"Jesse?" he called. And waited with the silence around him growing into alarm like mushrooms sprouting after a rain. He turned the knob, but the door was locked.

He took the front stairs to the front hall. Mrs. Fry was engaged in conversation there with the circus folk.

"Have you seen Jesse?" he demanded.

"Not since supper," she replied. She started to return to her conversation, then stopped. "Oh, but she may have gone strolling with Mr. Banes and Miss Hallows. I heard them ask her."

"Where? Which direction did they go?"

"Oh, uptown, I'm sure. I can't imagine Miss Hallows wishing to mix with the saloon crowd, can you?"

"No." He stood in thought a moment then retraced his steps to Boswell's room. Briefly, he told Boswell about the telegram. "If Jesse comes back here, don't let her out of your sight."

"Sure thing, Luke. I'll do my best not to let anything happen to her."

Luke left the boardinghouse on foot and started toward the quiet side of town. He searched a couple of streets, but found everything settling down for the night.

He headed toward the business district; everything was closed up tight except for the saloons and gambling houses. Here and there lamplight illuminated a patch of the street. There weren't many strollers out.

He passed the store that his sister Josie and her husband, Bart, owned and operated. Lights from the second floor shone down; lace curtains moved with the slight breeze in the opened windows. At the hitching post was his mother's buggy; Will's favorite stallion was tied there also.

Will and Mattie, Luke guessed, visiting. He thought briefly of running up and eliciting his brother's help, but that would take time and explanations. He decided against it and headed toward the main cluster of saloons.

On second thought, he retraced his steps to Josie's. After a brief knock, his sister answered the door. "Well, Luke! Imagine your calling—"

"Sorry, Josie. But I need to speak to Will."

Will stepped from the parlor into the tiny hall where Luke waited. "What is it, Luke?"

Luke didn't waste time on preliminaries. "Will, have there been any letters for me in the last day or so?"

"No, I don't think so. But Ma picked up the mail the other day when she was in town. What are you looking for?"

Luke lowered his voice and explained about the telegram. "It looks like the bastard has tracked us to some point. Anyway, I ain't taking anymore chances. I'm going to bring Jesse out to the ranch tonight." Luke lifted his hat and ran his hand through his hair. "When I find her, that is."

Josie and Mattie both crowded forward.

"Um, Luke. I think I may have your letter," Josie said. "I planned to give it to Will to pass on, but I forgot all about it."

"Where is it, sis?"

"Just a minute." Josie rummaged through her needlework basket.

"Why can't you find her?" Mattie asked. "Isn't she at Mrs. Fry's boarding house?"

"Usually, but she went strolling with the teacher and Banes, that new lawyer in town. I'm looking for her now, only when I saw Will's horse and the buggy here . . ." Luke trailed off as Josie handed him an envelope.

Tearing it open, he raced through the penciled lines.

Dear McCarthy and missus,

I take pen in hand to let you know of a dasterdly deed that happened here yesterday night. Three men came to our place looking for you claiming you stole from them. We wouldn't give them no direction for you so they burned my barn down and laughed after. It scared Effie bad. We done got away and got to town. They follered. We kept mum but Mr. Sizemore told them about the mules and Mehitabel. They was heading west last I heard. Hope this letter don't bring you and your missus no more trouble, but you needed to know.

John Pearson

A new, deeper understanding of Jesse's basic fears made itself felt. No wonder the girl trembled at even the mention of the bastard. To burn a man's barn merely for refusing to give information?

George didn't care about Jesse's rejection and would likely keep after her unless she was totally out of reach.

Or George was dead. The scoundrel would let her go only by a force he understood and acknowledged as greater than his own. And by gum, if a force bigger than himself was what it took for ol' George Jeter to give up a claim to Jesse, then Luke would provide it.

Without bidding a good-night, Luke muttered, "Gotta find her," and shoved through Josie's door, pounding down the outside stairs, his sense of urgency tripled.

Nearly a block away, several saloons were going strong. Three familiar people looking through a store window caught Luke's attention. He recognized Jesse's husky murmur and he could have sworn his heart did a leap to see her safe. His pulse slowed its pounding.

He stretched his stride to cover the distance between them in seconds.

"Jesse?"

She turned. "Oh, Luke . . . I thought you'd gone back to the M double C."

When he reached her, he paused politely. He didn't see any need to alarm everyone.

"Good evening, again, Mr. McCarthy," Miss Hallows murmured. "We were just admiring the hats in the window. There is such an adorable little navy blue straw that would compliment your wife's navy suit wonderfully."

"How do, ma'am," he responded, touching his own brim. He didn't bother to correct the woman; he was too concerned about getting Jesse out of town. "Mr. Banes."

"Luke," Mr. Banes replied. "What brings you back to town?"

"Well, I wanted to talk to Jesse." He let his voice carry his imperative and stared at her.

"What is it?" Jesse asked.

When Luke hesitated, Mr. Banes harrumphed and

Miss Hallows glanced between them. "Oh, please excuse me. We'll be walking just ahead, dear," offered Miss Hallows. "You take your time."

"It's all right, Miss Hallows," Jesse assured. "Luke will see me home."

"Oh, yes, of course. How silly of me," Miss Hallows replied, blushing.

"Yes, Miss Hallows, I'll escort Jesse home." Luke took Jesse's arm possessively. His relief at finding her calmed him, yet he knew his agitation showed.

For a moment Luke was tempted to take her to Josie's, which was closer than the boardinghouse. But his mount was there and the faster he got Jesse out of sight the better he'd feel, so he'd head them toward Mrs Fry's.

Jesse kept glancing at Luke. What was wrong? His skin appeared to have stretched around his features more tightly, and his face had a look of grim determination, an expression he'd seldom worn. "What is it, Luke?" she whispered.

"I'll tell you later, honey. Right now I want to get back to the boardinghouse."

But the words were scarcely out of his mouth before a heavy man stepped forward from the dark doorway of the closed drugstore. Only a shaft of light outlined his frame.

Instinctively, Jesse cringed back.

"Caught up to you at last, Jesse Mae," George spoke gleefully. His little eyes glinted in triumph. "Thought you'd got away fer good, din't ya?"

16

Jesse felt the blood drain from her face. After all this time . . . almost . . . yes, over three weeks. She'd been stupidly relaxed and unguarded. She'd worried about her relationship with Luke when she knew she shouldn't count on having that much freedom. Or that much choice. Now she'd brought George down on his head again.

George would kill him.

"I—" She swallowed. "I want nothing more to do with you, George."

"Well, ain't that too bad. I found ya now. You're gonna have a lot to do with me. A lot more, Jesse Mae."

"So you've found us," Luke challenged. He wondered where the Thomses were, but he dare not take his eyes off of George to look for them. He tried to push Jesse behind him, but she stepped to one side. "It makes little difference. You have no claim on Jesse."

"Shut yer mouth, cowpoke."

"Don't reckon I will. Jesse's my wife." Luke told the bald-faced lie without a blink of the eye. Next to him he heard Jesse's gentle gasp.

"Wife?" George nearly screamed. "Ya done it, huh, Jesse Mae?" He finished with a string of curses. "You was mine afore ya was his. Did she tell ya that, McCarthy? Did she tell ya how she used to meet me at night?"

"No, that's not true," Jesse protested, fighting back tears. His accusations made her sick to her stomach.

"That's about all, George," Luke said, his voice hard. "There's nothing more you can do about it."

"Can't, huh? You fergit what happened the last time?"

Several people had gathered to watch the conflict. Jesse didn't look closely at who they were, afraid to divert her attention. But George was a coward, and for him to admit that he'd done something underhanded in front of anyone meant that he felt safe from retaliation. In fact, this open challenge was totally uncharacteristic. Her actions seemed to have triggered something in him, made him bolder. Especially now when he had the Thomses' backing.

Swiftly, she searched the shadows of several buildings. The Thomses had to be around somewhere.

"Luke." Jesse tugged on his arm. She wanted to tell him not to get into a fight over her, but knew the words to be useless.

She wondered where Sheriff Carey had gone. Why didn't someone go after him?

"I didn't forget," Luke answered George. "But it doesn't change anything. Jesse's mine."

"The hell she is." George lumbered forward threateningly, his beefy hand resting on a gun around his waist, something Jesse had never seen him wear. He'd always favored a shotgun, before. He probably had a knife up his sleeve, too, for he always kept one there.

"Don't, George," Jesse said. "Luke isn't wearing a gun."

"Well, now, that's his bad luck, ain't it? Now get over here, Jesse Mae."

"She stays by my side," Luke said. "And we are leaving."

"Jesse Mae ain't," George insisted. His voice held his gleeful snarl. "Step up, men."

At his command, four figures emerged from the dark corners of the alley. Eli, dark, bearded, and with a glittering deadliness sparkling from his eyes, and Archie, bigger and dumber than George but no less evil, Jesse knew. The two others she didn't recognize, but they both wore low-slung gunbelts.

"George, please," Jesse began. Terrible fear raced up her spine. This was all her fault. Why hadn't she simply kept on traveling after Luke had reached his destination?

Five against one. Luke could never survive such an onslaught.

"Stand aside, Jesse Mae." George ordered.

Jesse took a good look at each man. Her stomach felt as though it dropped to her toes, but she refused to let Luke stand alone against five armed and dangerous men. "No . . ."

"Jesse, honey, I think it best if you move back."

"No, Luke, you don't have to fight for me. I'll—I'll . . ." Her lip trembled and she clamped down hard with her teeth to stop it. She took a step forward.

"Never, Jesse." Luke's hand clamped with bruising force around her forearm. "You damn well won't!"

George laughed and moved forward, his hand reaching. The evil sound chilled her despite the evening warmth. Even Archie smirked.

"You think yer gonna stop us from takin' 'er?"

"I am."

George chortled. "Yeah? You an' who else?"

"Me," said a deep voice in back of her. A man stepped up to align himself with Luke. He was tall, taller than average, and his shoulders, while not brawny, filled his shirt. Beneath his hat, a wisp of silver blond hair poked out, just like Luke's did. Jesse couldn't see the color of his eyes in the dim light, but the shape of them, and his nose, were like Luke's.

No one could mistake the resemblance. The man had to be Luke's brother.

Jesse felt a wave of shock. How much family did Luke have, anyway? He had a mother, and somewhere along the way he'd mentioned a sister. Was she around town, too?

Jesse felt a little better that she and Luke were no longer alone, yet guilty, too. Now she'd drawn Luke's brother into her troubles.

Nevertheless, they stood three to five, and Luke's brother was armed.

"Reckon you'll have to deal with me, too, mister," said yet another man who stepped from the growing crowd. "We don't take kindly to strangers comin' into Wayside Station and layin' a threat on our womenfolk."

Jesse didn't know who this man was, but again she was grateful for his help. Now they were four to five and two of them had weapons. The odds were definitely better.

"Yep," said another. "You picked a fight with the wrong family, mister. The McCarthys are our own. Reckon you just better leave peaceful-like if you don't wanta get run out on a rail."

"Or locked up," said someone else.

Jesse couldn't believe it. These men had come to defend Luke and protect her. They were Luke's friends and family. Her spirits lifted. Even though she was a woman and unarmed, she felt a part of them. Five, standing shoulder to shoulder.

It was a standoff. Except that Luke still did not have his own weapon. Jesse's panic shot sky-high. She was certain—she *knew*—that George would aim right at Luke if given even a slight opening.

"The McCarthys?" questioned one of the strange gunmen who backed George. "You the McCarthy brothers?"

"That's us," Luke answered.

"The ones that cleaned out that nest o' rustlers a few years back?"

"Yep."

The man turned to his companion. "This ain't our fight, Joe. I'm leavin'."

"What d'you mean, you're leavin'? I done paid you good money to back me," George roared. "Eli, don't let 'im leave."

Eli eased his gun out, but his uncertainty showed.

"Don't even try, Eli." The man turned and backed a pace. He dug in his pocket, pulled out a few bills, and flung them at Eli's feet. "I ain't a-goin' up against the McCarthys. C'mon, Joe."

Archie raised the shotgun he carried. Its barrel was leveled at a dangerous angle halfway between the two gunslingers. "Ya ain't goin'," he insisted in his high voice.

The man stopped. "I ain't a-tanglin' with these here McCarthy boys, I tell you. You'd have every lawman in three states down on you."

"He's right, George," Luke said. "I'd advise you to

get out of town while you can. You're in my territory now, and you've worn out your welcome."

Two of the men took threatening steps toward the gunmen. One fell back and turned to leave. Archie raised his shotgun. Some of the crowd scuttled out of the way.

"Sheriff's on his way," someone said from the crowd.

Jesse didn't take her eyes off George; she watched his glittering piggy eyes, stared at his mouth and the gathering of his muscles and flesh and intentions. Paralyzed with fear, she couldn't breathe, yet she knew. Knew when he would attack. In a lightning strike, she saw his left hand dip and a brief flash on metal.

"*Nooo!*" she screamed.

Jesse didn't know that she moved, yet she felt the slam of Luke against her back with the force of the sharp, excruciating pain. The wind seemed to be knocked from her, her breath gone. Shock, puzzlement crowded her mind. Was this it, then?

She looked down at the knife handle protruding from her shoulder, remembering the long narrow blade. Yes, she recognized it. George had lovingly polished it often in the Jeter household.

If she could've sighed with sadness, she'd have done so. After all the years of outwitting him, of playing every safety angle she knew, she supposed George had finally won.

But no. No, he hadn't won, because Luke was safe. Thank God! Safe . . .

The sadness lifted. Around her, the shouts and noise seemed muffled. She sensed a rush of activity, yet felt removed from it. Luke's voice spoke to her. She couldn't answer. Funny . . . she thought it would've been harder to let go . . .

Jesse slipped into unconsciousness.

*   *   *

Luke looked away from George for only a fraction of a minute. Only a fraction.

Jesse's scream hit him with the suddenness of a thunderclap; her small body slammed into him with a jolt.

He caught her automatically, without knowing at first what she'd done. Until he saw the knife. Until her blood spread. Covering her shoulder, seeping through his fingertips.

No! Oh, God, no . . .

Pandemonium broke out, but he only had eyes for Jesse. Flying fists, pounding footsteps, shouts, curses. They all went past him.

"Get the doc," he heard someone shout. Himself . . .

He went to his knees, taking her with him. Cradling her. With shaking hands, he shifted her, wrapped one arm around her back and braced himself. He stopped breathing. Taking a firm hold, he pulled the knife free. He dropped it as though it were a hot branding iron. It had been meant for him. Jesse had taken it instead.

Oh, Lord, his very soul begged. *Don't let her die . . .*

Immediately, a handkerchief was thrust into his hand. Will's, he recognized. He pressed it to Jesse's shoulder. Tightly. She couldn't lose any more blood.

We haven't had our chance . . .

The scuffling and fighting around him lessened. He scarcely noticed. Holding her like a child, he pushed himself to stand.

Will, his face in grim lines, waited for him. "Let's get her to Mrs. Fry's," he suggested.

Luke nodded.

A knot of men moved away from them up the street toward the jailhouse, pushing three prisoners ahead of them. Only three?

The scene too confusing, Luke let it go. He began walking toward the boardinghouse. Will shouldered a path for him through the few remaining onlookers.

"Oh, Mr. McCarthy, I'm so sorry," cried Miss Hallows.

He acknowledged her sympathy with another nod. Mr. Banes held Rosellen's elbow. She appeared shocked and distressed as well.

"I'll—I'll just run ahead and alert Mrs. Fry," Rosellen suddenly said, and whirled away.

"The doc?" Luke asked.

"Sandy's gone to fetch him," Will answered.

Josie and Mattie came along, seemingly from nowhere, with the buggy.

"Luke, climb in," Josie commanded.

"Mattie, you should—" Will began, frowning.

"Don't scold me now, Will," Mattie returned. "I'm all right. Luke needs our help right now."

"No . . . it's only a few more yards," Luke insisted. He couldn't risk the chance of jostling Jesse again by climbing into and out of a buggy for only a block's ride. Beside, she was no heavier than a child.

Dr. Reed met them at the boardinghouse door.

The yellow roses came into focus slowly. Her room.

An agony of pain sharpened her awareness. Someone shifted her shoulder. She whimpered.

"Hang on, sweetheart. Hang in there a little longer," Luke whispered in her ear, his voice the tenderest she'd ever heard. He seemed to share her hurt—a huskiness made him swallow. "Doc's almost finished."

He held her hand. Gently.

She shifted her gaze without moving her head. Mere inches separated them. Unshed tears stood on the edges of his lashes, seeming to magnify his blue gaze. Her lips formed his name, but she couldn't force a sound.

Dr. Reed gave her something to drink. She swallowed what she could, then closed her eyes. Comforted that Luke still held her hand, she squeezed his fingers.

Luke felt the gentle pressure of her fingers and his chest swelled with a world of tangled emotions. He'd have given his right arm to have suffered the knife wound instead of Jesse. Gladly. Yet she'd taken it for him.

He hadn't wept since he was a boy. Since his pa died. Now he could barely control his tears. Jesse loved him; no doubts left at all.

"You can relax, now, Luke," Doc Reed told him. "The wound is clean and it missed anything vital. Barring infection, she'll heal quick. Young and healthy and all."

"Thanks, Doc. Thanks a million." He felt too numb to accept relief yet.

"I've given her a tiny dose of laudanum. She'll sleep through the night. I don't have a nurse who can stay with her. . .." the doctor finished tentatively.

"Don't worry about it, Doc. I won't leave her."

"Thought not," Dr. Reed said, nodding. "Well, try to get some sleep yourself. She's going to need you for a few days."

He would need her forever, Luke thought as he gazed at her sleeping features. He wanted to trace her auburn lashes, to feel their feathery tickle, wanted to touch his lips to hers.

He contented himself with merely pressing his lips to her fingers.

From the hall, Luke heard the doctor speak to Will, and Will's low murmur. Then Josie's and Mattie's.

Will cracked the door, and Luke nodded. He laid

Jesse's hand against her waist and stepped quietly through the door.

"Did you catch 'im?" Luke asked his brother, the fire of rage coursing through his veins to every pore. He wanted to pull that sorry excuse for a man limb from limb. And then place him on a live anthill.

"Caught the big one right off. You were lucky, Luke. If it hadn't been for Sandy . . ." He shook his head. "Sandy knocked that shotgun up."

"George?"

Will stiffened his mouth in disgust. "Got away in all the excitement. Sheriff Carey's getting up a posse. Those two make-believe gunmen gave up without a fight."

"George got away? I don't understand it!"

"Too much commotion, Luke. With Jesse hurt . . ."

Nothing more was said for a moment.

"How is she?" Josie asked, her voice a soft whisper.

"Asleep. Doc says she'll heal right quick if she doesn't take on infection. She's gotta—" He broke off, clamping down on his overwrought emotions. Will laid a consoling hand on his shoulder. Mattie and Josie patted his back.

Drawing a deep breath to steady himself, he said, "I'm staying here until she's better."

Luke's family seemed to understand. He had been the happy-go-lucky brother, a constant tease to everyone who took only a few things in life seriously. Now, as Ma would say, the whole world seemed topsy-turvy.

"I'll tell Ma what happened," Will told him. "And I'll get back into town tomorrow. But I need to get Mattie home, now."

"Sure, of course you do, Will."

"I'm sure she'll be right as rain in a week or so, Luke." Mattie murmured her wish.

"I'll stay and help sit through the night, Luke," Josie offered.

"No, thanks, sis. You've your own family to care for, and the mercantile. I'll do okay, honest. Doc says she'll sleep through the night anyway. Tomorrow . . ."

Rosellen stepped forward. "I'll help, Luke."

"And I," said Miss Hallows.

Luke hadn't known they were there, in the shadows of the hallway. "All right, ladies. Tomorrow, I'd be right grateful. Tonight . . ."

Tonight he didn't plan on leaving her side.

Jesse woke the next afternoon with a terrible taste in her mouth. She couldn't open her eyes very wide, either.

"Would you like some water, dear?" asked a familiar voice.

"Yes." Her mouth felt like cotton.

A glass of water was placed at her lips. She sipped and rested, then sipped again.

The water refreshed her. She'd ask for more presently. When she had the energy. She felt so awful and couldn't remember why.

"More?" asked the same feminine voice.

She nodded, and the glass came again. She drank a little.

Her eyes finally opened wider. Luke's mother sat close by in a chair.

"Luke?" she whispered in a sudden panic. Memories flooded back, and fear as well.

"Luke's fine, dear, just fine. Is that what you wanted to know?"

Jesse barely nodded and let her nerves relax. Still, she wanted to see him for herself.

"I'm glad that you're awake at last, my dear. Are you in much pain? Well, of course, what a silly question for me to ask. Here, let me see if I can make you more comfortable."

With infinite care, she helped Jesse raise her head and placed another pillow there. "I'll just ring for some soup. You should have a little nourishment."

Mrs. McCarthy stepped out. Jesse heard the faint tinkling of a bell. Only a few moments later, Mrs. Fry, herself, came in with a tray. "Here you are, Annabelle. All ready for our little patient."

"Thank you, Sally. Please knock on Luke's door. I promised we would wake him the moment Jesse came around."

Mrs. McCarthy scooted her chair forward and lifted a spoonful of hot liquid. "Oh, this is hot enough to burn an elephant. We'll just let it cool a bit." She set it down on a small side table.

"Everyone has asked about you, Jesse. It's been hard to keep visitors out, in fact. But Luke . . . I practically had to call Will into town to eject him from your bedside this morning. He's been as agitated as a rooster facing a cook with a hatchet in one hand and a pot of hot water in the other."

Jesse smiled faintly in spite of herself. She could see where Luke got his sense of humor.

Mrs. McCarthy picked up the soup again.

"Wait, please," Jesse murmured. From the hall, she heard Luke's voice. Last night was a jumble of confusion in her memory. She wanted to see for herself that he was all right, wanted to be sure that he hadn't been hurt in last night's fracas. "Wait."

17

Jesse felt miserable; her shoulder hurt dread-
fully and so did her heart. Oh, everything was her
fault. She'd brought Luke nothing but trouble and
nearly gotten him killed.

She kept her gaze glued to the door. She had to see
Luke for herself before she'd know with certainty that
he was all right. Then she might feel better.

He'd tried so hard to keep George away from her.
But George had a mind like a tick—once he got a bite
of you he never let go. He wanted blood, he wanted
your life. And now Luke was a target because of her.

"Jesse." He came through the door with an anxious
swing, then stopped. He stared at her, his expression
as soft as butter.

Neither of them noticed Annabelle stealing quietly
from the room. Or the door closing.

"Oh, Luke," she said, working hard not to let her voice wobble. But her eyes pooled up and she bit her bottom lip. Still, the tears spilled down her cheeks. "I'm so sorry. So very sorry. Really, I . . ."

"Don't, Jesse, honey." He went on his knees beside the bed and took her free hand. "Don't cry. It's all over now. You're going to get well. Doc Reed said so."

"No, that's not it," she blubbered. "I nearly g-got you k-killed."

"Jesse, you saved my life!"

"But George—"

"George's turn will come," he stated flatly. "He'll likely hang."

"Hang? What do you mean?"

"Sheriff Carey's convinced that George and the Thomses are the ones who robbed the bank in Hinley a couple of weeks back. About the time we left there." He wouldn't tell her yet what they'd done to the Pearsons' place.

"George did that?"

"Him and the Thomses. They killed a bank clerk."

"Oh, my heavens . . ." She tried to sit up on her good elbow. The heavy bandages made her awkward; the pain made her wince. She ignored it. "I wondered where he was getting the money to—to come after me. Him and the Thomses. Oh, Luke! What have I done?"

"Jesse, honey, stop that," he demanded firmly. "Right now. It wasn't your doin'."

"But it's my fault. I—" A sob escaped her throat.

"It isn't! You're not responsible for what George and those wolverine buddies of his have done, do you hear? Or what kind of trash he is." He spit the words out in anger, wanting to pound something—like nails into a wall with his bare fist. Pulling George limb from limb might not be enough. The bastard had filled Jesse with a mountain of misplaced guilt, now, as well as making her so afraid she had to run for her life.

For the moment, he put his growing rage aside and as gently as he could, he wrapped his arms around her. "George has chosen his own path, honey. You had nothing to do with that. He's just not hiding under a rock anymore. He's an outlaw, a plain and simple rotten egg."

"An outlaw?" Jesse tagged the one word that held a real clue to what she wanted to know. "What do you mean? What else has he done? What—what happened after . . . after I fainted?"

"Well, three of 'em are in jail this very minute," he hedged.

"Three? Which three?"

"Archie and the two strangers. With the robbery charge, they're keeping the skunk in jail until someone from Hinley comes to identify him. He'll stand trial," he said with satisfaction. "The other two . . . Sheriff Carey plans to go through the wanted posters. He's determined to find a reason to keep them in jail, too."

"Where's George?"

She held his gaze.

"Um, that's the bad news, honey. George got away. And Eli. But the sheriff has a posse out looking for 'em."

She lay back and remained silent for a moment. "He'll come back," she said evenly. Too quietly. "He'll try again."

"I doubt it, honey." Nevertheless, he recognized the dread in her tone. The fear.

Annabelle tiptoed in and quietly took a chair.

"Oh, but he's vicious and mean. He came this far. . ." Jesse thought a moment. "Luke, I think I should leave here."

He shook his head. "Can't. Not without me."

"But if I'm no longer here, he won't bother you anymore. Or any one else in Wayside Station."

"He won't bother any of us again anyway," Luke assured her. "There isn't a man within fifty miles that wouldn't shoot him on sight."

"Nor a woman," Annabelle chimed in, picking up the soup bowl once more. It had grown quite cool, but she didn't think it mattered. She'd be lucky to get Jesse to swallow two spoonfuls, if she read the girl right. "We shoot varmints out here and bury 'em quick. And I can't abide a snake anywhere in my path. Now Luke, you let me feed Jesse here, and let her rest some more. Looks like you wore her plumb out."

When Jesse woke again, there was a small dish of blue lupines sitting next to her bed. They were a bright splash of color against the yellow wallpaper, she thought, and wondered who had placed them there. The slant of sunlight streaming through her window told her it was late afternoon.

A young woman sat in the chair beside the bed, a book in her hand. Her profile showed a delicate mouth, a small straight nose, and a squarish jaw. Fair skin and silky, dark blond hair told Jesse that she might be Luke's sister.

"Hello," Jesse said.

"Oh, hello." The young woman turned to her and smiled. "How are you feeling? Well, I know you're not feeling well, but is it any better?"

"Yes, a little, I think." The pain in her shoulder had reduced to a mere ache. If she didn't move. But she was uncomfortable and desperately wanted to change positions.

"Here, let me fluff your pillows," her companion

said as if reading her mind. "Luke brought those lupines by just a while ago. They're pretty, aren't they? He sent Crow to find them. He said to tell you he'd be by to take supper with you at the usual time. Ma and I had a hard time convincing him to leave at all, you know." She laughed, punching a pillow, then tucked it at Jesse's back. Jesse eased herself against the pillows once more.

"Imagine the scandal," the girl continued, "him in your room all night that way if . . . well, if you two weren't all but having the words said."

"Imagine . . ." was all Jesse was able to return, feeling a bit flabbergasted.

"Oh, I'm Josie Hanley, by the way. Luke's sister. Boy, am I glad to meet you at last."

"I guessed as much. You all look alike."

"Yes," Josie chuckled, "we sure do. But none of our offspring seem to favor the McCarthy bunch."

"You have children?" Jesse gazed at her in surprise. She didn't appear to have that frazzled look Jesse more often than not associated with motherhood.

"Yes, I have two little girls, Beth and Belle, seven and five. They're with Mattie for the afternoon. Will and Mattie have two little boys. They favor their mother quite a bit. They're all hoping for a girl this time."

"Who's Mattie?"

"Mattie is my sister-in-law. Hasn't Luke told you all about us yet? What a rascal. Usually, he shares. But lately, he's been so secretive, so close mouthed. Why, it was like pulling eyeteeth to get any information at all about you from him. You'd think he was guarding the location of the Dutchman mine or something. I just don't think it's fair."

"Not fair? I don't understand."

"Oh, well, you wouldn't, I suppose. It is only that he was such a scamp when Bart and I courted. He pestered and teased us to death." She laughed and wrinkled her nose. "I wanted the opportunity to return the favor."

Jesse found herself laughing back. Luke's sister was charming.

"Did you like the cologne Luke chose for you?"

"Hmm?" Jesse gave her a questioning look.

"Oh, didn't he give it to you yet? Me and my big mouth. I'm sorry, Jesse. Forget I said anything, please? Sometimes my mouth gets ahead of me."

"No, it's all right. I think I recall Luke giving me a package. Oh, dear. I was helping Emma get supper on the table and it was left on the dining room sideboard. I think. I planned to bring it up when . . . when I left to go strolling with Miss Hallows and Mr. Banes."

"Why don't I just run down and see if I can find it for you. I'll bring up some tea while I'm at it."

"Thank you, that would be nice."

Jesse stared at the ceiling. So now she'd met Luke's mother, his brother, and his sister. The women in his life delighted her, Jesse suddenly realized. They reminded her of the kind of family from which her mother came and had talked about. She wondered if there were more family members, and how many. His sister-in-law, of course, and his nieces and nephews. Mattie must be the one Annabelle had in mind when she questioned her about her skills at helping with childbirth.

Well, she wouldn't be able to do that, now, probably. She'd need a week or two to recover, and Luke's ma had said the birth time was almost upon the mother.

She sighed. Kindness and charm seemed to permeate Luke's family, and she suspected they didn't really need a housekeeper or a nursemaid. And Luke . . . Luke didn't need her, not really. He had family, friends, and a good job. And plenty of women if he wanted one of them. Why that upset her, she didn't know. After all she'd said about not being any young man's slave . . .

Everything had gone so wrong about her grand scheme of conducting her life the way she saw fit.

That hardly mattered now. She had to get well and leave this place. To try to elude George once more. Or face George down on her own.

That's what she had to do, she suddenly thought. She should've realized it before. Pushing herself to sit higher, she began to plan. First, she had to get a weapon.

Jesse had a run of visitors the following day.

Miss Hallows: "Oh, my heavens above, I was never so frightened in my entire *life,* Mrs. Luke, why, the whole episode just—just *exploded* with violence, and I thought my heart would jump right out of my chest and you . . . you were so *brave!* The obvious love you bear your young man . . . why, it's of classic propor-tions, so . . . *romantic!*"

Obvious? How could something be obvious to other people when the whole matter was a cloudy confusion in her own mind?

Rosellen Reed: "I am sorry to see you hurt, Jesse, truly, truly I am. It must pain you a lot. But Daddy says you'll heal quickly. I—I haven't been very friendly. . . ." The girl focused on the handkerchief she pulled at in her lap. "You must realize I've been a jealous cat. I—I wanted Luke, of course, and now you have him. Well, I'm sorry I wasn't more gracious about it. There, I've said it. Can we be friends now?"

Rosellen needn't apologize, Jesse told her. And certainly, they could be friends.

Mrs. Fry: "My, my, my. So our little mouse has become a town heroine. You gave us all quite a surprise, my dear, quite a surprise. Well, I for one am so glad to see it. You must think I've take dreadful advantage of your sweet, giving nature around the boardinghouse, but . . . well, I have noticed. You mustn't think I haven't. Now Emma misses your help and I shall have to do something to find another maid."

Sheriff Carey: "We'll do our best to catch those two that got away, Miz Jesse. Sorry you took an injury in the row." He tipped his hat to her, then to Annabelle, and left.

And the McCarthy women: "This clan has taken quite a shine to you, I suppose you know that. Hello, I'm the one you haven't met yet. I'm Mattie McCarthy, Luke's sister-in-law. May I sit down?"

"Please do." Jesse gazed at the tall brunette with huge brown eyes and wondered how she'd managed the stairs. She appeared ready to give birth at any moment. "You shouldn't have pushed yourself to come. Climbing the stairs as far along as you are . . ." she left off, shaking her head in wonder.

"I wanted to come. May I call you Jesse?"

"Oh, yes, if you like."

"We're going to be neighbors, you know, after you move out to the ranch, as well as sisters. It will be lovely having another woman close to my own age nearby. Especially in the winter and after Annabelle moves into town. We can visit often."

"Annabelle plans to move into town?"

"Didn't Luke tell you? Well, he'll get around to it soon enough, I suppose. There have been a number of other things to think about. Annabelle has been wanting to make the move for a long time, and now that Luke has finally made up his mind to marry, she's happy to leave the small house in his hands. She's an easy mother-in-law to have. So get well soon, Jesse. I'll love having you on the M double C."

"I . . . I . . . um, thank you." Jesse didn't know what else to say, thinking that in other circumstances she and Mattie might become the best of friends.

Josie breezed into the room. "Jesse, I brought you a piece of needlework and everything to do it with—I know you can't do it right away, but you must be bored to death with nothing to do all day but lie there. I hope you like the thread colors I've brought."

"That's very kind of you, Josie. I'm sure I will." Jesse glanced at the rich blues and golds lying against the white cloth. She hadn't done a piece of needlework since she was ten when her mother taught her how to do the various fancy stitches. It was an unheard-of luxury, to her way of thinking, to simply sit and work the piece. She smoothed out the printed flower design on the linen dresser scarf; it was lovely.

When would she ever have time to complete it? she wondered. By the time she healed, she'd be on her way west. But she could save it for a keepsake.

"Thank you, Josie. It's beautiful and I'll treasure it."

"Good. I have to get back to the store now. I'll drop in tomorrow."

By supper time, Jesse felt a complete fraud.

"Luke," she told him as soon as he came through the door. "You have to put a stop to this. Do you know what half the town thinks? They think we're already married."

He didn't immediately respond; he pushed aside the items on the small bedside table and laid down the supper tray. Two steaming bowls of chicken and dumplings sent a nose-twitching fragrance into the air.

"And, your sister Josie, and Mattie . . . they think we're only days away from I dos. What can we do?"

"Get married, of course."

"Luke!" She glared at him threateningly.

"I mean it, Jesse. We *have* to get married. As soon as possible."

"I don't agree." She wanted to pout like a child. He wasn't taking her protests or her concerns seriously. Then curiosity got the better of her. "Why do we?"

"Because it's just as you said. Half the town already thinks we're married."

"And how do you account for that?" she fumed, conveniently forgetting her part in the deception. "You led everyone to think it in the beginning. Every time I tried to explain that we weren't, someone interrupted or changed the conversation. And then you announced it in the street in front of everyone."

"Well, I couldn't give simple explanations when we first arrived. It was just easier to, um, let things stand. Besides, you were hiding out from George and, as far as I'm concerned, that's the best protection you had. To be married to me. Besides, in some areas, that announcement in the street makes it legal."

"What?" She sat higher on her pillow and watched him stir a piece of chicken around, letting steam escape. He'd said that part about a public announcement being legal with a straight face, yet she thought he couldn't possibly have meant it. He must be joshing. "Luke, you're fibbing. Aren't you?"

"Have a bite of chicken, honey. You must be hungry. You didn't eat much lunch, Ma said."

"Luke?"

"A little bite?"

Jesse opened her mouth and he placed the fork with its piece of chicken on her tongue, watching as her small teeth closed around the utensil. She began to chew. Gently, and without seeming haste, he fed her a bite of biscuit dumpling.

"All right," she said as she swallowed. "Now I want you to straighten the matter out. You must."

"I don't think so, honey."

"Why not?"

"Because you've ruined my reputation."

She blinked rapidly. "I beg your pardon?"

"Uh-huh, and then some."

"How could I?" Such an idea was ridiculous. Men didn't have those kinds of reputations. She asked suspiciously, "What have I done to ruin your good name?"

"Have another bite."

She raised her chin and refused to open her mouth. Luke exchanged his seat for a place on the bedside. "C'mon, honey, try some of this gravy. One of Emma's best efforts. She'll be hurt if you don't eat some of it."

He held out another forkful and Jesse's mouth began to water. She couldn't bear to hurt Emma's feelings, and she couldn't stand to be wasteful. She accepted the morsel, the gravy tasting rich and spicy, but her eyes never left Luke's.

His blue gaze held tenderness, but behind that was a flicker of staunch tenacity just as stubborn as her own. Or George's. But while George frightened her to her backbone, Luke didn't. Right now she was furious with him, but he . . . he was so . . . darned *appealing.*

"Why?" she demanded.

He stalled by forking a bit of chicken and dumpling into his own mouth. She watched his lips press together as he swallowed. "You've traveled alone with me."

"Only for a few days." Actually, it had been nearly two weeks.

"Been lovey-dovey with me. Boswell's my witness."

Jesse felt her face flush. "How would that ruin *your* reputation?"

"People would question my honorable intentions. They'd expect me to marry you."

"That—that's nonsense."

"Is it, Jesse?" He spoke in gentle demand as he put the bowl on the table. "They'd blame me for spoiling a young, pretty girl."

"But I—"

He leaned forward, placing his forearms on either side of the pillow. His face mere inches from hers, she felt captive to the emotions between them. She dropped her gaze, unable to sustain his.

"Would you really turn me down, honey?" He put his forehead to hers while one hand grasped a curl, winding it about his finger. "After my family has approved and all? After I've declared my undying love to the skies."

"You've done no such thing!"

"I'm declaring it now." His breath felt soft on her cheek. "Marry me, Jesse," he whispered against her ear. His lips nibbled at her earlobe. "You have such tiny ears. . . ."

"Oh, Luke. . ." Jesse wanted to cry because she wanted him so. He didn't play fair, he'd *made* her want him.

She nearly melted into a heap when his tongue ran into the inside of her ear, causing shivers to race down her body.

"I promise I won't beat you or anything."

Of course he'd never beat her. Not like George or a dozen other men might have. He had the most tender heart she'd ever known in a man. "Well, I—"

"My family all like you." His mouth traveled along her jawline. "A lot."

"That's very nice, quite . . . quite lovely, in fact. . . . But—" She tried to formulate her next objection, but her thoughts wouldn't come together.

"I'll be less than donkey's dung in my family's eyes if you say no and mean it."

He started around the other side of her jaw, his kisses growing hotter by the minute. She shifted slightly to lift her chin. Her desire for his mouth along the other side of her throat drove her to distraction. She felt it in her knees, in her toes and fingers.

How was she to resist this? Him? She was in a mighty dangerous position, she thought. In bed, in her bedroom with the door closed. On the verge of succumbing entirely, she desperately sought something to put distance between them.

"Whose? Whose eyes?" she whispered.

"In everyone's eyes," he continued. "I don't see how I could raise my head again in this town if you said no."

"Oh, Luke," she protested with a half giggle. Now, she thought, he was pressing the point a little too much.

He pulled back an inch or so. "It's true. And my boss . . . He's an upstanding man in the community. He wouldn't approve if we didn't get married. He'd blame the whole thing on me."

That stiff-necked, tough boss of his. She hadn't considered that aspect. She looked at him askance. "He wouldn't really fire you, would he?"

"It was close last time." He waggled his head and made a frustrated clicking sound. "I can't afford to make one more mistake, you know, and he don't allow for living in sin among the hands."

"But we haven't!"

"But he thinks we did."

"Oh, it is a tangle."

"See? We gotta set the date and it better be soon."

She thought a long moment, but it didn't seem to help her any. "If I say yes—"

"I'll make a good husband, Jesse, honey. I promise."

"Well, you know how I feel," she said sternly. "I won't be your slave, merely because I'm your wife."

"No, honey." His features were bland, but his eyes gleamed with triumph. And laughter.

"I insist on having my own enterprises." Luke had to understand that up front. She didn't want an argument about any of it later. "And the money I earn will be my own; you can't have it to gamble with."

"Yes, honey, I understand." He nodded gently, staring at the front of her nightgown. A corner of his mouth twitched. "You can keep all your own money that you earn from your, um, enterprises. I might have a few of my own."

"That's fine. Just dandy, in fact. But you'd better think twice about losing this good position. And if you're thinking of taking up homesteading for yourself or anything of the like, you'd better be prepared to work hard. I won't put up with a lazy man."

"No, no laziness around our house," he said in a quivery voice. Almost as if he held his amusement in. She suspiciously observed his attempt to firm up his mouth.

"And—Oh, Luke, you scalawag," she complained on a wail. He *was. He was laughing.* "You knew I wanted to remain on my own. . . ."

He gathered her to lay against his chest, careful of her injured shoulder. "I know, honey," he murmured in a conciliatory tone. "but you'll like being married. I promise you."

He pressed his mouth against hers, giving her a soul-shattering kiss that she thought—later, when she could think at all—might remain in her memory for a lifetime.

But so would her fears about George. Where was he now, she worried late into the night, and what was he planning? For as sure as she was that she loved Luke more than any creature or thing in all the world, she feared that if she remained with him she'd be the sure cause of his death.

18

Although she felt much better and could manage many things for herself after nearly a week, it was still easier to wear her nightdress and the robe Josie had brought her. When she awoke that morning, the boardinghouse seemed quiet, and she enjoyed the peace with no morning visitors.

But her peace was short-lived. That afternoon Sheriff Carey came to see her again.

"Afternoon, Miz Jesse. Glad to see you up and about. Doc tells me you're comin' right along and perkin' up nicely." He stood just inside her door, tentatively turning his brown hat in his hand.

"That's true, Sheriff. Thank you for inquiring. Won't you sit down?" She was a little surprised to see him.

"Well, I reckon I will, Miz Jesse," he said hesitantly. "If you're up to answering some questions."

"Yes, of course," she answered slowly. Luke said he had taken care of reporting everything to the lawman, and she wondered what she could add. "I'll answer anything I can."

His rather husky frame eased onto her one chair, while she faced him from the side of her bed. He cleared his throat twice before he said, "I wanted to find out a little more about this Jeter fella and his sidekick, Eli Thoms."

"All right. What do you want to know?"

"Well, Luke tells me you lived with Jeter's family back in Missouri, that right?"

"Yes, that's right. George's mother is my father's cousin. I lived with the family until a little over a month or so ago when . . . when I left."

"Uh-huh. And George?"

She sighed. She'd thought when she left Missouri she'd put an end to George's harassment. Now it seemed this thing was never going to be over. "It's very simple, Sheriff Carey. Even though I've constantly refused his attentions, George continues to feel that he has a claim on me. He loves making trouble, and now he has followed me, and. . ."

Jesse shrugged slightly, and bit her lip.

"Uh-huh. Did he ever have a run-in with the law back in Missouri? Or did the Thomses?"

"He never got caught at anything, but . . . Let me put it this way, Sheriff Carey. The Missouri lawmen were beginning to keep a close watch on George and the Thomses. Not that anybody could prove anything."

"Uh-huh . . . Well, from the description I got from the Pearsons, I reckon it was them that burned down their barn and chased them into that town they're close to in Nebraska."

Jesse's back went stiff. Her stomach turned over. "What? What did they do?"

"Got a letter from that Nebraska town lawman about it. Said three ugly sidewinders attacked the Pearsons after they wouldn't talk about where you and Luke had gone."

"Oh, Lord, please. Are they safe?" She began to shake. "W-was Effie and th-the b-baby hurt? Or John?"

"No, they got away. Now, Miss Jesse, I didn't aim to upset you none. Luke is gonna be awful mad at me."

"And . . . and they b-burned down. . .?" Tears rolled down her cheeks. Would George stop at nothing?

"Yes, ma'am."

"When? When did this happen?" She dashed her tears away, gritted her teeth, and renewed her vow. George had to be stopped; she couldn't allow him to harm anyone else.

"Um . . . about the time you arrived in Wayside Station, I'm thinkin'. They robbed the Hinley bank only days before that."

"They robbed a bank, too? Oh, yes, I remember now. Luke told me about it." They must have done that after she and Luke had almost run into them there. They must have backtracked to find the Pearsons.

"Yes, ma'am."

"Thank you for telling me of this, Sheriff Carey," she said, low and intense. "But I must warn you. Since you have Archie in your jail, be on the lookout for George and Eli to try to get him out. They're the kind of men who enjoy taking revenge and will stop at nothing to satisfy themselves at a wrong done them, as they see it."

She got up and walked to the window. "Oh, I must tell Luke right away. He has to be very, very careful."

"Don't worry too much about Luke, ma'am. He ain't no slouch when it comes to takin' care of himself, and 'sides that, he's being well guarded by his brother and the M double C hands."

Sheriff Carey didn't tell her that two of the M double C's men had been stationed at the boardinghouse since the night of her injury, nor did he mention that he had taken on two more deputies to give around-the-clock coverage at the town jail. He expected a lawman to come from Hinley soon to transport Archie back to stand trial.

"But will it be enough?" she nearly begged.

"Yes, ma'am, I believe it will," he told her in all assurance. She didn't understand, yet, the power the McCarthys wielded in Wyoming, he thought.

George and Eli found a hollow in the riverbank in which to hide. After the confrontation in Wayside Station, they'd retreated with all the haste of a charging buffalo. After two days, they'd gone west, settling in one of the wild canyons to take stock and bide their time.

At George's badgering, Eli sneaked back into town and sidled into the seediest saloon in town. He'd kept to a dark corner nursing a whiskey while he listened to the gossip. He heard how Archie had been locked up in jail and that woman, that McCarthy woman, as the speaker called Jesse Mae, was gonna pull through—thanks to the McCarthy clan and the doctor's quick action.

Eli didn't like it that Archie got taken. Neither did George, but George's hate toward Luke McCarthy, when he heard the news, grew even larger than his want of Jesse Mae. His wrath consumed him to the point where he thought of little else besides ways to hurt his enemy, ways to get even.

Eli liked getting even, too, but he wanted to set his brother free first.

Watching the stars come out, Eli threw down the tiny bone he'd gnawed to death, one from a little bird he'd caught two days ago. His belly growled. So had George's a minute before. They were down to their last supplies, and they had to decide what to do. An hour ago, he'd laid a plan under George's nose and waited for George's response.

"Well?"

"Worth a try, I reckon. He put a store by them bulls, I guess. Iffen we git Archie outa jail, then we c'n lay low an' try fer Jesse Mae agin."

"Sure, George, sure. But we gotta git Archie out, first. Reckon them McCarthys will figure it's to their good to help us if we got their bulls hid out so's they can't find 'em."

"When ya wanta do it?"

"Tonight's good. I know right where they's at. The M double C bunch is a-watchin' their front sides, but they ain't careful about this back end. Just two of us c'n sneak out them bulls from under their noses real easy if we play it quiet."

George dreamed of finding Jesse Mae somewhere alone; his thoughts dwelt on grabbing her off the street. He'd do it, too, he'd wait till he could. But getting the bulls would be only a start at getting even with McCarthy. And he was gonna do that, too. His little mouth parted in what passed for a smile. "Okay, we'll do it, Eli. But first let's git us some better eats."

"Where you thinkin' on doin' that?"

"Remember that place south a ways? It weren't no big place, jest one barn 'n' a house. Saw jist one ol' man when we went by to water our horses, 'member?"

"Yeah?"

"Well, them ol' guys often has a stash someplace. They don't spend it, they jest hide it away. See, that ol' guy had a gold watch chain. Noticed it right off, an' he saw me look. He got real nervous and pulled 'is vest down quick. I got a notion that mebbe he had more to be worked up over than only a watch."

Two mornings later, with Miss Hallows's help, Jesse put on her green dress and then sat on the side of her bed. In private, she counted her money with care. Two dollars and twenty-six cents.

It wasn't enough to get her to the end of the street.

She put it away, and walked to the front window. From her vantage point, she could see much of the shopping district of Wayside Station. Half a block away was Josie's mercantile store, and across from them was a gunsmith and saddle shop.

Necessity fought with sadness; she wondered if Josie would be willing to buy her harp and how much it was worth. She hadn't anything else of value.

When Boswell came to visit her an hour later before he left for the ranch, she was still mulling over her problems.

"Wanted to say so long, Miz Jesse, an' many thanks for all your nursin' care. Wished I coulda returned the favor. Real sorry you got hurt."

"I'm happy you're feeling better, Boswell. But you can do me a favor in return, if you will."

"Name it."

"Can you teach me to use a gun?"

Boswell sat down on the chair. While he was much his old self again, he still tired easily. "A gun, Miz Jesse? Well, reckon I could. What kind of a gun?"

"A pistol. I want to learn how to use a small pistol.

One that will fit in my pocket or my reticule. How much would such a gun cost? Secondhand, that is."

"Depends, Miz Jesse. On who's sellin' it an' what kind of condition it's in. What do you need one for?"

"I should think that would be obvious, Boswell. For protection." For Luke's and her own.

"But you've got Luke, now, Miz Jesse."

"It's Luke I'm thinking of, Boswell. George would've killed him that night. I can't risk putting him in any more danger."

"You still afraid of that George skunk, then?"

"Yes, and you would be too if you knew him like I do. He's . . ." There was no use trying to explain George's twisted character. "Anyway, would you please be on the lookout for such a gun? I'll find the money to pay you what it costs. But Boswell, this has to be our secret. I don't want Luke worrying about it. Okay?"

"Sure, missus. I'll find one for you."

His answer gave her some peace of mind, though not as much as she needed.

That evening when Luke came to escort her down to dinner, he handed her another package. "I brought you a fancy sling from Ma," he told her. "Here, I'll unwrap it for you."

As he unfolded the brown paper, she discovered a green checked square of cotton with a running embroidery stitch along the hem. In one corner was a set of three embroidered musical notes. It looked neat and pretty at the same time. "How very thoughtful of her." Jesse fingered one of the notes. The color matched her dress and made her feel less like an invalid.

"Ma said it was to give you a promise that your harp would be there in the parlor when you come."

"Oh. . ." Her heart jerked.

Brushing her hair aside, she turned her back for Luke to tie the new sling around her neck. It made her feel festive.

Luke ran a caressing hand down the cascade of her bright hair, then reached for the scarf. After he tied it, he kissed the back of her neck and then slid his arms around her waist and brought her small body tightly against his. Now that she'd agreed to be his wife, he didn't know how much longer he could stand not making love to her. He'd held himself in control all those nights on the trail and since. Now he thought he might burst with wanting her.

Jesse's injury might cause him some precarious balancing problems. He'd have to take extra precautions not to hurt her. Whether she'd admit it or not, she loved him and he basked in his plans on showing her what a husband's love could bring her. He'd teach her joyfully and with great delight.

He grinned to himself. Oh, how he wanted Jesse to know those joys and delights of being a wife. *His* wife.

"Mmm . . . You smell so good. Like lavender."

"It's the scent you gave me." Jesse felt his heat all the way down, knowing the very second when his body hardened in arousal. He rocked against her in gentle need, which caused her breath to catch.

"Do you like it?"

For a dizzying moment, Jesse wondered if he referred to the way he held her, but then realized he meant the fragrance. "Yes, very much," she murmured. "I remember my mother wearing it."

He nuzzled the side of her neck, moving his hand to cup the underside of her full breast. "Dr. Reed says you'll be up to traveling by Sunday. Let's be married Sunday evening."

"I think we'd better go to supper," she said. Her knees felt weak. She hadn't known her body could want something all on its own without her mind's permission.

"Promise." His fingers moved the slightest amount, only a brush of his fingers, but it made her wish there were no barriers at all, of clothing or anything else between them. That very thought shocked her and sent a jolt of desire all down her spine. He seemed to know it and responded by pressing against her more tightly. "Sunday," he urged in a husky voice.

"All right, Luke," she whispered. "Sunday evening."

"You can wear my wedding dress," Josie told her excitedly the next day. "I'm only a little taller than you, and we can give it a tuck just above the hem. It might be a little big about the waist, but we can fix that, too."

"Are you sure?"

"Of course, Jesse. You don't know how happy I am to have another sister."

Mattie had voiced a similar thought. Jesse had to admit that she'd filled a mother's role many times to the little Jeter girls, and been a sister to them when she'd had time. But this was the first time she'd been on the receiving end of so much generosity. Luke's mother, Josie, Mattie. And Luke himself. It embarrassed her that she had so little to bring to this family.

But she could still see to it that Luke didn't get killed.

Jesse eased her sore, still-bandaged shoulder into the cream-colored dress, letting the full skirt fall to the floor, then stood very still while Josie fastened it up the back. It was rather simple except for huge puffed sleeves made of exquisite lace. With Jesse's help, she moved to the mirror over the chest.

The dress was beautiful and complemented her hair and skin tones. The only problem that Jesse could see was that her fuller breasts pushed high above the dropped neckline.

She caught her lip between her teeth. "Oh, Josie."

"Now, that's not too much Jesse. It's . . ."

"Too much."

"I don't think so," Luke spoke from the doorway. His gaze met hers in the mirror. Jesse looked beautiful. "Wear it just the way it is, Jesse. For me."

The dress sure beat the hell out of anything she owned, Luke suddenly realized. That blue suit was good enough for travel, he reckoned, but he'd gladly burn anything else she kept in that beat up old carpetbag she bumped around with. She was down to two dresses, anyway, since the yellow one had been ruined by her injury. He'd seen the state of her nightdress as well. *That* would be the first to go.

He suddenly grinned, watching her blush all the way up and all the way down to where the material covered her skin.

"Luke, you ornery, cow-eyed good-for-little . . ." Josie sputtered. "Get out of here. You're not supposed to see your bride before the wedding."

"That's tomorrow, sis. Why can't I see her now?"

"Just because you can't, that's why."

He laughed, but dutifully disappeared from the doorway. Jesse heard his spurs happily jingling, seeming to accompany his good spirits down the hall.

The fitting left Jesse tired and her shoulder aching. Only minutes after Josie left, she fell asleep. An hour later, she sleepily answered a knock on her door. It was Luke again. He shoved a large package into her hands.

"I owe you this," he said, taking in her tumbled hair and unguarded, only half-awake gaze. He thought her totally vulnerable when he caught her thus, and deeply wanted to simply stay by her side until she'd gained more confidence with the world. He turned to scan the hall both ways. No one was in sight. He entered the room. "Where's Josie?"

"She took the dress home to alter."

"Good. Then I can have what I came for." He gathered her close and lowered his head.

His kiss tender and sweet, he lifted her clear of the floor and held her high. Jesse wrapped her good arm around him and let him have her mouth in sheer giddiness. Finally, he put her down and backed toward the door.

"Open your package, honey, or I might embarrass my mother by getting caught doing more than just kissing you. She's on her way up with something or other."

The package held the navy straw hat she and Miss Hallows had admired in the store window the night she'd been hurt. It was almost as elegant as the one she'd lost. Imagine Luke picking it out.

"It doesn't have a feather like the other one," Luke said. "But I thought it might do."

"Oh, Luke. It will do very well. It's just right, in fact. But you're not going to have anything left of this month's wage if you spend another cent. Now that's the kind of foolishness. . ."

He had the audacity to laugh. She glared at him.

"I'll collect my thanks later, honey. After we're married," he promised. He backed another step as he stared at her pink cheeks and pouting mouth. Another damned twenty-four hours to wait. He thought it might never come.

*   *   *

Dr. Reed said she could do without a sling if it didn't hurt, so she decided to leave it behind. It was time to be done with it anyway, she thought. Tomorrow she'd begin to exercise her arm, and as soon as Boswell found her what she'd requested, she'd start pistol practice.

Then it was time.

Josie helped her dress and put her hair up. The cream-colored gown fit her better now, and she felt positively elegant. At the hour agreed upon, she descended the front staircase to the parlor. That's where the family and few friends had gathered.

Luke met her at the door and took her arm. Two dozen candles lit the large parlor, and several vases of flowers filled the air with fragrance. Her quick gaze around the room took in the presence of Miss Hallows, Mr. Banes, Rosellen, and Mrs. Fry. And Boswell and Emma, standing in the back next to Sheriff Carey.

A few male faces she vaguely recalled seeing once before shared the wall space. Warmth flooded her heart as she suddenly realized it was they who had backed Luke and her against their adversaries. These were Luke's friends. Her gratitude was boundless.

Luke's family sat in the circle of chairs. His mother and sister smiled at her. She noted a few people seated next to them that she'd never met: the man and little girls who had to be Josie's, and the small boys that sat alongside Mattie who were obviously her sons. Luke's brother was seated next to them.

Fleetingly, she studied him. He was older than Luke; he wore a mustache and though his hair gleamed just as brightly, his eyes were so light a blue they appeared almost clear. They had a suspended quality, she thought, yet when he nodded to her, it was kindly done.

"Come along, Jesse," Luke murmured next to her ear. It gave her no time to greet anyone before she found herself standing in front of a little gray-haired man holding a huge Bible.

"This is Reverend Walensky, Jesse."

"How do you do, sir," she murmured.

The ceremony took little time. When the minister pronounced them married in the eyes of God and man, Luke tipped Jesse's chin up and very gently kissed her.

"Howdy, Mrs. Luke McCarthy," he said on a warm, husky note. He wore an enormously satisfied air.

Then Luke's family surrounded them, Josie laughing, his mother smiling as they kissed her cheek, Mattie joining them with awkward grace, men slapping Luke's back and pumping his hand while the children ran around noisily. Mrs. Fry announced that wedding cake and punch would be served in the dining room. Everyone trooped through.

Later, while talking with Miss Hallows, Jesse happened to glance at Mattie and noticed a tenseness flicker across her sister-in-law's face. A few minutes later, the expression returned. Mattie said nothing, but Jesse moved to sit close by. If she knew anything at all, she thought, she'd recognize labor when she saw it, and Mattie was experiencing childbirth pangs.

"Mattie, hadn't you better tell your husband?" she said under her breath.

Some of the men had adjourned to the front porch about twenty minutes before.

"Oh . . ." Mattie's brown eyes glowed and she made a little grimace. "You are very observant, aren't you? I suppose I should. I'm very sorry to cut your reception short, Jesse. I thought I could wait it out, but—" All at once, she took a sharp breath.

"I'll get him." Jesse excused herself and went searching for Luke and his brother. She found Luke in the parlor talking with Sheriff Carey.

"Luke! Luke, you must find your brother. Mattie's in labor, and if I don't miss my guess, she's going to need help very soon."

"Lord A'mighty, wouldn't you know it?" He took her elbow and turned her into the front hall. "Tell Ma and hang onto Mattie, honey, I'll be right back."

She'd turned to go when she heard him step to the front door and call, "Will! Will, we need you in here pronto!"

Will? Luke's brother was Will?

19

Will was Luke's brother! Not his boss, but his brother.

The significance hit her like a brick between the eyes. McCarthy equaled the M double C. She'd been a fool.

Anger flamed up, momentarily overtaking her concern over Mattie, even replacing her own joy of the day's happiness. She wanted to wring Luke's good-looking neck.

There had never been a possibility of Luke being fired from his job. Not even a pinhead of one. What was he on the ranch, anyway? She'd bet her next meal he wasn't a mere cowboy as he'd claimed, but a rancher, a landowner. Someone with assets.

Heaven help her, she'd been a stupid, blind, naive . . .

Jesse couldn't believe she'd missed it. The way the townspeople responded to him, to her. No wonder

Mrs. Fry thought her odd for wanting to earn her own way. And the sheriff, and others. The only excuse she had was that she'd been so up to the wall with worry over George's real threats of danger that she'd been blind to Luke's trickery.

Luke strode back through the kitchen door, unaware of her discovery, with his brother in tow. She glimpsed their faces, so alike. The McCarthy brothers. Strong, handsome men, both of them. And powerful.

Yes, powerful—hadn't there been reference to it when the fight had broken out? Those two strange gunmen wanted to back out when they realized who they were fighting. The McCarthy men had reputations of their own, it seemed.

"Where's Mattie?" Will demanded.

"Dining room," she murmured, her gaze flashing between the two men. She felt as though she hardly knew Luke any better than she did Will.

"C'mon, Jesse, honey. Looks like Mattie needs us." Luke directed her with all the assurance that she would do exactly as he wanted. A command to which any wife would respond, to get things done. She'd been getting things done all her life. For Bertha, for the kids, even for strangers.

She wondered if he had any intentions of honoring the agreements they'd made between them, that she could be somewhat independent within the marriage. Oh, drat it all. She felt betrayed in a way that was completely unexpected, a feeling of deep disappointment.

Luke had lied to her, while she'd been completely honest with him.

And, God help her, she'd fallen hopelessly in love with Luke. A handsomer-than-average cowboy, young and virile from the top of his curly head to the tips of his high-heeled western boots. His impudent smile could turn her to pudding without even a stir of the spoon.

Otherwise, how could she explain to herself why she'd done the unthinkable and married a *young* man when she'd promised her mother, promised herself, that she'd never fall into the trap of loving a man beyond herself?

Now she had to face the disappointment in her own judgment. And she wondered if Luke and Will were empire builders merely needing another woman to keep the enterprise going, to make babies and take care of the men.

She turned towards the back staircase, wanting to escape, yearning to hide for a little while to lick her wounds. But the sudden commotion from the dining room made itself felt. Josie rushed through the door.

"Jesse," her new sister-in-law said, "Rosellen says Dr. Reed has gone out to the Sanderson ranch. He won't be back for hours, if he gets back tonight at all. Ma asks if you can come now? Mattie's going to need you."

"Of course," Jesse responded. How could she refuse after all the kindness shown her? All week she'd hoped to find a way to repay it.

She took a fortifying breath and followed Josie to the family circle surrounding the expectant mother. Mattie had her own battle with which to contend, and she was exhibiting a mountain of stubbornness in doing it.

"I want to have this child at home, like the others," Mattie insisted. "There's time if we hurry."

Will, looking more distracted than Jesse had ever seen him, gritted his teeth. "Darlin', it'll take an hour to get home even if we hurry," he stated unequivocally. "We can't make it in time and I don't want our child born in the middle of nowhere. It will be better if we take a room upstairs."

With difficulty, Mattie pushed herself to stand. "Will, we're wasting time."

"Mattie!" Will protested adamantly.

Annabelle stepped forward. "Mattie, dear," she coaxed, "you had such a difficult time with little Christopher. Perhaps it would be best to stay in town to give birth. Jesse, here, has had experience with these things. We'll both be here to help you."

"Mother McCarthy, I—"

Jesse touched Mattie's arm and leaned forward to whisper in Mattie's ear. "Wouldn't you like your little girl to be born in the yellow bedroom with the yellow rose wallpaper? She will have a lovely entry into the world. And afterwards, we'll have tea."

"Do you think . . . ?" Mattie's eyes lit with amused hope.

Jesse nodded. For some odd reason, she'd called every one of Bertha's babies before they were born. She felt certain Mattie's baby would be a girl.

"All right. Will, help me upstairs, please."

Will gave Jesse a flash of gratitude, then swept Mattie into his arms and carried her upstairs.

"Jesse, you aren't up to this," Luke protested, a hand on her arm. "You've only recovered yourself. Let Ma and Josie take over."

From the parlor, Jesse heard Josie gathering the children together, including Mattie and Will's boys, in preparation for taking them home. Josie always did her part, she thought. She'd keep the kids safely out of the way.

She gazed up at Luke with a calmness she wasn't feeling. "I'm fine, Luke. And this is one reason I was hired, wasn't it? Because I know about birthing. The

M double C needed another woman on the ranch to take care of business. To perpetuate the family and its empire."

"Hired? Family . . . empire? What are you talking about?"

"The reason we married. Your boss *Will* wanted you to marry, and I have the best qualifications to become a ranch wife, don't I? Willingness to work hard, experience. To add to the family."

"Jesse . . ." He wore an expression of surprise and puzzlement. And hurt.

"I do owe you a lot of gratitude, though. You saved me from George. But you didn't have to marry me, Luke. I would've eventually come to work for you. But then, a wife serves for free."

Jesse turned her back and followed in her mother-in-law's wake.

Will was right, Jesse thought. His little girl would never have waited until they reached the M double C to be born. With her help and Annabelle's, Constance Jessanne McCarthy made a healthy and easy entry into the world. When Jesse finally laid the towel-wrapped little bundle in her mother's arms, Mattie thanked her with a grateful smile. A moment later, Will leaned down to kiss Jesse's cheek.

"Thank you, Jesse, honey," he said, sounding very like Luke. "My brother and I are both lucky men this day. Now run along to your husband. Reckon he needs you more than we do now."

Annabelle added her encouragement. "Yes, Jesse, go. You must be almost as exhausted as Mattie."

In truth, her shoulder ached abominably. She longed to lie down and sleep, but the yellow bedroom was no longer hers. She had nowhere to go except downstairs to where Luke waited.

Slowly, she descended the stairs. Luke met her at the bottom. The lower floor was still, the lamps turned low. "Where is everyone?" she asked, refusing to look at him.

"It's almost midnight, honey. Everyone's gone home or to bed."

"Oh." Aware that he studied her face, she let her gaze rest on the dark buttons of his vest, which matched the fine gray suit he wore. He'd removed his tie and unbuttoned his shirt, showing his long, tanned throat.

She let her gaze rise to his square jawline. The golden stubble that she'd become familiar with on their journey over the mountains gleamed. Her palm itched to find out how it felt.

He was her husband. Too good-looking, too charming—too close. Oh, why had she let her emotions run so wild? She'd betrayed herself, and now she'd never stop wanting him. Or loving him.

"I suppose we should let Josie know that everything's fine with Mattie and the new baby."

Luke observed the glazed look in her eyes and slid an arm around her waist. "Sandy'll go along to tell them," he told her. "It's our turn to go home."

"Who's Sandy?"

But fatigue overcame her ability to listen to his answer. Luke led her outside to where his mother's buggy waited, hitched to Rom and Rem.

"Oh, the mules."

He heard the gladness in her voice. She pushed herself to give them some affection, patting their noses and rubbing their ears. She loved the contrary beasts, and Luke was glad he'd given in to his sentimental feelings and brought them.

Luke lifted her into the buggy and wrapped a shawl around her shoulders against the cool night air. It was a moment before she noticed; she didn't own a shawl and looked down at it, stroking the silky fringe.

"Did you borrow this from Josie or Mattie?"

"Neither. It's yours."

"I don't own one," she replied with a note of puzzlement.

"You do now."

She didn't protest and closed her eyes at the rhythmic slow trot the mules exerted. Luke let her sleep. Explanations between them would wait until morning. He'd straighten out the misunderstandings then. How she'd come up with the notion he wanted her because he needed a wife to build an empire was beyond him. He wasn't building an empire, and neither was Will.

It had happened, though, he would admit. The M double C was quite a spread. He didn't know what Jesse'd say when she discovered she was the wife of a wealthy man.

A long sigh escaped her lips, and Luke glanced at her. Her eyes were closed, yet her murmur reached his ears with complete clarity. "Why did you lie to me?"

The plaintive question drifted quietly from her lips just as sleep overwhelmed her.

Hell! He hadn't meant it to become a lie.

Jesse stirred a little as he lifted her from the buggy and carried her into the house, but she didn't waken fully. Damn, the day had been too much, Luke fumed. Way too much. Her health hadn't caught up with all she'd faced today.

He'd been a selfish lout to push her, but he'd do it

again if necessary. Protecting her would be easier now that she was his wife.

He lay his bride in the middle of the big bed that had once been his parents'. Telling him it was the timely moving on of the life seasons, Ma had insisted he and Jesse have the house's largest bedroom, and since Ma planned to spend most of her time in town from now on, he didn't argue. Her best blue piece-work quilt, the one she usually kept in the cedar chest, covered the bed.

Jesse appeared almost lost in the middle of it, but he thought her the loveliest thing he'd ever seen. He removed her shoes, gently pulled the hairpins from her hair, then started on the long row of buttons down her back.

Abruptly, Jesse sat up in a panic, batting at his hand wildly. Her green eyes wide, she stared at him with terror. A low moan escaped her lips. It took him a moment to realize she was still asleep.

"Jesse." He called her name gently and curved a hand around her good shoulder.

She twisted away, as though she loathed his touch. Her action clamped his middle into a knot. What had he done? He couldn't stand the thought of her rejection, but he waited a moment to see what else would happen. Her gaze remained frightened as she crouched at the opposite edge of the bed against the wall.

What terrors in hell did she fight in her dreams? George? Likely.

"Jesse, honey, it's all right. It's me, Luke." He reached for her again.

She began to whimper. He stayed his hand.

"Honey." He lowered his voice another notch and spoke soothingly. "Jesse . . . Don't cry, sweetheart. You have nothing to be scared about. I won't hurt you, I promise." He put a knee on the bed and then, very slowly, the other. She didn't relax, but she didn't draw away any further.

"We were married today, remember?" He moved closer. "Think of all those nights on the journey home. I didn't harm you then, did I?" He tried again. "I only want to love you, sweetheart. Remember the fun we had on the trail? Remember the froggie song?"

He hummed a line. Her eyelids began to droop. He hummed more, making his tone as soft as a lullaby, as meaningful as a hymn.

This time she let him touch her, his fingers brushing her cheek. Slowly, he slid his arm around her once more and cradled her as her eyes closed entirely.

The unbuttoned bodice gaped wide, revealing even more of her white breasts above her undergarment. He yearned to see all of her and to hold her in all the ways a lover could. Then he spied the edges of the unbandaged ugly knife scar, still red and healing.

It hit him anew, and he stared at the reminder a long moment. It marred her lovely skin, yet he swore it would stand in his mind forever as her badge of courage. Jesse had taken that knife to save his life.

After a moment, he eased her down. Peeling aside the dress fabric, he laid his lips against her velvety skin, careful not to touch the wound. Dear God, what had he ever done in his life to deserve her?

Jesse smelled coffee, strong and hot. She opened her eyes.

Only inches from her nose, Luke's bare masculine arm rested on a jeans-clad upraised knee. Above the jeans, he wore nothing, giving her a glimpse of golden hair rippling along his chest. A paper stretched across his knees, his lashes flickered with his eye movement as he read. He sipped from a mug and she watched his muscles work; his arm bending, his throat as he swallowed. Her husband.

Feeling languid, she let her gaze wander. While not enormous, the room was good-sized. The walls were made of logs and chinking. They appeared freshly whitewashed. A tall, carved wardrobe stood in the corner, its door ajar. She glimpsed Luke's grey suit there and the lace sleeve of Josie's wedding dress. Her wedding dress.

An open window carried a fresh morning breeze and faint sounds of cattle in the distance; the air smelled of sage. A sheet covered her to her chin.

She shifted her gaze again and discovered that her husband watched her.

"Morning, Jesse."

"Morning."

"How d'you feel?"

"Fine."

"Is your shoulder painin' you any?"

"No."

"How was your rest?"

"All right."

She seemed to have no recall of her nightmare, so he asked, "Are you still mad at me?"

With that she sat up, ignoring the fact that she wore only her camisole and petticoat when the sheet fell to her waist. Slowly, she frowned.

"You can bet your best boots I am, you lying—"

"It wasn't an out-an'-out lie, honey. I only stretched the truth a little. Or left it out, maybe."

"—son of a weasel. Yes, indeedy, you left a lot out. Why? Just to see me make a fool of myself?"

"Well, I admit I was teasin' you a little at first."

"Teasing? You call fooling me into thinking you merely a hired hand with no ambitions for anything else only teasing?"

"You were so bent on believing it, Jesse. Remember? Do you recall what you said?"

"I know what I said, all right. I said I didn't plan to marry anyone."

"Least of all a gamblin' cowboy. Whereupon you gave me a look that'd singe a fella's tail feathers faster'n a campfire cook."

"I—" She had little defense for that, but her mind scrambled to find one anyway. It couldn't have been her fault. He didn't allow her time to think.

"Uh-huh, you did," he insisted. "Without even trying to find out who I really was, you lumped me in with all those galoots who you figured were no-good, lazy drifters."

It was true, Jesse'd done just that. So intent on her own plans the day she'd met him, and scared to her back teeth of George, she'd barely acknowledged Luke's help, even. Her fear and anger and disgust at all men had driven her to distraction.

Yet she wasn't quite ready to concede the argument. "What about later, when we were traipsing all over the countryside?"

"What about it? I asked you to marry me the first time in the cave, remember? And you turned me down. I was only a cowhand."

"Well, I married you anyway, didn't I?"

She noticed he'd shaved already this morning and his teeth gleamed with freshness. He looked relaxed and easy; he was at home where he belonged.

She was in his home, too. But was it theirs, together?

"And now I don't even know who my husband is," she complained.

A slow smile curved his mouth while an anticipatory sparkle lit his eyes. "Your husband is Luke McCarthy of the M double C brand. Anybody in Wyoming will tell you about our spread." He leaned toward her. "And there's no time like the present to get better acquainted, honey."

"Right." Jesse threw back the sheet and bounded off the end of the bed. "Where're my clothes?"

"Your clothes? Well, I, um . . ."

"Didn't you bring my bag from the boarding-house?"

"Honey, putting your clothes *on* wasn't exactly the activity I had in mind to get acquainted over."

"But I must see the place and how you grew up before I can understand you."

"That didn't seem to make no never mind before."

"What do you mean?"

"From that very first time that you kissed me I thought you understood me all too well."

"But I have to see your house," she insisted. "And the barns, and hen-house—you do have a henhouse, don't you? And whatever other work buildings there are on the place. How large is your vegetable garden? I need to know how much food preservation I'll need to think on . . ."

"Seeing all those things ain't getting to know me, honey. I want a wife in the ways that makes a woman a wife."

"Yes, I know. A wife . . ."

"I'm all-fired powerful hungry, Jesse."

She raised her chin, deliberately misunderstanding him. "I can't very well begin cooking your breakfast until I have something to wear."

"Oh, I don't know, honey. You look mighty fetchin' the way you are now."

"Luke McCarthy, don't be loathsome."

He sighed and left the bed. It didn't look as though he would get any loving this morning. Or be allowed to give it. Somehow, he'd missed his chance, and he sorrowfully wondered how soon it would come again.

He'd just have to make his opportunities count, he suspected. That's what Jesse had said once, wasn't it? That a body had to make the most of the opportunities one was offered. He grinned, feeling as right ornery as his sister and Jesse accused him of being.

So Jesse wanted to see the whole ranch, hmm? Well, that might suit him just fine. There were lots of places on the ranch that offered just the kind of opportunity he had in mind.

20

Jesse padded out of the bedroom, which she discovered opened directly into the kitchen. The room was twice the size of the bedroom, and its furnishings and equipment appeared old and well used, but shiny and sparkling clean. An open floor-to-ceiling cupboard held dishes, mixing bowls, pitchers, and canning jars. On the wall next to the stove, a rack held skillets, pots and pans, strainers, and other metal equipment. The third wall held a work counter with a basket of eggs and a pan of freshly baked biscuits. A huge table took up the room's center, already set for two.

She liked it. Even though it was crowded, Jesse thought the kitchen exuded warmth and peace, as though it held a wealth of good memories and a welcome for her.

"Coffee?" Luke asked her.

She nodded absently. Who had prepared this for them?

He set a mug of very black coffee on the table and nudged the creamer closer. "Sit down and I'll rustle up some eggs."

Jesse remained standing. "Um, I—I thought you wanted me to do that."

"Not this morning, Jesse, honey," he said, glancing over his shoulder. "You'll have plenty of time to settle in."

She watched him check the wood under the front burner before he placed a skillet on the stove. Reaching toward the back of the work counter, he brought forward two thick steaks, putting them into the hot skillet to fry.

Of course, he'd done his share of cooking over the trail campfire—why it should surprise her that he obviously knew his way around this kitchen, she didn't know.

"Who . . . who made the biscuits?"

"I did. They're light as a feather. Ma was a good teacher. Butter's just there."

Skeptical, she buttered and bit into one. True to his word, they were light and tender, fluffy in the middle and crunchy on the outside, just the way she liked them.

"Mmm, these are good. Are you sure you made them?"

He grinned and turned to look at her again. She was a pretty sight, standing in the middle of the kitchen wearing nothing but her underthings, with her bright hair tumbling down her back. He suddenly recalled how she'd looked with her petticoat high on her bare thighs that time in another kitchen. The picture felt burned into his memory.

However, she wasn't ready for lovemaking, he reminded himself, and kept his answer in neutral.

"Yep, I sure did. I can do lots of things well, Jesse. Lots that you haven't yet noticed . . . or chanced to find out."

"Tell me about the house," she requested. The way he looked at her made it easy to guess where his thoughts were, and she determinedly decided that that part of their marriage was just going to have to wait awhile. Until she could be certain she wanted—no, she wanted *Luke* all right, it was only that she had to know that the *marriage* was for real. Luke's turning out to be a rancher and landowner had thrown her. After all her misperception, she had to understand where she might fit into it all.

"This was the original cabin," Luke said behind her. He pulled out a chair and she sat down. His hand hovered over her shoulder, but when she shrugged away before he could even touch her, he let it drop. He went back to the stove.

"Ma and Pa came out here to Wyoming in the early fifties and built these two rooms when Will was a baby. Ma said, once, it was the happiest time of her life."

"I see. Where did they come from?"

"Illinois." Luke dished up the steak and eggs and set one plate in front of her, then sat down with the other. He indicated that she should eat and began on his own before he took up the story once more.

"Pa's family had a little money, and they staked him and Ma nicely when they came west. They started for the Oregon territory like thousands of others, but they got to this place and just never wanted to move on. Pa was like that, I reckon. When he saw something he wanted, he just never changed his mind. Guess I'm that way, too."

"When did your father pass on?"

Luke's voice took on a dreamy quality. "About a dozen years back. He came home from the war, but . . . he never really recovered. By that time Will had taken hold. We were blessed with good help. And Josie and I . . . well, we were right behind Will. Ma was our home front, and this kitchen. But Will and I ran the ranch. After Pa died, we just kept on."

"Have you had any Indian trouble?"

"Some. Not enough to make us leave. Ma made friends with a couple of families one winter when we fed 'em through a tough time. Grew up with Crow and Bear and they've ridden for us since they were tykes."

A knock on the front door ended Luke's tale. He rose to answer it, and Jesse scooted back to the bedroom. Her curiosity aroused, she cracked the door and listened.

"Sorry to bother you, Luke, knowin' it's your, um, um . . ." said an embarrassed young voice. "Well, see, Will's not home yet from town, an' Sandy went off yonder to the north section an' said he wouldn't be back afore tomorry, an' Crow thinks . . ."

"What is it, Pete?"

"The Herefords is missin'."

"Are you sure? Where'd you last see 'em?"

Jesse's attention sharpened. Where could Meshach and Shadrach have gotten to? She heard the slap of the door as Luke stepped through, and then his muffled voice. She crept into the kitchen and strained to hear what else the ranch hand had to say.

"Crow said they was down to the west crik yesterday evenin'. But this mornin' only that camel is there, an' seein' as how they's usually together and there's churned-up tracks, he said to come get you."

"You did right, Pete. Saddle up Paint. I'll be down pronto."

Jesse met Luke at the kitchen door. "What's happened?"

"Don't know. I have to leave for a while, honey." He strode past her into the bedroom and reached for his boots.

"Where is my bag, Luke?"

"Hmm? Oh, in the parlor, I reckon. Left it there last night."

She raced into the other room, scarcely giving it a glance as she concentrated on finding her clothes. She spotted the bag and raced with it back to the bedroom as Luke pulled on his shirt.

Opening it, she delved into the bottom, tossing her everyday petticoat and the blue suit aside in her search for her boy's clothes. "Wait for me, Luke. I won't be a minute."

He yanked his neckerchief from the chest. "It's best if you stay here, honey. Get some rest. Explore the house."

"No. If those bulls are lost, I'm going to help you find them." She untied and wiggled out of her lace-trimmed petticoat and pulled the denims up over her underdrawers.

She chose the damndest time to entice him, Luke thought. Except he wasn't sure if she was even aware that she set his blood on the boil. Having her down to only two pieces of clothing wasn't likely to cool his thoughts any or keep them on the task at hand.

However, he swallowed his wayward feelings and tried to discourage her. "I don't have time to argue with you, Jesse Mae. You ain't up to a long day in the saddle."

"I don't care if I am or not. I'm going." She shoved

her arm through the tan shirt. "I'll follow you if I must."

"Hellfire, did I get myself saddled with a stubborn little mule?" he muttered, half admiring the militant gleam in her eyes. He was torn between wanting her with him and wanting her to stay in bed and rest so she'd feel pert when he came home.

"Reckon you did, mister."

"Okay." He had to leave or he might get too side-tracked with wanting to kiss her. "I'll be down at the barn. Grab some of those biscuits and fill the canteens hanging behind the kitchen door. Five minutes, hear?"

He swung out of the door as she buttoned her top button and pulled the rolled-up man's hat from her bag. It was totally shapeless, and she thought it the ugliest thing she'd ever worn, but since it had saved her from the sun on the long trail ride, she was grateful to have it.

She plunked it on her head, tucked up her hair, and hurried to the kitchen, following Luke's orders to the letter. Only moments later, she stepped out of the parlor door. A log fence enclosed the ranch house yard, setting it apart, and accented by a half-circle drive. The McCarthy brand emblazoned the log above the entry: -MCC-

Beyond was the vast rest of it. She held her breath.

This was the well-known M double C. Mountains in the distance, rolling high plain all around. Barns, corrals, numerous other outbuildings across the road. A grove of trees a little ways off, and a large house beyond a creek. That must be Mattie and Will's place, she assumed.

She headed for the barn, where three men stood in the doorway. It wasn't hard to pick out Luke's lean form. The cowhands looked at her shyly and tipped their hats, but fell silent the minute she reached them.

Luke introduced her. "Boys, this is my wife. Jesse, that's Chunky and that's Pete."

"How do you do?" she replied formally. After that, she noticed that they seldom glanced her way, and she wondered if they felt uncomfortable around all women or just Luke's wife.

Boswell came around the corner leading three saddled mounts; a young spotted pony, a sleek brown mare, and his own gelding. He gave her a nod and a welcome familiar smile around his pipe. She broke into a smile of her own.

"Morning, Boswell."

"Here you are, Miz Jesse, you're on Sassy."

"Where's Rom and Rem today?"

"They're out to pasture." Boswell reached to help her mount the brown mare, but Luke forestalled him.

Luke handed the canteens and wrapped biscuits to Boswell and then lifted her into the saddle. Digging into his back pocket, he pulled out a pair of small leather gloves and handed them to her. Made of sturdy black leather, they nevertheless sported a decorative stitching. She looked at him in wonder.

"You need work gloves, Jesse, so your hands don't get cut up like they've been."

He seemed not to want a fuss in front of his men, she noticed, so she kept her voice low. "They're very nice. Thank you, Luke."

He nodded his acknowledgment of her appreciation and then took a moment to shorten her stirrups. Afterward he enclosed her ankle with his long fingers, an action of familiarity. His heat reached her clear through her boot. Intentional or not, it gave the signal that she belonged to him, a gesture in which he'd never before indulged.

He raised his gaze a brief moment, giving her the silent communication that he'd known exactly what he did. It shocked and confused her a little and gave her more to think on. As gentle as he'd been with her, Luke had just let her know that she belonged to him. And anyone else who'd watched the action. Her husband wasn't above telling the world to keep away from her.

Luke mounted and led the way past several buildings before nudging his spotted pony, Paint, into a trot. The three of them rode abreast for about thirty minutes, and then Luke took the lead down a long rolling slope towards a wide, shallow river. Normally, she would find it a pretty spot, Jesse thought, but at the moment she was too agitated.

Jesse spied Mehitabel, who stood alone near a cottonwood tree. Something didn't seem quite right. The animal stretched her neck and seemed abnormally skittish. Jesse threw her leg over the mare's saddle and slid to the ground before Luke could reach her. She approached the camel cautiously as she usually did to give Mehitabel time to accept her.

"Hello, girl. Hello." Speaking softly, she moved closer. Mehitabel stared but then let Jesse touch her. It was then that Jesse saw several very ugly slashes across the camel's neck and a few lesser ones on her body and legs.

Whip marks! A couple of them oozed blood. "Oh, Mehitabel."

Jesse felt her heart start to pound and she wanted to cry with outrage. She'd seen the like twice before: once after George had vented his wrath on one of the farm mules and then an old horse that had the misfortune to fall into his hands.

"Luke!"

He was there beside her. He touched Jesse's back for comfort, then examined the marks while Jesse soothed the beast with her low murmur. "Easy, girl, easy."

Although Mehitabel flinched, she seemed to know they were trying to help her.

"George did this," Jesse spoke with all the bitterness of months and years of piled-up offense. "Oh, poor Mehitabel. Luke, d'you suppose George got Meshach and Shadrach?"

"Might be likely." Luke's eyes had gone icy. "But by heaven, if he did, the bastard won't get far."

A rider came over the hill, and Jesse looked up. No more than twenty-five or so, the Indian rode as though he'd been born on horseback.

"It's Crow," Luke told her.

Boswell came up from where he'd been examining tracks by the river's edge. "Two of 'em. They went along the river, I guess. Can't see where they came out."

"I found it." Crow glanced at Jesse briefly but otherwise didn't acknowledge her presence. He spoke to Luke. "They came out up river about five-six miles. Two of 'em, all right. Not too smart. Didn't try to hide it."

"What else?" Luke demanded.

"Went toward the mountains." Crow shook his head. "They're greenhorn fools. Gettin' into that wild part."

"Ha! We'll get 'em." Boswell's face looked smug.

"How can you be sure?" Jesse wanted to know, looking from one to the other.

Luke stared in the direction from which Crow had come. His expression calculating, he balled his fists. "They've outsmarted themselves this time, Jesse. Where they've headed has too many dead-end canyons.

Not much water if you don't know where to look. If we hurry we can block 'em in. They can't come back this way without running into us."

"But can we get to them in time?" Her anxiety began to churn. She knew George. He might slit the bull's throats in revenge.

"In time for what, Miz Jesse?" Boswell asked.

"Before George does something drastic."

"Drastic? What d'you mean, Miz Jesse? You don't think—"

"That's exactly what Jesse does mean, Boswell. George is as mean as they come, a right nasty piece of work."

At last Luke turned to look at her. There was nothing left of the teasing, boyish charm. Once more, she was struck with the fact that Luke could be strictly business when he'd a mind to be, and right now his anger had reached red hot. "There's just one reason George and Eli might be keeping the bulls alive."

"Why? What reason, when he hates us so?" Jesse asked.

"Archie. Eli might just think that stealing our prize bulls will get his brother out of jail by way of a trade."

"But George wouldn't care a fig. He's bent on—" She stopped and flashed a begging question toward Boswell. What if George and Eli had taken the bulls to lure Luke into isolation where they could more easily kill him? She had to protect her husband. Had Boswell found what she'd asked him for? A weapon of her own?

Luke abruptly strode toward his horse, snapping out orders over his shoulder as he pulled out a jar of salve from his saddlebags. "Boswell, ride back to the ranch on the double. Send Chunky into town with word to Will, then pack supplies for several days."

"Uh, for how many?"

"Six. Now get cracking."

"For Miz Jesse, too?" Boswell's tone said he clearly couldn't believe Luke intended to take her along.

"Yep. Jesse, too."

Boswell headed for his horse.

"Crow," Luke snapped out. "Ride out and find Slim, Simeon, Dusty, and Miguel. And tell Bear to bring up extra horses and follow. Then meet us in the boulders up yonder."

"Sure thing, Luke." Crow took off at a gallop.

Luke began to apply salve to Mehitabel's cuts. But Boswell's and Crow's mount's hoofbeats had barely faded before Luke turned to her.

"What was it Boswell was supposed to do for you, Jesse?" His tone was rather casual. Too casual. Something bothered him.

"Why, I don't know what you mean, Luke."

His eyes narrowed. He pulled out his handkerchief to wipe his hand. "Jesse, don't lie to me. I saw that look you gave him. What was that all about?"

"Nothing, really, Luke," she said while fidgeting with her horse's reins. She wondered if she'd have the freedom to keep her own counsel in this marriage. It wasn't going exactly as she'd expected, and now Luke was behaving like he'd bit into a sour apple.

"Only . . . only, he said he'd try to find something for me." Luke adamantly waited for more and a peek at his face told her his patience was on a short fuse. "Oh, all right. He was going to find me a handgun."

"What for?"

"Well, I think that should be obvious," she told him with a note of disgust. "I don't own one."

"Jesse, I'll see that you have a weapon." He left Mehitabel's side and stepped closer to her. "You should have one here on the ranch, after all; you never know when you might run into a varmint. But why do you want one all of a sudden, and why didn't you come to me for it?"

"Um . . . I don't think . . ."

"And what were you gonna use to pay for it?"

"That's not any of your business." She gazed at him defiantly.

"Oh, no?" His brows lowered and anger laced his next words. "Everything about you is my business, now, Jesse Mae McCarthy, and we have to have one thing straight right this minute. You're my wife and I won't stand for secrets between us. Understand?"

"You can't expect me to—"

"Uh-huh, I do."

"Well, I . . . I—"

"Jesse."

She dropped her gaze and finally admitted, "My harp."

Luke was silent a moment, trying to read her face. His voice softened. "You'd sell your harp for a gun?"

"It's the only thing I have to sell." She started to turn away.

He'd known that. But she'd prized the musical instrument. He grabbed her wrist. "Why? Why, honey?"

"I can't take a chance, don't you see that?" she flared. "George wants to *kill* you. I felt too helpless before, I . . ."

Tears filled with desperation and love poured down her cheeks. Would he never understand? She would die a thousand times over if anything bad happened to Luke. She'd take that knife again without a second thought. Or a bullet. Whatever it demanded of her, she had to protect him.

"Oh, God, Jesse . . ." Shock at what she said, shock at what she implied . . . it all hit him anew, and his own wayward emotions melted.

He slid his long fingers to the back of her neck and used his thumb to tip her chin up. She hadn't been able to say the words, but she'd shown him her love once again.

Luke's thoughts shifted. George wanted to kill them both, he suspected. And the bastard probably thought he'd already done for Jesse when she'd stepped in to take that knife for him. Now she cried because she couldn't bear the thought of his facing more danger.

Luke thought he knew what she felt; he'd walked through hell those first hours after she was injured until he'd known she'd be all right. But she'd become unduly frightened of George. For her, George embodied all the attributes of Satan himself. He had to prove this snake was only a man.

"Don't cry, sweetheart." Wanting to comfort her, he laid his mouth against hers, tasting the salty tears, feeling the soft lips open for him. Whatever shyness or reservation she'd felt earlier was gone, he thought, and any idea of mere comfort fled his mind. She gave back all the passion he felt while she leaned into him and slid her arms around his waist. Her fingers dug into his back to pull him closer, sending his pent-up desire raging through his body, singing through his limbs. All logical thought left his mind.

He scooped her up with a swirl and strode a few paces toward the tall, thick grass not far from the creek and laid her down near the tree. The place afforded them a nest of their own. She didn't object.

Jesse glimpsed the raw hunger etching Luke's features and pulled his mouth down to hers once more.

She needed his kisses, even craved them. His hand rested on her breast, feeling sweet and erotic, before his fingers found her shirt buttons. Shakily, she searched for his, releasing the buttons one by one. He shuddered when she at last ran her palm over his bare chest, touching him lightly.

Then he fumbled with her jeans buttons and yanked at his own. A slight breeze lifted the smell of earth and grass to her nostrils while it rippled across her bare middriff.

"Luke," she whispered.

"Jesse, don't stop me. Not now . . ."

His voice stark, he tugged her pants down over her hips and went after the tie on her underdrawers.

"No . . . No, Luke, I won't, only . . ."

"What?" he said between kisses against her belly.

"Can you take off your guns? And your trousers, please?"

Whatever was to happen in the future, this was the now, Jesse hazily thought. She could no more have denied what they both wanted than to have refused to breathe.

Luke chuckled low in his throat at her polite request, elated by the husky passion he heard in her voice. "I reckon I could do anything to please my ladylove."

He shucked his clothes in less than a minute while Jesse watched with widening eyes. Eyes as green as the grass beside her, he mused. Her mouth bowed as it dropped seductively open, igniting him to flames.

"Now I know why women should wear skirts all the time," he mildly teased as he helped her off with her things in turn. She responded shyly with a bit of a giggle. He fell back on his elbows to look at her small form stretched beside him.

"Oh, Jesse."

He swallowed hard. He couldn't move. She was pink and white perfection, just as he'd suspected. Except for the ugly red scar. Yet it mattered only as a reminder. He wanted to . . .

"Oh, Jesse."

Her fiery hair tumbled over her shoulders almost to her waist while he buried his face between her breasts. She smelled of lavender.

Her touch tender, she cupped his head in her palms. Her thumb stroked his lower lip; Luke felt her touch deeply . . . oh, how he felt it. He gasped and pulled her thumb into his mouth. He heard her breath catch in turn. He brought her down against the length of his body, letting her feel his full arousal, letting her adjust to him, and then caressed her for long moments before he moved over her with care.

He made their joining as easy as possible for her, taking it slowly at first. In the end, she responded as wildly as he as they reached the pinnacle, wrapping herself around him with all the fervor that he could want. She held him as though she clung to life itself.

Her eyes closed against the noon sun. Jesse let herself float, sleepily wondering at this feeling of weightlessness. Yet Luke's knee over her felt very real and solid, his arm pinning her to him, heavy and warm. She drew a deep sigh. Their loving. She'd never known anything to make her feel so complete.

Oh, why did she have to fall in love with him? Against all her own best judgment. Now she was going to want this . . . this ecstacy for the rest of her life.

21

They climbed atop a huge boulder from which they could see a long distance.

"Will and I used to use this lookout point when we were boys," Luke told her. "Sometimes a band of Indians camped to the south of here. They don't come anymore."

He dropped to the hard stone and then cradled her between his legs to lean against him, his arm across her chest. His fingers lightly stroked her arm. He couldn't stop touching her.

She uncorked the water bottle and offered it to him. He swallowed deeply, then held it to her lips. She sipped, tipping her head back against his arm. He watched the movement of her mouth, and when a trickle of water ran down he leaned forward and caught it with his tongue. She shivered under the contact.

She said nothing. She'd made little conversation

since they'd left their spot downriver, and he wondered at her reticence. Had their loving made her shy? Hadn't she liked it? Was she sorry she'd married him?

"Look, there's Boswell leading the mules just coming along that ridge," he pointed out. "And Slim, Miguel, and the others. They'll be here in ten minutes or so."

Jesse nodded. He drew her closer so that he could nuzzle her neck. She didn't protest, yet he sensed her restlessness. Damn, he wished they'd had longer together before other people intruded. More time down in the long grass before they'd had to dress again. Their interlude, wonderful though it was, had been altogether too short. It left him wanting more. Much more.

And she'd remained quiet since.

Sniffing her hair, he slipped two of her shirt buttons free and slipped his hand through. Her softness filled his hand.

"They're closer," she murmured. Luke made a conscious effort to reel himself in, to put a clamp on his raging desire. He wanted her beneath him again. If only they didn't have serious business at hand.

He should be happy she had let him make love to her at all, and not be dissatisfied for what he didn't yet have. It had been . . . damn near perfect. She'd given him what he wanted. Yet something else, some quality of Jesse's still eluded him. And he wanted all of her.

He searched for what it was that bothered him, his thoughts circling. Jesse was his wife now, yet he was afraid she didn't quite believe it. As though there were things, or something, that wedged a gap between them.

Of course, she was still angry over his not telling her exactly who he was or about his total involvement with the M double C. And sure as shootin', a reminder was still coming over it. But he hoped it would be short and sweet, and then they could make it up with kisses. He'd make love to her again and show her how it didn't matter. After all, she couldn't fault him for having money when she'd expressed her desire to marry a man with enough wealth to provide for her.

No, that wasn't it. The elusiveness . . . It felt too much as though she'd given herself this morning as an act of . . . of contrition? desperation?

He mentally shook his head. No, that didn't quite capture it either. But her giving was a gift, nonetheless.

Then it dawned. That was it. She'd given him what she thought he'd wanted most. Her body. And she'd wanted him, too. But had her mind and heart been fully engaged in their lovemaking?

Luke drew a deep breath. For the moment, he had to put his own concerns aside. There would be time enough to think about them after they'd solved their problems with George, and he was itching to get it over with. Then maybe Jesse could find peace.

The oncoming men began their ascent up the long slope, so he stood up to show them where they were. Behind him, Jesse swiftly buttoned her shirt again.

"All set?" Luke asked Boswell when he arrived.

"Yep. Got everything. Sent Chunky into town like you said. Bear's coming along with a second string of horses. Said he'll catch up."

Luke lifted Jesse into her saddle, noting how right she looked on Sassy. The brown mare was a perfect mount for her. He'd let her know, soon, that the horse was hers. When the time was right. He thought her already too overwhelmed with new impressions and old worries.

"Let's ride," he commanded, fairly leaping onto Paint.

He nudged his horse into a trot, the other riders following suit. They followed the stream until they caught up with Crow, who waited beside a grove of pine.

Luke dismounted and turned to find Jesse had already done the same. While Boswell watered the horses, Luke and Jesse walked upstream with Crow.

"This is where they came out," Crow told Luke. "Two riders. Two cattle prints."

Jesse examined the tracks Crow pointed to. She had no trouble recognizing the bulls' hoof marks. And, almost lost in the weeds, a boot print.

"Luke, look here."

"Uh-huh. Looks like they dismounted for a bit."

"That's George's print. I recognize the way he walks." The track showed a deeper cut on one side, indicating the boot had a rundown heel with a notch in it and a rough side.

"Your wife is an observant woman," Crow said without looking her way, as though she wasn't there. "She'd make a good tracker."

"Yes, she has many talents and a great deal of spirit," Luke said and slid her a glance full of pride and teasing challenge. "To match her hair."

She didn't know why, but Jesse felt a warm glow at Luke's comments. Did he really think that? Did he really like her sometimes wayward spirit?

"What else have you found?" Luke asked Crow.

"The two men tuned north into the canyons, just as we thought. Found sign . . ." Crow trailed off and Jesse felt he'd stopped in deference to her.

"What sign?" Jesse prompted.

"One man used the whip."

"You mean on one of the bulls?"

Crow glanced at Luke, waiting for direction. Luke nodded.

"Yes, ma'am." Crow finally gave her a direct answer.

"Just like Mehitabel. Oh, the poor things. Meshach and Shadrach. How do you know?" She addressed Crow. "Where is this place? He didn't . . . he didn't kill it, did he?"

"No, ma'am. Found blood flecks. No carcass."

"When do you think this happened, Crow?" Luke asked. "We didn't discover the bulls missing till this morning."

Crow nodded. "Early. About sunup, maybe."

"That devil! He's a dirty rotten piece of garbage," Jesse exploded. "He's a horrible excuse for a man. I'd like to use a whip on him!"

"Calm down, now, Jesse. As long as he hasn't killed them outright, we'll get 'em back."

"But, Luke, you don't understand. He'll torture them. He loves that sort of thing. It gives him an odd sort of pleasure. It's only a wonder that Mehitabel got off so easy."

"I reckon Mehitabel gave as good as she got, honey. Or ran away. That likely explains the way she was found."

"Yep," Crow said. "That's another smart female."

"I wish we'd brought her," Jesse muttered plaintively. It seemed to her only right that the camel be with them when the crisis concerned the two bulls.

Luke was silent a moment. "Shall I send Crow after her?"

Jesse wanted to cry and rage, but it would do no good. "No, don't do that. Mehitabel will be better off where she is."

"I don't reckon we'll go any farther tonight," Luke said abruptly. It was still a couple of hours until sunset, and they could've pushed on.

But not Jesse. She was tuckered flat out. He didn't

think she had any extra strength to give on this trail ride. And he hadn't helped any, he admitted, by making love to her this morning. He'd been a selfish lout, a right self-indulgent fool to push her. It was a mark of her exhaustion that she hadn't put up a howl at their early camp.

Luke jerked his chin, and Crow turned and was gone in moments. He'd scout around to make sure the site was free of unwanted creatures. Luke then dispensed orders with a few quick commands and the men began to make camp.

Jesse started to unsaddle the brown mare, talking to the young horse. "Sassy. You're a pretty little lady. Where'd you get such a name, girl?"

"Named her myself," said Luke as he took over for her, giving her his impudent grin. "I like sassy ladies, haven't you noticed?"

"Are you referring to me?" She glanced at him over Sassy's back and raised her chin.

"I am." The corner of his mouth edged up.

"I never thought of myself as sassy," she said. "Just taking up for myself."

"You do that right well, honey. Don't reckon I'll get away with much for the next forty years or so."

"No, I don't think you should plan on it." His reminder that they were married and he expected to live with her for a lifetime felt a little unsettling. Forty years!

Needing to turn her thoughts, she asked, "What about the mare?"

"Trained Sassy as a filly. She's one nice little horse. You ride her as though she's always been yours."

"Always mine? What do you mean by that? I'm not used to . . . well, before I met you, I generally walked wherever I needed to go. I don't need to take your horse, Luke, when you need her for work. I guess if I have to ride, Rem will be quite enough, thank you."

"Un-unh, you don't understand, sweetheart." She still hadn't grasped the size of the M double C or his ability to provide everything she'd ever need. And, to be perfectly honest, he hadn't been very forthcoming about it. His idea of not wanting her to marry him for his money had gone way past where he'd wanted it to go.

Hell, the whole thing had blown up in his face like a whirlwind. Having Jesse help in a childbirth wasn't his favorite idea of how to spend their first night together as husband and wife. And now chasing ol' George wasn't the ideal honeymoon by any stretch of the imagination. Not a'tall.

But trail camping did offer some sweet opportunities. It reminded him of all those nights when he'd denied himself the chance to kiss her and hold her close. He'd honored her wishes and respected her chastity. Now that he had every right to, he planned to keep her as close as a mere two lips away every night. And if she hadn't liked the loving this morning, then he'd just have to make it so good she'd come to want it as often as he did.

He glanced at her pensive face as he threw down her saddle next to an outcropping of tiny white blossoms, then to where the men were spreading their things out down the slope to give them some privacy. He'd have to treat the boys to a drink, he reckoned, for their thoughtfulness.

He picked up what he'd been saying to her when his thoughts went maverick on him and finished his task.

"Out here you need to ride, Jesse, and we'll see to it you have several mounts to choose from. Country's too big to walk." He piled the saddles side by side, making a sort of wall.

"But I'm used to the mules."

"Jesse, you can have Rem and Rom both, since you like the dad-blamed mules so much." He took the reins off both mounts. "Do whatever you want with 'em. But I want you to have Sassy, too."

"She's a beautiful little mare, Luke. Are you sure?"

"As sure as the flowers in summer." He pointed to the carpet of white blossoms. "Roll out our blankets, honey. I'll be back in a few moments."

In truth, Jesse was more tired than she wanted to admit, but she daren't tell Luke for fear he might send her home. She fell asleep before he returned.

"Jesse." Luke half whispered next to her ear. "Wake up and eat something, honey. You haven't had a bite since breakfast."

"Tired," she protested.

"I know, honey, but you have to keep up your strength. Maybe I shouldn't have let you come after all."

That threat was enough. She sat up, rubbing her eyes like a child. He handed her a plate of beans and a piece of roasted meat and when she didn't immediately take a bite, he retrieved the plate, scooped up a spoonful and fed it to her.

"Stop," she mumbled when he tore off a morsel of beef. "I can do—"

"Now chew," he ordered as he placed it in her mouth.

"Luke . . ." she fussed while obediently chewing. Darkness had fallen. She must have slept for hours. She took the tin plate back. "I'll eat."

"Okay. Here's coffee. Watch it, it's hot."

"All right." She ate about half of what he brought her before she asked, "Has Crow come back?"

"Mm-hmm. Not ten minutes since. Would you like to visit the mules?"

"Oh, are Rom and Rem here? Yes, I think I would."

"Crow told the boys to bring them. Thought you'd like to have 'em close by." Luke had come to realize she felt a deep comfort in her friendship with the animals. By gum, he'd give her all of 'em she wanted if it would ease her way into their marriage.

"Oh, I'm going to like Crow," she said absently.

"Not too much, I hope," Luke returned teasingly.

"Only the proper amount, I do assure you," she said pertly. "I don't take up with men who aren't my best opportunities."

He chuckled. Even half-asleep she delighted him. "All right then, let's go." He pulled her to her feet and they strolled to the other side of the men's campfire.

"Evenin', Miz Jesse. Hope your sleep did you good." Boswell spoke to her from his spot around the fire. Several young faces looked at her, all a little shy and curious.

"Thank you, Boswell, it surely did."

"Evenin', Mrs. Luke," said another voice. She peered into the shadows to recognize who had spoken.

"Good evening, Slim. And the rest of you. Thank you for the supper. Whoever did the cooking, it was mighty good."

A young Mexican face beamed. The man doffed his wide brimmed hat. "Thank you, ma'am. It was a real pleasure to cook for a lady and not only for these unappreciative, down-at-heel range runners."

"Hey, look to who you callin' down at heel, you skinny, south-of-the-border . . . maverick," the speaker finished lamely, as though suddenly watching what he said.

A friendly argument broke out, but Jesse couldn't follow all of the jokes. Luke laughed. "Don't care who gets the better of this discussion, men, but just remember not to prance out your most colorful language. She don't need that kind of a show."

They left the men and found the horse tether. Jesse went down the line until she found the mules.

"Hello, there, fellas. I'm so happy to see you." Hearing her voice, they each turned toward her, Rom pressing his nose against her shoulder in greeting. She petted and rubbed their ears and seemed to relax. Luke hoped she felt better.

Afterwards, she strolled down the line, giving a greeting and a pat to every horse in the picket line, saving an extra few minutes for Sassy and Paint. Finally satisfied, Jesse headed back to the bedrolls.

"Ready to turn in?" Luke asked.

"I suppose so."

"All right. You go ahead and I'll be there shortly," he said as he stepped aside to speak to the men.

When Jesse reached the prepared bedrolls, she noticed they lay side by side with no space between. It seemed strange even though she and Luke had made love only a few hours before. She'd been all full of emotion and feelings, so much so that it scared her. She wasn't used to this married thing yet.

Stretching lazily, she then searched for her hairbrush, but couldn't find it. Had she forgotten it in her haste?

"Are you looking for this?" Luke asked her a moment later, holding it aloft.

"How did you know? And where did you find it?"

"I tucked it into my stuff while you changed into your riding clothes."

"Oh."

"Don't I get a thank-you?"

"Yes, of course. Thanks."

"Hmm. I was hoping for one of your more enthusiastic ones, honey. Like the time when I said we'd get your harp out of the freight office."

She flushed a little and dropped her gaze. "Well . . ."

Luke extended the brush out a few inches and waited to see what she would do next.

"Thank you, Luke," she said demurely. Very sweetly. Then she grabbed the brush, darted a kiss onto his cheek, and took off toward the river like a rabbit.

It was an out-and-out invitation to chase her, and he was glad to oblige. She was as quick as a little filly, but he wasn't a top cowhand for nothing, he told himself. He spun on his heel for the third time as she dodged him, and caught her by the back of the shirt.

"Gotcha," he crowed.

"Well, if I'd had my full strength back, you wouldn't have caught me so quickly."

"Uh-huh, and if I'd had my lariat, you'd never have gotten this far." He nodded toward the swiftly running river. "Did you want to wash?"

There wasn't much moonlight and she felt a little doubtful of the water's edge when she couldn't see what may be around. "Yes, I did. Would—would you stand guard for me?"

His pulses leaped. Would he? The husbandly task was more than welcome, and he was elated she'd asked. Still, he didn't want her unduly concerned. She shouldn't have to look over her shoulder every two seconds on the M double C for the rest of her life.

"Honey, none of my men would come near this place," he told her for future reference as he brushed a lock of hair from her cheek, "knowing you were bathing here. They'd respect not only you, but me and Will. But I'll stand guard against any four-legged varmints if it will make you feel better."

"I think I might like it better if I, um, know you're not far."

Inordinately pleased at the trust he heard in her voice, Luke made a husky plea of his own. "I might like it better if you invited me to join you."

"Oh, I . . ." Startled, she didn't know what to say. For seven long years she'd lived her life in fear and hiding from George, and even at times from the other Jeter men. When she'd thought of marriage, it had always been in terms of an older man who would make demands only on rare occasions. She never, in her wildest dreams, thought she'd be asked to bathe with a man.

Of course, she'd never dreamed she'd make love out in the wilds of Wyoming, either, with the kiss of a summer breeze, the stroke of tall grass brushing her bare skin, and the complete possession of a young lion of a man who carried her away from all reality.

"Don't you want me to?" His tone was soft.

"Well, I . . . I . . . Do you want to? I mean . . ."

"Uh-huh, I want to. But I won't if it upsets you." He leaned down to see her face more clearly in the deepening darkness. "Jesse Mae, I won't do anything" —he swallowed on an impossible promise— "before or unless you want to, too. Didn't you like it this morning?"

"Yes," she whispered.

Relief lifted a load from Luke's shoulders. He drew a deep breath. "Then was it too soon? Or . . . or too much?"

"I don't know about too soon, but I wanted . . . what happened. But I don't know what's too much or . . . or . . ."

Luke wanted to pick her up and run, wanted to laugh and shout in exhilaration. He found himself barely breathing.

"Would you like to find out? Down at the river? We can go upstream a ways. There's a bit of a pool there."

Slowly, she nodded her head.

22

Luke let Jesse sleep until well after sunup. He hated to wake her at all and, not for the first time, cursed his own weakness for wanting her near him. For not insisting she stay at home.

Yet their odd honeymooning pleased him beyond anything he'd imagined. If their first joining had been near-perfect, then last night in the river shallows had passed perfection. He'd teased her into total easiness about her nudity in front of him, telling her they were Adam and Eve for the night, let her scrub his hair, and in turn, brushed hers with long strokes, and finally, remained perfectly still while she explored his body. He'd kissed her toes, making her giggle, then worked his way up to her lips.

He'd carried her back to camp rolled in a blanket. She was asleep before he lay her down and barely moved from his arms all night.

This morning, though, he feared he'd exhausted her.

He traced her feathery auburn brows with one finger while the morning sun slanted onto her face. He had to wake her, and she wasn't going to like the decision he'd made, but the bulls had to be found and the ugly business of George had to be attended to. For her own sake, he had to send her home.

About an hour ago Crow had spotted a couple of riders behind them, one of them Will, they were certain. It would take about an hour for them to reach camp. He waited about half that time, and then a few moments ago, he'd sent the men on ahead with instructions for Boswell to return when Will caught up with them. Jesse would be more comfortable with the old man than merely with Will on the long ride home. Now he tucked Jesse's clothes underneath the blanket beside her body, letting his hand linger to stroke her warm bare skin.

"Mmmm. . ."

He heard the sensuous tone and cursed the fact he couldn't crawl under the blanket with her. "Rise an' shine, Jesse, honey," he whispered next to her ear. "Gotta go."

"Already?"

"'Fraid so. Have to find Meshach and Shadrach."

Her eyes opened and she sat up in a rush, instinctively holding the blanket close. "Oh, Luke! Why didn't you wake me sooner?"

"You needed the rest, honey. You ready to get up now?"

"Yes, of course. Where are the men?"

"Sent 'em on ahead. I'll catch up. But Sassy already thinks you don't like her 'cause she got left behind when the others took off."

"Sassy." She felt for her underthings and shook them out. "Where are the mules?"

"Crow took them with him. Don't worry, Jesse. We'll take good care of 'em."

If she hadn't been half-asleep, Luke thought, she'd have noticed his exclusion of her.

"I'm glad to hear that. Pour me some coffee, Luke, while I dress. I won't be a minute."

True to her word, she dressed in record time. She nibbled on the biscuit Luke brought her, rolled the blankets, then walked down to the cooking fire to kick dirt over it while Luke went to saddle the mounts.

Twenty minutes stretched into thirty. Jesse glanced toward the horses. Luke fiddled with a stirrup. It seemed to be taking him overlong, she mused, when they should be on their way.

Down trail, she heard a low whistle. Luke dropped Paint's stirrup. "It's Will," he told her. "And the sheriff."

They waited for the two riders to reach them.

"Catch any sign of 'em?" Sheriff Carey asked by way of greeting. His demeanor was stiffly serious as his hand rested on his sidearm.

"Sign aplenty," Luke replied. He pushed his hat back. "They wanted us to know they took the bulls."

"How many?" Will asked, his eyes cold.

"Only George and Eli, would be my guess," Luke replied, "unless they picked up any more partners out here in the canyons."

"Chunky said they'd done some damage to the camel." Will ignored Luke's sarcastic aside.

"Some. Looks like somebody took a whip to her with a heavy hand. Reckon she fought it, though, and ran back to the near pasture. That's how we found her."

"How is Mattie and the baby?" Jesse slipped her question in.

"Fine, Jesse, just fine," Will answered on a softer note. "Thank you for asking. And how are you making out? I didn't expect to see you among the hunting party after all the goings-on lately."

A quick glance at Luke suggested that Will's disapproval was directed at his brother instead of at her.

"I had to come. This has been my fight all along."

"Well, it's out of your hands now, Miz Jesse," the sheriff stated. "George Jeter and Eli Thoms are wanted by the law, and I'm here in my official duty. We just got word old man Sanderson's been murdered, out south of here. Men who did it tore up his place pretty bad. Took a wagon and foodstuffs, and the old man's pockets had been turned out."

"Old man Sanderson?" queried Luke. "How was it done?"

"With fists and a piece of stove wood, would be my guess. Pretty badly beaten."

"What makes you think it was George?" Jesse asked with a tremor.

Sheriff Carey shook his head. "No positive proof, but it seems likely to be them. Was two men. Sanderson had whip marks on 'im. Around his neck and his cheek. And we found a large hand print in the dust on the table. Not many men with that size of a paw."

Jesse felt sick. Another soul murdered? It seemed George's ugly nature had taken over completely.

"We aim to get 'em, dead or alive," the sheriff finished.

Had it really come to this, that George was being hunted down like a rabid dog? But given his uncontrollable character, she supposed it had been inevitable. She found it sorrowful only when she thought of Bertha. No matter what George was like, Bertha loved her son in her own lackadaisical way. On the other hand, the little Jeter girls would be safer; she had seldom allowed her fear for them to surface in her own need to escape the whole situation.

"What've the men found?" Will asked Luke. His gelding was restive, and he leaned forward and placed a hand against his neck to quiet him.

"Not much beyond the tracks. Crow thinks they'll hole up in one of the canyons."

"Unless they find the passage," Will remarked.

"What passage?" Jesse asked.

"There's an old outlaw trail in the mountains that can be reached through one of the canyons," Luke told her. "Ain't used much these days, leastways, not around here. A bunch of us cleaned out one of the hideaways a few years back."

Will let his frustration out with a heavy grunt. "Well, we better just hope to hell they didn't take the Herefords through there. It will take us better'n a week, possibly, to find 'em if they get into those back mountains. And all this travel ain't doin' the cattle any good, or us either."

"No, I reckon it ain't, so soon after bringing 'em home on foot," Luke conceded. He turned his attention to Sheriff Carey. "Are you planning to trail with us, then?"

"I'd like to, Luke. But I reckon I'd better get back to town. I might need to hire an extra jail guard after talkin' it over with Will, here."

"How about you, Will? Are you coming with us?"

"Nope. Reckon I'll leave it in your hands, Luke. I want to see Mattie settled at home before I take off for days. I'll speak to the men, though before I start back."

Luke nodded. "You can ride on ahead, Will. I'll be along after Boswell gets back down here."

Jesse's first sense of alarm hit her. "Why is Boswell coming back this way? Can't we just ride until we meet him?"

Luke examined her face intently. He couldn't put it

off any longer. "Jesse, I know you want to find Meshach and Shadrach as much as we do, but I'm gonna send you home with Will. Boswell can ride along."

"What? No—"

"You're not up to it, honey."

"That's not fair, Luke. I'm responsible for all of this. It's my fault. I've got to go."

He held up his hand, his anger rising. Why she felt guilty for what George did he didn't know, but he was beginning to understand her deeper thoughts. She'd been taking care of other people for so long that she still thought she had to fix everything herself.

"No ifs, ands, or buts, Jesse, and it ain't your fault," he insisted. "The trail's likely to get pretty rough from now on. You can't keep up right now, and I ain't takin' anymore chances on your recovery." Or safety, but she was likely to fight that one.

"But—" Jesse glared at him in silent accusation. How could he do this to her, send her home like he would a child? After last night, too, when he'd been so loving. Was this his idea of what marriage was about? He gave the orders and she blindly obeyed? It wasn't exactly what she'd bargained for, not at all, and he knew it.

Boswell rode up to them, halted, and said, "Okay, Luke, I'm ready." No one answered.

Jesse's hands tightened on her reins. What about Luke? It was *imperative* she watch out for him.

She was about to give him another scalding demand when she stole a look at Will and the sheriff. They pretended they didn't hear the argument by staring into the distance. But she knew they waited to see how she responded, waited to know if Luke "wore the pants in the family" or not, as Cousin Bertha would've put it.

Biting her tongue, she clamped her mouth shut. As

much as she didn't like it, she couldn't continue to argue or defy her husband in front of his brother or the sheriff.

Ruthlessly clapping a lid on her anger, she swung onto Sassy's back and reined her around smartly. "All right, Boswell. Let's go."

Luke watched her start down the trail, her back stiff. He knew she was angry enough to spit nails. He was only surprised he couldn't see little puffs of smoke coming from the top of her head. What went through his heart like a shaft, though, was that she hadn't bothered to say good-bye.

It was almost midnight when they rode into the ranch yard after dropping Boswell at the bunkhouse, yet a lamp burned in a window. Annabelle practically flew from the front door to help Jesse from her saddle.

"Oh, my dear. How could that rapscallion son of mine have done this? Taken you with him when you're still short of recovery. Chunky told me what happened. You're exhausted, and no wonder."

Jesse had her two feet on the ground, but she wasn't sure if they'd hold her. She silently commanded her legs to take her forward. "It's not Luke's fault, Mrs. McCarthy. I insisted on going."

"Well, come along into the house and we'll get you to bed." She turned to Will. "Any word on the Herefords, Will?"

"Naw, they haven't found them yet. They will, though, Ma, so you don't need to worry. Luke will find 'em. Got any coffee on?"

"Sure do, son."

As tired as Jesse was, she hardly knew how to behave when they entered the house. She felt awkward and shy; the few hours she'd spent there was as a stranger. This was Luke's home, and his mother's. She hung back.

"Jesse, I know just what you need, dear. You run along into your bedroom and I'll bring you a pan of hot water. I know you'll feel better for a quick wash. Then get into your night things. I'll be there in a shake."

Jesse murmured her thanks and did as she was told. If she felt like a child, she'd just have to think about it later, she decided. When she could think without falling asleep on her feet.

Moments later, she felt a wave of despair as she searched her old carpetbag for the second time. Her nightgown simply wasn't there. How could she have left it behind?

A light rap on the door brought her head up. "Come in," she answered. Since she'd had so little of it in the past, Jesse thought she should welcome the respect her mother-in-law showed by knocking before entering, but somehow she couldn't summon the energy.

"Oh, I see you're not quite ready yet," Annabelle said as she set a pan of hot water on the dresser. "Can I help you, dear?"

Jesse knelt on the floor beside her carpetbag. She swallowed hard and pretended to search once more; she couldn't let her mother-in-law see that she was close to tears over so silly a thing. Luke was right, she supposed. She wasn't quite up to snuff after all. "I don't know how I've been so careless, but I guess I've left my nightgown behind at Mrs. Fry's house. I suppose I'll have to sleep in my underthings."

"What about your new things, Jesse?"

"What new things?"

"Oh, dear." Annabelle smoothed a hand over her salt and pepper hair. "Well, it isn't my place to tell you, Jesse, but Luke filled up a whole drawer in that wardrobe," she nodded toward the huge piece of furniture that filled the corner, "with personal things for you. The top drawer, I think. Why don't you see if a nightgown is there?"

Curiosity and a warm glow brightened Jesse's lagging energies. She hadn't had many presents in her life. All at once she realized how many she'd already received from the man who was her husband.

Tentatively, she pulled open the top of three drawers. It was filled almost to overflowing with pretty but practical wear. Astounded as well as a little embarrassed, she glanced at Luke's mother.

"Excuse me, dear," Annabelle said hastily. "I must see to Will. Call me if you need anything else."

Jesse turned back to the chest. Three nightgowns, one made of fine foulard trimmed with lace and blue ribbon down the entire front center. The thin cloth made her blush to even think of wearing it. Of the other two, one was flannelette, obviously for cold weather, and the third a plain cotton one. Even it had tiny tucks from the neckline to the waist.

Also, she found chemises, bloomers, stockings, camisoles, petticoats, and one pink satin corset, like the one lent to her by Josie for the wedding. And a padded bustle in one corner. There were two sets of clothes, she noticed: one for dressy occasions and the other, with a greater number of items, for everyday wear.

What other treasures did the armoire hold, she wondered. Her curiosity getting the better of her, she opened the second drawer. Masculine, well-worn underdrawers, socks, shirts, and on top, a new man's nightshirt.

She examined the round neck and buttons down the front. For some reason she couldn't imagine Luke in that; she'd received the distinct impression he'd rather sleep in the nude. Had he bought it because of her?

The third drawer held sheets and towels. New ones.

Remembering the morning she had wakened in this room, she looked for Josie's wedding dress and Luke's suit in the top. They were there, hanging side by side. And two new cotton dresses, one in a bright blue stripe and one in a serviceable rusty brown, and a third dress, a soft, deep green silk. It had its own petticoat to match.

From a hook, a cotton sunbonnet made to match the blue dress hung from its strings.

She fingered the cloth of each dress, noting their simplicity, yet how well made they were. Somehow, she knew that Luke had chosen each one. Perhaps with Josie's help, but his choice, nevertheless. A wave of amusement surfaced; indecisive, her husband wasn't.

Her old dresses would appear rather sad next to the new ones, she thought. Then she abruptly realized something she hadn't noticed before. None of her old clothes had been in her bag except for the blue traveling suit. She wondered what had happened to them, and decided she'd investigate that tomorrow.

Through the door she heard Will leaving and Annabelle calling good night and decided she'd better get into bed, so she washed quickly and donned the plainest of the two nightgowns, the one with the tucks. She had just pulled the sheet up when another rap sounded on her door. She called for her mother-in-law to enter.

"Now, my dear, are you ready for the night? I've brought some warm milk to help you sleep soundly." Annabelle handed her a mug filled to the brim.

"Yes, thank you." She tasted the milk. It held a flavor of honey. "Mmmm. My mother used to put a little honey in a cup of warm milk at bedtime when I was small."

"Did she? Well, I must admit I always loved a little warm milk with honey at bedtime from my girlhood days, especially if I was overtired or not feeling well. I remember a friend and I—oh, Jesse, here I am rattling on while you can hardly keep your eyes open. Sleep, my dear, and don't let anything worry you. We have plenty of protection out here, you know. Will left a couple of the hands on night watch."

Jesse mumbled her thanks as Annabelle closed the door once more behind her. She'd been wonderfully cosseted by her mother-in-law, and the feather mattress under her was the most comfortable she'd ever experienced. But as she slipped into sleep, she heartily wished for Luke. The ornery, sweetly beguiling . . . weasel! He'd sure enough get an earful from her when he returned home.

All the same, she'd rather have been lying on the rocky ground beside him where she could feel his touch and know he was safe, than here in this feather bed alone. It was an odd sensation, this. Not feeling complete without him.

Jesse laid down the needlework Josie had given her. For the last hour she'd diligently tried to stitch the tiny leaves to turn just right on their stems, with only mild success. She'd never be much good at fine needlework, she concluded. She hadn't the patience.

Jesse didn't know how much longer she could stand this inactivity and rose to pace around the room. She hadn't heard Annabelle moving about the house for quite a while and wondered where she had disappeared to.

Yesterday, Annabelle had insisted she spend the

day resting, and by evening she wanted to throw the book she'd been reading across the room in frustration. Even her injury hadn't helped her deal with gentle activities in contrast to vigorous ones, and she thought she'd been better off if she'd had to do a full day's laundry or salt down hams.

Today had been a little different; Annabelle had taken her along when she went to make sure Mattie's house was in readiness for her homecoming tomorrow. Will had sent out a woman from town, Juanita, as a housekeeper, and Jesse stood by as Annabelle helped the new employee settle in. Jesse thought Will and Mattie's large house roomy and invitingly comfortable, yet she realized she liked the older one just as well, with its cozy, lived-in rooms.

Now, after two days, Jesse sighed with the waiting and useless frustration. Why hadn't they heard anything? There had been no direct word from either Will or Luke, and nothing from town to indicate any suspicious activity.

Jesse wandered into the parlor. Annabelle sat quietly reading by the window that looked out toward the ranch buildings. A black Bible filled her lap. She appeared contemplative and deep in thought. Jesse started to back away.

"Hello, my dear," Annabelle said, catching her just as she turned. "I suppose you're bored with resting, hmm? May I do anything for you?"

"Oh, I . . . please excuse me. I didn't mean to intrude."

"You didn't, Jesse. I always read a little Scripture in the afternoons. It comforts me, especially when the boys are gone and there's trouble brewing." She patted the open pages as though they were alive, then reverently closed the book and laid it aside.

"Come and sit down for a bit. We've had scarce enough time to visit since . . . well, my word, I'm not sure we ever did, properly, did we? What with one thing and another we've been on hilly terrain, so to speak. At the top of the mountain one day and down it the next."

Jesse sank onto the stool near Annabelle's chair. She really did like Annabelle, but it was as she'd said. They hadn't had much time to get acquainted beyond dealing with one crisis and another.

"There's a letter here for Luke from the Pearsons that Chunky picked up today in town. You might as well open it, Jesse."

"Oh, I couldn't." She examined the envelope curiously. "It's addressed to Luke." She bit her lip. The Pearsons? George had destroyed their barn, she remembered. And what else? Her heart ached for the hardship Effie and John faced once more.

"Luke won't mind, Jesse. You're his wife, after all, and you both count the Pearsons as friends, as I understand it."

"Yes, of course. Effie was most kind and generous when I . . . we needed help." She glanced shyly at her mother-in-law. "You know the story?"

"Luke told us all about it the night he got back, Jesse."

So Annabelle had known everything about her all along? Embarrassed and relieved together, all Jesse could murmur was a soft "oh."

After a moment, she allowed Annabelle to convince her it was all right to open the letter. She read swiftly, then glanced up with amazement. "They're coming out here to the M double C! Luke has offered John a place."

"Yes, he and Will agreed on it. There's a small piece of land a ways from here that already has some improvements on it. Will and Luke bought the homesteader out mostly as a favor a year back, but now we're all glad to pass it along to your friends."

"How wonderful! Oh, you are so kind. Luke is very generous, isn't he?" She couldn't help it. Her thoughts kept reverting to her husband.

"You know, you certainly do remind me of a friend I had when I was a girl," Annabelle continued to chat. Jesse thought it was to give them both something else to think about besides what Luke might be running into. "She was younger than I, but we shared a lot of time together at school. I've thought about it more than once since you were injured. It's not only your hair, either, Jesse, it's something . . ." Annabelle shook her head as though she hadn't quite captured it yet.

"Well, Mama always said I looked like my pa's mother except for my hair," Jesse chuckled. "Papa said it and my quick temper came from my mother's family. But I remember other folks saying I had eyes like Mama."

"That's it! Your eyes. They remind me of Elizabeth's."

Jesse felt goose bumps race up her arms. "My mother's name was Elizabeth," she whispered. "Elizabeth White."

"Oh, I don't believe it." Annabelle eagerly leaned forward, her hand on Jesse's. "Elizabeth White was your mother?"

Jesse felt very confused. "It couldn't be the same Elizabeth White, though. Luke told me you came west from Illinois. My mother came from Ohio. It was Papa who was from Missouri."

"But, my dear Jesse, I grew up in Ohio, too. I met Richard, Will and Luke's father later, after I was in school where I knew Elizabeth. Why, it has to be the same Elizabeth. You're so like her."

"Do you really think so?" Jesse responded, stunned

with the thought of a connection. Her heart lifted. "I never knew any of Mama's people, only a few stories of when she met Papa and how she grew up. I have her harp."

"Yes! I knew there was something more. Elizabeth was learning the harp. Oh, I'm sure it was the same Elizabeth White. Why, this calls for a celebration, Jesse," Annabelle said and quickly hugged her. "What a wonderful surprise. To find that the lovely new daughter-in-law my son brought me is the child of an old, dear friend."

Warmth crept over Jesse at the lively sincerity she saw in Annabelle's eyes.

"What shall we do to celebrate?" Annabelle said with a smile. "Oh, I know. Let's go into town tomorrow and attend the circus. I think the matinee is the last performance."

"But, wouldn't that upset Luke and Will?"

"Oh, pooh." Annabelle hopped up from her chair, excited as a chipmunk in an oak tree. "We have to keep our spirits up, don't we? And we have Chunky, and we can take one of the other boys. Sandy's a good man. He'll see that we're well protected."

Jesse grinned. She did like her mother-in-law. A lot.

"All right, Mother McCarthy. Let's go."

23

"*I can't believe I've been* such a dad-blamed fool," Luke muttered under his breath. Crow had just pointed out where the bulls and one rider had doubled back only a quarter of a mile from where they'd camped two nights before. They'd missed them by mere hours last night. Or minutes. Under cover of darkness, of course, but it still shouldn't have happened. He should have spread his men wider.

"Where's the other one?" he asked Crow.

"Gone north. Then east."

"To Wayside?"

"Maybe."

"Hell!"

Crow waited a moment for Luke to control his anger. "Wasn't the big one."

"It wasn't George." Luke felt a mountain-high relief flood him, recognizing the paralyzing fear that came with the idea of Jesse's being in danger again. "Then Eli. Must have gotten impatient to know what was happening with Archie."

"Want me to ride for the ranch?" Crow asked. "Or town?"

"Neither, just yet. If it's only Eli, he won't . . ." He shook his head and spread his hand. "I don't give a damn about Eli as long as he stays out of my path. The law will get him eventually. But George has a personal grievance, to his way of thinking. He's an all-fired mammoth threat to my Jesse. Let's stay on his tail."

They mounted and rode back to where the rest of the men waited. He gave his instructions in a clipped command.

"Slim, you and Miguel range wide to the east, Crow to the west, and the rest of you spread through the middle. Stay within shot range, but stay quiet, stay low. If you find the bulls, don't try to tackle the bastard that has 'em on your own. Use your guns only as a last resort. We want those Herefords back alive, and George might kill 'em if he thinks he's caught. Now go."

She and Annabelle at the circus! Jesse had never attended such a performance, and in spite of her worries, she felt excited by the prospect. She recalled Mrs. Fry's guests and all that they had told them about their acts. Trapeze artists. Clowns. And a real tiger.

At her mother-in-law's urging the next day, Jesse donned the blue striped dress with its bonnet to match. It made her feel elegant and ready for town. Imagine, three new dresses all at one time. She felt young and almost carefree.

Almost, but not quite. Part of her didn't like going without Luke. It didn't seem fair.

Annabelle covered her own anxieties rather well, but even so, Jesse felt her undercurrent of concern. Yet her mother-in-law wouldn't voice it nor allow Jesse to say much about it either as they drove to town.

They stopped off at Mrs. Fry's to see Mattie and the baby. Will, busily loading the buckboard with the three baskets of things Mattie had collected over the days of her confinement, looked up in surprise.

"Morning, Ma. Jesse. What are you two doing in town this morning?"

"Jesse and I simply had to have a diversion," Annabelle explained as she climbed down from the buggy. Jesse departed the vehicle as well, eager to see little Constance wrapped in a pink blanket and held in her mother's arms. Four-year-old Christopher dangled precariously over the back of the seat by his feet while three-year-old Daniel swung from the wheel. Automatically, Jesse laid a hand on Christopher's back to keep him from falling.

"And we thought we might take the boys and Josie's girls along with us," Annabelle added. "We'll attend the matinee and then bring the boys home with us afterwards. We'll be home before dark."

"Who d'you have with you?" Will asked, his eyes showing his concern.

"Chunky and Sandy."

"Sandy's good." Will approved of their escorts, then glanced at Mattie. "I reckon it'd be all right. The boys have been chattering like a couple of blue jays to go."

"Are you sure you want to take them, Mother McCarthy?

"Yes, of course. Don't we, Jesse?"

"Yes, Mattie, let them come."

"How about it, boys? D'you want to go to the circus with Grandma?" Mattie asked the dark-eyed boys.

"Hooray," Christopher shouted as he wriggled from underneath Jesse's hand and rolled into the seat.

"'Ray," echoed Daniel.

"I have Steve and Chute with me," Will said, tipping his head at the two young men standing casually by their mounts. "I'll send 'em back for you."

"If you think that's necessary, son," Annabelle acceded.

Jesse listened to all the preparations in awe. Men who worked for the M double C seemed to roll out from nowhere. Again, she wondered just how far the McCarthy ranch spread and how many men it employed. No wonder that scalawag Luke had insisted he could afford to hire her as a housekeeper. He could have paid her salary twice over, while she'd bit her lip nearly through worrying about where he was to find the money.

Slow as a snail on winter ice was what she'd been, Jesse thought as they took the two little boys up with them, exchanging the buggy for the buckboard to give Mattie an easier ride home. They headed toward Josie's.

With all this power and wealth behind him, how easy it would've been for Luke in the beginning to simply wait and board the next day's train with his bulls. To have reached his destination within a reasonable time instead of jaunting all over the countryside with her in tow. How easy to straighten the matter out with the train authorities, to have made a complaint of their mischief against George and the Thomses with Hinley's local sheriff, and then be done with it. He could have chosen a number of ways to handle his situation without getting involved with her. He could have ignored her, simply left her to solve her own problems.

Why, then, hadn't he? Why hadn't he done the easy thing, the sensible thing?

Her heart already knew why. Jesse felt a thunderbolt dazzle her mind, nearly tumbling her from her perch. It was easy to guess why when she listened to her heart. Luke loved her. He *loved her*.

Oh, she had heard him say it. More than once. But what were mere words? Her pa had said he loved her, and then abandoned her to the Jeters without a backward glance. George had said he wanted her. Yet his desire held no resemblance to love or caring. Bertha's husband said he loved his wife, yet he was too lazy to improve their living conditions from year to year, leaving Bertha and the children to live in near-squalor while he spent money on his own wants.

Luke was so different from the men she'd known. Luke had given her every consideration. He had backed his words with action.

"Here we are," Annabelle said. "Jesse, you sit with the children while I just run up and collect Josie and the girls."

"Yes, ma'am."

The boys clamored to go too, but Annabelle waved them down before she disappeared into the store.

Chunky eased in his saddle and gazed at the bustle of the town while Sandy dismounted and strolled up the street.

At the far end of the street a horn, drum, and tambourine sounded a lively marching tune. Two clowns followed, one riding a bicycle with a huge front wheel and one wearing a very tall hat, bowing to the people. Led by the woman Jesse had met at Mrs. Fry's boardinghouse dressed in a short costume whirling a long stick, the performers marched toward them. The tiny band drew the people along the streets into their circle with a marvelous sense of magical excitement.

Jesse and the boys all leaned forward to get a better view.

"I want the circus," Daniel demanded.

"Can't we go now?" questioned Christopher.

"Not yet," Jesse answered. "Your grandmother hasn't come with Beth and Belle. Don't you want to wait for your cousins?"

Daniel crawled into Jesse's lap, and then stood up to look over her shoulders. She held his little waist tightly.

The marchers, attended by laughing, running children as well as smiling adults, came closer.

"Let me down." Daniel twisted suddenly and jerked from her arms. She dived for him just as he had one leg over the side of the buckboard. She had him in a minute and settled against the backrest, only to discover that Christopher was gone.

She swiftly looked around her, spotting him as he ducked between two men and headed for the performers. "Chunky," Jesse called. "Sandy."

Sandy hurried toward her. "What is it, Miz Jesse?"

"Christopher," she answered, pointing toward where she'd last seen the boy. He wasn't there now.

"Chunky, you stay with Miz Jesse," Sandy ordered and sprinted away.

Annabelle came out of the store with Josie and the two little girls. "What's the matter, Jesse?"

"It's Christopher. He's—" Jesse spotted the child on the far side of the street peeping from under the belly of a nervous horse. He appeared to have no idea that he was in a dangerous position. She couldn't see Sandy at all. "Oh, here," Jesse said as she thrust Daniel toward his grandmother and leaped from the buggy.

On the outskirts of town, Eli rode toward the jail from the alley. He dismounted and left his horse behind the barbershop's shed and bathhouse next door. It was unlikely to generate suspicion there even if seen.

His luck was about to change. The circus parade made enough racket to draw most of the town's attention. He waited until the alley was deserted before approaching his objective, the one window in the jail's back wall. He made his way to it quietly and whispered. "Archie."

He heard a rustling, then a huge, beefy hand circled one of the lack steel bars. "Who's there?"

"It's me."

"Eli! It's 'bout time," Archie hissed in anger. "Where the hell you been?"

"Couldn't get here sooner, Archie. Town's swarmin' with lawmen." Eli glanced nervously over his shoulder.

"Why din'tcha jest kill some of 'em and get me outa here?"

"Ain't that easy, Archie. Look, jest lay low. George an' me are workin' on a plan." He didn't tell his brother that the plan didn't seem to be working. George was as stupid as a rock and thought of nothing but Jesse Mae.

"How soon? How soon ya gettin' me outa here?" Archie whined. "They're fixin' to mebbe hang me, Eli."

"It won't be long, Archie. What happened to them two-bit cowards that were s'posed to be gunmen we brung along?"

"They was let go three days back. Sheriff said he couldn't keep 'em any longer 'cause he couldn't find where they was wanted men."

Some of the excitement of the circus spilled around the corner as the clanging of symbols reached them. The parade passed down the street, taking the onlookers with them.

"Gotta go, Archie. Ain't healthy here in daylight. But I'll be back."

"When? When, Eli?"

"Tonight."

Jesse finally caught up with Christopher. He was none the worse for wear, but she thought it only by the grace of God, because the child dashed between horses' hooves and rolling wagon wheels like a little squirrel.

"Christopher!" She held her breath as he landed on his feet jumping from a grocery crate. "Your grandmother is waiting. Don't you want to go see the circus?"

"I'm watching the circus right now."

Most of the parade had moved on, and the child strained away as she caught his hand.

"But we have to get tickets and go to the big tent outside of town," she reasoned. "We can't see any of their tricks if we don't. Wouldn't you like to see the tiger?"

"A tiger?"

"Yes, I heard there's a tiger with the circus."

"What's a tiger?"

"Why don't we go along and find out."

"Okay."

Christopher at last allowed her to keep his hand, and they joined the stragglers to return to where they'd left the buckboard, Annabelle, and the others.

"You're my new Auntie Jesse, aren't you?" Christopher asked, scrutinizing her face.

"Yes, I guess I am." She smiled down at the boy. He was a handsome, brown-eyed child with none of the grubby look that seemed to characterize the Jeter boys no matter how she'd tried to keep them neat.

They passed the jail. The very fact that Archie Thoms was there made her shiver. She looked away. Then, perversely, she stared at the front of the building in defiance of her fear. It was only a building. Furthermore, it had a guard.

George should be in there, locked up tight. Where was he? More to the point, where was Luke? She fervently wished she knew that he was all right. If he hadn't forced her to leave him, she would know.

"My daddy doesn't like that bad man in there, does he?"

"No, I guess not."

"And Uncle Luke. He was mad as fire when you got hurted. Mama said Uncle Luke might blow that ol' jailhouse up."

"Well, I don't think he'd do a thing like that. Hurry, now." She glanced back over her shoulder nervously as they crossed the street. A half second's glimpse of a man between the buildings caught her attention. Small and dressed in black, he resembled Eli.

Jesse mentally shook her head; surely not. She must have imagined it. Eli and George were out in the wilds somewhere.

"Here we are at last," she said, pushing her anxiety down as they reached the buggy where Annabelle sat while Josie waited by the roadside. The other children were clamoring noisily to go.

"Christopher, you naughty little scamp," Annabelle scolded. "I swear you'll catch it if you do that again."

"I wanted to see the circus," Christopher defended himself, not understanding what all the fuss was about.

"Well, that's where we're heading. Now where has Sandy disappeared to? Oh, bother. Josie, Jesse, get in and let's be on our way. He'll catch up to us, and I don't want to miss the opening. No telling when another circus might come to Wayside Station."

Lifting the children into the back of the buckboard, Jesse climbed in beside them and forgot about the figure she'd seen between the jailhouse and the barbershop. Until later.

Jesse casually mentioned the sighting to Sandy as he rode alongside the carriage as they left town. She sat in the wagon bed with little Christopher asleep in her lap while Annabelle, on the seat, held Daniel.

They'd stayed to have supper with Josie and her family, so that now dusk had caught them on the way home. She felt perfectly safe, though. True to his word, Will had sent two more riders into town to escort them home. One of them, Steve, handled the team.

"Miz Jesse, why didn't you tell me sooner?" Sandy asked, a note of alarm in his tone. "I could have found the man. Or reported it to Sheriff Carey."

"Well, I suppose I really didn't credit that the man I saw was really Eli Thoms," she replied slowly. "I assumed Eli would still be with George Jeter."

Sandy said nothing more, but when the buggy rolled up to Will's house to deliver the boys, he mentioned it to Will. Her brother-in-law handed the sleeping younger child to Juanita before he lifted his older son from her lap.

"You saw Eli Thoms, Jesse?" he asked her.

"I'm not exactly sure, Will. I only caught a glimpse of the man. It seemed so unlikely that Eli would come into town in broad daylight. Besides, wouldn't he be with George somewhere?"

"Don't know, but I think we should let Ned Carey know about it. Have you heard from Luke?"

"Why, no. I was hoping you had."

Will frowned while Annabelle, taking one look at Jesse's face, said, "Luke will be home any time now, I'm sure, Jesse. After all, those bulls weren't that far ahead of them, and the rustlers, whoever they are, don't know this territory like the boys do. Luke will be home soon," she repeated.

"Chute," Will commanded the lean rider with the tied-down gunbelt, "ride back into town and let Sheriff Carey know that Mrs. McCarthy thinks she saw Eli Thoms in town today."

Jesse fervently hoped she hadn't steered anyone wrong. "It was only a glimpse, Will. I'd hate to send anyone on a wild goose chase."

"Don't worry about it, Jesse," Will assured. "Better checked and wrong than nothing checked and sorry."

In spite of Annabelle's honey-flavored milk, Jesse slept poorly. She rose at dawn feeling she needed to do something—anything—to resolve the troubles she'd brought down on the McCarthys.

She slipped out of the house before the sun was up and walked purposefully toward the barn corral. A lone lantern shone from the cookshack; she sidled away from it and the bunkhouse where male voices already hummed. Breakfast would be on the table shortly, she guessed.

She waited in the barn shadows until the clanging sounded to call the men to breakfast and listened as half a dozen men trooped into the dining room attached to the cookshack. Hauling her saddle out, she called low, "Sassy. Come on, girl, let's go for a ride."

By the time the sun popped over a hill, Jesse was almost out of sight of ranch headquarters. She twisted in her saddle to give one last look. Thankfully, no one had seen her leave, so no one had objected to her riding out alone.

Pointing Sassy's nose in the direction where she and Luke had left Mehitabel, she nudged her mare into a trot. Chunky had told her that he'd led the camel back there after keeping her close by for a couple of days.

Jesse felt perfectly confident about riding alone after all the riding she'd done in recent weeks. It didn't take her long to crest the last hill and race down the slope toward the river and the tall grass. The wind whipped through her hair, and all her hairpins went flying.

She rode around a curve and glanced about her. The camel didn't seem to be near the tree where they'd found her before. Avoiding the place where she and Luke had made love for the first time, she circled the area before heading west toward the huge boulders on the hilltop. Luke's lookout.

The warm sun on her back promised a hot midsummer day. Jesse remembered the heat in Luke's hands as he had caressed her that morning, and she longed to feel them again. It seemed like twice the time since they'd parted. For the dozenth time she wondered where Luke could be, and for the first time it overshadowed her anger at him for sending her home.

She dismounted and then searched for the footholds Luke had shown her in the largest of the outcropping boulders. Climbing it alone proved more difficult than she'd anticipated, but stubbornly, she kept at it until she reached the top. Dusting off her knees, she stood. Slowly, she began to turn in a tight circle, narrowing her eyes against the rising sun as she watched for any signs of Mehitabel.

A dozen or more longhorn cattle dotted a nearby hill, grazing peacefully, and the horizon beyond held more. She ought to head there. Perhaps the camel had sought company.

For good measure, she made another slow circle. Movement on a far hillcrest caught her atention.

24

Luke! Her heart picked up its beat. She wanted to shout with gladness at knowing he was home at last. Unknotting her yellow bandanna, she waved it aloft. The lead rider hesitated and then lifted his hat to return the wave. Sunlight gleamed on the bare head. Yes, it was her husband.

The rider kicked his horse into a gallop, outdistancing his companions in seconds. Jesse turned and slid her way down from the high perch. Swiftly, she mounted Sassy and pivoted her toward the direction that would bring her into Luke's path. It took a few moments for Luke to come into view again.

She reached the first part of the herd she'd seen from the boulder and discovered there were at least a hundred head there. Most of them had been hidden from view, she supposed, and hundreds more spread out along the shallow valley. Weaving her way, she came to the crest of the hill and waited.

Luke arrived in moments, a smile lighting his eyes. Without missing a heartbeat, he swept her from her saddle and across his lap, laying his mouth against hers in sweet, hot demand. She couldn't help herself. She gave the kiss back to him in kind.

"Mmm, Jesse, you're too damn real to be a mirage, thank God. Thought I might be going loco from wanting you," he murmured, and then took her mouth again. She responded by laying her palm against his cheek, her fingers stroking his ear.

His mount moved restlessly, and Luke reluctantly ended the kiss. He held her close, scrutinizing her face.

"What are you doing out here, honey? You're not alone, are you?"

"Not any more," she said with a mischievous giggle, snuggling closer.

"None of the hands somewhere beyond that hill?"

"Un-unh . . ."

He couldn't quite believe it. But a swift glance around showed him only cattle and countryside. "Damn, you shouldn't be . . ." Yet he couldn't resist one more kiss before he scolded her. The days they'd been separated felt like a month.

Jesse felt as scorched as if she'd put her hand onto a hot stove. His mouth and tongue explored hers, flooding her with desire.

The other riders came over the hill behind Luke. She heard them halt and tried to pull away, but Luke wouldn't immediately let her go. She hated to protest, but she was already embarrassed enough at what she knew his men saw. "Luke."

"All right." He sighed and let her sit up but his eyes

showed banked desires ready to flame at a moment's encouragement.

Sassy cropped grass a few yards from them. Luke nudged Paint over to the mare and swung Jesse into her own saddle. He bent, found her reins, and handed them to her.

He eased back in his saddle. "Now, Jesse, tell me what you're doing so far from the house by yourself."

"I've been a little worried about Mehitabel. I came to see her."

"Couldn't you have sent one of the men to bring her up to the house for you?"

"I'm used to doing things for myself, you know, not setting someone else to do my work."

"Uh-huh. Little Miss Independent, ain't you? Do you think no one else can do a thing as well as you?"

"No, of course not, but I'm quite capable of being on my own." What was making him so bossy all of a sudden, she wondered?

"I don't want you to ride out this far alone anymore," he grumbled.

"I wasn't lost, Luke," she argued. "Only I—" She stopped speaking and glared at him. She'd been lonely as a desert for him, but she'd be danged if she'd tell him that now. Besides, the toad still had several points against him for which she intended to extract finer explanations before she could fully forgive him.

"Well, where is the beast?"

"I don't know. I was looking for her when I saw you. Did you find Meshach and Shadrach?"

"No, not yet," he said, his tone short. His men came up to them and greeted her with a nod or a "howdy, ma'am" before Luke finished his explanation. "Trail doubled back this way. You haven't seen anything suspicious this morning, have you?"

"No, though . . ." She bit her lip, studying the tired lines around her husband's eyes. He was decidedly out of sorts at not finding the bulls and the culprits. Perhaps that really had been Eli she'd seen yesterday.

"Though? What is it, Jesse?"

"Yesterday your mother and I went into town. To see the circus's last performance, you know. Anyway, the circus people paraded down Main Street, sort of in farewell, I guess, and while I was watching, I saw someone who looked like Eli."

"You saw Eli in town?" His tone was incredulous.

"Well, I'm not exactly sure. I got only a glimpse. Anyway, Will sent Sandy back to tell the sheriff about it last night."

"I see. It was most likely Eli, all right. Crow found where he and George split up. That's why we're back toward home. Reckon we'll have to start again."

"Oh. Well, I wish we could find Mehitabel. I'd feel a lot easier if we could bring her back to the barn."

"Don't want you out here by yourself, Jesse. I'll help you find her." Luke turned toward his men. "Okay, fellas, you can go and have breakfast and then grab a couple of hours' sleep. But I want you back at the lookout rock by noon. With fresh supplies. Crow, you report to Will right off, and Slim, you ride up to the house and let Mrs. McCarthy know that Jesse is with me."

"Sure thing, Luke," Slim replied.

The others tipped hats or nodded and wheeled their horses, but not before Jesse caught a couple of half-hidden grins. They didn't expect them to really search for the camel at all, she supposed. She let her gaze drop while the color crept up her face.

"Where've you looked?" Luke asked her.

"Down by the river. By that cottonwood tree where we found her before."

"Let's try north a ways. Across the stream."

"All right."

Luke led the way. Jesse kneed Sassy to follow. They retraced the path that she'd taken and came out close to the river down from the tree. Slowing, Luke chose a low, shallow spot to cross and directed Jesse to watch her mare's footing. They paused to let the horses water, then started away from the river on the other side.

It was new territory for Jesse. She looked around at tangled brush and vines that lined the river in this section.

"Do the cattle get caught in that scrub sometimes?" she asked Luke, remembering how hard it was to keep their milk cow out of rough places back on the Missouri farm. One time it had taken her and two of the Jeter children half a day to climb down a rocky ravine after Molly.

"A few have a time or two. It's the dickens to get 'em out when they do. Most generally we have a man check this place every day or so, especially during calving season."

"I saw a lot of calves this morning. How many did you get this spring?"

"Oh, a thousand or so, I reckon," he replied casually.

"A thousand?"

"Yeah. Maybe two."

"Maybe two? Um, Luke, how big *is* the M double C?"

"Seventy-five to eighty thousand acres, I guess. Closer to a hundred thousand if we count grasslands to the south that we've been using. Some of it's high ground, like up ahead." He referred to the ground they climbed, growing more heavy with pine.

Jesse was speechless. After a while, she asked, "You don't think Mehitabel might've become caught in some of that brush, do you? Perhaps we couldn't see her."

"Jesse, I think we'd hear her if she'd wanted to be found, she—"

As if in answer, they heard a calf bawl. A moment later they found a few head of cattle, and Mehitabel.

"Well, I guess she became lonesome after all," Jesse said, laughing. They dismounted, and while Luke took a couple of minutes to check the cattle to see if they were all right, Jesse went to the camel. Mehitabel allowed Jesse to approach and pat her, but it was Luke who received her real affection. She preened and batted her long eyelashes at him like the best flirt in Kansas City.

"How are you, girl? Let me see those cuts, now." He ran his hand along her neck and withers. "They're lots better, that's good. Now how about coming on home, hmm?"

Luke tied his lariat into a halter. Mehitabel didn't exactly like it, but she accepted it at Luke's urging. They mounted and started back along the high ridge.

"What's that old building, Luke?" Jesse pointed to a small gray weathered building down slope from them.

"It's an old line shack that we used in the early days on the ranch. Will and I talked about replacing it last year, but time got away from us, I reckon. Should do it, though. Still need it from time to time."

They passed above it, descending the long slope at an angle. But they didn't go far before Mehitabel tugged at her halter and suddenly became fractious. Luke twisted in his saddle. "What's wrong, Mehitabel?"

The camel pulled harder. Luke stopped. "Maybe she's bruised herself." He slid from his saddle to look at the animal's legs and hooves. Mehitabel suffered his examination with indifference, but as soon as Luke tried to move forward, she gave out a loud bray.

"Can't quite figure it, but something's frettin' her. Maybe you should sing the froggie song, Jesse," Luke told her, only half teasing. "Stay here a minute, honey, while I have a look around."

Luke nudged his mount up the slope and began to make a slow circle.

"Maybe it's something else." Jesse murmured, and dismounted. She patted the camel's nose without encountering any resistance. It was almost too easy, she thought. "What is it, Mehitabel? What has upset you?" She began to hum the familiar tune. Mehitabel turned her head.

Jesse began to sing in earnest. On her own, the camel took a step; Jesse held on to the rope halter. Mehitabel shied and started down the slope in a more direct line toward the shack. Jesse had no choice but to stay with her.

She stumbled and slid and tried to sing while bumping along. Behind her, Luke shouted for her to hold on. And to keep singing.

". . . won't you marry me, mm-hmm . . ." Her breath came in short pulls and went out like a puffing steam engine, while her rattling song left her nothing to answer him with. So instead she started on the next line.

She heard the rumble of stones as Luke came back down the slope to reach her. Mehitabel pivoted and dodged. Jesse's arms were jerked almost from their sockets, and she felt a fleeting gratitude for the work gloves she wore, which Luke had given her. Her hands would have been raw without them.

Over her own noise, Jesse heard a low bawl of distress. It came from a distance, yet she couldn't tell from which direction. She saw no cattle. It hadn't come from Mehitabel.

"I have her, Jesse," Luke said as he clamped hold of the rope. She gladly let go of it.

Mehitabel stood still once more. Jesse tried to catch her breath. "What got into you, Mehitabel? Did you see anything that might have spooked her, Luke?"

"Nah, I didn't." Even as he spoke, they heard another bawl. Luke turned his head to listen. Mehitabel lifted hers, apparently listening also.

"Jesse," Luke whispered. "Sing . . ."

"What? Why. . .?"

"Just sing," he whispered insistently.

Jesse began once more. Another long, bawling answer. Then Jesse knew what had struck her as odd. The sound was muffled.

Stepping carefully, Luke led them closer to the cabin.

"A froggie did a-courtin' go, mm-hmm, mm-hmm," Jesse sang. She heard a louder answer this time. And Mehitabel acted even stranger than before, as though she couldn't hurry them enough.

Luke halted them while he gave the scene a careful once-over. From the rear, everything seemed serene. Except they heard the muffled noise of a . . . bull?

Luke put his finger to his lips. Immediately, she ceased singing. Jesse read the expression on Luke's face, full of disbelief, hope, and caution. Could it be?

Another bawl. Two? Two bulls?

Her pulse leaped. Meshach and Shadrach. Then where was George? It was unlike him to remain quiet.

Waving a hand to signal that she should stay out of the way, Luke dropped Mehitabel's rope. He made his way around the side of the shack, his gun drawn.

Jesse rubbed her hands down her thighs while her

heart beat hard enough for her to feel it all the way into her throat. Carefully, watching every step she took, she followed.

She'd just reached the corner of the shack and peeked around it when Mehitabel galloped past her. She glanced over her shoulder, her heart thumping, but she saw nothing untoward. Luke jumped to one side as the camel pranced to him, and he remained cautiously still. Around them, all settled into quiet once more.

Except for inside the shack.

The old boards creaked as Luke pushed open the door. A ribbon of sunlight slanted inside, right on the tan hides of the two Herefords. Rags covered their eyes, tied behind their shortened horns, and filthy, shredded rags covered their hooves. What remained of a rag muzzle dangled from one of them. The other one's was still in place, more or less.

"Oh, Meshach. Shadrach." She rushed in, tearing the dirty cloth from their heads. "Oh, you poor darling beasts," she crooned. "Poor, poor things."

Without regard to safety, she began to tear away all of the filthy rags. "To treat you so, when you're the pride of the M double C," she continued. "You're the kings of the fields, you are. How dare that skunk do this to you."

On all their travels, Luke had never before heard what Jesse said to the bulls, or how she'd talked to them; she'd whispered to them frequently, he knew, and often cajoled them. And the mules, too. So it wasn't only her singing that had charmed the beasts. It was simply herself.

Bemused, Luke observed in fascination as she led them peacefully out of the shack, still speaking in a low croon. Dang, he wished she'd give him some of that sweet talk.

"Oh, Luke, look at them. That blasted man hasn't been feeding them. They're hungry, poor things. And see here, see these scrapes and slashes. Oh, I could strangle George 'til the cruelty came out of him like . . . like that oozing mud squeezed up after the mountain rain."

Luke shook himself back to reality and went on his haunches to examine the legs and hooves of the Herefords. He ran a hand down their sides and back, checked their neck, eyes and ears. "George didn't do too much damage here, Jesse. Just neglect and pushing them too hard. They'll still be, um, healthy enough to make themselves daddies."

"George should be horsewhipped. And then tarred and feathered." She stomped over to throw the rags down inside the cabin door.

Luke thought he'd never seen Jesse so angry. She put him in mind of a little red hen with ruffled feathers. He'd seen her mad before, but never with blood in her eye. "Remind me never to mishandle an animal in your company, Jesse Mae McCarthy," he told her, swallowing his laughter. "You get downright ornery mean over it, don't you, honey?"

"I don't care. If I get my way, I'm likely to string the snake up all by myself. Where d'you think that copperhead has gone?"

At least her anger seemed to have wiped out her fear, Luke mused. Yet she had a right to her fears. They were valid enough. He now thought it very likely that George had gone looking for her again. Or gone to ground; he could be anyplace. And she'd been out on the range by herself earlier.

By damn, that put him into a sweat.

"Don't know, honey. But I reckon we'd best start for home. It'll take us half the afternoon to coax the Herefords along. They'll want to stop and eat."

He didn't say that he wished for a pair of eyes in the back of his head. Or that he wanted to check his guns but wouldn't for the added anxiety it might cause her.

Though he didn't want to leave her even for so short a time, he let her stay with the bulls while he gathered up their mounts. He turned his back and swiftly examined his weapon and counted his ammunition, already knowing what he had, but checking it anyway.

"You know it was Mehitabel that found them," Jesse remarked once they were on their way down the trail. The path that led to the tiny cabin had faded over the years, yet now that they were alert to it, Luke saw a few prints that showed recent use.

"Yep, guess it was. She's quite a girl."

"Uh-huh. We have to reward her some way, Luke. She's a wonderful beast."

At that, Luke did chuckle out loud. "No one will ever dispute your word on it, honey."

They herded the bulls in front of them, unconcerned for once that they would fight each other. They only wanted to eat and drink, Luke knew.

They were about to step from the edge of the trees, when a sudden gunshot whined into their midst.

And hit its target.

Luke threw himself around, his heart in his throat. But Jesse, looking shocked and pale, stared back at him. It was neither of them.

One of the bulls was down. The other bawled frantically while Jesse slid off Sassy and knelt at the bull's head faster than Luke could command her to keep down. Mehitabel danced her protest and dashed away.

Luke didn't spare a glance to determine which of the bulls it was after he saw that the bullet hadn't hit Jesse. His gun drawn in a flash, his glance searched every bump and rock in the area around them. A drift of smoke directed him off to the left.

"Oh, Meshach," Jesse cried as tears rolled down her face. Blood gushed from the wound in the bull's neck.

Luke pinpointed his spot. The attack had come from behind a low outcropping of stone and brush.

It came again, a bullet whizzing wide past Luke's ear.

"Keep down, Jesse." Luke threw the command even as he returned fire and then vaulted from his saddle and knelt in front of her. The only cover was a hundred yards to the right. Behind him, he heard the downed bull thrash once and Jesse's soft cry.

She leaped to her feet, her fist shaking a wild challenge. "George Jeter, you're the biggest, ugliest coward that Satan ever spawned. Hitting and shooting poor defenseless animals for the sport of it."

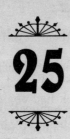

25

Frightened anew, Shadrach bolted out of sight. Mehitabel made a wide circle, trailing her rope halter between her feet. She was in danger of choking herself if she caught it in anything, but Luke wasn't in any position to chase her.

Jesse was crying so hard she could barely see, but she didn't care. At the moment, her anger overcame every sense of self-preservation.

"Jesse, don't!" Luke reached for her, but she stepped away just short of his fingers.

She dashed the tears from her eyes. "Come out in the open, you simpleminded oaf. C'mon, you wanted me. Well, here I am. C'mon."

She moved out further. "Why don't you face me, George? Or shoot again."

"Jesse, dammit, get down!"

Another shot rang, whipping the air beside his cheek. Wide once more, Luke noted.

"Ha! You aren't any good with a gun, are you, George?" she spit out, almost with a dare.

"Jesse, for the Lord's sake. . ."

"You're only good at torturing helpless animals or when you sneak up on somebody from behind," she yelled. "Catch someone unaware with a knife or a whip, that's what you like. You like to hit with your fists and show how big you are when someone can't defend themselves."

Grass jerked around the rocks where George was hidden. Luke watched George's clumsy progress as he made his way from one side of his shelter to the other. The brim of his hat edged above the stone and Luke felt his nerves tighten. The man was about to make another move.

"Where's your shotgun?" Jesse challenged. "Did you lose it? C'mon out, George, face me."

Luke made a frog leap, tackling her around the legs. Jesse slammed into the earth face-down. She had no breath left. She couldn't move.

Luke landed on top of her and ducked as another shot was fired. Closer. His hat took the impact and whipped away with the force and wind. He lay as if he were dead.

"Quiet," he whispered in Jesse's ear. He kept as still as he could, but raised his glance just as George crept around the edge of the rocks. It took all his nerve not to move. He had to make George come out into the open for them to have an even chance.

From the corner of his eye, he saw a tall brown flash. Mehitabel. The camel raced behind George in a circle.

Luke waited until George raised up. His nerves and

muscles gathered. Then he stood erect, ready to shoot.

"You're dead, McCarthy," George roared. He cocked his gun.

But Mehitabel struck, her long neck snaking out while her teeth sunk into George's shoulder. A scream tore from George's throat as his gun went off, the bullet discharging into the ground. George fell to his knees.

Luke raced forward. George twisted and raised his pistol, aiming at the camel. Luke took aim at George.

Before he could fire, Mehitabel bared her teeth, shook her head and pranced to the side. George, already off balance, tried to rise. At the same time, Mehitabel's rope caught between two rocks and went taut, slicing across George's face heavily.

Ignoring his scream, Luke tweaked George's weapon from his hand and placed his own gun against George's temple. "Move and I'll let the camel at you again."

George's dirty hands covered his gashed cheek and nose. Blood poured from between his fingers. "Don't. . ." he whined.

Jesse was on her feet and running, her fists flailing. Luke glanced briefly at her face, and then amended, "Or maybe I'll let Jesse have first crack at you, you bastard."

Jesse hiccuped with grief. "Y-you murderer—hic—I h-hope you hang—hic—from the tall—hic—est tree in three states." She passionately wanted to hit him, yet brought herself up short. She couldn't hit even George while he was hurt.

"None of it woulda happened iffen ya hadn't a run off from me," George snarled.

That did it. Without premeditation, Jesse hauled her fist back and popped him in the mouth. And then grinned in satisfaction as George glared at her in hatred.

"Get the rope off Mehitabel, Jesse," Luke snapped out.

"Gladly!"

"Naw, Jesse Mae, don't . . . you cain't hang me without no trial," George cowered away as Jesse laid a hand on Mehitabel's halter. "McCarthy, ya cain't . . ."

Jesse turned away in complete distaste and disgust and removed the rope halter from Mehitabel. She and Luke ignored George's whining as they tied him with it.

The sound of running horses came from across the hill. Jesse looked up to see three riders approaching.

"It's all right, Jesse. They're M double C men."

Letting relief wash through her, Jesse turned on her heel and headed toward Shadrach, walking in long strides. Behind her, she heard Sandy, Chute, and Crow as they began to question what had happened.

Shadrach grazed about a quarter of a mile away. Jesse needed the moments of quiet to gather herself. Poor Meshach.

Jesse folded her legs beneath herself and sat limply, never taking her eyes from the Hereford. Shadrach ignored her in favor of cropping grass. Jesse wished she could gain peace as quickly after the day's horrible upsets.

Yet as she sat, letting her mind begin to quiet, she occasionally heard drifts of the men's voices. Luke's tones stood out, and she knew she'd always be able to pick his voice from others. He was her husband and they were alive. Both of them. And she could find no anger left toward him.

After a moment she realized he'd called her.

"C'mon, Jesse, honey. Let's go home."

"What about. . ?" She couldn't bring herself to look at Meshach's poor body again, nor at George.

"The men will take care of what's necessary. They'll haul George into the jail and someone will bury Meshach. And by the way, they caught Eli last night. They found old man Sanderson's watch on him. He's in jail with his brother."

"I'm glad. What now?"

"I think it's time we just go home."

Jesse drew strength from the sound of Luke's voice and grabbed his hand tightly as he slipped his arm around her shoulders. "You don't have to be scared anymore."

"I'm not." She glanced up into sky blue eyes filled with love. "Not any longer, not of anything . . . with you."

She thought his smile reflected the brightness of the sun. His tone lightened. "D'you suppose you can live with me for a lifetime then and be a young man's darling?"

For the first time in her life, Jesse fluttered her lashes. "I suppose I might consider it, if you promise not to be lazy. I won't put up with a lazy man, you know."

Luke chuckled. "Mmm, no. No laziness allowed in the McCarthy household. Which reminds me . . ." He lifted her to Sassy's saddle, his hands lingering on her waist. "I have several, um, enterprises to get caught up on, it seems to me, and I wouldn't want you to accuse me of being lazy in, um, certain husbandly chores."

"Oh. Well, if you're really pressed to see that they're taken care of, perhaps we shouldn't be late for supper. I've been rather poorly lately, you know, and Annabelle has been insisting on my retiring early to bed. Right *after* supper."

Luke mounted, then nudged Paint into motion. Her invitation was the best he'd ever had from Jesse, and he didn't plan on it going to waste. It would take them an hour or more to reach home, probably. And thirty minutes to bathe and shave . . .

To hell with after supper. He'd make time *before* supper.

He heeled his mount into a faster trot. On her own, Mehitabel fell into line behind them. Letting out a bawl, Shadrach ran to catch up.

Luke flashed her a broad grin. "Jesse Mae McCarthy, you'll find me the most enterprising of husbands—I think you might count on me taking up your time before supper."

"*Before?*

"Uh-huh. After all, I must make the best of all my opportunities."

Epilogue

"*Jesse Mae McCarthy, you* aren't wearing your skirts that short!" Luke stood in the bedroom door observing his wife as she held her new pink silk anniversary dress in front of her while facing the long mirror. The hem barely reached her knees.

Since her hair had faded to a soft white, pink flattered her extremely, Jesse thought. She was pleased with the dress; it would be just the thing for tomorrow's celebration. "Well, I like it. Mattie helped me choose it."

Luke let his gaze travel down her skimpily clad back. Her white shoulders under the thin straps of what passed for a chemise these days were inviting, and in those new shorter bloomer things, her fanny appeared only a little plumper now than when he'd first noticed it forty years before. The sight of her had never ceased to pleasure him over the years.

He wondered if they'd be missed for the afternoon if he simply shut and locked the bedroom door against their five grandchildren and two sons. The grandchildren often had their cousins in tow, Will and Mattie's seven and Josie's two. They'd been overrun with the young'uns for the last week, and he was growing a little tired of the invasion.

"It's too short," he insisted, though not seriously.

"Is that a problem? You said only the other day that my legs are still shapely and pretty." She extended one and pointed her stockinged toe, flashing him a flirtatious glance over her shoulder.

That did it. To hell with the family. His sons and their wives could find their own activities. As for the children, they'd have to make do without them for now.

"They're damned beautiful and you know it." He quietly snapped the door closed and locked it, then moved into the room and sat down in the big armchair beside the bed, never taking his eyes from her. "But I don't necessarily need to share that knowledge with every other galoot in Wayside Station."

"Well, I think the shorter fashions are very practical." She hung the dress back in the armoire and reached for her shirtwaist. "They allow more freedom of movement and—"

With very little effort, Luke reached an arm around her waist and hauled her crosswise onto his lap. He immediately brushed the shirtwaist from her shoulders and caressed her soft skin.

He lowered his head for a kiss and took his time with it. She answered with her own kiss. "Mmm, you feel so nice," she murmured, snuggling her face against his neck.

He held her tighter, running his hand up her thigh.

"You feel more than nice, honey. You feel deliciously sinful. And you're right. These modern clothes allow for more freedom. . ." His fingers found their way under the elastic. "These things you can wear for me anytime, honey."

"Feeling a little neglected, are you, Luke?" she asked teasingly.

"A lot neglected, you little scamp," he answered as he nibbled her ear. "The kids take all your time when they're all here. Hell, they leave me in the dust."

"As if you minded," she laughed. "They love it when you teach them to rope and ride, especially little Luke. He's most interested in the cattle. I think he's the one to follow in your footsteps here at the ranch."

"Uh-huh, think you're right on that. Though time will tell. But forget the kids for a moment, honey. I've got something for you and I can't wait 'til tomorrow to give it to you."

Luke pulled out a jeweler's box from his shirt pocket and handed it to her.

Glancing at his face, Jesse thought his eyes were still the bluest of any she'd ever seen. His hair, like hers, had faded, but his expression of teasing laughter and love nearly outshone the sun. "What, another bauble? Really, Luke, you spoil me."

"Open it, honey."

She did so. Against the velvet lay a gold charm bracelet, full of so many charms it jingled when she lifted it. Tiny silhouetted animals. She looked closely. A camel, two bulls, two mules, a cat. Five circles, each with the name of a grandchild, two larger ones with the names of their sons, Richard and Keith. The largest one of all was inscribed.

Laughter shook her tiny frame and her husky voice

held a catch as she murmured over his sentimentality, "Oh, Luke . . . It represents how we met. . . ."

"Read what it says, Jesse."

She glanced at him once more and reached for her spectacles from the nightstand beside the chair. Tipping the gold circle toward the light, she read out loud. "My darling for all time," and from the lower edge, "From the old man."

Her laughter rippled out, attracting two youngsters who had wandered into the kitchen looking for a snack.

"What are they doing in there?" asked seven-year-old Cynthia as she brushed back a lock of golden hair from her blue eyes. Her cousin, nine-year-old Luke, had his ear to their grandparents' door.

"I don't know, but grampa just said something about 'best opportunities.'" He listened a moment. "Now it's all quiet."

Little Luke took a step away from the door. "C'mon, Cindy. I'll race ya to the corral."

$1,000.00

FOR YOUR THOUGHTS

Let us know what you think. Just answer these seven questions and you could win $1,000! For completing and returning this survey, you'll be entered into a drawing to win a $1,000 prize.

OFFICIAL RULES: *No additional purchase necessary.* Complete the HarperPaperbacks questionnaire—be sure to include your name and address—and mail it, with first-class postage, to HarperPaperbacks, Survey Sweeps, 10 E. 53rd Street, New York, NY 10022. Entries must be received no later than midnight, October 4, 1995. One winner will be chosen at random from the completed readership surveys received by HarperPaperbacks. A random drawing will take place in the offices of HarperPaperbacks on or about October 16, 1995. The odds of winning are determined by the number of entries received. If you are the winner, you will be notified by certified mail how to collect the $1,000 and will be required to sign an affidavit of eligibility within 21 days of notification. A $1,000 money order will be given to the *sole winner* only—to be sent by registered mail. Payment of any taxes imposed on the prize winner will be the sole responsibility of the winner. All federal, state, and local laws apply. Void where prohibited by law. The prize is not transferable. **No photocopied entries.**

Entrants are responsible for mailing the completed readership survey to HarperPaperbacks, Survey Sweeps, at 10 E. 53rd Street, New York, NY 10022. If you wish to send a survey without entering the sweepstakes drawing, simply leave the name/address section blank. Surveys without name and address will not be entered in the sweepstakes drawing. HarperPaperbacks is not responsible for lost or misdirected mail. Photocopied submissions will be disqualified. Entrants must be at least 18 years of age and U.S. citizens. All information supplied is subject to verification. Employees, and their immediate family, of HarperCollins*Publishers* are not eligible. For winner information, send a stamped, self-addressed № 10 envelope by November 10, 1995 to HarperPaperbacks, Sweeps Winners, 10 E. 53rd Street, New York, NY 10022.